In Praise of *Chasing a Blond Moon* (2003, The Lyons Press)

"Top-notch action scenes, engaging characters both major and minor, masterful dialogue, and a passionate sense of place make this a fine series."
—*Publishers Weekly*

"An absorbing narrative twists and turns in a setting ripe for the corruption that inevitably occurs when obscene profits encounter a simpler way of life."
—*Dallas Morning News*

In Praise of *Blue Wolf in Green Fire* (2002, The Lyons Press)

"A gripping plot, replete with memorable surrounds and spiky characters, makes this second in the series (after Ice Hunter*) an excellent choice for most collections. A good pick also for readers who enjoy outdoor mysteries by such authors as Nevada Barr or Dana Stabenow."*
—*Library Journal*

"This second Woods Cop procedural is well written, suspenseful, and bleakly humorous while moving as quickly as a wolf cutting through winter woods. In addition to strong characters and a compelling romance, Heywood provides vivid, detailed descriptions of the wilderness and the various procedures and techniques of conservation officers and poachers. The tricky, evasive behavior of federal officials recalls the atmosphere of The X-Files, *while the police procedure and banter evoke K.C. Constantine's Mario Balzic series. Highly recommended."*
—*Booklist*

In Praise of *Ice Hunter* (2001, The Lyons Press)

"Crisp writing, great scenery, quirky characters and an absorbing plot add to the appeal of the memorable first entry in a promised series of Woods Cop mysteries."
—*Wall Street Journal*

"Heywood builds his surrounds slowly . . . peopling his novels with memorably idiosyncratic characters and conveying an overall sense of reverence for nature. An engaging read and a promising series debut."
—*Library Journal*

JOSEPH HEYWOOD

ICE
HUNTER

A WOODS COP MYSTERY

THE LYONS PRESS

GUILFORD, CT

AN IMPRINT OF THE GLOBE PEQUOT PRESS

Copyright © 2001 by Joseph Heywood

First Lyons Press paperback edition, 2005

The Lyons Press is an imprint of The Globe Pequot Press.

10 9 8 7 6 5 4 3 2 1

Printed in the United States of America

ISBN 1-59228-654-2 (paperback)
ISBN 1-58574-225-2 (hardcover)

Library of Congress Cataloging-in-Publication Data is available on file.

*This novel and those to follow in the series are dedicated to
the elite corps of more than two hundred men and women who
wear the gold badge of conservation officers and
serve the people and natural treasures of Michigan
in ways and to degrees those of us who are served
can hardly imagine.*

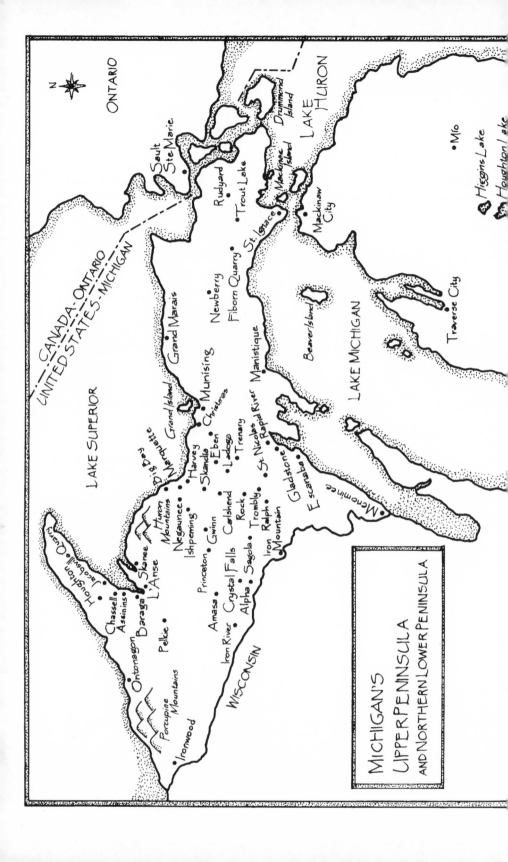

MICHIGAN'S
UPPER PENINSULA
AND NORTHERN LOWER PENINSULA

ICE
HUNTER

· THE PAST ·

· 1 ·

It was the week after his sixteenth birthday, four days after deer season had opened. Michigan's Upper Peninsula was blanketed in heavy wet snow. His father was out on patrol and Grady Service was buttoning up for the night when he saw headlights flash across the front of the house and heard a car window open and slam.

Grady went to the front door and peered out though the curtain.

There stood Conservation Officer Pease DuPlechet, his father's closest friend and one of the old man's regular drinking buds. Like his father, DuPlechet was a World War II veteran. A gunner on a destroyer at Okinawa when kamikazes struck, he had earned the Navy Cross stubbornly manning his gun through the bloody attack. He was a small, pug-faced man with leathery skin and a whitewall haircut.

Usually Pease just came in but this time he stood there fidgeting.

When Grady opened the door, DuPlechet flicked away his cigarette and stood rigidly. "Grady, your dad's dead."

The boy showed no emotion. The old man had always taken life head-on. The only son was expected to do no less.

"No varnish on this, kid. He stopped up to the Two-Woof Camp and had one too many. On the way out he stopped to help some hunters and got hit by a truck. He shouldn't have been boozing on the job, but that's done now and it's never gonna get said again. You've got a right to know the truth."

"Thanks." The only word Grady Service could manage.

DuPlechet handed him his father's wool overcoat, the amorphous garment COs called a horseblanket. "He'd want you to have this," his father's friend declared. "You want me to stay?"

A gorge rose in the boy's throat. "I'll be all right." He had always been all right and always alone, his father out chasing poachers or drinking with his friends. He watched Pease DuPlechet drive away, closed the door, turned on a light, and looked at the coat, which was stained with blood.

No tears were shed, no sorrow racked him, and he did not mourn.

He behaved the way the son of Gibson Service would be expected to behave.

Conservation officers and DNR personnel came from all over the state to the funeral in Negaunee, where his father had been born. The cemetery was crowded with dignitaries, uniformed officers, and reporters. Michigan's governor gave the eulogy.

Silken words were purred over a cold corpse, the congressman declaring his father "an original and a hero." The surviving son stood stiffly in the bloodstained green overcoat, not hearing the words and thinking that he was even more alone now than before.

· 2 ·

It was late in the third period of the annual battle with Michigan Tech, whose ice hockey team soared among the elite of the country every year while Northern Michigan University's new varsity program struggled to earn respect in the NCAA hockey community. They had played twice in two years and Northern had been twice humiliated, but tonight the teams were playing evenly and scoreless.

Grady Service had played hockey most of his young life, and now as a senior he was captain of the green-and-gold-clad Wildcats. As a left-winger his job was less scoring goals than punishing the opposition, a job he undertook with passion. His opposing winger was a muscular Canadian from Toronto, a two-year All-American who would no doubt move on to the National Hockey League when he graduated. The winger, Toby Blanck, had size and speed and the disposition of a wolverine guarding a fresh kill. For two periods Service and Blanck had shadowed each other relentlessly, each hammering the other every time the puck was touched. Both of them played with a ferocity that caused others to veer clear of them at every opportunity.

Service felt his coach tap his shoulder pad to tell him he was up next, then lean down to whisper, "We need a dinger, Grady."

The line changed on a whistle for an offside and Service moved into position beside Blanck.

"Your asshole a little tight?" Blanck hissed as they waited for the linesman to drop the puck.

Service said nothing. When the puck was dropped he leaned into Blanck and tied up his stick as the puck was flicked backward. He immediately disengaged and cut toward the boards, keeping his head up. Blanck was caught by surprise by the burst of speed and grunted to catch up. Service heard the other player's skates crunching the ice in pursuit.

The puck bounded softly off the boards onto Service's stick. Realizing that Blanck had him lined up, he cupped the puck gently with his blade, dug his skate blade edges into the ice, and let the pursuing winger's momentum carry him past. With Blanck beyond him, Grady

Service cut straight to the slot, looking for his center or the other wing to pass to, but no green socks appeared in his peripheral vision. No choice but to try to split the two defensemen, who were trying to pinch him. He dug hard, pushing the puck ahead of him, his mind racing as knowledge and instinct mixed.

Blanck would be right behind him in angry pursuit, but Service did not let his presence cut into his concentration. He aimed for a point between the converging defenders then slid the puck outside to the right, rammed his left shoulder against the left shoulder of the nearest defenseman, and bounced past him, gathering the puck back to his stick. Grady found himself one on one against the goalie. He faked to the keeper's catching glove then cut sharply to his own left, flipping a sharp backhander low over the goalie's stick.

He did not see the puck go into the net. He heard the start of a roar from the fans and then felt himself driven hard into the boards behind the net. As he bounced off he felt fists pounding on the side of his head. He dropped his gloves, took a stride to get separation, and saw the wild eyes of Blanck. There was no time to think. He grabbed Blanck's sweater with both hands, freed his right hand, and began punching wildly.

The next thing he knew Blanck was on his back unconscious and bleeding as teammates pulled Service away.

Grady watched from the penalty box as trainers carried Blanck off the ice on a stretcher. He shuddered at the huge stain of blood coagulating on the slushy ice behind the net.

The locker room was bedlam afterward. His coach gave him the game puck. Northern had won 1–0, its first win over its archrival. It was a meaningless victory. Tech was headed for the playoffs and Northern had long ago slipped out of contention for the postseason.

After showering and getting dressed, Grady stepped out of the locker room to find a man in a baggy suit and garish flowered tie waiting in the tunnel. The man wore a charcoal-gray fedora with a small red feather in the hatband.

He looked at Service's bloodstained green wool coat and said, "You'll need a new coat when you hit the Bigs. I'm Billy Veach, head scout for the Red Wings. We like your game, Service. Tell the truth, we don't care much for the college game, but we've watched you a long time and we think you can play. We're going to draft you this summer and you'll get an invite to camp in the fall. What to you think about that?"

"I don't know," Grady Service said.

Veach, an NHL all-star in his playing days, looked perplexed. "The hell you say?"

"How's Blanck?" Service asked.

"The sawbones are looking him over, eh? Overrated, that bugger. Good size, but a pretty boy. You put him in his place."

"I'm not proud of it," Service said.

"Hey, breaks of the game, Service. You give and you take."

Service headed for the opposing locker room and Veach followed, slipping a card into the young player's coat pocket.

Tech's coach was John McInnes, a legend in college hockey. As soon as he saw Service, he said, "Toby's gonna be okay."

"I didn't mean to hurt him."

"Hell, we all know that. You just did your job, and he took the first swing. Let's mark her down to frustration and be done with it." The famous coach stuck out his hand. "Good luck in the NHL, eh?"

But Toby Blanck was not okay. His skull was fractured and he was critical for nearly a week before pulling through. A surgeon was flown up from Ann Arbor and operated, declaring afterward that he had put a metal plate in the player's head and his hockey career was ended. Grady Service watched the developments from a distance and made up his mind that he too was finished with the "game." He graduated that year, got his degree, volunteered for the Marine Corps, trained at Parris Island and was shipped to Vietnam, where the violence was not in the interests of a mindless game.

· 3 ·

Department of Natural Resources Director Eeno Tenni stood wringing his hands as the wash of the blue and white state police helicopter swept across the empty parking lot.

Conservation Officer Grady Service stood behind the director and next to Lorne O'Driscoll, chief of law enforcment, the DNR's division charged with enforcing the state's fish and game laws.

The call to the Higgins Lake meeting had come late the night before, while Service was patrolling north of the village of Ralph, near Flat Rock Creek. It was early October and black bear season was under way; Service had spent a long day checking hunters and their bear dogs. The call for the meeting had come down not through channels but directly from the chief. Despite a poor sense of humor, O'Driscoll was widely respected by the state's conservation officers. He set high standards for the force and would not allow such standards to be compromised.

It had been a brief telephone conversation. "The governor wants to see you at the CCC at zero eight hundred." The CCC was the Civilian Conservation Corps Museum at the north end of Higgins Lake in the north-central part of the state, a five-hour drive from Service's home halfway between Escanaba and Marquette. "Be in proper uniform," O'Driscoll warned tersely before hanging up.

Service didn't have to ask the subject of the meeting. He had known this was coming. All that had been in doubt was when.

There was a chill in the early-autumn air as Service and his superiors stood in the parking lot that served as a convenient helipad. In the distance the hardwoods were fading to pastels, while towering white pines maintained their dark green. A sloppy vee of geese passed over the tree line, their sounds drowned out by the approaching helicopter.

Governor Samuel Adams Bozian hopped out of the state police chopper and strode purposefully toward the men, his wispy silver hair whipped by rotor wash.

The governor was an undistinguished, rotund man who had been in politics since college. He appeared soft but was well established in his first term as a formidable politician with a firm hold on the state's reins and a burgeoning national reputation.

Eeno Tenni rushed forward to greet the governor, but Bozian ignored him and marched directly on to Service and O'Driscoll.

"Service," the governor said, fixing his hard blue eyes on the conservation officer. "This meeting is off the record. I'm here as a father, not as governor."

"Yessir," Service said, knowing full well that Bozian was always acting as governor.

Bozian's son had been a probationary conservation officer, and in one of his rotating assignments had been sent to Grady Service, whose job it was to train and evaluate him. All probationary officers spent a year in such rotations before being declared qualified to handle the demanding and taxing work of a fully certified CO. Getting to this point was tough for any candidate. Of five thousand candidates, only four or five a year made it all the way through probation to full duty. The governor's son, Samuel A. Bozian III, was called Trip, looked nothing like his father, and lacked all of his father's fire.

In July Service and Trip Bozian had been called to a private campground near Rapid River to handle some rowdies, who turned out to be very drunk members of a Flint motorcycle gang called the Blood Moon Barbarians. As motorcycle gangs went the Barbarians were more unruly than dangerous, and Service had bumped heads with them before. They usually showed up somewhere in his district in July, after the Fourth, which was a good thing because on Independence Day the campgrounds tended to be filled with families.

The two COs' arrival had been greeted by a cacophony of drunken catcalls and a long string of profanity.

Service recognized the group's leader, a man in his thirties with a stringy blond ponytail and a small gold dog bone in his nose, which gave rise to his nickname, Nosebone.

The diminutive and muscle-bound leader stepped forward to meet Service, grinning the way he always did.

"Bone," Service said.

"What's happenin', officer?" the biker replied.

"Your crowd's over the top, eh?"

The biker grinned. "Just enjoying the beauty of nature."

"You're gonna have to break it up and dump the beer, Bone." No doubt some of the bikers were on drugs too, but Service was neither stupid nor heroic about such confrontations. Two against many were lousy odds. They'd need more backup to shake them down. Better to calm the scene now and, if circumstances warranted, call in help later to check for illegal substances. Mostly he just wanted to shut them up and be finished with it.

"Dump the brews? The state gonna pay us back?"

"It'll be cheaper to dump the alcohol than call in a lawyer and make bail," Service said calmly.

Nosebone had a long rap sheet, but Service could see that this wasn't one of his dark moods. He'd bitch, dump the alcohol, get his troops in order, and the COs could be on their way.

"Yah, I guess," the biker said. "Gettin' so you can't have a little howl anymore."

"How it is," Service said, not unsympathetic to the biker's feelings. "You got a problem with the laws, talk to your state rep. I just enforce the laws they give me."

"Yah," Nosebone said.

The exact sequence of what had occurred next was stuck in Service's mind. Trip Bozian sort of swaggered up to half a dozen bikers and ordered them them to put down their beer cans. Service noticed too late that the probie's gun holster had been unsnapped.

"Fuck off," one of the bikers growled at Service's partner.

Trip Bozian fumbled for his firearm, and before Service could intervene the weapon was out and the probie's hand was shaking. The PCO ordered the bikers to move, but the men stubbornly held their ground. When they didn't respond, he fired one round into the ground across the front of them, kicking up small clods of hard dirt.

The shot caused a momentary scramble as the bikers retreated, roaring in one voice.

"Fuck this," Nosebone said. "Barney Fife can't shoot at us like that."

Service was in a difficult position. Bozian had made a major mistake, drawing his weapon and discharging it, but he couldn't let the bikers react and he couldn't reprimand Bozian in front of them or this would split them and give an edge to the rowdies.

"Dump the suds and call it a night," Service said with a steely voice to the biker.

Nosebone studied him momentarily, tipped his can, let the foamy beer run out, and told the others to do the same, which they did, but not without grousing.

"Time for you to take your herd and clear out," Service said.

"We paid ahead," the leader complained.

"You shoulda thought about that before you turned loose the menagerie."

"The what?"

"Move out," Service repeated, and after taking a moment to consider his options Nosebone gave the signal. The bikers went to their hogs, cranked them up, and departed, several of them doing dirt-spewing wheelies and playing cowboy in pathetic displays of opposition.

When they were gone, Service found Trip Bozian trembling badly. He carefully took the probationary officer's weapon away from him, pushed in the safety, returned the weapon to the man's holster, and snapped it shut.

The governor's son looked devastated. "I fucked up big time, didn't I? Oh man," he said, moaning softly.

Service didn't answer right away.

Rather than let the young officer go home to brood alone, Service took him into Rapid River and bought coffee at an all-night gas station.

They sat outside on a picnic table and talked.

"You have to report this," young Bozian said.

The question was purely rhetorical. "What happened?"

"I'm not cut out for this," Trip Bozian said.

Before Bozian had arrived for his rotation with Service, he had been briefed: Other officers had noticed that the young man showed a great deal of anxiety in tight situations, and often less-than-adequate judgment. The jury was still out on his ability to do the job. Bozian's previous failures had been minor, but this error was a strong indicator that the governor's son was indeed not suited for CO work.

"I'd rather get bounced than hurt somebody," Bozian lamented.

Service didn't lecture because there was no need. The probie already understood that he wasn't suited for the nerve-racking job.

Still, Service didn't say anything. He would make his report, but it would be somebody else's call on young Bozian's fate. Given that his father was the state's chief executive, Service had a hunch he might be kept on and shielded.

It came as a surprise when the governor's son was dropped quietly from the program, but he knew that eventually the department would have to contend with the governor. He'd guessed that eventually the governor's wrath would be vented in his direction.

That moment was now.

"What the hell happened with my son?" the governor demanded again.

Service took a deep breath before replying. "He couldn't cut it, Governor."

"You encountered violent elements, and my son met force with force," the governor declared.

Service wondered what Trip had told his father. "Sir, we encountered some rowdies, and your son drew and discharged his weapon outside department rules."

"You were both being threatened."

"No sir. We were in discussion with the subjects and it was under control. Our rules of engagement are clear," Service said. "There were no weapons in evidence and no overt threat, only a crowd of drunks. Your son overreacted."

"That's *your* version," Governor Sam Bozian said.

The implication was that Service was wrong and expected to recant. "Those are the facts, Governor."

"And based on your version, you recommended my son's termination."

Chief O'Driscoll intervened. "Governor, Officer Service simply reported the facts, which he is required to do. The decision to terminate Trip was mine."

"The shot did not hurt anyone," the governor said. "Nobody was injured."

"That's irrelevant," Chief O'Driscoll said. "Civilians were needlessly endangered. Your son experienced previous problems during his probationary assignments. He lacks the requisite self-control to deal with ambiguous and potentially explosive situations."

The governor stared at the chief of the law enforcement division. "My son was railroaded," the governor said angrily.

"If so, sir, your son laid the tracks himself," O'Driscoll countered.

Director Tenni sucked in his breath and cringed, expecting one of the governor's legendary verbal assaults, but Bozian simply stuck out his finger and shook it at Service. "I have a long memory, Officer Service."

Service didn't like the threat but knew enough to keep quiet. His chief had impressed him by stepping in the way he had when clearly the governor wanted his scalp.

Bozian marched back to the helicopter, which quickly lifted off, its turbines screaming and pelting them with dust.

"Thanks for the support, Chief," Service said to O'Driscoll.

"The next time you are ordered to report in uniform, it will be the proper uniform," the chief replied icily.

Service was wearing the same overcoat his father had worn during his career as a CO. Modern uniforms had superceded the old shapeless horseblanket coats years before, but Service clung stubbornly to the old one.

"Young Bozian was not cut out for police work," O'Driscoll said. "Lose the coat. That's an order."

Service had no intention of disposing of the old coat. Michigan had been the first state in the union to hire a full-time salaried game warden back in 1887, and in more than a century since then game wardens—now called conservation officers—had fashioned a proud and honorable record. For more than half their history the COs had worn horseblankets, and Service wore his father's coat to honor those who had gone before him.

Service watched his superiors get into the chief's truck and drive away, leaving him alone, which was how COs lived a great deal of their professional lives.

A museum employee was standing near Service's truck smoking a cigarette.

"Was that Clearcut?"

This was the nickname the pro-business governor had earned among state employees and conservationists.

"In the flesh."

The man chuckled. "He's sure got plenty. Pretty unusual the governor meeting up here like this. You get a medal or something?"

"More like a kick in the ass," Service said.

"You don't look none the worse," said the man.

Service took out a cigarette and lit up. He was signed out for the rest of the day and he had to pass the Manistee River. He decided this was a good day to fish for chinook salmon, which were beginning to fill the river. In a way he felt sorry for Trip Bozian, but the young man was simply not up to the job and knew it. He would land on his feet. The governor would take care of his son. He'd also take care of Service if the opportunity came, he told himself as he began to map out his plan for the day's outing. He would fish into darkness, then drive the five hours back to his district, sleep in the truck, and greet tomorrow's bear hunters bright and early.

·THE PRESENT·

· 4 ·

He drove the tote road with his lights off, as he almost always did when he patrolled, and suddenly the conservation officer saw a glint of light and knew there was a vehicle snugged into the side of the overgrown lane ahead. There was a smidge of moonlight, but not quite enough. The silhouette looked like an older Caddy. Grady Service checked his watch. Ten straight up. McCants would be along any moment and they would be needing privacy to cut from the lane over to the Sand River to get set up for poachers. Kids, he figured. Didn't they have homework any more? Definitely a Caddy. He slid out of his double-cab and walked stealthily toward the vehicle ahead.

He was several feet from the Caddy when he heard the springs squeaking. He thought, When a Caddy's rockin', don't come knockin'. Midnight, windows down. He approached from the left rear panel and peered in before clicking on his light.

The woman had light-colored hair. She was a top-rider, her chin jutted out, head back. Great, he thought.

He shone his light into the backseat. The woman didn't flinch, but there was plenty of scrambling beneath her.

"Whose vehicle?" he asked.

"Mine," the woman said, squinting directly into his light.

"Can I see your operator's license, registration, and proof of insurance?"

"We don't need a license for what we're doing," the woman said. She didn't take her eyes off Service and she didn't move either. She was a cool customer.

"I need to see your license," Service said. "Please." Conservation officers were expected to be calm in all circumstances and taught to be polite, nonthreatening. But the book didn't cover walking up on backseat boffers.

"All right," the woman said, irritated. She crawled over the back of the front seat and slid behind the steering wheel, making no attempt to cover herself. Service observed a well-defined tan line. Artificial, he decided. Or a flatlander. There hadn't been much sun so far this summer.

Service switched his light to the backseat. The man had a thick neck and covered his face with his hands. Despite the attempt, Service recognized Jerry Allerdyce and felt his skin crawl.

The woman thrust her license and registration out the driver's window.

"Stay here," Service said.

"You care if we finish up while you do whatever it is you do?" she asked.

He didn't answer and fought a smile as he walked back to the truck. He called the county's centralized dispatch to check plates and find out if there were any outstanding warrants on the driver. Her record was clean and clear. Her license said her name was Laudonia Capacelli, with an address in Royal Oak, a Detroit suburb.

Seeing Jerry Allerdyce did not sit well. He had not thought about the Allerdyce family in a long time. Jerry was the eldest son of Limpy Allerdyce, now serving a stretch in Jackson. Jerry was tall with angular features on a triangular face, long hair in a ponytail, and a ratty goatee. It was hard to understand Jerry and the woman in the Caddy, but Grady Service had seen enough life to know that expectations and reality rarely intersected. What attracted a particular woman to a particular man was impossible to generalize. Given Jerry's reputation with women, however, Service was nearly certain that Cadillac Lady was not unattached.

Back at the Caddy he handed the woman her documents. She was still in the driver's seat. "Get dressed and go."

"We like it here. No law against it, is there?"

"Leave it alone," Jerry said in a pained whine from the backseat.

"Never mind," the woman said. "Mood's sorta shot, I guess."

"Find a more private place next time," Service said.

"We thought we had," she said haughtily.

Service walked back to his truck, got a cigarette, lit up, and stood outside. People, he thought. In this job you just never knew what was next.

The Caddy made a lugubrious stop-and-go turnaround on the lane and came back toward him. The woman had not bothered to dress. She leaned out her window, smiled, and winked as the automobile slid by.

Service waved her on. Down the road they could be arrested for exposing themselves, but that would be the county's problem. He had his own business to attend to.

Ten minutes later he heard another vehicle moving up behind him, lights out. McCants.

As soon as she got out of her truck, she said, "Was that Caddy back here?"

"Coitus interruptus," he said, holding out a pack of cigarettes.

There weren't many smokers left among other COs. Especially among the young ones, who seemed annoyingly health conscious. CO Candace McCants was an exception. Four years on the job, she was Korean born, five-six, a muscular 160. He liked working with her. She wasn't afraid of anything and had inordinate common sense, a rare combination.

"Kids?" she said, lighting her cigarette.

"Something like that."

"You write 'em up?"

"For what?"

She laughed. "Getting more than us?"

"People wanna bonk in the boonies, no problem for me. We've got enough to do tonight."

"What did the guy look like?"

He jabbed her shoulder. "Jerry Allerdyce," he said. "Ready to work?"

"Jerry? Yuck!" she said. "Lemme grab my gear."

Service was dozing when McCants touched him to wake him.

"What?"

"Doors slamming."

Service blinked to clear his eyes and mind and hit the ON button. They had a surplus Russian night-vision scope bought from a forestry professor at Northern Michigan who ran a side business selling surplus Russian military equipment, offering it to sportsmen at huge profits but at cost to COs. The equipment was excellent, all digital, and would hook into a VCR. Whatever happened, they could freeze-frame and print excellent black and whites. The state also issued American-made night scopes. Most COs preferred the Russian models.

Through the lens, the world appeared in shades of green.

"Who is it?" McCants asked.

"You don't wanna know."

"Jesus. The Veldcamps?"

"In the flesh."

"I hope not literally. We got them here last year. Same damn spot."

"They haven't done anything yet."

"They will," she said. "Bone stupid. Can you believe they're back in the same spot?"

"Maybe they believe lightning won't strike twice in the same place."

"If so, we are definitely going to mess with their minds tonight."

The Veldcamps were first cousins, both in their early forties. They lived together in a cabin below Gwinn, the place surrounded by discarded tires and automobile parts. They were both members of some half-baked militia group and longtime poachers. Taking away their hunting and fishing privileges didn't stop them from doing what they had always done. In some ways Service could sympathize with them, but the law was the law.

From their blind in the tag alders beside the creek, Service could see the Veldcamps wriggling into their waders, like too small casings for way too much sausage.

Last year they had arrested the pair for firing shotguns into a school of spawning whitehorse suckers. Now that the suckers were back for their June spawning run, so were the cousins, as predictable as the sun every morning and not as welcome.

The creek rose from a spring pond about a mile above where they were hidden and flowed down to a culvert under the hard-packed dirt road. Just below the culvert was a wide bend and a hole where suckers tended to stack up. Service had seen as many as a hundred fish at one time here. This was the only such place for a good thirty miles and not ten miles from the Veldcamps' cabin, a natural gathering place for fish, poachers, and law officers.

Service watched the two men wade into the stream. Then the splashing and cursing began.

"What?" McCants asked.

"I'd say . . . softball bats."

"Idiots," she said disgustedly.

"*Your* idiots, this year."

"Let's just shoot 'em."

"Out of season."

"I meant just in the legs."

"*Out of season,*" he repeated with emphasis, smiling.

"Ooh-kay," she said with mock disappointment.

"Be careful," he told her. She answered with a soft grunt.

While she cut over to the road, Service put down the night scope and made his way quietly through the tag alders to streamside.

The two men Bambied when Candy's spot lit them up.

"Who?" one of them said.

"DNR," McCants said, moving toward them. "Put the bats on shore."

Sonny Veldcamp poked his bat into Win Veldcamp's chest, knocking him backward into the water. "I *told* you these fucking bats were too loud!"

McCants stepped down to the streambank. "Put it down, Sonny."

"Oh Christ! It's that gook bitch again," Sonny Veldcamp yelled. He immediately took a step toward her, brandishing the bat.

McCants stood her ground.

"Drop the bat," Service said from behind Sonny.

"Fuckers!" Sonny screeched. He lunged for McCants but as he put a foot up on the bank, she gave him a sharp kick in his support leg and sent him back into the water.

Service hopped into the water and pushed Win Veldcamp under the surface long enough to make his point. Win came up snorting water from his nostrils.

Sonny stared into the light. "We *own* these fish, you fucks. We pay taxes."

McCants laughed out loud. "You have to have a job to pay taxes, Sonny."

"We're Americans, rice nigger."

Whoops, Service thought.

McCants stepped toward Sonny, took hold of his shirt, and jerked him forward. He went down like he'd been headshot. She dragged him onto the grass, folded his arms behind him, and cuffed him.

Service pushed Win forward to join his cousin.

"You're not gonna arrest us," Win said. "We got no fish."

"You like hockey, Win?" McCants asked.

"What of it?"

"It's like spearing."

"Huh?"

"Intent alone will draw a penalty."

"What spears?"

"Bone stupid," McCants said.

"Shit, man." This from Sonny.

"Quiet," McCants said. "The UN troops in the woods may hear you."

Militias believed that the United Nations was conspiring to take over the United States and had troops hidden all around the country.

"You hear that?" Win asked Sonny.

"Give 'em Miranda," Service told his colleague.

Ordinarily they'd just write a ticket for a court date, but the Veld-camps were multiple offenders and likely to go hermit. They were set up to watch the sucker hole all night so they called the county, who dispatched a deputy to whom they transferred custody of their prisoners. When they got back into their blind, they opened thermoses of coffee.

"Rice nigger," McCants said. "That's a new one."

"The cousins have a gift for language," he said.

She laughed. "How many hours until we can stop having fun?"

"Quiet," he said. "You'll ruin business."

After a while she asked, "How have you done this job for twenty years?"

Service said, "Just like cons, one minute at a time." Being obsessive didn't hurt either, he told himself.

The remainder of the night was quiet. They returned to their vehicles before sunrise, McCants looking as fresh and alert as if she had just had a full night's sleep. Youth, Service thought. All these kids joining the department. Young and competent. His youth was long gone and he needed to work harder just to keep up with them. It wasn't that he loved the job so much as it was all he had. Raised on duty, dipped in it, fire hardened in too many ways. Truth be known: This was all he wanted.

The night left him tired but not sleepy. He knew how to take care of this. As he drove back to his place, he ticked off his duty list for the next day. He'd sleep this morning. Then head over to the Mosquito. It had been a few days since he had been in the area, and to protect it you couldn't leave it alone too long. This had been one of his old man's axioms and now it was his.

· 5 ·

The Mosquito River passed lethargically under US 2 to merge with Lake Michigan through a channel that bisected a series of low scabs of cobble and indestructible grasses. The river, which was seldom wider than thirty or forty feet and much narrower at the mouth, was stained orange by tannin from the hemlock forest upstream. From the highway bridge it looked like just one more shallow, slow-moving, mosquito-infested trickle, an appearance that belied its reality. The river ran more or less north to south through an area called the Mosquito Wilderness Tract. At the bridge it was a shallow, sluggish stream suitable only for suckers and spring smelt runs, not the sort of place to attract a casual sportsman motoring past at cruising speed. The name on the sign at both ends of the bridge added to the river's image of inhospitability.

On several occasions Grady Service had fought Lansing's tourist-hungry bureaucrats, who wanted to put up signs to mark the tract as a wilderness area. So far he had succeeded in stopping them, but he had no doubt that the fight would go on. Ironically, the damn state outlawed billboards, then erected its own obtrusive signs all over the landscape. It made no sense, but he had learned over the years that Lansing's policies seldom made a great deal of sense.

The Mosquito Wilderness was one of the state's natural jewels, and it needed to be guarded as such. In his twenty years as a conservation officer Service had done everything in his power to see that the Mosquito was protected. Poachers and bushwhackers were not treated gently, and he pressed every charge he could. He also made sure the word was out: Screw with the Mosquito and you are fucked.

He had even talked the Mosquito Wilderness Preservation Association into creating a homepage on the Web, where it was prominently noted that the wilderness was a mosquito- and blackfly-infested hellhole as well as the single most heavily patrolled area in the state by COs and other law enforcement officials. He didn't care if it wasn't true; it was the most heavily patrolled area he had responsibility for and that's what counted. In law enforcement perceptions were often more compelling than reality.

Half a mile north of its outlet the Mosquito turned fast and twisty and was filled with wild brook trout whose beauty often left him speechless. Most of the area had never been logged and was filled with trees that were hundreds of years old, coyotes and bears, deer and moose, bobcats, martens, and mink.

He supposed if he had loved the women in his life with half the ardor he felt for the wilderness, his life might have been different. But he had never had a great deal of luck with women, and he was certain that this was due to his own deficiencies, not theirs. He had a tendency to get focused on one thing and exclude everything else. Often that one thing was protecting the Tract.

The failures of his love life aside, he knew with certainty that he loved the Mosquito Wilderness. His father had guarded it before him, and it had fallen to him to steward it for the next generation. Like most of the state's conservation officers, Grady Service took his responsibilities seriously and passionately. It was not so much about doing a good job as it was about upholding a sacred trust.

Parking his truck at a trailhead, Service locked up and headed into the bush on foot. There was a general belief among poachers and others in the state that conservation officers seldom ventured far off the roads. It wasn't true, and Service made sure that he covered the most isolated areas of his beat on foot as often as possible. It was impossible to calculate the PR value in word of mouth of a CO suddenly appearing in an area many miles from the nearest road. Over the years people got to asking how fewer than two hundred officers could be in so many places at one time. He had even had state troopers ask him the question, and he always answered with a provocative laugh.

Tonight there would be long light, until nearly 10:30 P.M. And tonight, if he was lucky, there would be no fishermen to check. He could take advantage of having the river to himself.

The last quarter mile to the river was swampy and choked by tag alders and wild vines. Service rarely followed established man-made or animal trails. Experience had taught him that it was better to take compass headings and strike out, making his own way. It was harder going, but it let him move unobserved and appear seemingly out of nowhere.

Fifty yards from the river he saw fresh bear scat near a fallen white cedar. The previous winter had been particularly harsh and the spring even worse, with a series of ice storms and high winds that knocked down anything with the slightest weakness. Like life, he thought. He was not afraid of bears, but it was early summer and he had no desire to play tag with a fiercely protective sow with cubs. He quietly moved on and steered a more direct route to the river.

There was nobody in sight when he reached the water, but he sensed someone close by. Tucking his fly-rod case into a hollow snag he had used for years, he worked his way down to a bend in the river with a deep hole on the outer curve, a place he called the Geezer Hole because of the very old and very large brook trout that lived at its head. It was one of the wider places on the river, with a large gravel bar mixed with reddish blue clay in the center and the greenish orange river racing by in long smooth glides on both sides. The purple color of the clay was unusual and had always seemed odd to him, but nature had her own ways and rarely shared her reasons.

An older man was hunkered on one knee at the far end of the gravel bar. No rod, just a camera around his neck and a strange hammer in a leather belt holster. He was scribbling furiously on a little notebook balanced on his knee.

"Hi," Service called out.

The surprised man looked up and fumbled at putting his notebook away.

"DNR," the CO said.

"I'm not fishing."

"I can see that."

"I'm just looking around."

The man was nervous. "What exactly are you looking for? I know the area pretty well. Might be able to point you."

"I don't think so."

"Where are you parked?"

"On the highway," the man said.

On the highway? It was a good ten miles of hard walking away — *if* you didn't get lost, which most people did.

"Are you camping in the tract?"

"Haven't decided," the man said.

There was no evidence of a pack or any gear other than the camera and the hammer.

"You have to stick to designated sites in the tract."

"I know the rules," the man said irritably.

"The nearest camping area is three miles south."

"Yes, I know."

With experience, you developed intuition about people. Something was definitely hinky with this guy.

"Have you got a compass?" Service asked.

"Yes, in my pocket."

"Best use it. I'd hate to have to mount a search."

"Don't worry," the man said. "I know what I'm doing."

Service wanted to ask more questions, but before he could say anything the man got up, pivoted, and headed downstream, splashing carelessly as he went. So much for fishing the Geezer Hole, Service thought.

The man's brusque manner and unfriendliness had Service's curiosity at full glow. He decided to follow, but first he waited. Most people believed that a trail couldn't be followed in moving water, but they were wrong. This bottom had a lot of loose stones and enough clay, sand, and silt to make it fairly routine to follow just about anybody. Worst case, he could leapfrog ahead and watch for debris and clouds of sand tumbling downstream. If the water stayed clear, he would know the man had gotten out or stopped above him. He waited ten minutes and began to follow. This time Service decided to take the most direct line. What was this guy doing?

It didn't take long to see that the man had gotten out less than a hundred yards below the Geezer Hole. There were wet spots on the top of a dry log. An experienced man would wait until dark and get out, hoping that the lack of light would cover his sign. And animals didn't step on logs; only men did. This guy had jumped out fast. Their encounter had spooked the man. If his vehicle was ten miles south on the highway, why was he headed west? Definitely hinky.

The man's tracks showed that he was moving fast, using the trail for a while then going off trail, sort of zigzagging. It took an hour to find where the man had parked a vehicle. It was gone, of course, but it had been there. Judging by the width of the wheel base, it was a full-size Bronco, a Blazer, or a Ram, all models no longer in production.

Now Service was really curious. Cutting north, he jogged quickly back to his truck, drove out, and circled back to the road where the stranger was most likely to have come out. He found tracks that fit the ones he had seen back in the woods; the pattern showed a left turn. Service drove along the road for thirty minutes, but decided to give it up. The man hadn't done anything wrong. He had just acted strangely. So it went. Submitted to the same test, he would no doubt also fail.

It was time for home and sleep. Tomorrow he had to be in court on a case from an arrest he had made last September. Time in court was usually a pain in the ass, and this would be no different.

At the house Cat met him on the porch and hissed ostentatiously. He had found the animal in a bag of eight newborn kittens that somebody had drowned. Why this one survived was beyond him, but it had and had turned into a feline misanthrope. Which made it an animal he could relate to.

"Okay, food coming up, you four-legged ingrate. Put your claws back in their sheaths."

For most of his career in the Department of Natural Resources, Service had lived in a pop-up camper that he moved from campground to campground, but five years ago he had bought property close to the Tract and built what he called a house. Others called it a shack, or worse. But the opinions of others rarely concerned him; the place suited him. It was two stories with one large room on each level. The upper level was for expansion but so far remained empty, a place for Cat to dismember mice and voles and hold forth over lesser creatures in nature's violent chain. On the ground floor he had a kitchen area, a bathroom behind unpainted doors he had propped up to serve as screens, his communications equipment, and a dozen OD military surplus footlockers. He slept on a thin mattress on three of the footlockers set end to end.

As soon as he shed his uniform, he checked his messages. There were the usual whinings of residents and a couple of calls from local stoolies, but only two calls interested him. Lisette McKower said she wanted to meet him tomorrow after court at the Duck. McKower was a sergeant and his protégé as well. He had trained her a long time ago and she had moved up. He wondered what she wanted.

The other call was from Luticious Treebone.

He called Treebone's home number in Detroit.

"This is the Tree," a booming voice answered.

"How's Hoffa?" His friend's pit bull.

"Bad tempered, which is just how I like my dogs. S'up, man?"

"You called me, remember?"

"Right, just wanted to see if you were payin' attention. I've got some time off. I'm thinking maybe I might mosey north and do some fishing. You up for it?"

"Tree, you hate it up here."

"Then I'll just ride along with you. Change of scenery will do me good. Kalina's mother is coming to town."

"No guts?"

"Discretion, baby. There's a time to wail and a time to bail. A man don't wanna get the two bollixed up, dig?"

Service laughed softly. "I'll line up some footlockers for you."

"You don't own a bed yet?"

"I refuse to join the conspicuous consumptionists."

"Man, you need to join the human race." Treebone laughed. "I'll be there day after tomorrow. I can let myself in."

"Watch out for Cat."

"Maybe I'll bring Hoffa to deal with the hairball."

"Cat will eat him for lunch."

"See you soon, man."

Service and Treebone had finished college, Service at Northern Michigan, where he had been only a fair student and a competent hockey player. Treebone had played football and baseball at Wayne State and graduated cum laude. They had both been on the verge of being drafted, so they volunteered for the marines, met at Parris Island, and served together in the same long-range recon unit in Vietnam. They had been through hell and rarely spoke of the war since. When they got back to "the world," they had both joined the Michigan State Police; two years later there had been an opportunity to transfer to the DNR and they had both accepted, but within a year Treebone had taken a job with the Detroit Metro Police. He was now a lieutenant in charge of vice. They had remained close friends now for more than twenty years. Tree wanted to ride with him? His friend had something up his sleeve, because he did not venture voluntarily into the U.P. without a compelling reason. Tree's idea of wilderness was Belle Isle on the Fourth of July.

Service thought about eating but didn't feel like cooking. Court tomorrow. He would need sleep to cope with that bullshit.

As soon as he settled onto his sleeping pad, the phone rang.

"Service."

"You're not out stomping around the boonies?"

It was Kira Lehto. "I've got court tomorrow."

"You sound beat."

"No more than usual."

"Did you lose my phone number?"

"You know how it is." She ought to. She was a well-known and highly respected veterinarian with a practice she called an ark—meaning she took on whatever came her way, rarely asking if people could pay before she took care of an animal. Just about every conservation officer and ranger in the central and western Upper Peninsula called her when they needed help. They had dated for the better part of a year, but many of their nights together had been interrupted by emergency calls, either for her or for him. The last couple of months they had begun meeting during the day when they could both break away from duty for a couple of hours.

"I'm sorry."

"No you're not," she said, her tone a well-delivered jab. So far, she seemed to understand and accept him, showing no interest in changing him, which made her unique. So far. "Will court take all day?"

"Could be. A violet I plucked last September. From Detroit. He's bringing his own asshole lawyer up to fight it." Violet was the term Service used for violators.

"Iffy?"

"You never know. Tree called. He's driving up the day after tomorrow. His mother-in-law is invading."

She laughed her hearty laugh. "Want to bring him over for dinner?"

"I don't know what time he'll get in."

"Okay, see you guys Thursday. I miss you, Grady."

"I miss you too."

"We ought to think about a vacation and take a couple of weeks, you know, go somewhere real."

"And leave all this good stuff to the bad guys?"

"You've got a job, Service. I'm trying to give you a life."

"That's a big challenge," he said.

"I'm up to it. Thursday night, then?"

"We'll be there."

"Good luck in court."

"Thanks." He suddenly felt guilty and lonely. "You want me to drive over tonight?"

"I think we should just wait," she said. "Celibacy makes the heart grow fonder. Besides, you have to face a bad guy in court."

He grunted. "Okay, Thursday night. Tree can spring for the wine."

"Be safe, Grady."

Safe? Did that term ever apply to this job? Had he ever had a job that was safe?

On the Freedom Bird from Da Nang to Seattle, Treebone and he had ridden in silence nearly halfway across the Pacific before Tree mumbled, "I think we're gonna survive, man."

"If the plane doesn't crash."

"You're a sick motherfucker."

His friend hadn't been wrong. You had to be a little sick to deal with the kinds of people they both dealt with now. If you weren't twisted when you started, you got that way over time.

After hanging up, Service walked onto his porch. It overlooked Slippery Creek. Its clay bottom and loonshit edges hosted a nice population of robust brown trout that didn't grow long, but got fat and thick. The DNR had planted hatchery stock many years before, and they had taken hold; now the strain was nearly native and reproducing on its own. He hated the rubber fish that the state's stew ponds produced for public waters, but the state was in the business of managing unnaturally high game and fish stocks for the benefit of the people. Sometimes the artificiality of the whole endeavor depressed him, but there were times when things seemed wild enough that he allowed himself to be pleased. The fish in Slippery Creek had gotten lucky and found a niche because few people knew they were there—and even those who did were mostly not interested in the considerable physical effort necessary to work the water. You needed to be an acrobat to wade a clay bottom. Or a fool.

From the berm that bordered the stream he could hear the tree frogs trilling. Males calling frantically for females, advertising their availability. He thought about calling Kira back, but went inside and settled onto his pallet. He had court tomorrow and this was one sleezeball he wanted to see put away.

· 6 ·

Service rarely had trouble sleeping, but he had not slept well last night. He could not get the man in the Mosquito Tract out of his mind and decided that he would have to keep a closer watch in the future. Most work you did because it came with a paycheck. But there were some things you would do for nothing, and clearly the Mosquito fit this category. His old man had died protecting the Tract and he was damn well not going to let it slip away on his watch.

The courthouse in Marquette was made of plum-red sandstone hauled over from the quarry in Jacobsville in the last century. The now-defunct quarry was at the far southern tip of the Keweenaw Peninisula, maybe the most isolated spot in the state. An annex had been built onto the old building and looked like square fungus. Things used to be made to last. Now buildings seemed to be built on the assumption that they might stand only twenty or thirty years. Build it, use it, tear it down, build another. This throwaway mentality seemed to carry over to too many facets of life. It made more sense to build for keeps. It used fewer resources and gave a solidity to things that modern life often lacked. He knew he was stubbornly old fashioned in some ways. Kira called him a reactionary.

The district court in the annex handled misdemeanors, and this was where most COs did their court duties. But this case was a felony and being tried in the circuit court in the old building. The venue pleased him.

The charges also included a federal ding for use of a silencer, but this case was being tried in the state circuit court first. They had enough to put the defendant away without the silencer count; if they could get him on the other charges at the state level, the feds would jump in next to try to bend the man for information about where he had gotten the device. The Bureau of Alcohol, Tobacco and Firearms rarely passed a chance to follow up on such opportunities. The DNR and other state agencies almost always cooperated.

The judge was Onty Peltinen, a forty-year-old University of Michigan freak who drove a maize-and-blue conversion van and hung four gigantic yellow-block M flags off his front porch on game days. The judge always wore a blue suit, a yellow shirt, and a yellow-and-blue striped tie. If not for trout, Peltinen would no doubt be riding herd over a court nearer to Ann Arbor. As it was, he fancied himself the new John Voelker, the judge from Ishpeming who had written under the pen name of Robert Traver. Peltinen fished for brook trout in his free time and wrote exaggerated accounts of his self-absorbed exploits for obscure trouting journals. He was a short man with razor-cut pale brown hair and a handlebar mustache that sometimes seemed red. No doubt Peltinen liked presiding in the same courtroom where parts of Voelker's *Anatomy of a Murder* had been filmed.

Service had no idea what sort of a judge Peltinen was technically, but he had shown good sense in his rulings and appeared to be an unabashed friend of natural resources and COs. Probably because Service and other COs told the judge about great places to find trout. There were precious few like Peltinen nowadays and whatever his peculiarities and proclivities, they could be forgiven. Especially in the U.P. where everybody tended to skate in the more extreme bands of the eccentricity spectrum.

Deputy Prosecuting Attorney Joe Doolin met Service outside the courthouse. They both lit cigarettes.

"Fuckin' pain in the ass," Doolin said, "this no-smoking shit. Someday they'll pass laws so's a body can't even smoke in the bloody bush. Mark my words."

"They'll have to catch me," Service said.

Doolin looked at him and grinned. "I expect that might be a problem for the no-smoking cops."

The deputy prosecutor was sixty-seven, of average height, with a crooked nose and missing the lobe of his left ear. Nobody asked how the ear had been injured, and Doolin never volunteered. He had grown up in Ishpeming, been a trouting pal of John Voelker's, gone to school in Illinois, practiced law with a big firm in Chicago, gotten fed up with cities, and returned home to Marquette. In recent years Service had noticed more and more big-timers suddenly deep-sixing their careers and coming home or relocating to out-of-the-way places where the pace of life was slower. Doolin called the trend downshifting, and Service thought that was about as good a description as any. Sometimes he wished he could downshift, but what would be down from where he was, a hermit in Alaska?

"You ready for this doozy?" Doolin asked.

"Let's press on," Service said, flicking his cigarette away and opening the door for the prosecutor.

There were the usual preliminaries before Service was sworn in for the state and took his place in the witness chair. It was an expansive room with a stained-glass cupola overhead and balconies with glass-fronted bookcases filled with law books bound in red and gray. The carpet was red with green squiggles that looked to Service like snowflakes. The walls were gray with recessed white plaster alcoves and small columns with gaudy gold leaf. The old court's nearly black hardwood paneling and heavy, ornately carved railings made him think of all the people who had sat in the seats for more than a century, following essentially the same process as today. Things were different now, but the law still had force, and this comforted him. In some ways the cavernous room looked like the inside of a cathedral, but the justice sought here was for this life, not the next.

His old man had sat here many times, doing the same job.

"Good morning, Officer Service," Doolin opened.

Judge Peltinen sat behind a raised black wood desk. There was an American flag nearby and seven white globes on posts on the front corners of the desk. He looked small behind the official barrier.

The conservation officer nodded.

"You were the arresting officer in the case of *State versus Schembekeler?*"

"I was."

"Excuse me," Judge Peltinen said, interrupting with a hopeful look on his face. "Is the defendant any relation to the legendary Glenn 'Bo' Schembechler?"

Schembechler had been U of M's football coach for many years and was one of Peltinen's personal heroes.

"No, Your Honor," Doolin said, answering quickly before the defense could jump in. "Different families, no connection, even the spelling is different." Leaning toward Service he whispered, "I knew *that* was coming."

"Just wondering," the judge said wistfully. "Okay, Joe. Sorry to butt in. Let's move on. I just had to ask."

"Understood, Your Honor. Go Blue."

"Go Blue," Peltinen said brightly.

Doolin turned back to Service and rolled his eyes so that only the conservation officer could see.

"How long have you been a conservation officer?" he asked.

"Twenty years."

"Before that?"

"I had two years in the Michigan State Police and three years in the U.S. Marine Corps after college."

"During your police career, how many tickets have you written?"

"I don't know." Why had Doolin asked that?

"Thousands?"

"Objection," the defense attorney said. "Leading the witness and this line of questioning has no point." The attorney was from downstate, some subspecies of Detroiter. He wore a shiny black suit with gold flecks, a scarlet tie, and gold-rimmed pilot's glasses. His name was Hardin Bois.

"Mister Bois," Judge Peltinen said, "you're new in my court and to this area and I need to tell you up front that up here we do things a little differently. If you have good cause for objection, by all means raise it. Otherwise, shut your trap. This ain't gonna be on CNN tonight. We assume you know your stuff or you wouldn't be here, so do your client a favor and jump in when it makes good legal sense. We trout fishermen don't like to waste time on dead water. Am I clear?"

"Very clear. Thank you, Your Honor." The attorney's face reddened.

"You've written thousands of citations?" Doolin repeated, turning back to Service.

"Probably."

"You have a lot of experience with violators. Am I correct?"

"Yes, that's correct."

"How many of your cases have come to trial?"

"This makes about twenty."

"Only twenty in twenty years?"

"Yes."

"Is that normal for officers in your position?"

"No. Most are in court more often." Most COs who wrote a couple of hundred tickets in a year could expect six to eight of their busts to go to court. The fact was that no CO spent much time in court unless there was a complex case. His record was better than other COs', but only marginally. Doolin would not bring this out.

"I would say that this attests to your thoroughness at your job."

"Objection," the defense attorney said.

"Sustained," Peltinen said. "Dammit, Joe, we all know Grady and

we all know he's a fine officer. Can we just keep this thing moving?"
The judge moved his hand like he was turning the crank to a reel.

"Yes, Judge."

Service guessed that Peltinen had brook trout on his mind.

"Officer Service, please tell the court what happened on September
29 of last year."

"It was six weeks before the gun season for deer and two days before
bow season and I was on patrol. Several times over the summer I had
seen a large buck with a pretty fair rack in fields along the edge of the
Mosquito Tract. This was up near the headwaters of the river. In our
training, and this gets reinforced by experience on the job, we learn that
when we see a trophy animal we should assume it will become a target
for poachers or illegal takers. It's like following the money in other
criminal matters. Our currency is wildlife. Having seen this animal several times, I decided to patrol the area regularly, alternating the times
when I was there."

"To look for poaching activities?" Doolin asked.

"My primary intent was to let my presence deter illegal activity."

"Does deterrence work?"

"It's a central precept of law enforcement."

"Continue, please."

"It was 7 P.M., not long until dark. I saw the animal in the same
area where he usually was, at the edge of a field, barely out of the woods.
Suddenly, I saw the animal's hindquarters flatten. Then the buck got
up, made a twisting jump to the right, and jumped down into the
swamp. Deer don't behave this way unless they've been startled, frightened, or hurt."

"Are you an expert on white-tailed deer behavior, Officer Service?"

"I'm not a biologist, but COs accumulate a lot of experience ob-
serving animal behavior, and our experience makes us knowledgeable."

"You're also a tracker, correct? In fact, you are a nationally known
tracker who is sometimes asked by other state and also federal agencies
to lead various searches."

"Yes, I can track."

"In fact, you are a member of a Native American group called the
Shadow Wolves. These are trackers who have proven themselves in their
profession, and you are the only Caucasian who has ever been inducted
by the group. Is this correct?"

"They don't exactly induct you."

The Shadow Wolves had been created by Ted Owlfeather, a Cherokee who worked for the Texas Rangers. Owlfeather brought together six Native American trackers, called a press conference, and proclaimed them the best in America.

A few years later Service was on his way home from spending New Year's with Treebone and his family in Detroit. Despite a heavy snowstorm, he kept to back roads. About a mile north of Caffee, at the entrance to Fiborn Road, he found an older-model green Torino station wagon with its nose stuck in a snowbank forty yards off M-40. Three doors were standing open, and the interior was piled with blowing snow. He brushed off snow to find a Kansas license plate. He called in the number and was informed that the vehicle had been stolen from Liberal, Kansas, on New Year's Eve.

Service drove into Caffee and talked to the man who ran a wrecker service. He was unaware of the Torino and checked around. Nobody knew anything. The Mackinac County Sheriff's Department had not gotten a call about a car in trouble, and Service decided to investigate. Where were the people who had been in the vehicle?

Long-abandoned Fiborn Quarry was a mile or so north up the narrow lane from the Torino's resting place, the quarry a source of limestone in the nineteenth century. Service took his snowshoes and emergency pack and started down the lane, but it was drifted over; other than a deer trail or two crossing over, there was no sign anyone had been down it. If the people in the car had not headed toward the village of Caffee, they would have moved into the pines, where the snow wouldn't pile up so fast. Why they would head this way escaped him, but after a few minutes he cut a trail in the pines, called in his location, with his hand-held radio and continued following three sets of prints. The trail petered out in drifted-over open areas, but each time it disappeared he rediscovered it farther north in heavier cover where there was a protective canopy and easier footing.

Late that day another snowstorm moved in, but he pressed on. Perhaps the people had been hurt when they plowed into the snowbank and gotten disoriented. They were heading away from the road and civilization and into the deep swamps that surrounded the Hendrie River. Without equipment and know-how, most people wouldn't last long in this weather. He melted snow in a water purification device and ate the energy bars he kept in his emergency food supply. The state police and Mackinac County Sheriff's Department tried to mobilize to help him, but the storm stopped them. He continued north on his own, afraid that if he didn't push on, the people would die.

It took three days, but he finally smelled smoke, and when the snow relented a bit he saw smoke from a small fire going under some cedars. As Service approached, a gunshot sounded. Service yelled to identify himself but got another gunshot in answer. He alerted the state police, who wanted him to hold off and wait for backup, but he could hear frightened female voices coupled with an angry male voice and knew he could not wait. Having no idea what he was dealing with, he moved cautiously. The man took several shots at him as he maneuvered. Eventually he could see where the fire was and shot into the tree above it, dislodging a pile of snow that plopped on the fire and put it out. The man came forward trying to fire a rifle, but it was jammed. Service met him in thigh-deep snow and broke his jaw using the heel of his hand.

The man had robbed a bank in El Paso, Texas, two days before Christmas and disappeared despite a national manhunt. He had carjacked the Torino and, because of the storm, gotten all the way to the U.P. without detection. The women were frightened and suffering from exposure, but survived. The bank robber was returned to Texas, where he was also wanted for murder. He was later executed. Service never learned why the man had gone north into the swamps or spared the women.

In the wake of his hunt, Wansome "Wally" Purple, an Ojibwa from Rice Lake, Minnesota, had called Service to inform him that he had been chosen for the Shadow Wolves, a group he had heard of but knew nothing about. As it turned out the group's founder, Ted Owlfeather, objected to his induction, but Owlfeather was no longer in charge. Service went to Pine Ridge, South Dakota, to meet the other members. There was no formal ceremony and they drank heavily for nearly forty-eight hours, but Purple knew how to publicize things so there had been a good deal of national and state publicity about Service's new status. This was about two years before he got Trip Bozian as a probie, and Service suspected that his status with the group had made it tougher for Bozian to retaliate. He had talked occasionally to Wally Purple and two or three of the other Wolves since South Dakota, but had not seen them again. Once in a while he read in the newspaper about something one of them had done. His membership, he decided was strictly honorary, which suited him.

"My point is that you are a skilled and proven tracker, correct?"

Doolin's voice brought him back to the present.

"I usually find what I'm looking for."

"Is it true that you have never failed to find a lost person that you've been looking for?"

"Objection," Bois said for the defense. "This is irrelevant."

"Your Honor," Doolin said, "tracking requires attention to detail and powers of observation beyond what we normal folks possess. A tracker needs knowledge, wilderness skills, keen eyes and ears, and a fine analytical mind. I'm trying to establish Officer Service's competence in this regard, and his success rate is the measure of how effective he's been at using these critical skills."

"Overruled," Peltinen said from high above. "Witness can answer the question."

"Have you found every lost person you've ever searched for?"

"Yes." Which was true, but too damn many of them weren't alive when he finally got to them. He knew Doolin would not ask this.

"And you use your highly developed skills to track animals and violators as well, is that correct?"

"I do."

"Okay, let's go back to the Mosquito. You saw the buck go down, then get up and flee?"

"Correct. I thought someone had taken a shot."

"You heard the report of a firearm?"

"No, but I saw how the animal reacted."

"This led you to investigate further?"

"Yes. I circled on the presumption that a shot would most likely come from the animal's downwind side. I hiked in about a quarter mile and cut trail."

"Cut trail?"

"I saw fresh sign that someone had been there."

"What signs?" Doolin asked.

"There were deadfalls arranged in a vee, a pretty typical makeshift blind. There was also evidence of some scraping on the top log, a rest for a weapon. The grass behind the blind was pressed down. And I saw heel indentations to indicate that somebody had been sitting there."

"Could you tell how recently the place had been occupied?"

"Yes, only minutes before. Some bent grasses were recovering their elasticity."

"You say there were boot prints?"

"Yes and the left heel had a distinctive nick in it that made it easy to read on the ground."

"Then what?"

"I followed the trail."

"In the footsteps?"

"No, trackers always offset six to eight feet to one side or the other. Otherwise you can spoil the evidence."

"Please continue," the prosecutor said. "What did you find?"

"The trail led me to where I had last seen the buck. The animal's tracks were fresh and there were patches of deer hair on the ground, but no blood. I believed the animal had been grazed, perhaps along the spine, which would account in part for the way its back legs splayed when it went down."

"But there was no blood."

"Right, no blood."

"Meaning the animal might not have been struck at all?"

"No, there was hair. It had been struck."

"How do you account for the lack of blood?"

"Even with a kill-shot, an animal may not bleed right away. It depends on the nature of the weapon used and, if it's a firearm, the caliber, the cartridge load, and the site of the wound. An arrow, for example, rarely shows blood after a hit. It penetrates and causes massive internal hemorrhaging, which leads to shock, which eventually kills the animal. You often find no blood until the animal is down and nearly dead. Deer shot in the gut or heart by a rifle don't always bleed immediately and often can travel a long distance before there's a blood trail. The hair tufts and the animal's behavior told me it had been hit."

Service waited for Doolin to lead him, but Doolin's eyes had glazed over, so the conservation officer continued his testimony.

"The boot tracks led toward the hair on the ground, so I followed the tracks. There was a low ridge running south, and I figured the deer looped right and the shooter was trying to move on a parallel course, using the high ground to get a second shot."

"What did you find?"

Welcome back, Service thought. "I heard a shot."

"You heard a shot. A loud shot?"

"No, it was muffled."

"Like it was a long way off?"

"No, it was muffled but close."

"But a rifle makes a very loud sound. Even a plinker like a .22 makes an audible crack, am I correct?"

"Some make more sound than others, but this was baffled."

"Baffled? You mean like a silencer?" Doolin's face showed astonishment. It was an act for the jury. Doolin enjoyed the drama of the courtroom stage.

"Yes." Service expected the defense attorney to object, but he was sitting silent in his chair, staring off in the distance.

"You have experience with silencers?"

"Yes."

"During your tenure with the DNR?"

"I was a sniper in the Marine Corps."

"Our U.S. Marines use *silencers?*"

"Yes, for some special missions and tasks. I've also worked with federal agencies that use silencers, and I've been through an FBI course on using and identifying weapons with silencers."

"So you knew there was a silencer."

"I knew a firearm had been discharged and that the sound was muffled."

"What did you do after the shot?"

"I went toward the sound. Below and to my left I saw the buck thrashing around on its side. In front of me there was a man with a weapon in the position of port arms. I asked him what he was doing."

"Then?"

"He turned in my direction and leveled the rifle at me."

"How did you respond?"

"I turned on my tape recorder."

"Your recorder?"

"Right. It's attached to my belt. It's Swedish-made and can pick up the sound of a butterfly running into a tree fifty yards away."

"That's an exaggeration."

"No, it's fact."

Everybody in the courtroom laughed. Except the defendant and his attorney.

"Do all officers carry recorders, Officer Service?"

"I can't speak for all my colleagues. I got the idea from videocams on state police cruisers. COs generally work alone and often among armed people. If something happens to me, I want there to be some record to give somebody a starting point."

"You mean, if you were dead?"

"Or too injured to keep going."

"Is it legal to record this way?"

"Yes."

"Does the court have the tape?"

"It does," Service said.

"Are you paranoid, Officer Service?"

"No, I'm careful. I saw the shooter's rifle pointed in my direction. So I turned on the recorder."

"Did you feel threatened?"

"The shooter told me to depart."

"What were his exact words, please?"

"He said, 'Split, fuckstick.' "

"Was there an 'or else'?"

"He raised his weapon at me."

"And what was your response to this threat?"

"I looked down toward the buck and yelled, 'Run, deer, run.' "

"Run . . . deer . . . run?"

"I wanted to divert the shooter's attention."

"Did it work?"

"Yes."

"Tell us what happened."

"He looked away and I charged and tackled him high so as to get inside the rifle. That way he couldn't use it. We collided pretty hard and we both tumbled down the embankment. The fall separated us, but it also separated him from his rifle."

"What happened next?"

"He pulled a knife."

"What did he say?"

"He said he was going to cut off my testicles and stuff them in my eye sockets."

"Were you afraid?"

"No."

"Why not?"

"He was a yapper. I'm not afraid of people who start talking when they try to threaten you. The dangerous ones don't say anything. Besides, if it looked like I couldn't handle him, I could always run away."

"You'd do that?" Doolin feigned surprise.

"Lickety split, if that's what the situation dictated."

Observers in the courtroom laughed. Even Peltinen grinned.

"Where was your sidearm during all this?"

"In its holster."

"You never pulled your sidearm?"

"No."

"But he was threatening you."

"Drawing my weapon is a last resort. We're taught when we draw to shoot to kill. I didn't think the situation required that. Besides, his leg was broken."

"From the fall?"

"Yes, I could see how it was bent. He was so jacked up on adrenaline that the pain hadn't hit him yet. And he was still on the ground."

"What did you do?"

"I told him to set the knife down and push it out of his reach."

"Did he comply?"

"No, he threw it."

"At you?"

"It passed three feet to my right, chest high."

"In other words, he was not complying with your order."

"Correct."

"Then what?"

"He put his hands up to his face and started to cry."

"Cry?"

"Weep, bawl."

"Did he say anything?"

"He said none of it was his fault."

"What did you say?"

"I told him to put out his hands. Then I cuffed him and read him his rights and told him I was going to call the county EMS."

"Did he resist?"

"No, he kept yelling that it wasn't his fault. I advised him to remain silent until he got a lawyer, but he kept yelling that it wasn't his fault and that everything had been caused by intoxication brought on by sweets."

"Sweets?"

"Hostess Twinkies."

The people in court began to snicker.

"He actually said this?"

"Repeatedly."

"Did you find any Twinkies?"

"No."

"Any wrappers?"

"Just one, near the deadfall blind."

"Did he say it was his?"

"Yes."

"What did you do?"

"I added littering to the charges."

This time everybody in court laughed out loud and raucously. One individual even applauded.

Judge Peltinen pounded his gavel and said, "Order, please. Let's not act like a buncha ridgerunners." But even Peltinen was grinning.

"Any other . . . *Twinkie* . . . *evidence?*" Doolin asked, trying to subdue a smirk.

"No. I searched him, checked his trail and his blind, his vehicle. After EMS transported him, I got a search warrant and checked his cabin. No Twinkies. In fact, there were no sweets of any kind in his cabin except granulated sugar."

"Did the defendant act intoxicated?"

"No."

"Did you use the Breathalyzer?"

"Yes. It was normal, blood alcohol of zero."

"Did you believe him, that sugar got him loopy?"

"Objection," Bois said. "Not qualified."

"Sustained," said the judge.

Doolin moved on. "Officer Service, are you aware of a case in California where a jury found a man innocent on the grounds that he committed murder while temporarily insane from sugar intoxication?"

"I wasn't aware of the case at that time. I am now."

"Do you have an opinion on that defense?"

The defense lawyer jumped up. "Objection. The witness is not qualified to provide a legal opinion."

"Sustained," Peltinen said.

"As a citizen do you have an opinion?"

"Yeah, California ain't Michigan."

"Meaning?"

"If it smells like baloney and looks like baloney, it's baloney."

Several people in court snickered. Including some members of the jury, who sat in high-backed benches to the judge's left. Peltinen shot them a hard look, but they kept smiling.

"Had you met the defendant before September twenty-ninth of last year?"

"No."

"Officer Service, have you ever been wounded in the line of duty?"

"I have."

"How many times?"

"Three times."

"Firearms?"

"Yes."

"Have you ever shot anybody during your DNR duties?"

"No sir."

"You showed admirable restraint, Officer Service."

"I did my job."

"If another officer had encountered the defendant, the outcome might have been dramatically different," Doolin said.

"Objection!" Bois shouted.

"Sustained. Dammit Joe. You've made your point."

"Sorry, Your Honor. I'm finished with the witness."

The judge looked at Hardin Bois. "Your lick."

The defense attorney straightened his tie as he stood up.

"Officer Service, did you *see* Mister Schembekeler discharge a firearm? Please answer my question."

"I heard it."

"Officer, I asked if you *saw* my client discharge his firearm?"

"No."

Bois turned to face the jury. "In fact you did *not* see my client discharge a weapon. What you heard could have been another weapon, am I right?"

"It was his."

"But theoretically it could have been another. Did you find spent cartridges?"

"No."

"How do you account for that?"

"I don't."

"So you did not see my client discharge a firearm of any kind and you found no spent cartridges, is that correct?"

"Yes."

"Officer, were rounds missing from the defendant's clip?"

"No, because—"

"You've answered the question, Officer. Thank you."

Doolin would circle back to this one.

"If you did not see Mister Schembekeler fire a weapon—any weapon—and you found no cartridges, then you must agree that theoretically there could have been another shooter."

"Theoretically."

Bois smiled at the jury. "Thank you, Your Honor."

"Redirect," Peltinen said, checking his watch.

Doolin asked, "Officer Service, how could there be no rounds missing from the clip?"

"Because there wasn't any clip. It was a single-shot weapon." Doolin was hokey, but he was good.

"Had the weapon been fired?"

"It had."

"How do you verify this?"

"My nose and a test."

"Was this test done?"

"Yes."

"When?"

"On scene immediately after the apprehension."

"And the result?"

"It was positive. The weapon had been fired."

"Thank you. Did you recover a slug from the dead animal?"

"Yes. It was the same caliber as the defendant's rifle, but the bullet was too fragmented for ballistics."

"Can you explain this to me? Our jury probably understands this stuff, but I don't."

Doolin played every angle. "This caliber with this powder load makes the bullet tumble. When it strikes something hard, it shreds."

"Have you had previous experience with this caliber?"

"Yes, it's poachers' favorite flavor."

"Did the defendant deny the weapon was his?"

"No."

"Did the defendant say he had shot the animal?"

"No. He only said that it wasn't his fault, that he had been intoxicated by sweets."

"How did you interpret this?"

"He had shot the animal, but was not acting rationally."

"And his weapon was equipped with a silencer, which is against federal statutes."

"Objection," Bois said angrily. "There is no charge on a silencer in this case."

Peltinen grimaced. "Overruled. Answer the question, Officer Service."

"Yes, silencers are illegal."

"Officer, have you ever arrested other suspects when you did not see them shoot?"

"Many times."

"And all those arrests stuck?"

"Objection," Bois said. "Irrelevant."

"Sustained," the judge said.

"Did you hear any other shots that night?" Doolin asked.

"None."

"If we are to believe the defense, there would need to be two poachers in the woods at that isolated location, both with the same weapon, same ammo load, and each with a silencer, is that correct?"

"That seems to be his theory."

"What're the odds of that?"

"Objection," Bois said with a raspy growl. "The witness is not a statistician."

"Withdrawn," Doolin said. "Officer Service, in your twenty years with the DNR how many silencers had you encountered in the field before this situation?"

"None."

"This was the first one in twenty years?" Doolin looked surprised. It was more playacting.

"Yes."

"Your first ever, and defense counsel would have us believe that there were two?"

"Objection!" Bois shouted again. "Leading the witness."

Doolin slicked his hair back with his left hand and said, "Thank you, Officer Service."

"The witness is excused," the judge said.

Doolin piped up, "Your Honor, the defense is going to haul in a battalion of medical experts, and I see no reason for Officer Service to remain here. He has plenty of other duties to attend to."

"Fine by me," Peltinen said, "but I would like for him to sit tight for a few minutes. Can do?" he asked, glancing at Service.

"Yessir," the CO said, taking a seat in the gallery.

"Good," Peltinen said. "Mister Bois, I know you got yourself some fancy tech-talkers all lined up to snow us rubes, but I've done some research myself. A friend of mine from the U of M, he's a big-shot internist now, board certified, AMA, all that. He went to the AMA for some scientific information, and they said there's no such thing as intoxication by sweets. Is your client a diabetic?"

"Yes, Your Honor, and he is insulin dependent."

"Thank you. Since he didn't go into shock, we can rule out that pesky Twinkie. See, a diabetic goes into shock and can get cuckoo when his sugar is too *low*. If the diabetic gets too much sugar, he goes off the air, not on a shooting spree. I know this is going to be a controversial ruling and naturally you've got the right to appeal, but we get too many folks trying to play games with the court these days and I don't like it one bit."

"Your Honor," Bois whined, his voice strained.

"Put your butt on that chair, counselor. I am directing a verdict of guilty. We don't play games up here and we've heard enough baloney. Out east this sort of thing is called junk science. Which means it isn't science at all. I'm not going to insult the intelligence of this jury or waste anybody else's time jawing over a buncha horsebleep."

"This will be overturned," Bois said angrily.

The client looked dumbfounded, but Service knew it was an act. The jerk had concocted this whole thing before he poached, and it was a crime that the system had to take it this far. Even if the man appealed and won it was going to cost him a fortune, and right now all Service wanted was justice, in whatever form was possible.

"Maybe it will, but after you and your client get done talking to the feds, I doubt you'll be singing that song. Bailiff, please take the jury to the deliberation room."

They were out less than fifteen minutes.

Guilty on all charges.

When the verdict was announced, the judge set a date for sentencing. The feds were waiting to take custody of the defendant outside the courtroom.

Grady Service stopped by the defendant and leaned down. The man suddenly threw himself at the CO. The bailiff, a security guard, and two burly court employees pulled the two men apart.

The Duck Inn was a tavern at a dirt crossroads ten miles south of Marquette, a worn-out place where COs, rangers, loggers, cops of all flavors, and lawyers gathered after business hours.

"What did you *say* to him?" Doolin asked, hoisting a beer in salute.

"I didn't say anything."

"No?" Doolin's eyebrows popped up.

"I gave him a Twinkie."

Doolin's beer exploded down his chin as he began to laugh.

Sergeant Lisette McKower came into the bar thirty minutes after Doolin and Service arrived. She stood in the door and made eye contact with Service, who followed her to another table where they could have privacy.

McKower was five-five, 120, with short brown hair, a long neck, and tiny hands. The first time Service saw her he thought they'd sent him a cheerleader, but she had been twenty-four, had spent three summers as a USFS smokejumper, and it turned out that she was smart and as tough as moosehide. Nothing rattled her.

"You eat?" she asked.

"What happened to your diet?"

"Put your sarcasm away, Grady. How'd court go?"

"Guilty on all charges. Peltinen directed the verdict. The feds have him now."

"Twinkie defense," she said, shaking her head. "We've heard some strange ones in our day, but that's a top-fiver for sure. I'm going to order, okay?"

He held out his hands. "Yes, Sergeant."

She clucked at him and signaled for a waitress, ordering two bacon burgers with the works and a large order of fries. "How's Kira?"

"In the holding pattern."

She shook her head. "Why is it that good women are always attracted to bad boys?"

"I resent the implication."

"You'll always be a bad boy, Officer Service."

Their relationship was a delicate blend of professional and personal, and there had been a time for a month one fall when it had been hot and intimate. After it ended, there had been some hard feelings and embarrassment, but over time they had stayed close friends.

"If you say so, Sergeant."

"Grady," she said, studying him, "Allerdyce is getting an early release."

Service stared at her. Limpy Allerdyce had spent the past seven years in Jackson at the State Prison of Southern Michigan, a maximum-security, walled prison built a long time ago. Allerdyce was one of the most notorious poachers in the state's history, and Service had put him away time for attempted murder. Allerdyce was the leader of a tribe of poachers, mostly his relations, who lived like animals in the far southwestern reaches of Marquette County. They killed bears and sold gallbladders and footpads to Korean brokers in Los Angeles for shipment to Korea and Taiwan. They killed dozens of deer, took thousands of fish, and got substantial money for their take from buyers in Chicago and Detroit. Despite their income, the clan lived like savages. Service had not expected Allerdyce to be turned loose for several more years.

"That explains Treebone."

"What about Tree?" she asked.

"He called and said his mother-in-law was coming to town and that he wanted to get away, but I think he knows about Allerdyce. When are they kicking him loose?"

"Tomorrow."

"Tree," he said, with a tone, half angry, half admiring.

"Live with it, Service, some of us actually care about you."

"They assign a parole officer yet?"

"I assume so. You want to talk to his PO?"

"It wouldn't hurt. If Limpy's out tomorrow, there'll be a big welcome-home bash tomorrow night. I wonder if his clan will even recognize him?"

"How's that?"

"It'll be the first time they'll have seen him clean since his last stint in the jug."

McKower chuckled. "They had to force-clean him in jail during the trial."

"I'm going to pay him a visit."

"That's a spectacularly stupid idea," McKower said.

"It'll be purely social, you know, welcome the rehabbed citizen back to the community."

"The last time you showed up where he didn't expect you, he put a shotgun slug in you."

"All the more reason to go. Animals like this, you show fear and you're screwed. I'm not going to be walking around looking over my shoulder."

"It's your call, but for the record, I'm against it."

"Noted."

When the bacon burgers and fries came, McKower devoured them. She dipped her fries in mayonnaise.

When she finished eating, they ordered coffees to go and walked outside together.

"Congratulations on the Twinkie deal," she said.

He smiled. "It was sweet."

"God," she said. "I *hate* puns."

"I'll take Tree with me to visit Limpy."

"That's better than going alone, but it's still a stupid idea."

"Some system we have, paroling a piece of shit like this," he said, grumbling.

She patted his arm. "Be careful and if you go, call me afterward. Tell Kira she has my sympathies."

"Yeah," he said. "Why don't you and Jack join us for dinner Thursday night? Tree will be there." Jack was Lisette's husband.

"I just might do that," she said.

"Kira's going to cook."

In the years since he had trained her, she had eaten his cooking many times and always complained that he didn't make enough to feed a flea. He never disputed this; when he decided to cook, he preferred quality to quantity. If Kira cooked, there would be enough, and Lis would love it.

"It's my turn for a night out and Jack's turn to take care of the kids, but I'll be there," McKower said.

He watched her drive away from the Duck Inn and lit a cigarette.

Most fish and game violations grew out of unchecked emotions, not evil. Most murders were like accidental violations, not intentional, the perpetrators being victims of location as much as anything else.

Some churchgoing, Boy Scout–leading wrench-twister from Flat Rock saw not one, but two eight-point bucks and before he could think: *bang, bang.* Accidental violator.

A woman from Owosso gets a two-day fun pass from her old man. She's up on the Middle Branch catching trout. Nice ones. Big ones. Eager ones. One. Five. Ten. Limit reached, but God are they ever biting! Geez, can't quit now. Just a few more. Like, this happens only once in a lifetime and the hubby will never believe me. Just this once, I'll take them home. Twenty-two trout. Whoops. Accidental violator.

Hubby and honey have too much to drink. He says, Yip. She says, Yap. She pushes. He punches. She slaps back and screams. He reaches for the Ginsu. Ohmigod, what have I done! Common emotions in uncommon circumstances got out of hand. This was life and not something you could legislate against. Most folks were sorry after it happened, murderers included. You wrote them up or arrested them. They paid the fine or did the time and most would never do it again. It was a fact that few murderers ever killed again, and it was the same with accidental violators.

But Limpy Allerdyce was no accidental violator. He had no normal emotions. He was a predator in human form, a demon, a shape-shifter, a crow pocketing a bauble at Kmart, a wolf taking easy and helpless prey. He was cold-blooded and calculating, most of his children sired from his other children, a dirtbag who took and did as he wanted with no remorse. Service had once found him teaching some of his younger kin to skin rabbits while they were still alive. Another time he had dumped poison into the pond of a dairy farmer who had shot a deer on public land he considered his. After the nearby school district got a court order saying he had to send his kids to school, Limpy had mailed pornographic photographs to schoolboard members. He had done time for assault and battery, for stalking, and for a dozen other crimes, not to mention dozens of misdemeanors for illegal hunting and fishing and trapping. In Limpy's twisted mind, all that mattered was what he wanted and if you didn't agree, you were in deep trouble.

And he was getting out.

But not for long, Service told himself.

· 7 ·

Cat was asleep in Luticious Treebone's lap when Service got home. It had been a long day, talking to people, making arrangements for Allerdyce's reception.

"Nice dog," Service said.

"You'd hurt your own cat's feelings?"

"*That* animal has no feelings. The Asians have the right idea about cats and dogs: food."

"Still the hard case," Treebone said, flashing his smile. "I shoulda brought Hoffa," he added.

"Cat would've killed him. You're here because of Allerdyce."

The huge vice cop shrugged and scratched the cat's plump cheeks. "I figured you couldn't avoid sticking your face in his. You just don't get diplomacy the way I do."

"Some things just have to be done."

Nearly eight years ago Service had followed Allerdyce four consecutive nights, wanting to catch him alone, but he was usually with several of his miserable offspring. The night he finally got him alone, Limpy's choice of fish bait was half a stick of dynamite. Ignited at the right depth, dynamite doesn't make much noise in the river and stuns fish like nothing else. In Vietnam he and Tree had occasionally used grenades for the same purpose.

That night they were on the lower Escanaba River, in the warmer water below St. Nicholas. Limpy touched off two charges in a deep hole and netted walleyes into his aluminum boat with a long-handled salmon net. Service waited on shore, and when Limpy beached the boat, he stepped forward to challenge him.

The conservation officer had no idea where the shovel came from, but it caught him hard, breaking his right shoulder. Service tried to roll over when he fell, but a shotgun blast caught him in the left thigh. He was lucky it was a slug and a 20-gauge. It ripped out a chunk of meat but didn't break the bone or take out the femoral artery. When he came to, Allerdyce was long gone. Charges were filed and a warrant issued, but Limpy disappeared.

Service's wounds kept him in the hospital nine days, and he had nearly three full months at home recovering after that. Eight years later his shoulder still ached when rain or a low front was moving in.

While he recuperated, every police agency in the state searched for Limpy. Service knew they'd never find him. Limpy could live off the land indefinitely, but he had one major weakness: his appetite for women. He couldn't go long without, but he wouldn't be stupid enough to go where he might be grabbed. Maybe.

Service used his downtime to work his informants. Limpy's favorite women were his own daughter Vicki and daughter-in-law Honeypat. Neither of them lived in the compound with the rest of the odious family. Vicki lived in Gwinn and Honeypat in a house trailer in the Cyr Swamp west of Helena. Allerdyce wouldn't be dumb enough to venture near a town. Service staked out Honeypat's trailer.

Every afternoon he left his truck in a friend's garage at Little Lake and hiked nearly five miles through the Cyr Swamp, knowing that sooner or later Allerdyce would show.

The first two nights Honeypat's lights were on. The third night the trailer was dark from dusk on and Service heard them inside, but he was not ready to make his move.

The next two nights all was normal again at the trailer, and again on the third night Allerdyce came. Service did not see Limpy arrive and had no idea what direction he came from, but there was no doubt he was there. They went at it with the exuberance of bobcats in heat. Again, Service held back.

After three repetitions, Service knew he had the pattern. Every third night.

On the next rep Service made his move. Using the noise of their passion as cover, he moved up to the cinder-block steps of the trailer's door. When Allerdyce stepped out, the conservation officer reached up, got the front of his shirt, and pulled him down. Before Limpy could react, Service twisted his arms behind him and cuffed him. A naked Honeypat came shrieking out behind Allerdyce and jumped at Service, who sidestepped her, drove his foot into her nearest thigh, grabbed her hair, and pulled her into the ground. Before the two lovebirds recovered their wits, they were both handcuffed.

A call to the county brought deputy sheriffs with help. The prisoners were placed in separate squad cars.

Allerdyce sat with a grin on his face. "Ole Honeypat's some sweet pussy," he told Service. "You want some o' that, help yourself. She don't care who, even the law."

"Maybe after she's had a shower," Service said.

"Soap breaks the seal," Allerdyce said. "God give us a seal on our skin to keep off the germs. Break the seal, you get sick. You seen a bear take a bath?"

"They swim."

"Not with soap," Limpy said with a grin. "Check the Bible on that." Allerdyce looked up at him. "You been out there skulking a while?"

Service nodded.

"Thought so," Limpy said. "Had me a feeling, but you know how it is when you get the pussy-wants. How'd you figure it out?"

"Process of elimination."

Allerdyce grunted. "Guess it don't pay to have favorites."

"Probably not," Service said. It always amazed him how hardened criminals would engage in weird conversations after they were in custody. It was as if nothing had happened.

"Guess you healed up okay."

"Good enough."

"Me, I'm a fast healer too. You know, I coulda killed your ass that night, but the way I seen it, we were both just doing our jobs. You'd do good to remember that."

"Considering where you are now, that blade cuts two ways."

Limpy looked up and grinned toothlessly. "I guess it does at that."

It had taken six months to try him, and he had been gone seven years since then.

Service got two Strohs from the refrigerator, took a seat beside Treebone, and gave his friend one of the beers.

"You'd rather play with Allerdyce than face your mother-in-law?"

"I'm just here to help."

Service said, "We have to do this my way, Tree."

"There's no rules for cockroaches, my man."

"I don't break the law."

"Shit," Tree said with an expansive grin. "Bending ain't breaking."

"I'll decide how much bend there'll be."

The two men clicked their beer cans together.

Treebone said, "I always follow orders."

"When they suit you."

"Where would we be if we always followed orders in She-it-nam?"

"Point taken," Service said.

Most of the Allerdyce clan lived in a compound on a narrow peninsula between North and South Beaverkill Lakes. The area was a long way from civilization, not the sort of place you just stumbled across. With water on two sides and swamps on both ends, it was difficult to get to. There was a two-track from a US Forest Service road down to the compound's parking area and then a half-mile walk along a twisting trail from there into the camp itself. The surrounding area was dense with cedars, hemlocks, and tamaracks. In terms of isolation, it was a fortress.

Approaching from any direction other than the tote road and trail was difficult, but over the years Service had done some prowling around and had learned the family's trail system.

It took nearly five hours for the two men to move into position. They could smell smoke from the camp and hear the sound of rifles being fired into the air. The celebration was under way.

"Sounds like the boys and girls are havin' a high old time," Treebone said. He wiped perspiration off his forehead and slapped at the mosquitoes and insects swarming around them. "Bugs here big enough to *shoot*."

Service ignored the insects and discomfort. "You understand what we're gonna do?"

"Yup."

"Don't take this lightly and don't overdo it. They've got weapons and some of them are felons. That's all we need."

"Black Man and Robin ride the redneck trail," Treebone said. "I love this shit."

"These assholes aren't the Insane Latin Counts, but they have their unique style. Don't underestimate them."

"You worry too much. 'Is You Is or Is You Ain't My Baby?' "

This was the title of an Aaron Izenhall song. Izenhall had played alto sax with Louis Jordan and the Tympany Five and their breakneck boogie-woogie was one of Treebone's great passions.

Service used his handheld radio to make a quick call to a contingent of deputies waiting to move in. They were in the woods in their vehicles a couple of miles from the compound's parking area.

"One-ninety, this is DNR 421. We're moving in."

"Good hunting, 421."

"Let's get it done," Grady Service said to his friend.

" 'Let the Good Times Roll,' " Treebone said softly. Izenhall again.

Service walked slowly through the woods. Why writers talked about a silent forest was beyond him. Tree frogs sawed and crickets chirped and blended into a white-noise buzz that masked their movement. Off in the distance he heard crows on their night perch. The closer they got, the louder the camp frenzy sounded. Somebody was playing a fiddle and somebody else whanging a drum, *whack-whump-whacka-whack*, with no discernible rhythm, and now and then a weapon was discharged. When Service got close enough, he saw the clan bunched loosely around a huge bonfire, and the scene made him shiver. They were mostly naked, screaming and dancing herky-jerky around the fire. The muzzle flashes of rifles fired upward added sparks to the smoky air.

Limpy's tribe.

The camp comprised a dozen or more construction trailers and blackened log cabins, situated more or less in a circle. The din from the celebrants was amazing; the sounds from the people gyrating around the fire were barely recognizable as human.

Ten feet from where Service stood he saw a man with a woman bent forward, her hands clutching a rickety chair back. They two were squealing and grunting like pigs as they copulated.

The CO worked his way from cabin to cabin until he saw Limpy sitting in a metal rocking chair near the bonfire. There were clan members gathered around him. The king and his vassals.

Service used the darkness to get as close as he could, sucked in a deep breath, and stepped boldly into the fire's flickering light.

The noise stopped almost immediately. All eyes locked on him. A dog bayed pathetically. There was no other sound but the crackling from the bonfire and the frantic trilling of tree frogs in the distance.

Allerdyce, who was a small man when Service had last seen him, looked even smaller now. He was shrunken and wizened, his skin sallow and hanging loose, his eyes black beads sunk deep in his triangular skull. He wore a beard now, and his hair was pulled back into a dirty gray ponytail. "You," Allerdyce said calmly.

"I thought I'd pay my respects, Limpy."

One of the vermin near the fire pointed a lever-action rifle in the conservation officer's direction, but the old man motioned him away.

"Honeypat's here, you want some pussy," the patriarch said. "Remember her? Ever'body dings 'er. I expect one more won't be makin' no difference."

Honeypat stepped from behind a group of people. She wore no clothes, and her black hair and her eyes were wild. She had aged twenty years in the past eight. She was in her early thirties now and looked fifty.

"That's generous, but Honeypat looks like she could use a long rest."

"That one don't never need no rest," Allerdyce said, letting loose a long belch. "Coming here wasn't too smart, eh?"

"I figured you'd be looking for an escort back to Jackson, Limpy."

Allerdyce stared at the fire and rocked back and forth. "You think you can put me back in there?"

"You've already broken your parole, Limpy."

"How's that?" Allerdyce asked, ever so slightly raising an eyebrow.

"You are gathered with armed ex-felons. I've witnessed the reckless discharge of firearms. You want me to keep on with the list?"

"That's just so much chickenshit," Allerdyce said.

At that moment Luticious Treebone emerged from the background, stepping up to the other side of Allerdyce.

Allerdyce looked over at Treebone and said, "Youse brung a nigger here to my home?"

"This nigger's glad to make your acquaintance," Tree said.

"I ain't done nothin'," the old man said. "I been away."

"You're under arrest," Service said to Allerdyce. "Put your hands out in front of you, Limpy."

Allerdyce was deathly still, his eyes darting around, a crooked grin forming.

"Are you deaf?" Service said.

"Put out your hands," Treebone added.

The old man did as he was told. Service cuffed Allerdyce and radioed for backup while Treebone stared down the crowd with a leer.

Service transmitted, "One-ninety, this is DNR 421. Come on in."

There was the muffled *wah-wah* of sirens in the distance.

"Take you an army and a nigger to get an old fart like me?" Limpy asked, looking up.

"You should understand," Service said. "You do what you've got to do."

"I ain't goin' back," Limpy said.

Service didn't argue with him. He helped him up from his rocker, frisked him, informed him of his rights, and started him east toward the trail.

"You best leggo, fish pig," Honeypat said, jumping in front of him. "He's stayin' with *us*."

Treebone stepped toward Service, withdrew his pistol, and touched it to Allerdyce's head. "Here's the deal, ma'am. You can have him without his ugly, toothless head, or he can go with us and keep it. You pick."

Honeypat glared at the gigantic vice cop.

Four deputies came huffing into the camp.

"Nigger," Honeypat shrieked.

"Work on your vocabulary, sister," Tree said. "That shit's getting old."

The deputies stared in amazement at the Allerdyce clan. "Fuck," a deputy named Linsenman said to Service.

Limpy suddenly jerked free from Service and ran, screaming, "Scatter!"

The clan burst apart like a covey of quail, going in every which direction.

Tree swept Limpy's spindly legs before he could get three steps. Allerdyce went down like a sapling under a logger's double-bit ax.

The deputies didn't have to move. Service had anticipated the breakout attempt and had deployed the cops in two waves. Only four had come into the camp. The rest were in the surrounding woods, waiting.

Minutes later, seven other deputies came out of the woods, bringing the fleeing Allerdyces back at gunpoint.

Service led a silent Limpy out of camp to where the county police cruisers waited and stuffed him carefully into the backseat of the first squad car he came to.

"You ain't got me yet, young fella."

"Get him out of here," Service told Deputy Linsenman. "And keep him apart from the others." The others were being stuffed into other cars and a police van.

It took the rest of the night to go through the camp. They found sawed-off shotguns, dynamite and blasting caps, illegal game and fish, and, in a shallow grave dogs had dug open, a newborn baby wrapped in rags and stuffed in a green plastic trash bag.

The baby had numerous deformities and had not been long dead. The sight turned Service's stomach.

"Was a weak one was all," one of the women explained. "Poor thing just couldn't make it. How God planned it," she added.

It was a misdemeanor not to report a death.

With considerable interrogation and games to get them blaming each other, there were enough charges to put many of the clan members away, some of them for a long time. But this was secondary. During Limpy's long absence, the family had been almost docile.

It was just after daylight when Service and Treebone got to the Marquette County Jail to do all the paperwork, talk to some of the suspects, and sort out charges.

Grady Service stopped in to see Limpy, who was housed alone in a single cell.

"I got grandkids," Allerdyce said. "What's gonna happen to them?"

"Social Services will take good care of them."

"I take care of my own."

"Not this time, Limpy."

"I don't want to go back to that place."

"You should've thought of that before you went back to the camp."

"Them are my people."

"You're a convicted felon on parole, Limpy. You know the rules."

"A man's got a right to be with his family."

"Not *your* family."

"You make a trade?"

"I don't need to."

"Maybe I got something you'd be likin' to have."

"Thanks, but I like my women with more than two teeth."

"I'm serious."

"So am I. Enjoy your stay, Limpy. Before long you'll be back home in the Jack."

"Humanity," Tree said, shaking his head as they got ready to depart.

· 8 ·

The two men bought wine and flowers in Marquette before stopping at Service's cabin to shower and change clothes. Kira Lehto lived in a small frame house less than a quarter mile up the road from her veterinary clinic. The house had two large bedrooms, a huge modern kitchen with an island, which she had added at great expense, and a screened porch that wrapped around three sides. Lisette McKower had gotten there before the two men. Lehto and McKower were on the screened porch drinking martinis from glasses with six-inch-long stems.

"How far ahead of us are you?" Service asked, as he and Treebone pushed open the porch door.

"Way far," McKower said. "We're women."

"Oh man," Tree said. "That feminasty shit again."

McKower raised her glass in a toast, then got up and gave Treebone a long hug.

"You, in a skirt?" he said, grinning. "You've actually got *legs*."

"Don't let word get around," she said in a low voice. "You two look pretty satisfied with yourselves."

"It was some sort of postapocalypse git-down," Treebone said. "Nek-kid redneck booty and all of them doin' the deed and howlin' at the moon. It was like Devil's Night in Detroit, only greener."

"That doin'-the-deed part sounds good to me," Lehto whispered as Service kissed her on the cheek.

Service glanced in McKower's direction. "Allerdyce made noises like he wants to make a deal," he said.

"As in, what for what?"

"We didn't go into details. I figured it would be better to let him sit and contemplate going back to Jackson."

Sergeant McKower looked thoughtful. "Seven years inside. It's not unthinkable he has something to trade."

"Not likely anything to interest us."

"I'll make sure Doolin knows," she said. "You never know."

It was a relaxing evening. Treebone regaled them with stories of pimps and hookers, crack houses and the antics of his four daughters, and he had them laughing until their stomachs ached. Lehto served carrot soup with dill and sour cream, grilled skirt steaks with parsley-jalapeño sauce, red potatoes, steamed corn, and blueberry cheesecake.

Tree got too far into the martinis to turn back before the wine, so Service appointed himself designated driver.

"Lisette can drop Tree at your place," Lehto said, running her hand along the outside of his right thigh.

Service was tempted, but there was a part of him always pulling against what he wanted.

"We've got to go into the Tract in the morning."

Treebone hummed a few bars of "Beans and Corn Bread" and insisted McKower dance with him.

"That's not dance music," she said.

"Is for me."

"What would your wife say?"

"She says I dance white, which, no offense intended in present company, is not a compliment."

He faked a stumble as they danced.

"Your wife's right," McKower said.

Treebone roared with laughter.

"He'll be a big help in the morning," Lehto told Service.

"He heals fast."

"Good thing," the veterinarian said.

They had a perfunctory kiss good night by his truck. "How about Saturday at the usual place?" he asked. "On your lunch break."

"You could just stay here tonight."

"I can't."

She made a face and hugged him less than enthusiastically.

On the drive home Treebone mumbled, "Ain't no law against it."

"Is that you talking, or your booze-bro inner twin?"

Tree grunted. "Blood kin fucking. No law against it. Can fuck and howl at the moon all they want. Just can't get married."

"You make that up?"

"You think that's the first time I've seen that shit? What I wanna know, who s'posed to be makin' the laws in this state?"

"Good question."

"I hate the woods," Treebone grumbled. "Makes people go crazy."

Service felt the same way about cities.

✻ ✻ ✻

They spent the next morning driving the perimeter roads of the Mosquito River Wilderness. Treebone mostly leaned against the window and took Motrin tablets every couple of hours. Each time Service found a parked vehicle he stopped and called in the license plates. By year's end he would have to turn in his truck for a new model that would carry an electronic package enabling Lansing to track his vehicle's whereabouts every minute of the day. The system was tied in to the Global Positioning System network of satellites in stationary geosynchronous orbit above the earth. Some COs already had the system and were using tuna cans to disable the antenna so that they could avoid Big Brother's unbroken attention. Service knew that when his time came, he'd have his own tuna can primed for duty.

Service hoped to come across a full-sized Bronco, Blazer, or Dodge Ram, but no such luck.

They stopped for lunch on US 2 at a place called the Rose River Eatery. The corpulent waitress had coarse gray hair tied back in a bun. She handed them each a menu and said, "I'm your waitress, not your server."

Treebone took more painkillers, washing them down with ice water. "You got greens and black-eyed peas?"

The waitress laughed. "We got pasties," she said. "That's the only soul food above the bridge."

"I don't eat titty tassels," the Detroit policeman grumbled. "There is some very weird shit up here, Grady."

"We prefer to think of our eccentricity as quaint."

"I don't see how you can stand it here. What exactly were we doing this morning?"

"Checking things out."

"They pay you for this?"

"Twice a month, man."

"One time, we found this pimp down by Fort. Had a stiff in his trunk. A real stinker. Was his number one girl. She died from an OD of black horse and he said he couldn't stand to part with her. Said she was a good earner."

"Very colorful. Your point?"

"We sent all our pimps up here, man, they'd die in days."

"Put that idea on paper and send it up the line."

"I might just file my papers," Treebone said, taking another long pull of water.

"Retire?" This was unexpected news. Service raised an eyebrow.

"When I joined the department, we were at war with the city. Cops then were like ten percent blacks, ninety percent whites. We were an occupying force and hated by the people we were supposed to be protecting. Few years further on we were seventy percent brothers and sisters. Now it's back down to just over half. We're going backward and I just don't feel like fighting that shit all over again."

"You'd be okay on your pension?"

"I've got nineteen with DMP, one with the DNR, two with the state, and three years with the crotch, which also counts. I won't be throwin' garden parties at the *Dee*-troit Yacht Club, but we can get by. There're a lot of private security firms now, and they pay real green for real experience."

"You could live without this?"

Treebone laughed. "Man, you're the only motherfucker who *needs* this shit. Not only is this not a great living, it's a shitty life too."

"I don't mind it."

"That's why your old lady up and split."

"There was more to it than that."

"That's what *you* say. So what were we looking around for this morning?"

Service told him about the odd-acting man he had encountered on the Mosquito River.

"No law against being strange, man. There was, that waitress would be doin' hard time."

"I'm just curious is all."

Treebone shook his huge head. "We've been down that road together. I'm gonna hit the road for home tonight, stop at the bridge, do the state a favor, maybe blow that motherfucker to kingdom come."

"Your prejudices are showing."

"Man, it took all my life to learn how to read crazy black people. We don't need redneck ridgerunners takin' over the Lower Peninsula."

"Thanks for your help with Limpy."

"Somebody's got to look out for your sorry ass. An' while I'm thinking of your best interests, why don't you marry your dog doctor and get it over with? Fish pig and dog doctor: Now, *that's* a match made in heaven. Seriously, she's a fine lady, Grady. Just this once, use your brain instead of your Johnson."

Service smiled but did not answer. He cared a great deal for Kira

Lehto, but he wasn't going to rush things. They had known each other less than a year.

After lunch they stopped at the US Forest Service office near Indian Lake and used the copier. Service handwrote a note telling people to alert him if they saw any Broncos, Blazers, or Rams on the Tract roads, and he asked that the USFS people write down the license numbers. Then they circled the wilderness again and dropped more notes at several houses along the perimeter.

"How many miles you drive a year?"

"Right around forty thou."

"You're lucky you don't have piles and butt blisters."

After they got back to the cabin and his friend was gone, Service got out his briefcase and began writing his daily narrative report. Most of the time he didn't mind doing the paperwork that went with the job, because the reports reminded him of the importance of what he was doing. More to the point, they helped him keep score, and Grady Service was a man who always kept score.

Cat hissed and swatted at the phone when it rang at 3 A.M. Service scrambled to answer it before she knocked it off the table.

"Service."

"This is Maridly Nantz. I'm sorry to wake you, Service, but we have a fire in the Mosquito." Nantz was district fire officer for the area that included the Tract. This was her first year in the district, and Service had only met her once.

"Where?"

"Ten miles upriver from US 2."

He tugged on his pants while they talked. "How big is it?"

"I'm not sure yet. I'm just leaving and I thought you'd want to know."

"On my way."

"You know the department's policy on fires," she said. For a moment he was irked to hear what sounded like a warning from a first-year fire marshal.

"I know the policy," he said grimly. The new USFS policy on fires was to let them burn themselves out and run their course, unless human habitations were threatened. The government had decided that fire was a natural phenomenon, like a bad winter or a tornado. Service understood the policy as it related to other places and other forests, but not to his Mosquito Wilderness Tract.

"But if the opportunity presents, we can do something, right?"

"We'll see when we get there. That's all I'm promising."

"Thanks for the call, Nantz."

He had learned long ago that fear was often worse than reality. There was no sense burning yourself out with might-be's. They would deal with what they found. He also thought about Maridly Nantz, trying to picture her. They had met briefly when introduced by Doke Hathoot, the Tract's supervisor. She had medium-length dark hair, a sharp nose, thin lips, an angular jaw. He guessed her to be in her early to midthirties. In some ways she looked very girlish, which made him wonder if she had what it took to deal with a crown fire. If she was like too many of the fire officers he'd worked with, though, she'd stay a season or two then move west to where the real fire challenges were, and if she did he couldn't blame her. Michigan didn't have that many major fires, and if fire was your passion, you wanted to be where the action was.

It was not a large fire. Two, maybe three acres. But it was centered right on the Geezer Hole where Service had seen the man, and he was immediately suspicious. By the time he got to the fire, Nantz and a dozen forest service workers had pretty much contained it with pulaskis, a piss pump, and a small bulldozer. "We could've let it burn out, but I thought this would be good practice for my people."

"Thanks," he said. She didn't have to contain the fire but she had, and whatever her reason, he appreciated it. "Who reported it?"

"A man by the name of Voydanov. He lives out on County Road 909. He said he was walking his dog and smelled smoke. He called it in on a cellular. How did we live before those things?"

"Where is he now?"

"At home." She gave him the address.

"Cause?"

"Too early to tell," she said. "Not lightning, though." He understood. The vast majority of forest fires were ignited by lightning strikes. "I've alerted forensics." The state police forensics people were located in Negaunee, a town west of Marquette, and covered the entire U.P.

When Service knocked on Voydanov's front door, a dog with a deep snarling bark started in. Eventually the porch light came on and, when the old man finally opened up, Service was eye to eye with a black Great Dane, its head the size of a Shetland pony's. Voydanov was in his eighties, bent over and slow moving. Service took a step backward when the dog rammed its snout against the door.

"Don't mind Millie," the old man said. "She's just noise."

Just Noise had saliva cascading from her cavernous mouth.

"Can we talk about the fire?"

"Sure."

"Outside?"

"You don't like dogs?" The old man gave him an inquisitive look.

"I don't want to upset her," Service said.

"She's not upset. She's just curious. Like a kid."

A 160 pound kid with fangs, Service thought. "Outside, please?"

The old man stepped outside.

"You reported the fire?"

"Yep."

"Wasn't it a little late to be walking your dog?"

"My wife died last winter and the truth is I can't sleep for beans. If it's bad, me and Millie go out to the Tract and walk around."

"I'm sorry about your wife."

"It went fast," he said. "I guess that was good for her."

Service sensed the man was about to slip into a melancholy reminiscence. He asked, "What about the fire?" to get them refocused.

"Almost down to the river when I smelled the smoke."

"Did you see anybody?"

"Nope. Rarely do out there."

"You're certain?"

"Just Millie and me."

"Did you drive back to the trailhead?"

"We walked. Good for both our hearts."

"Did you see any tire tracks?"

"Always tracks on that road. Besides, it was dark, and I don't need a light when I got Millie."

Service considered asking more questions but decided against it. "I hope you can get back to sleep."

"Are you kidding? I'm too excited."

"Maybe warm milk would help."

The old man chuckled. "Hell with that. I had me some Jack. You want a snort?"

"Thanks, but I'm on duty."

Voydanov looked skeptical. "I never knew that to stop a game warden. When I was a young man, the wife and I used to bring our kids up here. No house then. We used to camp in tents during deer season. There was a game warden used to stop by and have a swig or two. He was a good man. Helped me haul out a deer one time. Name was . . . Service. He was a great big fella, like you."

"He was my dad."

Voydanov cocked an eyebrow. "That so? He still around?"

"No, he died."

The old man looked sorry. "Too bad. He was a good fella. What killed him?"

"Timing," Grady Service said. He couldn't bring himself to tell the old man his father was a drunk who'd died because he'd been having a swig or two with his admirers and informers. "And location. The combination."

"Never heard that one before."

"Thanks for calling in the fire." Service started to walk across the yard.

"You want to know about the truck?" the old man called after him.

"What truck?" Service asked, stopping and turning back.

"You know, one of them four-wheel doodads. Big sonuvabitch."

"I thought you didn't see anyone."

"Didn't see a person. Saw the truck was all."

"At the trailhead?"

"Nope, short of there. Saw it when Millie and me walked in."

"Can you show me where?"

"Sure."

The old man comforted the dog before they left, then moved slowly out to Service's truck. Voydanov wore gaudy green plaid pajamas and scuffed leather slippers that were too loose and made slapping sounds when he walked. They drove down the access road. Voydanov stopped Service at a spot a quarter mile short of the trailhead, off to the left of the road.

"It was back in there maybe a hundred yards. I seen a glint of metal and me and Millie walked back partway to take us a look."

"Did you notice the the license number?"

"Even if I'd paid attention I had nothing to write with. I just figured it was a night fisherman. Sometimes they park back there and cut across to the old log slide. You know it?"

Service knew the landmark. It was upriver from the Geezer Hole, a place where a century ago loggers briefly slid their logs down a steep embankment to the water. It was the one area of the wilderness that had been scarred by man and it was still eroded, this despite a substantial investment in bank stabilization all along the stretch.

"But you didn't see anybody?"

"Nope. And whoever it was musta left between when we walked up and came back from over toward the fire. That little fire girl give me and Millie a lift home. You know, the pretty little gal with the big bazooms?"

The old man might be old, but not too old to notice Nantz's bustline. "What color was the truck, sir?"

"Dark."

"Black, blue?"

"Just dark. I couldn't make out no color."

Service was pretty sure he'd gotten all he was going to get and reminded himself that when he was dealing with old folks in the future, take his time and ask every question, including the most obvious ones. Elderly people had their own rhythms, did things in their own time, lived in their own inner worlds.

"Okay, thanks. Let's get you home."

He dropped Voydanov off and watched the old man walk to his house, then drove back to the site and parked so nobody could get back to the spot and ruin any evidence.

Nantz pulled up in her truck around daylight. She was covered with soot and her eyes were red. "You want coffee?" she asked. "I don't do fires without my coffee." Service wondered how many fires she had fought, and where. He stood by her truck as she poured coffee into a thermos cup. "You run out of gas?" she asked.

"I thought I'd wait here for forensics," Service said, pointing. "Voydanov saw some kind of vehicle parked back there. He saw it on the way in, but he thought it was gone when you drove him out."

She studied a set of fresh tire grooves pressed into the ferns. "Well, a ghost didn't leave those."

"Did you got a read on the fire?"

"Just a preliminary." She got out of the truck and unashamedly pulled her yellow Nomex shirt over her head, not bothering with the buttons. Her breasts were stuffed into a tiny green athletic bra. She was not a subtle woman, Service thought as she reached into the truck and poured more coffee for them, his into the thermos top, hers into a wrinkled Styrofoam cup. "The POO's in the southwest corner of the site, near the river." POO, point of origin. "There's evidence of an accelerant."

"You found something?"

"A pattern, which is enough until the techs take a closer look. Did we get a license number on that vehicle the old man saw?"

He shook his head, noting she had said "we." Most fire marshals tended to protect their authority and turf. Nantz was different.

"Too bad. Probably end up writing this one off as unsolved."

"Thanks for putting your people on it."

She smiled. "It was small and this time I had the bodies. If we go red flag and get us a bad boy, you know how that will go down." Red flag was the code for the worst possible fire conditions.

He understood and it made him sick. It was true that forests regenerated themselves over time, but it took a century or more to restore a forest to its original state—if it made it at all. Lumber companies and loggers lobbied Lansing for all fires to be fought, and this was one of the rare instances where he agreed with the timber people. Not with their reason, but the result. The timber folks wanted trees to cut, and fires stole these. But the Mosquito was not open to logging and if a fire broke out there, the timber industry would stand silently by and let it burn.

"Let me know how the investigation goes," Service said.

"Sure. It'll be a few days, earliest. Maybe we could get together over a few beers."

"Maybe," he said.

When he backed his truck up, she was putting on a fresh shirt.

"Keep your shiny side up," she called out.

"You too."

She gave him a smile as a good-bye.

Their "regular" meeting place was a township cemetery. Its long looping drive passed by a creek with clear water. The cemetery was no longer in use and had a chain and lock across the entrance. He and Lehto had keys. The chain was down when he got there, and he locked it after he drove through. There was a rare grove of majestic red cedars by the water. A large green Hudson's Bay blanket was spread on the ground.

Service plopped down beside her. The sun was unseasonably hot and the sky blue and cloudless.

"You work all night?" she asked, studying him.

"There was a fire in the Mosquito."

"I can tell," she said. "Do you have to go back?"

"No, it's out and the investigators are on it." He took off his shoes and socks. "I didn't have time for a shower."

"I like you natural."

He ignored her, finished undressing, walked down to the water, waded in, and sat down gingerly. When he got out he came back to the blanket and lay down on his stomach.

"I called you this morning," she said.

She settled in beside him and kissed his shoulder.

"What say we unloose the moose and get the edge off?" she said.

"I never met a woman who talked like you." More to the point, he had never met a woman in such a rush.

"Gets you going, eh?" she said, laughing lasciviously.

He rolled on his side and pulled her to him.

He was asleep, his arm draped over his face, napping lightly. He felt Kira's finger tracing the line of one of his scars.

"Nice nap?" she asked.

"Did I snore?"

She rolled her eyes.

"Sorry."

"I'm not. You know, if we hadn't done it in the dark the first time, we might not have done it at all. I've never seen so many scars. Have you noticed that I've never asked about them?"

"I noticed."

"Have the other women in your life been curious about them?"

"Some were, some weren't."

"How do I add some and some?"

"You're the scientist."

"I haven't figured you out yet," she said.

"Is that bad?"

"No, but I'm nosy."

"I'm pretty simple."

She laughed in his face and poked him in the chest. "Bullshit, Service. You are a complete mystery."

"Not to me."

"I worry about you, Grady. For God's sake, you wander around the woods all night with crazies and sleep on footlockers! That's *not* normal."

"I think of it as training."

"For what?"

"Life. If you get too comfortable, it's too hard to go out and do what you have to do."

"That's twisted."

"It's reality. People who get too relaxed stop producing."

"You're not a factory."

"In some ways I am."

"A shrink might have some fun with that."

"Shrinks have fun with everybody else's problems."

"Ah, my modern Luddite."

"Whatever that is," he said.

"Okay, I've put this off long enough. Now I'm asking. Tell me about the scars."

There was no point in arguing. He propped himself up on his elbows.

"Bottom to top. Left thigh, that's from Allerdyce, 20-gauge shotgun slug. Left ab, Vietnam, rocket fragment. Right ab, AK-47 round, also Vietnam. It hurt like hell. Left forearm, a fifteen-year-old squirrel hunter accidentally potshot me with a .22. Upper right thorax, Vietnam, grenade. Upper left arm, deer hunter with a 30.06; he took exception to my presence in his woods."

She touched the upper center of his belly. "That one?"

"Grandma, .410 shotgun slug."

Her mouth was agape. "Jesus, Grady! Your grandmother *shot* you?"

"Not exactly."

She poked him again. "We're making good progress, Grady. Don't go south on me now."

"Why is progress important?"

"A relationship is either going forward or backward. It doesn't stand still."

"That sounds pretty arbitrary."

"Trust the doctor on this, Grady. About Grandma?"

"She used to plink woodchucks that came up to her garden."

"You're too big to be mistaken for a woodchuck."

"I stepped in front of the round."

She sat up and stared at him. "Stepped . . . as in accidentally, right?"

He shook his head. "I wanted to see what it felt like."

She sucked in a breath. "You *what?*"

"I was curious. It was like an experiment. You know about experiments."

"You could have been killed!"

"I wasn't."

"How old were you?"

"Thirteen."

"Jesus, Grady." She put her head on his chest. Neither of them talked for a while. He wasn't sure if she was angry, shocked, or both. Her mood shifts could be mercurial.

"I don't want to know any more about your scars," she said solemnly.

"I've never been shot in the back," he told her.

"That's enough, Grady. I don't like the implications of any of this."

"My ex-wife said I had a death wish."

"Was she right?"

"Not usually."

"You're not particularly adept at comforting a lover," Lehto said.

"We were married four years and she never complained. One night at dinner she said, 'I'd like another helping of cauliflower and a divorce.' I looked at her. She said, 'You have a death wish and I don't want to be a young widow.' She left after she finished her second helping of cauliflower. She was already packed."

"Baloney," Lehto said.

He made a sign over his chest. "It's the absolute truth and as close to verbatim as I can make it."

"Where did she go?"

"Away. She never said and I never asked. She filed for divorce in Nevada and after that, who knows?"

"Did you love her?"

"Not after that cauliflower business."

"Don't joke," she said. "We're having a serious discussion. You never tried to get her back?"

"Nope."

"Would you have taken her back if she came back on her own?"

"I don't do hypotheticals," he said.

"C'mon, Service. Open up."

"Maybe."

"You know, she might have been right," Lehto said. "So she became a young divorcée instead of a young widow. Practically speaking, what's the difference? Alone is alone. She must've been really afraid of losing you."

"That's illogical," he said.

"These things don't have to make sense."

"See!" he said, brightening. "It was that way with Grandma's shotgun too."

"That poor woman. She must've been shattered."

"She called me a fool. My old man took her shotgun away from her and gave her a ticket."

"You made that up."

"Only the ticket part," he admitted. "But it wouldn't have surprised me."

She lay her hand flat against his penis and pressed. "You thinking what I'm thinking?"

"What?"

She took him in her hand. "What do I call him?" she asked in a whisper.

"What the hell are you talking about Kira?"

"It's an important move forward in our relationship," she said. "Personal names for our private parts. It's what couples do when they start to fall in love. It's in all the textbooks."

"Not any textbooks I've read," he said, adding, "my ex and I didn't have any personal names for anything."

"I rest my case," she said. "You're not with her anymore."

"And you think *I'm* crazy?"

"I don't want to talk anymore," Kira Lehto said.

"Okay by me."

They dressed slowly after their lovemaking. Dressing was the only thing Kira did slowly.

"We needed this," she said.

He smiled.

"Excuse me, but that was an invitation to make a date for the next time."

"Whenever you want."

She put her hands on her hips and thrust out her jaw. "I'd like to hear some want from your end. This isn't an open-ended take-it-or-leave-it kind of thing for me, Grady." Her voice had suddenly risen to a high pitch.

"Why're you mad?"

"I'm *not* mad. I'm disappointed. I care about you and I want us to spend more time together. Normal time, not so-called quality time, which is a loser's term for something is better than nothing. I thought you wanted the same thing," she said with frown. "No, I take that back: I'm disappointed in *me*."

"I don't understand what the problem is."

"Your grandmother was right about you! You *are* a fool!"

Her truck tires spit gravel when she departed.

He had a sour stomach. Why did his relationships always go this way? What did she want, a billboard on US 41 to let her know he cared about her?

*   *   *

When he drove across a bridge over Wallen Creek he saw a woman in blue waders and a lavender vest, casting a fly into a pool by the road. Her bronze Maxima was pulled off the shoulder of the road. It had Lansing plates. There was a bumper sticker, a navy blue fish with the words LOVE 'EM AND LEAVE 'EM.

He got out and eased down to the rock-strewn shoreline. She was twenty feet away.

"Hi," the woman said warily. She had reddish blond hair, round cheeks, a nice smile, her hair in a neat French braid that stuck out the back of a red-and-black baseball cap. The hat had a LANSING LUGNUTS emblem on the crown.

"Do any good?"

"Just some dinks, but it's fun."

"Rainbows?"

"Yep, you wanna check my license?"

"No." He saw she had a wedding ring. "Your husband with you?"

She paused before answering. "No."

"Does he fish too?"

"When he can get away. He travels a lot in his job." She was giving him a suspicious eye.

"Is that a problem for the two of you?"

She laughed nervously and unconsciously stepped back. "Are you coming on to me?"

"I'm just curious."

He could see her evaluating him. After a bit, she waded to shore, brushed the dust and debris off a flat-topped boulder with her hand, and sat down.

"I'm Jerrijo Burke," she said, extending her hand.

She had a solid grip.

"Grady Service."

"Chuck travels a lot. Fifty percent a year on the average. Some years it's worse. I used to be a CPA in a good practice. Now I just do taxes for friends. It makes me a little fishing money and keeps me in the business."

"Downshifting?"

She smiled. "Getting back to basics."

"You're happy?"

"What's this about?" she asked, her eyes declaring concern.

"I'm trying to work something out."

"Yeah, I'm happy," she said.

"Him too?"

"He hates being gone all the time, but sure. We're both happy."

"You miss each other when you're apart?"

"Of course, but we've learned to focus on our time together, not our time apart."

"That works?"

"It seems to," she said, with a deep laugh. She dug her fishing license out of her lavender vest and held it out to him. "Check me, okay? I want to be official."

He gave the gaudily colored document a cursory look. "You're legal." He gave it back to her, noting that it was a shame that the state under Sam Bozian had done away with trout stamps as a way to save money.

"I've never met a game warden before and I just wanted to make it official. What's her name?"

"Who?"

"Look, officer, you started this. Your girl, her name."

"Kira."

"That's a nice name. Do you love her?"

It was time to shift the subject. "Do you want to catch some big brook trout?"

"Who doesn't?" she said. "Big as in how big?"

"Well, fifteen-inchers aren't uncommon."

"Jesus — excuse my Greek."

"You go west to the next intersection and turn right. Go about two miles. You'll see an old barn on the right. There's a faded sign for Redman chaw. There's a gate across the road. No lock. Open it and drive to the end of the two-track. You'll see some birches in a big clump across an open field. Walk over there and go down to the river. It's the upper part of Wallen. Fish guys have been planting triploids, sterile males. They grow like crazy. Usually they put them in brook-trout-only lakes and try to raise trophies. This is a new angle on that. Use a Green Stimulator or a Long-Legged Skunk and the bigger and bushier, the better. Around five, switch to a Green Caddis, say a twelve. Come sundown, forget it; they won't hit anymore. This afternoon, fish the shadows under the cedar trees where they hang over the runs."

"Is it private land?"

"Nope, it's just not publicized. Be sure to close the gate behind you."

"I don't know what to say. This is a really odd moment."

He smiled, "I know. Thanks for talking to me."

"Are you sure you're okay?"

"Enjoy," he said.

He watched her drive away and thought any other day he'd drive up and hear her laugh as she hit big one after big one. What had Treebone said, a fish cop and a dog doc? Lots of people had jobs that kept them apart, but somehow managed as couples. He drove around feeling unsettled. He did not like how he and Kira had parted.

"Focus on the time you have," he said out loud. Kira wanted more time. So did he. Maybe it was time to make time. Shit or get off the pot, his old man used to say.

He made two stops on the way to Kira Lehto's office.

Her receptionist looked up at him when he walked in. "Doctor's in surgery."

"Cancel her appointments for tomorrow."

"What?" the young woman asked.

"You heard me."

"I can't do that without confirmation from the doctor."

"Yes you can."

Lehto was suturing a jagged laceration that zigzagged through a patch of shaved skin on a large brown mongrel. She wore a surgical mask decorated to look like a dog's snout, green scrubs, pale yellow latex gloves. She glanced at him when the door opened and said, "Scrub in, Officer Service, or stand clear."

Her surgical assistant pointed to a sink. "Disinfectant, then soap and water. I'll glove you and mask you when you're done."

He did as he was instructed but stayed back from the table.

The sutures were in. "She got mixed up with a porky. I have to pull some quills from her face," Kira said to him. "Want to hold her head?"

"I can't," he said. "A porcupine did that to her belly?"

Kira Lehto raised an eyebrow. "She tried to run away and got hung on some sharp metal in a barn. What do you mean, 'can't'?"

"Can we just talk about this later?"

Lehto looked at her assistant. "Did he say 'can't'?"

"It sounded that way to me."

After the dog was placed in a post-op cage and her assistant had gone to do something else, Lehto peeled off her gloves and dropped them in a stainless-steel can. "Why are you here, Grady?"

"Making the most of our time together."

"Jesus, Grady. Get to the point."

He hesitated, "I canceled your appointments for Monday."

"You did *what?*"

He took her hands, but she resisted instinctively. "Come with me," he said.

She cocked her head to the side. "Have you gone crazy?"

"I'm not qualified to diagnose." This time when he pulled, she followed.

They went into the reception room. The receptionist looked at Service with annoyance.

"Did you make the cancellations?" he asked.

"Not until the doctor says so."

"It's okay, Jean. It's . . ."

"Call it a unique personal emergency," Service said.

The receptionist started to get up. "Are you all right, Doctor Lehto?"

"She's not good," Service said. "She's *fantastic.*"

Lehto laughed. "I'm fantastic," she said, smiling at her receptionist, who looked flustered.

When Lehto saw the suitcase on the front seat she said, "That looks like mine."

"It is," he said, moving it to the small bench behind the bucket seats.

"Where are we going?"

"Home," he said sheepishly.

Dr. Kira Lehto crossed her legs and her arms, looked straight ahead, and smiled. "So far this is one damn interesting day."

When they got to his place, he opened the back of the truck and began to unload.

"That looks like my bed," she said.

"It is."

He set it up in the main room and when it was done he got a glass of water, drank it down, went over to the bed, and began to take off his clothes. "Is this moving forward or backward?" he asked.

She began unbuttoning her blouse. "It's too early to predict ultimate direction, but the rate's rather promising."

Late in the night, after he made bacon, eggs, and toast, they sat at his tiny table across from each other.

"Well?" he said.

"You're afraid of dogs?"

"Stop laughing," he said. "It's not funny."

"I *can't* stop," she said, as tears ran down her cheeks.

The telephone rang at 6:30 A.M. and they looked at each other and Service got out of bed and went to the phone and turned the receiver upside down in the cradle.

"One good sign after another," Kira Lehto said, patting the mattress.

· 10 ·

All the next day they made love, cooked, puttered, and talked, and on Monday Grady Service asked Lehto to move in with him. It was an impulse, he knew, but he convinced himself that this was the right thing to do for both of them.

Lehto told him his house was as barren as an army barracks and it wasn't what she considered to be normal bachelor emptiness; it was something entirely different. He could tell she didn't like it.

"It's pathologically empty, Grady. It's like nothing in your life sticks to you. Even your cat doesn't have a real name."

Service felt a twinge under her criticism but was surprised that he wasn't more offended by anything she said. She was candid and affectionate at the same time. They had dated for nearly a year, but after the past thirty-six hours together he decided that he was only meeting the real Kira for the first time. There was a rational, practical side to her and a wide-open, almost reckless side. She ranged between pensive and manic, one moment making a list of the groceries and other things they would need and an instant later pressing wildflowers in one of his books. It was as if she were two people in the same body and having thought this he laughed, because she had said more or less the same thing about him. Maybe it was the same with everyone. Certainly his ex had turned out to be someone else.

She agreed to living together on the condition that they split time between her place and his. She said she could get a telephone device that would automatically transfer their calls, which meant they could be either place and still take care of their professional responsibilities.

When he dropped her at the clinic he felt a brief tug of separation, but she patted his face and said, "Tarzan may now get after the bad guys. It was a wonderful interlude, Grady. I only wish we were leaving on a real vacation, away from everything." They both laughed and he drove away feeling happier than he could remember feeling. Despite this, her words about vacation gnawed at him. He couldn't remember the last legitimate vacation he had taken. In his time off he found plenty of things to do. Why did you have to go somewhere else to do that?

His afternoon would be spent at the District 3 headquarters in Escanaba. He was scheduled for refresher training on PPCT, pressure point control tactics, wherein COs would go through the motions of sharpening their ability to bring troublesome violets to their knees using a minimum of physical force and some practical body mechanics.

His first call of the morning went to the fire warden, Nantz.

"Well, it's man-made," she said. "I was pretty sure, but the lab has samples from the POO and will run mass spec to try to pinpoint the compound. Maybe that'll help, maybe not. The state forensics people got tire prints from the truck Voydanov saw. They're definitely from a full-sized SUV. Which make is anybody's guess. We caught the fire in time. I guess we should be satisfied with that."

"I'm not," he said.

"Neither am I," she said. "I'll keep you in the loop and anytime you wanna have that beer talk, just say the word."

"Thanks, Nantz."

When he got through to Lisette McKower she asked, "Where have you been?"

"Personal time. I've got PPCT this afternoon."

"You're supposed to keep your supervisor informed. Parker's been trying to reach you. He's in a real snit."

Sergeant Charles Parker was McKower's counterpart and Grady's direct supervisor. Each of them oversaw half the COs in the district.

The first time Service worked with Parker was the morning after a severe thunderstorm. They had been called to a residence near Trenary. The residents had gotten up in the morning to find three dead deer under a large maple tree behind the house. Despite the rain, the grass around the animals was black, and two huge branches had broken off the maple's main trunk. Parker ruled immediately that the animals had been killed by a lightning strike, but Service had doubts, and as he walked around the scene his eyes kept returning to the garage where ATVs and snowmobiles were stored along with the longest spool of insulated electrical wire he had seen since Vietnam. He had asked the residents what the cord was for and was informed it belonged to their high school junior son, who had it for some kind of science experiment. His supervisor was antsy to resume their patrol and Service finally agreed to move on, but that night he went back and confronted the family's high-schooler, who reluctantly confessed to setting up a booby trap, baiting it with apples and corn. When the deer wandered into the grid, he tripped the juice, killing them. There had been a lightning strike into the tree early that evening and the boy decided that nobody would be the wiser if he conducted his experiment. His parents had been bowling in Escanaba when the events took place. Service cited the boy for illegally killing deer and for creating an illegal fire. He went back to the office that night and filed his report and the next day had Parker on the phone, asking him why he had gone back after he had decided the cause was lightning. Service said the ground pattern didn't look right and he just wanted to be sure. Parker had already told others about the incident and how he had proclaimed it lightning before Service could decide. He had never forgiven Service for making him look bad, but he had also pretty much left Service alone after that.

"I was with Kira. You want those details too?"

"Don't push, Grady. Allerdyce wants to talk, but he told Doolin the only one he'll talk to is you."

"I'll head up there right now. See you this afternoon?"

"You want me to pull you out of class?"

"You're a pal."

He heard a long pause on the other end. "Grady Service, do I detect happiness in your voice?"

"I gotta go talk to Allerdyce. Later, Sergeant."

"Assuage Parker," she said. "He's your supervisor."

"I know, I know."

Limpy was wearing baggy, patched, and faded county orange coveralls when a guard brought him into the interrogation room. He looked even smaller now, as if he were wasting away by the day.

"Your old man was a boozefish," Allerdyce said. "Understand, I ain't tryin' to put the man down. Not at all."

"Not a real good start to building a trusting relationship, Limpy."

"See, I knew him good back then. I was just a snot-nosed kid and he run me in now and again, but I knew him. The way it worked, he'd haul my ass out of the woods and I'd tell him shit I heard."

Limpy had been one of his father's informants? "My old man's gone. Are you going to start telling me shit you've heard?"

"No, I'm gonna tell me shit I *know*."

"You know how it works. You tell me what you have and I talk to the prosecutor and then we see what it's worth."

Allerdyce grinned. "You ever wonder why I never hit the Skeeto?"

Service thought he knew. "You knew I'd be there."

"Shit," Limpy said. "You fuckin' pup. It was out of respect for your late departed old man. He loved that place, so I always left it alone. And he stayed out of my neck of the woods. See, that's how your old man and me worked it; titty for tat."

"My old man didn't cut slack for anyone."

Limpy was perturbed. "Your old man, he give a name to every deer over there in the Skeeto. One time he caught Monkey Bill Hurley in there with a jacklight and two spikehorns and broke all his fingers with a crowbar. Your old man was a hardass sonuvabitch, boy. Them crooked fingers got Monkey his name. 'Fore that he was plain old Bill Hurley, a half-assed jacklighter on his best day, and afterward he had him a new name and was put out of business 'cause you can't shoot no piece good with monkey fingers. Your old man took his living and give him a name."

"Get to the point."

"Point is, I know shit you don't know you don't know."

"That doesn't make it worth anything."

"Yah? Well, the gov'mint don't own the whole Skeeto. You know that, smartass?"

Service had no idea what Allerdyce was talking about. "That's it?"

"Like you said, we're buildin' trust here. You start with that, see if you want more."

"Time for you to crawl back in your cage, Limpy."

"You think you could get me a few minutes alone with Honeypat?"

Service shook his head and signaled for the guard to fetch the prisoner.

Doke Hathoot was the superintendent of the Mosquito Wilderness Management District, which included the Tract and some adjacent properties. He'd once been a CO, but had transferred to the parks branch of the DNR and moved up. Law enforcement wasn't for everybody. He was a bit of a bootlicker, but had always proven a good man when it mattered.

Service telephoned Hathoot from the Marquette County Jail.

"Super here."

"This is Grady Service, Doke. I heard something today that doesn't make sense. Does the state own all the property in the Tract?"

"Every square foot."

"Why would somebody think differently?"

"Was it some academic egghead?"

"No."

"Well, whoever it is, they're dead wrong. Somebody is mixing up ownership and leases."

"Leases?"

"There are a few forties in the Tract that carry ninety-nine-year leases. When the state bought all the property back in the early 1900s there were some stoneheads who refused to sell. The courts could've condemned the property, but the governor back then didn't want the bad ink, so he and his people worked out a lease deal and it was ratified by the legislature. The vast majority of the contracts went kaput when the lessee died, but there are a few ninety-nines still in effect, and these are worded so that the lease passes to the lessee's survivors for the term of the lease. Technically the lessees can build on the property and use it pretty much any way they want until their time is up, but back in the forties or fifties all the lessees agreed to keep the land in its natural state. So the leases still exist, but it doesn't matter. We own the land, they aren't using it, and the legal status is more or less moot."

"Do you know the locations and expiration dates?"

"Not off the top of my head. It's been so long since anybody asked me about this I'm going to have to dig around. I'm not sure where the information is anymore. Why do you want to know?"

"I'm not sure. A hunch, maybe. Can you get the lokes, names, and expiration dates for me?"

"I've got to be at a meeting tonight in Traverse City with some NRC members and Una's coming along and we're gonna take a few days off, so it'll be the end of the week before I can start in on it for you." Una was Hathoot's wife. It was well known that she hated the Upper Peninsula and took every opportunity to urge her husband to get a transfer to somewhere "civilized."

"That's fine."

The NRC was the Natural Resources Commission, the policy-making and oversight board for the Department of Natural Resources. Since Sam Bozian had been elected governor, old-line NRC members had been replaced by the governor's well-heeled pals. There were few genuine conservationists left on the commission, and as a result it had become a subject of scorn from the state's media, the DNR, sportsmen's groups, and environmentalists as well.

"Mind if I ask what your meeting's about?" Service asked.

"It's your standard dog and pony. I figure they're trying to plan next year's meeting schedule and they're looking for a unique place to get away to for their annual planning soiree. Everybody with a wilderness property has been asked to meet with them and give them a rundown on what we are and how we do it." Hathoot added, "This doesn't have anything to do with our fire, does it?"

"I don't think so."

Hathoot chuckled. "If I was the one who started it, I'd sure hate having both you *and* Nantz on my butt."

"She's a dogger?"

"As fanatic as you. That's a compliment."

"Have a good one in TC, Doke."

Service knew that unless they got lucky and got the vehicle and license number, or some other kind of traceable hard evidence, they'd never get the firebug. Tracking a man on foot was one thing; finding a vehicle was entirely another. He wasn't sure the lease situation had any bearing, but Limpy had been right and that made it worth a little more attention.

There were seven COs in the PPCT refresher course: Service; Candace McCants, who covered the northern half of Marquette County while Service took care of the southern part; Gordon Terry from the Porkies; Val James from Iron County; Cathy Ketchum from Newberry with her husband, Joe Ketchum, who worked up toward Grand Marais; and Leo Robelais, who worked the Les Cheneaux Islands and Drummond Island. They were all seasoned vets and he had worked with each of them at one time or another. In the old days, before Lansing started putting tracking devices into CO vehicles, all the COs in the Upper Peninsula, and some from the Lower as well, would meet each year at the end of deer season some isolated camp somewhere in the backwoods and party for three days. They called these events Howls, and though they were officially outlawed now by edicts from Lansing, they still went on, if somewhat toned down from the old days. This year Gordie Terry would host the event somewhere in the rocky hills south of the Porcupine Mountains.

There were also two probationary conservation officers in the class: Sarah Pryzbycki, who was currently under the supervision of the Ketchums, and Dan Beaudoin, who had once been a navy SEAL. Pryzbycki and Beaudoin had brought good records from training assignments in southern Michigan. As probies, they would spend a year moving from area to area working with different COs, learning on the job, adjusting to different styles, and being evaluated daily. It was a taxing year for most probies, moving every two to four weeks and working the most distasteful and routine assignments. The word was out that these two would make good COs, and Service saw immediately that they fit in well.

Sergeant Ralph Smoke was the class instructor. Smokey worked out of District 6 in Mio and over the years had taught nearly every CO in the state how to handle physically unruly people. Smokey was short and muscular with a Hitler mustache and an occasional stutter, but he knew his job and the others listened.

After twenty years on the job Service had been through every kind of training the DNR had, the fad shit and the real stuff. He believed in training. You could always learn something new or reinforce old knowledge, and if he got one idea at a training session, it was time well spent.

Still, he had too many things he'd rather do than spend the afternoon putting arm twists and fingerlocks on his colleagues. As far as he and other veterans were concerned, the use of pressure points was pretty limited. A CO's main weapon was his brain, and his ammunition language and ability to talk to people. To be effective, you had to learn to size up people and situations quickly and talk them into a safe and calm place. You had to learn to listen as if your life depended on it because there would come a time, sooner or later, when it did. If suspects bolted, which they sometimes did, you ran them down and tackled them, or kicked their legs from beneath them, and usually when they hit the ground the fight was gone. If you had to resort to PPCT or anything else physical you were already behind the power curve and on the precipice of failure.

McKower waggled him out of class before they went outside for practice.

"Did you talk to Limpy?"

"I think he's playing some sort of screwy game with us."

"Shall I pass that analysis on to Doolin?"

"Not yet. I want to play along with him for a while, see where it takes me."

She said, "It's your call." Then, "I got my score back on the lieutenant's test."

He was surprised and showed it. "I didn't know you took the LT test."

"They want me in Lansing next week for the interview."

To advance to sergeant and lieutenant in the DNR you had to take a written test; if you scored high enough, a grueling interview followed. Those with the highest scores and best interviews got put on a waiting list. When a lieutenant's job opened, the most qualified got the first call.

"You'd move?"

"It goes with the territory."

"Yeah," he said. He still thought of her as his youthful probie of long ago. "What's Jack say?" Her husband was a self-employed electrician.

"He says they need juice other places, just like here."

Jack was a no-nonsense guy. Not much of a sense of humor, either. Service had always thought she deserved better, but she never complained and in the final tally it was none of his business.

"The kids?" She had daughters, nine and four.

"You know how kids are. They won't want to move, but if we do, they'll adjust."

"I guess," he said.

She said, "You're not taking this very well."

Service said, "Sorry."

McKower had been a sergeant for six years now and although he was not one of her direct reports, he had come to depend on her. She had been a great field officer and was an effective sergeant who knew how to lead and direct. She'd make a great lieutenant and down the road she could probably run the whole Law Enforcement Division, but he just wasn't ready to part with her.

"I'll let you know about Limpy. Guess I'd better get outside in the dirt."

McKower laughed and squeezed his arm. He walked outside and Candy McCants jumped in front of him, screaming, "I know PPCT and I am a lethal weapon!"

Service raised his hands in mock defense. "I know first aid and I'm not afraid to use it!"

After that, the group pretty much went through the motions. Sergeant Smoke lost his temper and told them they all had to buy beer for him after class.

When Service got home, Kira's truck was parked in the place where he usually parked. He immediately thought about moving her truck, but gave it a second thought and reminded himself, Use the time you have.

"I'm home, honey," he shouted as he pushed open the front door.

Lehto was sitting on the bed, wrapped in a blanket. "We have the flu," she said.

"We?"

"I figure twenty-four hours for you," she said with a raspy voice.

"I'll make chicken soup," he said.

"It won't help. It's a virus."

"And fern tea."

"Fern?" She made a face.

"You'll see."

She moved to the table in her blanket while he boiled water and heated chicken soup from a can. She kept the blanket tight around her and shivered continuously.

"I ought to put you back in bed."

"Maybe you should sleep on the footlockers tonight," she said.

He shot her a look. "No way."

She sipped the tea tentatively. "It tastes . . . fresh."

"Most people use the leaves. I use them too, but this month and next you throw in a few nuts to add flavor."

"I like how you know stuff," she said, sniffling. "It's a turn-on."

"Yeah, well, Mister Know-It-All learned something today he didn't know before. The state owns all the land in the Tract, but some parcels have been leased out to private individuals for ninety-nine years."

"So?"

"So, just when you think you know everything about something, you find out that you don't."

"So?"

"You sound like a kid saying, 'Why?' The so is this: What else don't I know about the Tract?"

"Life and death hang in the balance," she said sarcastically.

"You get surly when you're sick."

She said, "We'll see how you well you handle it when your turn comes."

"I don't get the flu," he said.

She gave him a look. "It's a virus. It's neither intimidated nor dissuaded by hardheadedness."

"It won't affect me." He kissed the top of her head.

"Don't," she said.

"Would you like your soup now?"

"Don't patronize me, Service."

"I'm just taking care of you, honey."

A tear formed in her right eye. "I know and I'm being a bitch."

"You're just being sick."

"Same thing," she said.

She ate all the soup and made sounds of appreciation.

In bed that night, he spooned in behind her.

She said, "I parked in your place on purpose. I wanted to see how you'd handle it."

He said, "I thought about moving your truck."

She sighed. "But you resisted the urge."

"So far," he said. "It's not morning yet."

She put an arm around his neck. "We are doing *so* good."

Maridly Nantz sounded tired and unhappy when she called Service. "There's been another fire," she said wearily.

"Been?" He was trying to wake up and sort out her words. Usually he was instantly awake in the night, but not this time.

"About five acres," she said, "but it's contained and we're sitting on it tonight in case hot spots flare up. I think you'd better come take a look. I'll meet you at the old log slide."

"The fire was near there?"

"The fire *was* there," she said.

"Rolling," Service said. Nantz had a cool head.

Kira asked, "What is it?"

"Another fire in the Tract."

"Oh no."

"Go back to sleep," he said.

"You don't have to twist my arm," she said, folding a feather pillow over her head. He gently squeezed her foot when he was dressed. No response. She was an instant and deep sleeper.

The log slide. The night of the Geezer Hole fire, the old man called Voydanov said he thought the driver of the vehicle he'd seen may have been fishing the log-slide area. Why had he thought this? More important, Service thought, why hadn't he asked Voydanov more about his reasons for thinking the stranger had been fishing? Got to get yourself focused, Service, and stay that way, he chided himself as he raced the truck down dark gravel roads.

Nantz was soot covered and frowning through bloodshot eyes. "It's too damn early in the summer for this. It hasn't been dry enough for natural causes and the tourists don't invade until the Fourth," she said angrily.

They waded into the river and stood in knee-deep water. The bottom was loose cobble, which made for unsteady footing. They shone their lights up the steep embankment on the east side. It was denuded of vegetation and blackened by fire. Tendrils of smoke plumes curled upward from the charred ground.

"It came all the way down to the water's edge," he said.

"I think it started down here by the water and burned upward," Nantz said, correcting him. "The wind was west-northwest at about four knots, gusting to eight. Behind our backs. We have to climb up to see the rest."

Service followed her downstream to where the land dipped down closer to the water; they got out and cut back to the northeast on a gently rising game trail. He was impressed that she seemed at ease walking in total darkness. Most people couldn't deal with it; many conservation officers labored to overcome natural fears of the night. When they closed in on the southern edge of the fire site, Nantz switched on her light.

"There," she said. "See it?"

There was a fire line, three feet wide, scraped cleanly down to the mineral earth.

He was surprised. "You and your people worked quickly to contain it."

She got down on one knee, keeping the beam of her light on the earthen scar as she pawed at the dirt. "We didn't dig this," she said disgustedly.

What was she trying to say? "No?"

"Whoever started this used the river on one end like an anchor and dug a line around the other three sides. They even chain-sawed some trees to keep the fire from jumping the line. It looks like they didn't want it to spread. They made a fire, but not too big. I don't get it."

Service understood what she was describing, but couldn't imagine a reason. "You mean it's a deliberate, controlled burn?"

"It sure as hell looks that way," Nantz said.

Service examined the fire line again. "Were your people up here?"

"No, one of them spotted the line where it came down to the river on the north end. As soon as I saw that, I came up here alone and checked to the south and east and found that the line was all the way around the burn. I kept my people back. I didn't want them bollixing any evidence. They're downriver now, in a clearing. I'm on watch for hot spots."

"As usual, you're right on top of everything."

"This deal pisses me off."

"We should hole up and wait for first light," he said. "Is arson coming?"

"They've been notified."

"When will they be here?"

She shrugged. "First light at the earliest. They don't like working nights. We can brew some coffee by the river. I have chow coming in the morning for the crew. You bring your fart sack?"

"I can doze by the fire."

"Don't let me fall in," she said.

Service built a small pit fire using green wood to make heavy smoke. They both doused themselves heavily with DEET in an oily preparation. The mosquitoes were bad, and billowing smoke would keep them at bay. Blackflies wouldn't attack until sunrise; nothing would stop them when they came, and it would be well into July before they were finished.

Nantz lay down on her side, using a small pack for a pillow. She looked over at Service.

"How'd you find this one?" he asked.

"I was downriver at the first burn and smelled smoke."

"You were out here?"

"I wanted to walk the other area when it was cold. Another fire," she said. "Goddammit!"

Service got water from the river for coffee and set the pot on a small gas grill she had brought in.

Nantz was asleep before the coffee was ready. He found himself staring at her. She was good at her job, committed, too good for this to be her first time. Like some women in jobs that used to belong exclusively to men, she could be pretty abrasive and aggressive, but she was a dedicated professional. Her behavior reminded him how tough it was to be a woman in what was still largely a man's world. He could remember when the first female COs were hired and all that they had gone through to prove themselves. Some couldn't deal with it and moved on, but many stayed and some of them were now sergeants and lieutenants; some, like McKower, might very well run the whole show someday.

Service didn't sleep. He kept the fire going all night and swatted at bugs. At first light he left Nantz and began scouting the fire line, looking for tracks, tool prints, anything to give them a lead. The blackflies were thick, but he tried to ignore them.

Nantz showed up during his second circuit. Her face was smudged, her hair matted and greasy.

"Anything?" she asked.

"Not so far."

"Figures," she said. "Whoever dug this line knew what they were doing. It looks to me like they intended to keep the site clean."

Logical conclusion, Service thought. "Is it safe for us to move into the burn yet?"

"Safe, but let's wait. My people will make a sweep soon and they'll go over the ground methodically. We should wait until they finish. Besides, some of the bigger rocks in there may still be hot."

He looked at her, thinking he had misheard. "What rocks?"

She told him to get on a nearby snag and pointed into the burn. "See those outcrops?"

It took a minute for him to focus, then he saw them. Granite. In fact there seemed to be a dozen or so in a rough, curving line. Between them were charred white and gray, chalklike stones. What the hell was this?

"I never saw rocks here before. Not like those," he said, stunned by his own ignorance.

"I'm not surprised," she said. "There's only a couple of places in the Tract like this—this one and another back east a bit. They could all be connected down deep. Glaciers moved through here and dumped all kinds of shit on the bedrock. Hell, in some places you've got to dig down two, three hundred feet to hit bedrock. The fact is that underground, everything is connected in one way or another. The granite here is what makes for the steepness. Back when loggers briefly used this, they probably understood the rocks would hold up and this would be a great spot to dump their take into the river."

Service wasn't listening. Granite *here*? It was yet another instance where he suddenly understood that he still had much to learn about his wilderness. Every time he thought he knew it all, he found out that he didn't. The price of hubris, he chided himself. How did she know so much about the Mosquito?

"Why would somebody intentionally burn this over?" he asked.

"Crazy people have crazy reasons," Nantz said, "but they're still reasons."

He grunted and wondered if the stranger with the camera and hammer was connected to this. "Aerial photos might help," he said.

"I can try," she said. "Why?"

"I'm not sure. Different view, maybe. Sometimes a little distance or time or a different angle help us see more clearly."

She shrugged. "It can't hurt and it's early in the season. I still have budget. If the fires get going this summer I can always appeal to overspend. I'll get on it right away. You going to hang in here?"

Her understanding of budgets tagged her as veteran. "For now. This was about five acres?"

"That's a WAG, but it's close enough for government work."

"How long would it take to dig a fire line around five acres?"

"That depends on the severity of the burn, the number of people working, the weather, their experience, and their equipment."

"Let's say there were one or two people."

Nantz rubbed an eye socket with the back of her hand. "There are a lot of roots and crap and it's steep as hell in parts. I'd say one or two days of hard, steady work."

"Meaning somebody would have to be here for a while before they torched it. If they wanted to avoid involvement, they'd wait to dig the line straight through, then set the fire and split."

"Makes sense to me," she said, studying him. "What's your point?"

"If somebody was here for a couple of days, or came in several times to dig a little at a time, they'd risk being spotted."

"Witnesses? That's a long shot."

"Long shot or not, we have to consider the possibility."

"How?"

"Use the media maybe."

"Reporters seldom get anything right," she said disgustedly. "Make that never."

He continued to think out loud. "If somebody was here more than a day," he said, "they probably came in and stayed. They wouldn't come and go. They'd want to minimize discovery. That's what I'd do."

"Yeah," she said. "Meaning they'd have a camp nearby?"

"Not a permanent camp, but a temporary resting spot. And they'd be dropped off rather than park in the area and risk their vehicle being spotted."

She wiped her mouth. "I think I'm following you." The sparkle was returning to her eyes.

"One person would be a lot less conspicuous than two or more."

Nantz nodded. "So the guy gets dropped, treks in, stays till the job is done, lights the fire, and hikes out to be picked up."

"It could be just like that," he said.

"More than one person would make it a conspiracy," she said.

"Maybe, but the second person might not know what the first one was up to."

Nantz motioned for him to follow. She took him to a tree stump just inside the fire line. "That's fresh. Done with a chain saw and, judging by diameter, not a small one. The second person wouldn't be blind to such a huge chain saw." She showed him the top part of the tree on the other side of the line. The bottom had been trimmed to keep it off the fire line.

She was right. "Yep. Two people at least."

"Should we look for a place where somebody rested or staged?"

"We'd probably never find it," he said. "All they'd have to do is get up in a tree."

Nantz's radio squawked. She answered with her name.

"Fire sweep," she said to Service. "Okay," she radioed. "My people and the arson crowd will sweep the burn."

She led him to the southern edge of the burn behind where the sweep began. He saw eight people spread about twenty yards apart. Service recognized the chiseled features of Sergeant Robo Peterson, the UP's chief arson investigator. Peterson looked over from the center of the line and saluted, but immediately returned his gaze to the smoldering ground ahead.

Service and Nantz squatted to observe.

Someone shouted from the west side of the sweep line.

"It's Bravo," Nantz said. "She's second in. Let's move."

Service followed her. She crossed the burned ground as gracefully as a deer.

Bravo was a tall black woman with her hair done in intricate cornrows. She held a baseball cap in her hand and looked glassy eyed. When Nantz got to her, the woman pointed over her shoulder and vomited, spewing on Nantz's leg. Nantz immediately put her arm around the woman and bent her forward at the waist. She looked at Service and nodded for him to check ahead.

The area was rocky as hell, but he was surprised to see a narrow crevice among the granite outcroppings. At the bottom he could make out the figure of a human being, but it was eight or ten feet down and on its face. And the rocks were hot. He took off his shirt, spread it out and wrapped both hands in it, and then climbed down using the shirt to protect his skin. At the bottom he found that the body was badly charred, its clothes burned off. Nantz appeared above him.

"Call the county," he said up to her.

Service checked for a pulse. None. He knew from experience not to disturb the corpse. Too much experience.

"Dead?" Nantz asked calmly from above.

"Nantz, make the call," he said sharply.

She left and Service climbed back up the same way he had come down.

Several people had gathered on top, but Nantz was shooing them away to continue the sweep.

"The ME will eventually pull the body out," he said. "Don't let him leave until I get back."

"Where are you going?"

"To talk to Voydanov."

Bravo was still on her hands and knees gagging. Nantz looked down at her, then at Service. "Catch you later?"

Voydanov's damn dog raised a ruckus, but Service heard the octogenarian tell the animal to hush.

" 'Nother fire, eh?" the old man asked when he opened the door. He immediately stepped outside and closed it behind him. The dog stopped barking, but continued to scratch at the door from inside.

The sound gave Service the willies. "You knew about the fire?"

"I seen the vehicles and equipment going by."

"Did you walk your animal last night?"

"Nope, me and ole Millie parked ourselves in front of the TV."

"The last fire, when you saw that vehicle parked back in the trees, you said you thought the driver might be fishing at the log slide. Why?"

Voydanov grinned. "Path of least resistance, I guess. Park there an' you can walk a circular route, along the contour to the log slide. It's longer that way, but it's also faster. You go direct and you have to bust a gut down through the bush. My kids and me used to hike around the contour. Pretty open walking all along that route."

Stupid me, Service thought. As a CO he spent so much time off trails that sometimes easy routes didn't register. It had never occurred to him that the stranger he'd met had come downriver, but now he realized that he may have. His mind that night had been locked on fishing for his own enjoyment, not on his job. Dumb. When he was a kid his old man had taught him to bodycheck. Said, "Forget the bloody puck and lock your eyes on the man's chest." He hadn't done that this time. Good thing the old man was gone; he'd be disgusted by his son's performance.

"Have you seen any other vehicles?"

"Not around here."

Service evaluated the answer. "Somewhere else?"

"No cars, no trucks."

"Some other kind of vehicle. ORV or ATV?"

"Just that chopper."

"You saw a chopper here?"

"Not here, back in the woods. I thought it belonged to you people."

"By the log slide?"

"Nope, farther up."

"Our chopper. Markings?"

"Nope, just a chopper and the bird."

The bird? Talking to Voydanov was like traveling a labyrinth with a blind person leading. "What bird?"

"Under the egg beater."

"There was a bird *under* the chopper?"

"Right, flying right under it, like a fat old goose, long neck and everything. You ever see that movie about some Canadian girl teaches geese to fly, then leads 'em down south with one of them udderlights?"

Movie, udderlight? "Ultralight?"

"That's what I said. Damn birds flew right along with that kid."

"You saw a bird flying with the chopper? How close?"

"Underneath, maybe fifty feet, maybe a hundred. Close."

"Upriver from the log slide?"

"Yep, a mile or so, maybe two."

"When?"

The old man pursed his lips in thought. "That would be the day before yesterday, right after sunrise."

"What color was it?"

"Mostly gray, with a long neck."

"I mean the chopper." Geez.

"Blue but not like a bluebird sky."

"With DNR markings?"

"Nope, no markings at all. I just assumed it was you fellas. Who else would be hovering over the Mosquito?"

"And this was yesterday?" Service asked, testing him.

"Couple of days ago, right after sunrise, early in the morning." Me and Millie was fishing.

"How long was it up?"

"One hour, two, but not covering a bunch of ground."

"Hovering?"

"More like moving real slow. He'd fly north, then south. Maybe a

hundred yards apart each time. Maybe more, but that's close. He was being methodical."

Service fought his frustration. "What shape was the chopper?"

"It was a Huey," Voydanov said confidently.

"Are you sure? There are all kinds of choppers."

"This was a UH-1H Iroquois, made by Bell, single engine, old fart.
Bell called them the Indian name, but the grunts called them Hueys and
if they didn't have weapons they were called Slicks."

"How do you know so much about Hueys?"

"My son flew one in Vietnam. Two tours."

"He make it back?"

"His body did," Voydanov said sullenly. "Part of him's still over there,
I think. Guess that damn war done that to a lot of our boys."

Service gave the old man a business card. "You think of anything else,
call me. Anytime, okay?"

When Service got back to the burn at the log slide, the medical examiner was still working on the body and photographs were being shot. Service got a cup of coffee from the cook fire, which Nantz had rekindled. He
left the ME alone to do his thing. Science types could be quirky and
needed their space to do their jobs. Nantz came over and sat beside him.

"ID yet?"

"No," she said.

"Voydanov told me that he saw a chopper upriver of here two days
ago, a dark blue machine with a bird flying underneath it. The old man
thought it was ours. Is Forest Management doing any work in here?" Forest Management was the DNR group charged with taking care of state forests and the group that controlled fire marshals like Nantz.

She puffed her cheeks. "Not that I know of. A bird beneath a helicopter? That's weird. Was the old guy sober?"

"He's just old, which sometimes is a lot like being drunk."

"You think the chopper is connected to this?"

"I don't want rule out anything yet."

"Roger that," Nantz said.

Eventually the body was recovered and carried out. The stiff was in a
black body bag, strapped to the litter.

The medical examiner was Vincent Vilardo, an internist from Escanaba appointed ME by the county board of supervisors.

"Hi, Vince. We know who it is?"

"Not yet. No wallet, but he's still got fingers and teeth. I expect we'll find out quick enough."

"Can I take a look?"

Vilardo unzipped the bag.

Service found himself staring into the charred face of Jerry Allerdyce, the husband of Honeypat. Limpy's son. This thing was getting more and more complicated and confused.

"You see a ghost?" Vilardo asked.

"It's Jerry Allerdyce, Vince."

"One of Limpy's mutts?" Everybody in the U.P. law enforcement community knew about the Allerdyces.

Service nodded. "Do me a favor and run prints to be sure, but we need to hold off on a public ID for a while."

Vilardo shrugged. "Just make sure you clear this with the county and your chain of command, eh?" he said. "We can say we aren't releasing the name until we notify the next of kin. Arson will go along with us."

"I appreciate this," the conservation officer said.

"There's something else you should see," Vilardo said. He unzipped the body bag farther.

The body reeked and its chest was charred to a shiny black sheen, but Service could see a huge hole over the heart area. No fire caused this.

"Just a preliminary," Vilardo said, "but I'd say subsonic, explosive-tip bullet. Shot in the back. The entry hole is teensy, but the bullet played havoc when it came out the front."

A homicide? "Time of death?"

"You'll have to wait. Seems to me somebody doused this poor bastard with gas and lit him."

"Are you telling me the body was the POO?"

"Peterson says no, that this was in addition to the starting point."

"Thanks, Vince."

"Grady, you should drop by for dinner sometime, we'll have some potato gnocchi with sweet pepper sauce. It'll melt in your mouth. You stop, okay? Rose would love to see you." Rose was his wife. Vince was the chef.

Nantz hiked out beside him, her shorter legs keeping pace. "What next?"

"We get those aerial shots and you get some sleep."

"I'll get on it," she said. "If you need help, call me. You need *anything*, call me," she added with a raised eyebrow.

"I will," he said, trying to avoid her eyes as he got into his truck. He immediately got on the radio. "Delta County, this is Marquette DNR 421." This was standard department commo. There were two sergeants in his area and one lieutenant. The LT was DNR 400. The sergeants were Charlie Parker, 402, and McKower, who was 403. The people who reported to Parker were 421, 422, and so on. Service reported to Parker, a fact which didn't set well with either of them. McKower's people were 431 and up. In the DNR, people had numbers, but county sheriffs and state cops went by the numbers of their vehicles. Communications tended to be pretty confusing to rookies in any uniform, and to everyone during a crisis.

"Go ahead, 421."

"Patch me through to Joe Flap, in Gladstone." He gave her the number.

Flap was an old-time CO, a true horseblanket who until retiring several years ago had been one of the few contemporaries of his father's still on the force. Flap was an experienced pilot who still flew an occasional mission for the DNR and always pitched in during deer season. Flap had flown combat in Korea and for the USFS in the West after that. He had also flown supplies to bush outposts in Alaska and Canada. He had crashed so many times and had so many close calls that other pilots called him Pranger.

The patch went through quickly.

"Joe, this is Grady Service. I need your help."

"Air or ground?"

"Information."

"Cost you a six-pack of Old Milwaukee."

"I want to ID a chopper. Navy or dark blue Huey, no markings. It was seen two days ago over the Mosquito."

"You think it's down?"

"No, we just want to know who was flying it and who owns it."

"Never seen it."

"Could air traffic control paint it?" Service asked.

"That depends. Talk to Lonnie Green in Escanaba. He works the tower at Delta County; he's the local ATC feed. Good man. I think they keep radar tapes nowadays."

"Thanks. You'll get that beer."

"I'd better, and soon. I'm sixty-seven and getting older by the minute. I die, just plunk that six-pack in my coffin, okay?"

Service laughed and got a patch to Lonnie Green. He explained what he wanted and arranged to meet him. They met on US 41, just north of Rapid River. Green was a short, trim man with pale eyes, shiny pink skin, and a head of thick, unkempt white hair. Service spread a map on the hood of this truck.

"Two days ago there was a chopper up here for an hour or two. This was in the early morning. Is there any way to track it?"

"Do you know the altitude?"

"Low, right down on the deck."

"Well, that's a bitch. Below twenty-five hundred feet we have a hard time, unless it's way out over the lake."

"It was well inland. But you do have tapes?"

"Voice and radar. We keep the tapes for fifteen days and if nothing comes up, we tape over them. Thing is, if this guy is VMC —"

"VMC, you mean VFR?"

"Same-same. New term, visual meteorological conditions. If he's VMC, there's probably no way to find him. FAA reg fourteen CFR allows for all sorts of jobs to be done without filing flight plans, especially if they're local. That fourteen CFR covers all sorts of stuff."

"Pilots can just go up and do their thing?"

"As long as the weather cooperates. Most of your shoe clerks don't care to fly when the soup is in."

"Shoe clerks?"

"Amateurs, blue-sky flyboys. People file flight plans or they don't. Or they file false flight plans. Sometimes they use real call signs, sometimes not. Sometimes they use their transponders, sometimes not. Sometimes we get a body paint, sometimes we don't. We also paint flocks of birds and even the occasional Amtrak if it's up on a hill. And if the weather's bad, forget painting aircraft; all we paint is rain or snow."

"It's dark blue, a Huey with no other markings."

"Radar doesn't see markings and unless a bird skates by the tower, we can't see either."

"Sounds like there's not a hell of a lot of control," Service said.

"Puts a choke-hold on your sphincter, doesn't it?"

"You mean somebody can just take off and do what they want?"

"Well technically, if they're VMC. Reg 19 CFR 122.32/33 requires them to land back where they started, even if they don't file a flight plan. The reg is mostly a formality and gets treated as such."

"Meaning locals ignore it."

"Bingo. I'll see what we have and get back to you, but no promises. Is this urgent?"

"I don't know yet. We're investigating a fire."

"I'll do it quick as I can. Do you have a time for the sighting?"

"We have a report that it was just after sunrise." Service gave Green his card and reminded himself how COs were more and more being asked to act like a bunch of junior executives, handing out calling cards.

Service tried to remember if Jerry Allerdyce had been at his father's compound the night they had arrested Limpy. He hadn't been among the detainees.

Honeypat's trailer looked abandoned, but Service drove up the long two-track and parked nearby. The woman emerged from the door as soon as he stopped. She was shoeless, wearing black pantyhose and no blouse. A faded GREEN BAY PACKERS championship cap was tilted backward on her head.

"It's you," she said disgustedly. He noticed that her front teeth were shorter than her incisors, which hung down like fangs. "I got company coming and it won't do for a fish cop to be hanging around."

"Get dressed, Honeypat. We need to talk."

She didn't argue and he followed her inside. She put on a diaphanous silk robe, which hid nothing, sat on a bowed couch, crossed her legs, and lit a Camel.

"So talk," she said.

"Is Jerry the company you're expecting?"

She sneered. "No way."

"Where is Jerry?"

"How would I know?" she said. "My s'posed to keep track?"

"Was he here last night?"

"He ain't here any night. We're whaddyacallit . . . separated."

"How long?"

She frowned. "Since he knocked up some teenybop twat over to Iron Mountain. He done her doggy on the back of his Skidoo last New Year's Eve."

She was clearly peeved, which made no sense. While her husband was making it with some teenager, she was sleeping with his father. He wondered if this was a cause-and-effect thing, then put the thought out of mind. It was what it was.

"Have you filed for divorce?"

She tapped a teetering ash into a beer can. The only ashtray in sight was already overflowing with butts. It said SOO ANTLERS. "Haven't gotten around to that yet."

Which technically made her next of kin. "Honeypat, Jerry's dead."

Her eyes flashed momentarily, but her face remained impassive. "Yah?"

"I expect you and Limpy will want to make funeral arrangements when the body is released."

"Pitch him in the dump for all I care."

It was curious that she asked no questions. "I'm sorry to have to bring you the bad news."

"I guess I won't be needing to pay no lawyer now."

So much for that, Service thought. He wondered how his ex would react if she heard of his death.

"Can I call anybody for you?"

"Just split," she said. "I got company coming."

"Could be your husband was murdered."

The woman fumbled her cigarette.

"Did Jerry have a problem with anyone?"

"Besides me? The asshole had problems with everyone."

Service put a business card on her grimy kitchen counter. "Call me. I need to know who he hung out with."

She laughed strangely. "He hung with any chick would drop her gear," she said through clenched teeth, her first sign of real emotion.

The pot calling the kettle black? "They'll hold his body a while and they won't announce his identity until the preliminary investigation's completed. There will be an autopsy. You got the name of that girl in Iron Mountain?"

She mashed her lips together.

Meaning, Get lost. "Call me if you change your mind," Service said.

He passed a red truck on his way out. He recognized the driver as a barber from Marquette. Married.

Limpy was tight-jawed when Service met him. Honeypat apparently had called ahead and given him the news about his son.

"You hear about Jerry?"

"Hear what?" Allerdyce asked.

Lying through his teeth. "He's dead."

Allerdyce wouldn't look at him.

"He was shot in the back."

No response, no questions.

"He was in the Mosquito, Limpy. After he was shot, somebody set him on fire. Could be they knocked him out and torched him while he was still alive. We don't know all the details yet."

"That's all?" Allerdyce said, still not looking at him.

"The county isn't going to release the body for a while."

"I gotta go," Limpy said, getting to his feet.

Service stepped outside the jail and had a cigarette. The bank clock said 5 P.M. He called Kira from a pay phone.

"Are you okay?" she asked through a deep sniffle. "What happened with the fire?"

"It's out, but we found a body in the fire. It looks like he was shot."

"My God," she said. "I never thought about COs handling that kind of stuff."

Most people didn't. "I'm not handling it. But he was on state land, which makes it my business. One more stop and I'm headed for home. Do you feel any better?"

"Still shaky, but recovering, and of course you're immune."

"Yep," he said. "Be there soon."

On the drive back to Honeypat's, he radioed Nantz. "How's Bravo?"

"Shook up. It's her first like that."

"Happens to all of us," Service said. He had noticed that Nantz hadn't shied away from the corpse, and he again wondered what sort of experience she had.

"Even you?"

"Plenty of times."

"Macho with feelings," she said. "I like that. The aerials will be shot tomorrow if the weather cooperates."

"Make sure they go upriver from the log slide too," Service said. "One to two miles."

"What's up there?"

"I don't know, but that's where Voydanov said the chopper was."

"How do we pinpoint a spot?"

"Good point," he said. "I'll head down there in the morning."

"I'll join you," she said.

He wasn't going to argue. "Park where we were today, five A.M.? Tell the pilot we'll be in place to guide him at ten A.M. See you there."

"Count on it," she said.

* * *

Honeypat was sitting on the stoop of her trailer, drinking from a can of Colt .45.

"You okay?" he asked.

"I just got off twice," she said. "That helps."

She was incredibly blunt. "I really want to talk to that pregnant girl."

Honeypat shrugged. "You'll find her at Limpy's camp. Her people kicked the slut's ass out after the bunny bit it."

"What's her name?"

Honeypat's eyes went glassy. "Saila Kalinen."

"I appreciate this."

She nodded curtly.

"Who'd Jerry hang out with?"

"He was a loner, except for pussy. Like Limpy."

"Did Jerry work?"

"Not regular. Tended a little bar, sold some venison, logged some pulp."

"What bar?"

"I don't remember. He never lasted long. He'd work, ball one of the waitresses or the boss's wife or daughter or mother, get himself canned. Ask around, they'll all know him."

"Who'd he log with?"

"Some guy named Ralph. An old pal of Limpy's. He lives over to Christmas, I think. There were others too, but I never knew their names."

"Was Jerry a good logger?"

She stared off at the forest. "One of two things he was good at. He could work like a dog when he set his mind to it."

"Are you going to be okay?"

"I always am," she said.

Kira waved through the window and opened the door. A huge black thing bounded out and Service instinctively turned away and braced himself against the fender of his truck.

"Bear!" he shouted.

"It's a Canary Island mastiff," she said. "Her name is Newf."

"Tell it to get back."

"She likes you. Her owners are moving down to Midland and can't keep her. They dropped her off today. I told them I'd find a good home for her. Tell her to sit. She's very well behaved."

"Sit," Service said tentatively.

Newf flopped down and panted.

"Get her away."

"She won't bother you."

Service slid cautiously along the side of the truck, jumped onto the porch, rammed through the door, and slammed it behind him. The dog continued to sit.

Kira kissed him on the cheek and hugged him. He looked out the door again. The dog was still there.

"You can let her in," she said.

"Like hell."

Halfway through his soup, Service went to the door and opened it. "Come on," he said.

The 130-pound animal walked through the door, her tail wagging, went to Kira and looked at her.

Service said, "Sit." The dog did as instructed.

When he finished his pasta, Service said tentatively, "We can't keep her."

"I know," Kira said.

"I mean it," he said.

"Of course you do," she said, patting his hand.

· 12 ·

The dog shadowed Service around the cabin in the early morning, staying close and watching, but not interfering.

"Take her along with you today," Kira said sleepily from the bed. "She'll be good company."

"I can't. It's against regs."

"Don't be so contrary. Just tell her what you want. She's better trained than you."

His legs felt rubbery. His fear of dogs was entirely irrational, but it had always been there; he had tried several times to conquer it, to no avail. "Okay," he said, pushing open the front door. The mastiff followed him out. When he opened the passenger door, the dog jumped up and sat down. It was embarrassing to be a conservation officer afraid of dogs.

"You'll do as I say," Service said to the dog as he slid behind the wheel.

The dog woofed softly, taking him by surprise. "You don't understand a damn word I say. That was coincidence."

The animal woofed again and stared at him.

"This is my truck and I'll do the talking." Damn Kira.

Nantz's truck was already there when Service pulled in. Her feet were sticking out the driver's window. The sky was suggesting gray, morning twilight under way.

"Skeeters will make you their breakfast," he said, tickling one of her bare feet.

Her feet recoiled slightly. "I've got a lot of testosterone," she said. "It keeps skeeters and men away."

He smiled. "I doubt that. Were you here all night?"

She sat up, pushing a lock of hair out of her face. "I kept dreaming my forest was burning. Needed to be here. This job is making me crazy." She opened her door, put on her socks and boots, got out and stretched. She sniffed one of her armpits and made a face.

Her forest?

"I could use a bath," she said spying the dog in his truck. "Who's that?"

"Her name is Newf. I'm just watching her until she has a home. You interested?"

"No way." Nantz opened his truck door. The mastiff jumped down and licked her hand and rolled on her back.

"She's friendly. Soft."

"Let's go," Service said. The dog immediately got up and trotted ahead, stopped and looked back to make sure they were following. When he nodded, the animal ran on, but constantly circled back to keep them in sight.

"How long have you had this dog?" Nantz asked.

"One day, and she's *not* mine."

"If you say so," Nantz said.

It was going to be a hot, muggy day. Usually the humidity didn't settle in until July. They cut over to the river above the log slide, crossed and followed the eastern bank north, looking for some sort of landmark with which to guide the light plane that would take the aerial photographs.

At 9 A.M. the dog began barking loudly and wouldn't shut up or come when Service called. He went to her and found her perched on a granite outcrop more than six feet tall. The dog wagged her tail.

"Good girl," Nantz said as she caught up. "There's a row of cedars north of us. The pilot should be able to see this," she pointed out. "We couldn't have picked a better spot."

"Pure luck," he said. "That's all."

Nantz slid off her pack and looked around, wiping sweat off her forehead with a purple kerchief. "Just this one outcrop," she said. "What's it doing here?" The top of the granite was discolored, an off brown. The rock was similar to those where the fire had been, only this was a single outcrop and not a dozen.

"They'll never see it from the air," Service said.

"I've got smoke," Nantz said. "I wonder how much more granite is around here?"

Service had never noticed granite anywhere in the area before the fires began.

The dog trotted down to the river, waded to a shallow gravel area beside a log near shore, and loudly began slurping water and pawing at it.

Service checked his watch and scanned the sky. "We have an hour to wait, give or take."

Nantz nodded and followed the dog into the river.

What was it his old man used to say? The Tract has everything if a body learns how to see. Some father he was, rarely home and then spouting psychobabble and scientific terms and him with barely a high school diploma. Tiger Service he was called. He had served in the Pacific as a marine sharpshooter. In life, Grady had never been close to his father, though he realized later he had adored him. Now look. He was also a former marine and a combat vet and now a CO, not to mention the latest Service to be the self-appointed Tract keeper. Just like the old man. How had this happened?

Nantz peeled off her shirt and began splashing herself with river water. After a few splashes, she sat on the log, took off her pants, and lay them over the log.

Service looked away.

"It won't be long till there's a plane with a camera overhead," he said.

She said, "They've never seen a girl in her skivvies?"

"Jesus, Nantz."

"Okay, okay," she said.

The dog was pawing in shallow water fifty feet downriver.

Nantz moved to a deadfall less than ten feet from Service and sat down. She had no modesty. He tried again to look away.

"Damn dog," he said. "She'll stink up my truck."

"She's just exploring. Leave her alone," Nantz said. "You ought to appreciate adventuresome females."

The dog splashed back upstream and dropped a mouthful of pebbles at Nantz's feet.

"Thank you, girl," Nantz said, rubbing the animal's dripping snout. She reached into the water and grabbed a handful of the pea gravel and picked through the stones in her hand. "Nice," she said. "We girls like pretties, right Newf?" The dog wagged her tail and ran off into the river to explore some more.

Service took two energy bars out of his pack and tossed one to her. She caught it with a flick of her wrist.

"Wow, a breakfast date."

"This isn't a date," he said.

She held up the bar. "It says right here, Breakfast date bar."

"Let's talk about the search."

"Yessir," she said, waving a sloppy salute at him. "Whatever you say, *Sir!*"

She let him do the talking, nodding as she nibbled on her breakfast bar.

"How the hell do you know so much about the Mosquito?" he asked, surprised that the words had slipped out.

She eyed him before speaking. "I grew up in Cornell," she said. Cornell was a farming village on the Escanaba River, a spot that had been made into a quality fishing area. "I got my B.S. in forestry at the University of Colorado and an M.S. in ecology from Oregon. Two summers as a hot shot out of Oregon, three as a smokejumper in Alaska. I did my master's thesis on the Mosquito ecosystem. I spent a summer here and I think I walked every square foot a hundred times. I wasn't searching, just looking. It's amazing what you notice when that's your only goal. I had a publisher in Eugene who wanted to publish the thesis, but I said no. The one conclusion I reached was that this area can't stand a lot of human intervention and if I published I was afraid it might draw more people in than are already here. After the master's, I got a job with FEMA. I was assigned to Denver, but they sent me all over the place. It seemed like I was always in on the cleanup. After three years, I decided I'd rather fight and contain, not mop up. I heard there were openings in Michigan not far from home, and here I am. Since I arrived this spring I've spent every spare minute out here, looking around, surveying the turf, getting reacquainted. I guess I'm sort of partial to it."

Service wasn't sure what to say. He found it unnerving, even offensive, to think that someone else might know the tract better than he did—he, its self-appointed guardian.

Nantz was on her back on the log in the morning sun when the plane made its first pass. She didn't hurry to get dressed, and pulled on her shirt as she talked to the plane on her radio.

"Air One, this is Nantz. You see us?"

"That's a negative," came the reply.

"Popping blue smoke," Nantz said. She peeled the tab off the lid of an olive-green can, shook it to stimulate the chemical reaction, and placed it on the ground. Blue smoke began to pour out and drift almost directly upward.

The plane waggled its wings when it passed over.

"Got blue smoke," the pilot called. "What's the plan here?"

"Start a mile above us," Nantz said, "fly down the river to three miles below where we are now. Can you get us a half-mile cut to the east of the east bank?

"That what we want?" she asked Service, who nodded.

"Roger that," the pilot said on the radio. "Anything else?"

"Thanks, we're gonna head out now."

Service was staring at Nantz.

She said, "I like it when you look at me."

"Not you," he said. "The ground."

"Oh, great," she said.

"Look down," he said.

"For what?"

"Come over here by me."

She did as she was instructed and sat beside him on the ground.

"See where you were? Tell me what you see."

"Nothing," she said.

"Wait."

"Jesus, Service. If we're gonna play games, let's pick one we both like. Want some of my ideas?"

"Just look," he said.

She stuck her chin in her hand. Ten minutes passed. "Okay," she said. "I give."

"A sparkle," he said. Then, "Follow me." He told her to sit in one place and he moved a few feet farther on and stood there.

Almost immediately she said, "I see it." She went to where the sparkle had shown, and bent down to pick up pebbles. "Dog rocks," she said. "Newf brought these to me." She reached for her shirt pocket and saw there was a hole in it. "God, I hate to sew," she said. She retreated slowly, retrieving the small stones until she could see no more. She held them in her fist.

Service came over and looked at them. One stone was sort of clear and greasy, about the size of a large peppercorn, and rounded.

"It's glass," Nantz said dismissively. "The river rounds and polishes broken glass. Personally I prefer agates."

"Glass," he said. She gave him the stones. He absentmindedly deposited them in his shirt pocket, removing the compass that he kept in there. Then he saw it wasn't working right. The needle was spinning slowly, not locking on north. Peculiar, he thought, but not unusual in the Upper Peninsula, where iron deposits sometimes played havoc with magnetic compasses. But there wasn't any iron ore near here. He didn't need the compass and put it in his pack.

After the long trek back to the trucks, Nantz said, "I'll get the aerials to you just as soon as they arrive."

"See you then," he said. Newf jumped into the front seat beside him. She was wet and smelly. "You travel with me, you gotta keep your yap shut," he said. "What goes on the road, stays on the road. Got it?" The dog tilted her head and panted, then woofed and her ears drooped.

Service said, "Okay, deal. You wanna stick your head out the window?" He reached over and rolled the window down partway. The dog rested her nose on the glass.

Service drove to Hathoot's office, which was not that far away. The superintendent was sitting in his receptionist's chair, talking on the phone.

"How was TC?" Service asked after the man hung up.

Doke Hathoot shrugged and led him into his office. A folded map was stretched out on a round conference table.

"The leases are in blue," Hathoot said. "You can see we've whited out those that have expired and control passed back to us."

Service studied the map. There was a blue parcel half a mile east of the fire and another one about a quarter mile east of the outcrop he and Nantz had found this morning. Curious.

"You got names for me?"

Hathoot went over to his desk, got an envelope, and handed it over.

Service opened it and read. The parcels had originally been granted to Cyril Knipe. They were near the river and both now leased to a man named Seton Knipe, his address listed as Pelkie. There was no way to tell how old the man was, and there was no address or phone number. The lease would expire in 2007.

Service wrote down the coordinates of all the leases and all the information he could find on the lessees. There were only five left, and three of the parcels were on the eastern boundary, next to a perimeter road.

"If there's a ninety-nine year lease and the lessee dies, rights pass to the survivors, right?"

"Right. We talked about that. The families get control of the property for the duration."

"Could they sue to retrieve the right to use the land, build a building, whatever?"

Hathoot looked puzzled. "People can sue for anything, but guess I'd better check with our legal beagles on that one. Why?"

"I don't know yet. I'm just trying to learn all I can. You heard about the new fire?"

"New fire?" Hathoot's eyebrows popped up and he looked surprised.

"Five acres at the log slide. Intentionally set. We found a body."

"Holy shit."

"The victim had been shot."

"Double holy shit."

"It's under investigation now and nobody is talking about it yet."

"Did you identify the deceased?"

"Not yet." Service wasn't sure why he didn't tell Hathoot he was pretty certain it was Jerry Allerdyce, but he had learned over the years, starting in Vietnam, that when stuff started going funny, you needed to withdraw into yourself and trust few others. "Your briefing go all right?"

"The usual crapola," Hathoot said. "The governor wants even fewer state employees and he wants to up the state income, but reduce taxes. 'How the hell do you do that?' I asked the NRC guys. By selling off state land, they said. Did you know that DEQ has been ordered to okay licenses and leases with minimal investigation before they approve development grants?"

"I've heard rumors." Clearcut Bozian seemed intent on letting business do anything it wanted in the state. He was not surprised by Hathoot's revelation, but it irritated him.

"Before it was just a practice from above. Now it's in writing."

"Don't tell me they want to sell the tract." Service felt his anger rise.

"Holy shit, no! We're still a gem in the state's crown jewels. Me, I'd do it the other way and buy property and real estate for the state and the future. This would cut down on rural incursions and let us put some substantial parcels back together, but in Lansing they think they'd lose tax revenues, so they want to sell public land for cash and to jack up the tax base. The thinking is to lower the rate, but get more people paying. Bureaucrats."

"They come after the tract," Service said, "and they will have a war on their hands."

"If they do that, count me in with you. And if you need more on the leasing situation, just call me."

✻　✻　✻

Kira sounded out of breath when he reached her at her office. "I'm glad you called!" she said. "I just got a call from a woman in Rock. Something about an eagle and her dog in her backyard. Meet me there?"

"Sure," he said. He wrote the address on the back of his hand with a ballpoint pen, a habit acquired in Vietnam.

Kira's truck was parked in front of the house, which was on the edge of a marsh not far from the Tacoosh River. Newf wagged her tail when she saw Kira, but Service told the dog to stay and she did.

There was an older woman with the veterinarian. She had on a faded shapeless sundress and blue flipflops with her hair in a ragged black hair net, creating the appearance of a helmet.

"They've got Mac," the woman keened. Her eyes were red from crying. "I turned a hose on 'em, but it didn't do no good."

"Her dog McClellan," Kira whispered to Service as they headed behind the house. "Named for the Civil War general who didn't like to fight. That should make you feel good."

"It's still a dog," he said.

In the backyard two very large, angry adult bald eagles were on top of a bloody brown dog. One of the raptors had hold of the dog's neck; with the other set of talons he was locked to the other bird. They were pecking at each other and pounding away with their wings.

"Get me a broom," Service said.

The old woman fetched.

Service poked tentatively at the birds to switch their attention to the broom, but they were too filled with hate for each other.

The broom was not going to work. "You got your tranq gun?" he asked Kira.

"Yes, but I don't have a clue about a safe dose for eagles. I don't want to kill them. How about cold water?"

He nodded while he cautiously continued to try to separate the birds' talons with the broom.

Kira lugged the bucket of water and Service tossed it and the birds suddenly lifted, but took the dog with them. The CO instinctively grabbed the brown dog and the eagles let loose, flitting upward, showering a small rain of feathers. Service and the suddenly freed dog fell to the ground. The dog shook its head, saw Service, and lunged snarling at his chest, but the CO managed to knock the animal aside with an elbow as he scrambled to his feet.

"Don't, Mac!" the old woman shrieked.

Mac wasn't listening.

The dog was losing blood fast, but crouched to attack, trying to marshal its strength, its ears flat. Kira grabbed the owner and pulled her back. Service wondered if he could get to the broom, but suddenly Newf banged into his leg, knocking him off balance, and planted herself between him and the brown dog. The two animals stared at each other silently until the brown dog finally collapsed on its side.

Service exhaled in relief and backed up, calling Newf, who came to him reluctantly and kept staring back at the other dog. He had learned a long time ago never to run away from an angry or injured animal.

Kira returned with a blanket and talked softly to the injured dog while she carefully wrapped it. She told Service she needed to get the animal to her clinic.

"Help me, Grady."

He was nervous but grabbed the brown dog's front. Kira got its hindquarters and they carried the animal to her truck, where she gave the animal an injection and used a towel to wipe blood off her own arms.

"Do you want me to follow you back to the office?" Service asked.

"No, I'll be fine." She kissed him and got in her truck. "I'll take Newf and see you at home." She opened her passenger door and Newf jumped in and sat down.

Service dug into his shirt pocket, asked for her hand, and put the pebbles from the Mosquito in her hand.

"What're these?" she asked with a smile.

"It's your reward for pulling that woman back," he said.

She looked at the stones, then at him. "I *love* sparkle-arkles, baby. You'll get *your* reward tonight," she added, lowering her voice. "If I can stay awake." Then she winked and started her engine.

Service lingered by the passenger door and stared at the dog. "How did you get out?" he asked.

The animal woofed and wagged her tail, looking back as Kira drove away.

There were black hairs on the edge of his truck window on the passenger side. The dog must've squeezed her way out. "Okay, dog." he said to himself, "I owe you."

The county dispatcher relayed Service by radio to Gustus Turnage, a CO in Houghton.

"Gus, Grady."

"Yo."

"I need information. There's a man over your way in Pelkie. His name is Seton Knipe." Service spelled the name. "Get me an address, phone number, and a read on him."

"How soon?"

"Quick as you can. Do you know him?"

"No, but Knipe's an old name around these parts. Dough from mining and logging. Iron mines, I think, somewhere in the distant past. Maybe some real estate in recent years."

"Let me know what you find out, okay?"

"Wilco. How goes the battle?"

"Day by day."

"Yeah, well, eat your Twinkies," Turnage said with an audible chuckle.

The word was out on his court exploits, Service knew, and it made him feel good. When you took down a bad guy, it gave all the good guys heart.

He called ahead to the Marquette County Jail, only to learn that Limpy was refusing visitors. There was no point in bugging the old bastard. Instead, he turned southwest and headed for Limpy's camp. When he parked, he saw a lookout dart into the woods.

Service didn't get far down the trail before Limpy's brother Eddie came toward him. Eddie had done half a dozen short stints in various U.P. county jails for fish and game and assault violations. He was a few years younger than Limpy but looked nearly as bad. He was toothless and balding, his face lumpy with acne scars, his back bent. Still, he had strength enough to lug along a baseball bat.

"You're not welcome here," Eddie said.

"I want to talk to Saila."

"Jerry's dead. Just leave the girl be."

The word had obviously traveled fast. "Jerry was murdered, Eddie. We need information."

"We know how to take care of our own."

"Yeah, well, you didn't do so well with Jerry."

Eddie turned without a word and led him into camp.

Acrid wood smoke hung in the air. Several people milled around casting angry eyes at them.

The girl met him on the porch of a run-down shack. She was tall, five-ten at least, with spindly legs and arms and an enormously protruding belly. The other clan members gathered near the porch.

Service said, "Folks, can we have a few minutes alone?"

The crowd dispersed reluctantly.

The girl had a pretty face but aged eyes, and he couldn't blame her.

"I'm sorry about Jerry," he said.

"I keep thinking he'll come walkin' up the trail any minute."

"He was murdered, Saila. Somebody shot him and set his body on fire and he is not coming back."

"That don't change what I feel for him."

"He was in the Mosquito Wilderness Area when it happened. When did you last see him?"

The girl thought before answering. "Two, three days ago, I guess."

"Was it two or three? This is important."

"He sorta comes and goes, ya know?"

"Did he say where he was going?"

"Just that he had a job to do."

"Did he say when he'd be back?"

"Probably yesterday."

"What kind of job?"

"For some guy."

"Do you know who?"

She shook her head and clasped her hands together. He understood the body language. She was shutting down.

"Do your folks know about Jerry?"

She barely moved her head. "They don't want me and our baby."

"You should call them," he said. "Your baby ought to have grandparents. Did Jerry work with this man before?"

"I don't know," she said. "We don't put our noses in other people's business."

This was a Limpyism. "Do you know what kind of work it was?"

"No, but I seen his chain saw was gone."

"What make was it?"

"I don't know that stuff. It was yellow. Had a long blade, ya know? Jerry took real good care of his guns and tools."

But not people, Service thought. "Anything missing besides the chain saw?"

"No, just that. He's real particular about that saw. He'll use other people's tools, but not their chain saws. Wouldn't loan his, neither."

"This other guy, did he pick Jerry up?"

"No, I think they were gonna meet at the Happy Jet."

"In Gwinn?" It was the only bar he knew with this name, but he needed to make certain and help her to keep talking.

"Yah, Jerry likes the Happy Jet. I haven't been in there yet, but I hear it's way cool."

If you liked bikers and meth freaks. "Did Jerry have his own car?"

"He had Limpy's truck and he took real good care o' that, too."

Service couldn't think of other questions. "Thanks for talking to me, Saila. Call your parents. Things get said when people are mad or upset, but time tends to calm things down. They'll be worried about you when news of Jerry gets out."

She nodded, but he had a feeling she wouldn't call.

Eddie Allerdyce walked out of camp with Service. "You think they're gonna let Limpy out?" Had Limpy told his brother he was offering to trade information? It wasn't likely. The family would not like it if their leader were known to be cooperating.

"I don't know," the CO said. "He violated parole. You know who Jerry was going to work with?"

"I did, you can bet we'd already be hunting that bastard."

Which meant he knew that Jerry had gone with somebody. "Let the law handle this, Eddie. You people have enough problems."

"You're a decent guy," Eddie said. "Limpy told us that. He don't got no hard feelings, eh? He didn't mean to shoot you that time, ya know? It just sorta happened."

"What's Jerry drive?" Service asked.

"He's got my brother's truck."

"Did you see Jerry leave with his chain saw?"

"Nope. I didn't see him leave at all."

"Maybe he was going to do some work with Ralph."

"Limpy tell you that?"

"I'm just asking." Eddie didn't need to know he'd gotten the information from Honeypat.

"Ralph lives near Christmas?"

"Down to Ridge, but he don't welcome visitors."

It wouldn't hurt to leave Eddie with a little hope. "Tell your people if they clean up their acts, Limpy may have a chance. You keep on doing what you've always done and they won't send him back to you."

Eddie said nothing.

Ridge was a tiny farming community southeast of the village of Christmas. Like most COs in the U.P., Service knew of most the villages and little clusters of houses that served as population centers, but he had never been to Ridge and radioed CO Jake Mecosta for help. A member of the Baraga-L'Anse Ojibwa, Mecosta worked out of Munising and was one of the few Native American COs in the state. Most of the tribes and bands had their own police and CO forces, and few of the Indians moved into the state ranks. Service wasn't sure why. Mecosta agreed to meet him at the public boat launch on Christmas Beach in Bay Furnace. Christmas was a fine example of Yooper schemes to make money. A Swede from Munising had bought land back before World War II and had built a factory to produce year-round Yule gifts. The business had burned, but the town had kept the name. You could still buy Christmas trinkets in gas stations and restaurants. And you could gamble at the tiny Indian casino called Kewadin, which meant north wind.

Jake Mecosta was leaning against the front fender of his truck, chewing a toothpick. Nearing fifty, Jake was six-six, with short salt-and-pepper hair and skin the color of cherrywood.

"You're a long way from home," Mecosta said with a grin when Service pulled up beside him. You hunting Twinkies?"

"Something like that," Grady Service said.

"I heard Allerdyce got out and you already put him back in."

"For now. I'm trying to get some information about his son Jerry."

"Jerry? That one's dumber than a Sioux tryin' to ride a bicycle," Mecosta drawled. The Ojibwa had fought for nearly a century and a half against the Sioux, driving them from Upper Michigan, Wisconsin, and Minnesota onto the Great Plains. Hard feelings persisted on both sides.

"You know Jerry?"

"I busted him once for stealing black walnut trees."

That sounded like Jerry. "I've heard he used to work for a man over this way, a friend of Limpy's. Named Ralph. He supposedly lives near Ridge."

Jake Mecosta spit out his toothpick and grimaced at the mention of the name. "Ralph Scaffidi," he said.

"*The* Ralph Scaffidi?" Scaffidi was a Detroit mobster who suddenly became major news when FBI investigators leaked information to the media that he had knowledge of the Jimmy Hoffa disappearance in 1975. "What's Scaffidi doing up here?"

"The official word is that he's retired," Mecosta said, "but I talked to Wink Rector and he didn't say so in so many words, but he left me with the impression that Scaffidi was exiled up here by the mob. He's got a couple of punks living with him, but if Rector is right, they're guards, not servants."

Wink Rector was the FBI's resident agent for the Upper Peninsula. He had an office in Marquette and a house on the Chocolay River.

"Have you met Scaffidi?"

"No, but a couple of times the wife and I have seen him and his shadows in Foggy's." Foggy's Reindeer Room was a bar in Munising. "Are you actually gonna go see him?"

"I guess I have to."

"Better you than me," Mecosta said with a sly grin.

Directions in hand, Service left his colleague at the boat launch and drove south toward Ridge. Scaffidi's house was half a mile down a tree-lined, hard-top driveway that looped in front of the structure. The new house was huge, made of cedar logs and sited on a small hill overlooking a swamp. The house looked bright orange in the sun. A mown and manicured lawn stretched all around the house. Service expected KEEP OUT signs but found none.

Service had barely parked when an old man with silver hair ambled out the front door. He wore a golf shirt with an emblem that said KEY BIS-CAYNE YACHT CLUB.

"Mister Scaffidi?" Service said as he got out.

"I am he," the man said. He face was tanned, his hands wrinkled with age. He had pale brown eyes that were alert but betrayed no emotion. Service saw somebody else lurking behind the screened front door.

"Grady Service, DNR."

Scaffidi nodded. "A fish dick," he said with a teasing grin, "but not local. Mecosta's our local guy. What brings you out to the sticks?"

Jake had said he'd never met the man, who anticipated Service's thoughts. "I've never met Officer Mecosta, but I make it a point to keep track of such things. How about a cup of espresso? A warm drink cools the body on a hot day. I've got a new machine sent from Milano."

Service agreed and followed Scaffidi onto the porch, where they sat at a small round table. An unopened Sunday *New York Times* lay in the middle of the table.

The old man sat down and said over his shoulder at the door, "Carlo, two espressos, please, and cut the lemon peel fresh, *capisce?*

"I'm glad you're here," Scaffidi said, turning back to Service. "I've tendered invitations to your colleague Officer Mecosta, but he hasn't bothered to respond. I have a lot of concern about this brouhaha over feeding deer. A fella's gotta bait deer, well, that's like hunting sheep in the barn, am I right? This bovine TB thing is a mess, but until the state puts down its foot and says no more feeding, it's just going to keep spreading. The government's got to look out for all the people, am I right? Not just the connected few."

Scaffidi was referring to a continuing controversy between farmers, the DNR, State Agricultural Commission, Farm Bureau, other groups, and some wealthy people in the northern Lower Peninsula who had hunt clubs where they fed deer year-round to keep them on their properties. Bovine tuberculosis was carried in the air from cattle to deer. Some scientists believed that putting out huge piles of corn and other feed caused animals to congregate, which helped bovine tuberculosis to spread. The DNR's director insisted there was no hard evidence of this, but the division's own wildlife chief had called for a statewide baiting and feeding ban.

"I'm sorry," the old man said. "You don't make the regulations. You just enforce them. Forgive me for running off about this, but I care very much about our natural resources."

A muscle-bound young man in running shorts and a Honolulu blue DETROIT LIONS football jersey brought two tiny cups of espresso and eyed Service suspiciously.

"Carlo's one of my assistants," Scaffidi said. "He's a good boy, loves the woods. It's hard to find young people to come up here and work." Jake Mecosta said Scaffidi's helpers were keepers. Carlo certainly looked the part.

Service watched Scaffidi rub the lip of his cup with lemon peel and followed his lead.

The espresso was bitter.

"I had to do it again," Scaffidi said, "I wouldn't touch this crap, but I'm an old man and the doctors want to take away all my pleasurable habits. A man's gotta hang on to what he can, am I right? I get one cup a day. So what can I do for you, Officer Service?"

"I need to know if a man named Jerry Allerdyce sometimes works for you."

"He has, but not recently. Is there a problem?"

"Jerry is dead."

The old man didn't bat an eye. "That happens to all of us."

"He was shot."

"Has that been in the news?"

"No sir, not yet."

Scaffidi stared at him. "I'm retired."

The statement caught Service by surprise and left him momentarily flustered. "I didn't mean . . ."

The old man raised his hands. "I know you didn't. Jerry was a wild kid. He did some jobs for me, took down pulp, cut firewood, hauled stuff here and there. He'd work hard for a few days then get some beer and disappear. I tried to understand, tried to teach him good habits, that work is work and play is play, but he wasn't the kind to listen. My niece is staying with me. She's getting a divorce and it's messy. She and Jerry, well, I don't have to paint you a picture. I found them back in the woods one day. Like rabbits, they were: I had to cut him loose." Scaffidi pursed his lips and shook his head.

"When was this?"

"Late last month. My niece was here maybe two weeks before I caught them. I thought, okay, she's been married a long time to a crumb, she's sowing some wild oats, and what's the harm, but I don't like to mix family and help. I'm old school."

"That's the last time you saw Jerry?"

"Four weeks back, maybe five. I made it clear he's not welcome here socially or otherwise. I wish I could be more help. I hate this kind of thing coming up here. In Detroit . . ." He threw up his hands. "That's a different planet, but up here is peaceful, like the Garden of Eden," he added with a beneficent smile.

"How did you meet Jerry?"

"His father told me about him."

"How do you know Limpy?"

"Many years ago my car broke down and he stopped to help me. We did favors for each other from time to time. I was still living in Detroit then, but he went off to prison and I haven't seen him since. You're the officer he shot, aren't you? I thought I recognized your name from the papers back then."

Scaffidi was very well informed and though he was superficially friendly and polite, there was more to him, something Service couldn't quite nail.

"Limpy was released early, but he's back in jail."

Scaffidi nodded. "Some people, it takes a long time to unlearn things."

A reference to himself? Service wondered.

"I'm sorry about Jerry. He was likable, but unreliable."

Service pushed back from the table.

"More espresso?" Scaffidi asked.

"I have to move on, but thanks for talking to me."

The old man walked down to the truck with him. "You gotta go?"

Service nodded. "Thanks again."

The old man looked into his truck. "I see they haven't saddled you with one of the Big Brother computers yet." The coming DNR satellite system was not public knowledge yet. Scaffidi was very well informed.

"Not yet."

The old man grunted. "The Web, satellites, cell phones, digital, the whole world's going electronic. It's not for me." He tapped his temple. "In my day this was the only computer that mattered."

And still is, Service thought. Scaffidi might be aging, but his mind was sharp.

"Do you like trout?" the old man inquired.

"Yes."

"Good, good." The old man tugged at his arm. "Please, this won't take a moment. I want to show you something." Service tried to resist, but Scaffidi was persistent and said finally, "I won't bite."

They walked down the lawn behind the house to a pond with two fountains. "It's fourteen feet deep and well oxygenated. Doesn't freeze in winter." The old mobster spread out his hands. "I got brook trout like *this*! You get some time off, drive over, and I'll show you. It's no-kill, but I have an excellent camera and a friend who does fantastic mounts with fiberglass. We measure the fish, send him the pictures, and back comes a work of art."

"I might do that."

"Bring Officer Mecosta with you. I have the utmost respect for the work you and your colleagues do."

Scaffidi's attempt to be smooth made Service skeptical.

"In my pond I got a brookie will go nine pounds," he said. "This is my life now. Fish, woods, deer, the animals, wildflowers. Winters I'm in Key West." Service wondered if the old man was trying to posture and, if so, why?

As they got back to his truck Service saw a Cadillac coming up the driveway. It stopped behind his vehicle, and a dark-haired woman got out. She had long legs and long hair the color of india ink. She wore a red silk sundress and had several strands of beads around her neck. Long earrings dangled from her ears.

"Good, good," Scaffidi said. "Judy Pellasi, meet Officer Service."

She extended her hand, and shook Service's firmly. He saw a faint laugh in her eyes. Scaffidi's niece hurried up the stairs, her high heels clicking on the porch boards, and disappeared inside.

Scaffidi touched the conservation officer's sleeve. "All set, Officer?"

"Thanks for the espresso."

"Don't forget about those brook trout," Scaffidi said.

"I'll call first," Service said. The old man was obviously lonely, and maybe Mecosta was right about his being in exile.

Service used his cell phone to call Treebone at his office in the 1st Precinct, near Greektown in the center of Detroit.

"Vice," Treebone answered.

"Grady."

"What's up? You don't make social calls."

"Ralph Scaffidi."

"Ralph the Shovel," Treebone said with a laugh. "Lotta people down this way think he planted Jimmy Hoffa. What about him?"

"He's living near Munising. I need a profile."

"You in your truck?"

"Rolling along at double nickel."

"This shouldn't take long. I'll call you back."

Twenty minutes later, as Service approached Trenary, his friend called back.

"Here's the scoop. I talked to OCTF." The Organized Crime Task Force comprised personnel from the FBI, DEA, and Detroit Metropolitan Police. "Scaffidi was so much smoke in the Hoffa deal. He was a CPA, alleged dealings with the bent-noses, but he was never a made man. Strictly a service provider on the periphery. When Jimmy H went MIA, some people in New Jersey floated Scaffidi's name. The Feebs turned him inside out, but it was no go. He was a sideshow, a red herring."

"The media played him up big."

"Pencils, man. They gotta scribble about something. Don't get me wrong. Scaffidi's no angel, but he's not in the main line. Laundered some money, did this, did that. Sort of a mob utility man."

"Has he been down?"

"No, man. He's been bounced plenty, but that's all. Teflon, see? He's dirty, just more efficient than his pals. Word is that he's smart as hell. OCTF said he got disgusted because of the Jersey mob's little game and closed his biz. You sure it's him up there?"

"I talked to him not thirty minutes ago."

"The OCTF gang says he's slick. It's like dealing with Mister Rogers."

This fit. Scaffidi was not the least bit threatening. "He ran a laundry for the mob?"

"The Feebs think so. They worked with the IRS but never got enough for an indictment. The grand jury looked at him beaucoup times and passed on him. He has the big bucks, but it all looks legit."

"Big bucks from accounting?"

"He speculates, invests, buys, sells — like that."

"Speculates on what?"

"Pork bellies, bull testicle futures, soybeans, gold, who knows?"

"But he's retired now."

"That's the word."

"Up here people say he's got mob minders. That he's not here by choice."

"I didn't get that impression from OCTF. They know he's there, by the way."

"Do me a favor?"

"I'm a giver."

"See if you can ferret out more details on his business interests. Has he ever been implicated in a whack?"

"I'll dig, but the way it's told here, he's superficially clean. I'll do what I can. Why the interest?"

"Limpy's son Jerry turned up dead."

"You think Scaffidi is involved?"

"Just checking things out." Scaffidi had ordered Jerry away to protect his niece, but knowing Jerry, he might not have kept away.

"Okay, man. Stay off the trails."

"Always."

Service stopped for coffee at the Trenary Home Bakery, known far and wide in the U.P. as the THB, which was both a bakery and a restaurant, the latter in an old Red Owl grocery store building. The floor was made of red and black tiles. It was like being transported into the fifties. He ordered Trenary toast, the Finnish form of cinamon toast called *korpu*. The bread had a shelf life of months and could be eaten only if dunked.

He thought hard about Scaffidi. Jerry Allerdyce had worked for him, but not recently—according to Scaffidi. Jerry had boffed Scaffidi's niece. Was this enough to cost Jerry his life? Scaffidi was on the periphery of organized crime; no doubt he had the contacts to have such things done. Jerry cut wood for him. Wood had been cut in the tract around the fire where Jerry's body had been discovered. Service decided that Ralph Scaffidi deserved further attention. Until he had something solid to grab on to, he needed to keep all options open. After a final bite of toast he decided to pay a visit to Wink Rector, the resident FBI man in the U.P.

It was late afternoon when Service drove up Wink Rector's street near the town of Harvey, where the Chocolay River dumped into Lake Superior. The house was in a plat of new homes, two stories with two-car garages and well-watered lawns. Rector was tinkering with his sprinkler system.

"King Twinkie," Rector greeted him.

"I just visited Ralph Scaffidi."

Rector looked surprised. "Why?"

"Jerry Allerdyce was murdered. I had information suggesting he was doing some work for Scaffidi."

"Was he?

"Odd jobs, but Scaffidi canned him back in May."

The FBI agent clucked and shook his head.

"I got the feeling that the people there with him weren't there by his choice," Service said.

"They're not."

"Rumor is that the mob exiled him up here."

"Bullshit. He helped us with another investigation and made some people unhappy." Rector pushed up the end of his nose. "That kind of people. The Bureau didn't give his name to the news. The New Jersey mob did that to push the investigation back into Detroit and deflect it from them. It didn't work, but it screwed up Scaffidi's life big time. He's alone and he wanted protection. We set him up with a private security firm from Detroit. They send him a couple of guys, they last three or four months and leave and then they send him replacements, but he pays the bills. It's not like witness protection. Did he show you his pond?"

"I saw it."

"He's a nut about hunting, fishing, conservation, all that stuff. The pond is state of the art and when he says there are big brookies, believe him. Hard as hell to catch."

"His niece is staying with him."

"You mean Miss Leggy?" Rector shook his hand for emphasis. "She doesn't hurt the eyes, does she?" he said in a conspiratorial tone and glanced over his shoulder. "The wife hears me, I'll be dead meat."

"What's she doing living up here with Uncle Ralph?"

"Her soon-to-be-ex-husband caught her with an anchorman from a Detroit TV station and filed papers. It got messy, and she's wild as hell. It's not my job to judge people."

"Scaffidi said Limpy helped him with a car problem once."

"That's the story. A flat tire on M-28. Talk about fate, Limpy and Scaffidi. They became pals. Go figure. Scaffidi has an M.B.A. from Detroit-Mercy and a master's in civil engineering from Purdue. Opposites attract."

"That's all there is to it?"

"Limpy's pure dirt, but as far as I know they were just pals."

Rector's wife, Barb, came out of the house. She was wearing an apron over shorts.

"The steaks are ready, hon. Hi, Grady. You want to join us for dinner?"

"Sorry, Barb. Duty calls."

She smiled, said, "Cops," and went back inside.

Service thanked Rector for his help and headed for Gwinn, which was south and thirty minutes away. He was tired from all of the day's driving, but he wanted to check out a couple more things.

Service called the county dispatcher and had him run Allerdyce's name. He got back a plate number and description of an '85 Ford pickup.

Next he called Bob Bagilvo, Gwinn's police chief. "This is Grady. I'm heading into town. Meet me at the Happy Jet?"

"Got an ETA?" the chief asked.

"Thirty minutes."

"I'll be there."

Bagilvo was waiting in the dirt parking lot of the bar, which was a non-descript two-story building with wood paneling up about eight feet. A yellow sign on the side said WELCOME HUNTERS. It was always there, even though the gun season for deer was only two weeks long. The sheriff was a short man with a thick neck, shaved head, and a Fu Manchu mustache.

"What're we looking for?" Bagilvo asked.

"Limpy Allerdyce's pickup. We think Jerry Allerdyce was using it and he's dead."

"I heard," Bagilvo said. "Why're you doing the legwork on this?"

"Related matter," Service said, giving the small-town police chief the plate number and vehicle description. The truck was not in the bar's parking lot, or in the immediate area.

"Can you and your people check town and put out a BOL?" Cop talk for be on the lookout.

Bagilvo said he would and Service headed for home. His day had lasted nearly sixteen hours already. There was no overtime for all this, and the union steward was always monitoring COs' biweekly time reports. As usual, he'd falsify his, claiming only the hours the union contract called for rather than the actual time he had worked, which was always more. The horseblanket days were better; back then COs worked whatever hours it took to get the job done and if you were underpaid, you didn't care, because the work had a purpose. You took time off when natural breaks came, not when somebody arbitrarily wrote it into a schedule. Philosophically, Service accepted the function of unions, but he did not like being organized.

He found Kira waiting on his cabin porch for him. Newf stood beside her, wagging her tail.

"How's the eagle dog?" he asked Kira after their kiss.

"I'm keeping him for a couple of days, but he should make it. Newf was brave, wasn't she?"

"I guess," he said.

The dog wagged her tail when she heard her name.

"The brown dog panicked," Kira said.

"So did I," Service said, making her laugh.

It was Service's turn to cook, but Kira had already made a small pork roast with wild rice. "I was beginning to think I was going to dine alone," she said. "Want to talk about your day?"

"The usual," he said.

After he did the dishes and showered they went to bed, cuddling close, but his mind was on Jerry Allerdyce.

· 13 ·

Bagilvo called early the next morning. Allerdyce's pickup had been found west of Gwinn in the village of Princeton, a long-ago mining town now inhabited by old folks and Air Force retirees from the nearby base that had closed a few years back. It now housed various state prisons and the Marquette International Airport. Bagilvo had been the town's chief of police for a long time; when one of his people located the truck, he anticipated what Service would want and immediately alerted the county and state police lab from Negaunee. Kira offered to take Newf, but Service put the dog in the truck and took her with him. When he arrived in Princeton, Limpy's pickup and the area were crawling with people.

"Got anything?"

"Not yet," Bagilvo said.

"Was there a chain saw in the truck?"

"Nope."

Which could mean that Jerry had moved it to into another vehicle. *If* he'd ever had the saw. *If* he had met anyone. Still so many ifs.

"Anybody talk to people who live around here to see if they saw anything?"

"My people are knocking on doors right now."

"Make sure we get prints," Service told a nearby lab technician.

"Take it easy," the man said. "Let cops do cop stuff, okay?"

Service apologized. He had the politically bad habit of assuming command of whatever he was involved in. This had irked many people over the years.

"Let's eat," Bagilvo said. They drove separately to the Sweete Shoppe in Gwinn.

"You look tired, pal."

"Summer's starting," Service said. "People come north, think they're free, let it all hang out."

"Hell, summer hasn't even started. You got to learn to pace yourself or that job will kill you. They couldn't pay me enough to do what you do," Bagilvo said.

It was not an unfamiliar sentiment, yet Service and most other COs wouldn't trade their jobs for anything. Usually.

Service got to the county jail just after lunch. Limpy was brought to an interrogation room. He had a toothpick in his mouth, but few teeth.

"Jerry had a job with someone and took his chain saw along. We found your truck near Princeton, but no saw. We figure Jerry got picked up. He sure as hell wasn't out at that fire all by himself."

Limpy said nothing as he gummed the toothpick, making it dance.

"You were right about the Tract. Parcels were leased to people when the Tract was first established. Some of the leases are still in effect. They're for ninety-nine years. I have names."

Limpy looked mildly interested. "Yah?"

Time to float a name, see if Limpy reacted. "Two parcels, forty acres each, are leased to Seton Knipe of Pelkie."

"That so?"

"Why'd you tell me about this, Limpy?"

Limpy grinned. "When you work out a deal, let me know." He stood up. "You think I could get out of the hoosegow to go to Jerry's funeral?"

"We'll see what we can do." It might be a while before there could be a funeral, Service knew.

"Maybe me and Honeypat could get it on too."

"Don't push your luck," Service said. "If you're playing with us, you're never gonna get out."

"Yah, yah," Limpy said as he walked away wheezing. "I'm shakin' in my mukluks."

Service stopped at Strawberry Lake and parked at the public boat launch. As fishermen came and went, he checked their licenses and made sure they had personal flotation devices or life jackets. They all did. Newf greeted the anglers like old friends, her tail wagging. While he was there, a helmetless boy in a red T-shirt raced an ATV down to the launch, saw Service's truck, swerved sharply, almost tipping over, and raced back up the road, spitting gravel. Service followed a dust cloud and pulled into a double-wide trailer built back among young white pines in neat rows.

A man came out. He was tall and shirtless, with the muscles of an iron-pumper. He had an earring, forearm tattoos of wiggling hula girls. His blond hair was cut short in front and grown scraggly in back. His Jeep Cherokee had a logo from Hamtramck and a DETROIT LIONS decal.

"Did you see a boy just drive in on an ATV?" Service saw a long, flat-bed trailer, the kind used to haul ATVs, beside the trees.

"Nope."

"Is the boy your son, sir?"

"Fuck off," the man said with the shadow of a grin. No doubt the kid was already inside, or out back, watching. Men sometimes did stupid things to win their sons' affections.

"I just don't want your kid to get hurt. He's too young to ride without supervision, and he wasn't wearing a helmet."

"Must be somebody else," the man said.

Service knew from experience not to argue. Some behavior patterns were predictable. The CO got back into his truck and when he reached the main road, he turned away from the boat launch, drove half a mile, pulled his truck into a side road where it would be out of view, got out, locked it, and went back to the road.

It didn't take long for the helmetless kid in the red shirt to come zooming by at forty miles an hour or more. Service crossed the road and cut through woods and fields to the double-wide trailer, where he hid to await the boy's return.

When the boy in red came back into the driveway about twenty minutes later, he shut off the ATV and started to get off, but Service ran from hiding and grabbed the kid's arm, scaring him.

"W-w-where'd you come from?" the kid stammered.

The father came running out of the trailer, huffing, his fists cocked.

"There's no truck," the kid squealed at his father, his eyes wide.

Service looked at the father. "Sir, I want to see your license and this vehicle's registration."

"Don't you have poachers to chase. You gotta pick on a little kid?" The man was angry and hyperventilating.

"A child's safety is as important as our work gets, sir. License, please."

The man looked for a moment like he would lose his cool and take a swing, but he managed to get back some control of himself and fumbled to dig out his wallet.

Service asked the boy if he liked riding and the kid said it was "cool." Service lectured him gently about safety and wrote the father a ticket for several offenses, including failure to supervise a minor, no helmet, riding off a designated trail, and no spark arrestor on the ATV, a mandatory device designed to stop the vehicle from starting grass fires that could spread.

The man looked at the ticket and said, "Jesus H. Christ. How much will this shit cost me?"

"Less than a funeral for a dead child," Service said.

"Don't give me that horseshit," the man said. "You're stealing from me."

Service had had enough. "Sir, if this happens again — if *anything* happens again — you'll do time and the court will condemn your machine."

"What's that mean?"

"It means the court will confiscate the ATV and sell it at a public auction."

"Geez, I just bought that thing," the man said with a whine.

"Good, now you know how you can keep it."

When he got into the truck he called dispatch to tell him where he was and looked over at Newf. She was panting from the heat. He knew he couldn't keep bringing her along like this and locking her in the vehicle.

Treebone called on the cellular as he drove east.

"You cruising the boonies?"

"I think of it as immersing in a population-challenged environment."

"That's a fact. Scaffidi's only other business is Wixon Inc., a company that sells heavy equipment to construction companies."

"What sort of construction?"

"Mostly highways. Apparently that's what got the feds to bite on the shit floated by the Jersey boys."

"Anything other than highways?"

"That seems to be it. Scaffidi is the majority owner, but he stays out of day-to-day stuff."

"Thanks, Tree. Any decision on pulling the plug with the DMP?"

"Gonna stick for now. You want to hear a good one?"

Treebone loved his stories. "Woman named Shelley used to work the line at Ford, turning tricks during her shifts. This got her canned, but I guess she liked the institutional biz. Worked herself a deal at Hopewell Receiving. Rented an exam room for her johns, eighty to a hundred a day. The hospital administrator took half. Shelley was there three years. He billed her out as physical therapy, made themselves major green, see. Somebody got onto it and at the arraignment the judge asks Shelley if she's licensed for PT and she looks at the judge and says, 'I was born with all the license I need, Your Honor!' "

Treebone laughed so hard he began coughing. "How could I leave all this? By the way, Scaffidi's company just won a big contract up your way. Equipment for a mining company."

Heavy equipment and a mining company? No link to Jerry Allerdyce there. Service drove slowly down the dirt roads of southern Marquette County, looking for illegal trash dumping activity. He did this every couple of weeks. It was fairly mindless duty and for the moment didn't put him jaw to jaw with some idiot with a room-temperature IQ. It would be nice, he thought, to have the freedom to stay on one case, but his duties were varied and you had to do what you had to do. When it came to trash, locals were worse than tourists. They would pull any scam to draw welfare, but they wouldn't pay a penny for legitimate services. Down one of the roads, on a crescent moon pull-around, Service saw a green trash bag and got out and opened it. Newf sniffed the bag briefly and trotted off to find something of more interest. The bag was filled with glossy four-color porn mags. He stacked them up. Thirty-one, and all but two with the subscriber's address carefully cut away. Two were enough.

Henty Digna came to the door of his house.

"Can you step outside?" Service asked.

Henty reluctantly followed him out to the truck. Service showed him the bag of magazines and told him where he had found it.

"Sure it's my subscription, but I didn't dump that stuff. No fuckin' way. You know how much those rags cost? I think my brother copped them. He's an asshole. Your people know him."

"Harry Digna?" Service fought back a smile. He knew Harry very well indeed.

"Yah, can I have my books back now?"

"Sorry, I need them for evidence."

Harry Digna. Service grinned as he started his truck. Harry was a hard-luck cheater and a harder-luck hunter. Twice in six years, as COs stalked him, Harry had fallen out of a thirty-foot-high treestand and broken both his legs. Service had gotten him the first time and Candy McCants had gotten him the other time. Both times Digna had been found with a Chinese assault rifle slung around his chest. Both times during bow-and-arrow season when all guns were illegal. Assault rifles were illegal at all times. Now Harry walked with two canes and worked as a butcher at the IGA in Gwinn.

When Service walked into the grocery store, people stared at him. A woman at the meat counter had silk forget-me-nots braided into her hair and greeted him. "What'll it be today?"

"Is Harry Digna around?"

"Out back. We got a load of beef in today. What's he done this time?"

Service ignored the question and went to the back of the store. Digna was splitting beef carcasses with a band saw. He wore goggles and leaned against a sort of metal sawhorse for support.

"Turn off the saw," Service said, making a hand signal. The butcher's white apron was greasy and spattered with blood. "How they hanging, Birdman?" Digna's pathetic tree accidents had earned him the nickname among COs.

Digna looked irritated. "Don't call me that. I don't even hunt no more."

"What you mean to say is that your hunting privileges no longer exist. Did you steal your brother's skin mags?"

The butcher's eyes narrowed. "He loaned 'em to me. What's it to you, eh?"

"Harry, I have your mags in my truck. They were dumped on Blue Spruce Road. Your brother says you took 'em, and you admit to having had them."

"My word against Henty's," Harry said defiantly.

"You're the one with the record."

Digna's shoulders slumped. "We'll get prints off them and we'll know that you dumped them. That's against the law, Bird. Why're you always breaking the law?" This was not exactly true, but Service knew that with many suspects a bit of pressure would pry the truth loose pretty quickly. "Illegal dumping isn't a small thing, Bird. There's a big fine and we make sure it gets into the papers."

"You mean like the *Mining Journal*?"

"That one and others. Maybe TV too. Your name will be right out there for everybody to see. Think about the headline. 'Birdman Dumps Onehander Mags.' "

"You can't do that. My old lady will flip out."

"Did you dump them?"

Harry Digna's chin dropped and he mumbled, "I couldn't dump them in the garbage at the house. The old lady wouldn't like that. You gotta give me a break." The butcher held up a chunk of frozen meat. "You like steaks?"

"Are you trying to bribe me?"

"No, no—no bribe. I'm just making conversation."

"It sounded like a bribe."

"Swear to God, it wasn't a bribe."

"Good," Service said, "a bribe is serious and can land you in jail. You've got enough problems as it is."

"No bribe," Birdman said, dropping the meat like it was on fire.

"You know Jerry Allerdyce?"

"Yah, sure. So what?"

Of course he knew him. Birdman ran with a bad crowd and he was known as a loose-lipped gossip.

"He's been logging with someone. I want you to ask around, get me a name, and we'll leave this deal with you returning the magazines to your brother."

"If Jerry hears I'm asking around, he'll kick my ass."

"Would you rather have this in the papers? It's your choice."

"No, man. I'll do it."

"You'd better come through for me, Bird. Either I get a name from you and it checks out, or we take you to court and everybody will know about this."

"You'll get a name, I swear."

"It has to check out."

"I know, man. It will."

Service said, "Bird, Jerry was murdered a couple of nights ago, so you're going to have to be real careful."

Digna grabbed the edge of a metal table to steady himself up.

"I'll be in touch, Bird."

Afterward, Service returned to patrolling the back roads. Birdman was too stupid to be a professional violator. Limpy was bad, but he wasn't stupid.

When he called in to dispatch he learned that Nantz had called.

He reached her at HQ on his cellular. His, not the DNR's.

"I got the pix," she announced. "You want to take a look?"

They met at a roadside park between Marquette and Escanaba.

They used a picnic table to spread out the photographs, anchoring them with sticks and stones. Newf kept prodding Nantz's hand with her nose, wanting attention.

"You can't quite see the upriver outcrop," she said to Service as she tapped one of the eight-by-ten black-and-white photographs. "All you can see is the area around the log slide where the fire cleared it out."

Service took his time. "It forms a sort of a rocky circle in the burn area."

"Yep," she said.

"You'd think that rocks in a shape like that might mean something."

"Could be," she said. "I took geology, but it was boring." She rolled her eyes.

"You make a lousy grade?"

"Nah, I aced it. I aced everything in college. Four-point start to finish."

"Really?" he said with a laugh. Somehow he wasn't surprised. "I guess we need to get these to an expert on geology."

"No, what you want is a petrologist. They study the history of rocks."

"It's that specialized?"

"How many angels can do the horizontal dance on the head of a pin? Science advances in stages. Experts think they know all there is to know and some upstart sees things differently and this changes the whole she-bang. It's always been this way. When Columbus sailed to America, navigators had known for a hundred years that the earth wasn't flat. But the crowns of Europe financed voyages and they wouldn't finance anything the church didn't approve as being theologically sound, so the navigators knew the truth and ate shit from the church so that they could do their jobs. Sometimes science knows the truth, but politics and religion complicate things."

Service suddenly wondered how long chasing fires would satisfy Nantz. "Quackademics are a pain to deal with. Where do I find one of these petrologists?"

"Try Tech."

Michigan Technological University was in Houghton. It was one of the top engineering schools in the country, its specialty mining in its various forms. The college had grown up out of the prosperity that followed iron and copper discoveries in the central and western U.P. in the last century.

"Just call the geology department, tell them you're with the DNR and you want photo identification help."

It irked him to have her telling him how to do his job.

"If you tell them you need a petrologist, they might even think you know what you're doing."

Service grinned. "That would fool them."

"Do you and Newf want to get a beer and stuff?" she asked.

"No time now," he said.

"Well, I'm gonna keep asking," she said. "I don't quit easy."

Was she coming on to him? Since his wife had left him, he had gone through long spells without women and other times when he was seeing several at the same time. When he was a boy, sex had seemed a mysterious and sacred thing, but as an adult it seemed as if the act was no different than eating; when you were hungry, you got yourself a meal. But now that he and Kira were growing closer, he had this old feeling coming back, one that told him he needed to be true to her. Even so, he had not told Nantz about Kira. Keeping his options open was an old habit he wasn't proud of.

Lonnie Green was at his office at the Delta County Airport. "This is Service. Any luck?"

Green coughed to clear his throat. "Well, the good news is that we had a radar paint all right, right where you said it would be, and when you said it would be there. The return is intermittent, but we estimate that the chopper was there more or less for forty-five minutes. That's the time between the first paint and the last one."

"What's the bad news?"

"We can't find a blue Huey, which doesn't surprise me, but we did make an effort. There's no call sign, of course, and no flight plan. But I sent a bulletin to airports in the Yoop, Wisconsin, Minnesota, and downstate Michigan. Nobody can tell us about a blue Huey. The thing is that there are lots of small airports and no towers and one hell of a lot of VMC fliers. Hell, there are farmers who fly small fixed-wings off grass strips built in their hay fields, and businesses that have their own birds for local stuff. Unfortunately, ATC is primarily concerned with commercial traffic, so that's where we focus. The rest, well, they're just out there, and as long as they're not low-flying, buzzing, causing trouble, or about to bust the Canadian border, we don't pay much attention to them. Like you guys, we've got limited resources and we can do only so much."

"Meaning that's it?"

"Not entirely. We could still get lucky. Other stations are on alert. If this bird flies again, somebody will eventually see it and report it."

"You think we should take this thing to the media?"

"If your bird is involved in something illegal, the bad guys will also hear the report and repaint the chopper, stop flying, or take it apart, crate it up, and ship it somewhere else in the country."

Service felt consternation. The chopper painted on radar, which meant it existed, but not officially. It made him wonder how safe air traffic and passengers really were and how much ATC boiled down to window dressing. Why was it that the stuff he got involved in was never easy?

"Thanks," he said.

"Listen, instead of the media, why don't you alert the Coast Guard, state police, hospitals with choppers, and your own people and ask all of them to watch for your bird?"

"Good advice. Thanks for the help."

Service tried to call Lisette McKower but was told by the district office that she was "not available," a standard answer designed not to pin down an officer's location when the officer didn't want to be disturbed. Before he could get off the line, his call was passed to Sergeant Charlie Parker. This he didn't need.

"Officer Service?" Parker said officiously. "Geez, I used to have a Service who worked for me, but he disappeared."

"Lay off," Service said.

"You're not the Long Fucking Ranger, Service. You're part of an organization and I'm sick of your bullshit. Check your spelling: There's no i in team."

"It's 'Lone,' " Service said. "Not Long."

"What was that? Are you correcting a superior officer?"

"How am I not doing my job?"

"You're not keeping me informed, that's how you're doing. I hear all sorts of shit second and third hand."

"You're getting all my reports on time, right?"

"Don't give me that passive aggressive junk. I had my way, you'd be out. We need team players, Officer Service, not *dinosaurs* like you."

Which all boiled down to Parker wanting information from his subordinates in order to horn in on the credit for what his people did. As a CO, Parker had been a loner and not overly effective, doing only the easiest jobs and avoiding any sort of dangerous work. How he had gained rank was one of the DNR's great mysteries. And now that he was a sergeant he wanted total control over everyone under him. It wasn't that Parker was a bad guy; it was just that he wasn't up to the standard that Service felt should define the CO force.

"I'm doing something wrong," Service said, "you know what you can do."

"What I know is that stunt you pulled with Limpy."

Service said nothing.

"I've also heard that you've been interfering in a murder investigation and carrying around an unauthorized animal. You've gone too far this time."

Somebody must've complained about Newf. "Charlie, I've got work to do."

"Don't hang up on me, Officer Service. I'm warning you."

Service hung up and took a deep breath. What a doofus. He looked at Newf and said, "Don't sweat Parker."

A call came in from a man who had found a dead cat near Carlshend. Sometimes cats and dogs mixed it up with rabid wild animals, so Service went to see him. Normally the county animal control people handled this kind of thing, but he was close and it didn't hurt to monitor these things. It was early in summer for a rabies outbreak, but you never knew.

The man lived in one of a cluster of houses on a dirt road near an area where there was an abundance of skunks, which were sometime rabies carriers.

"You called?" Service said, when the man came to the door.

"Damn right. You wanna see the animal?"

The man had it on a shovel beside the house.

"Where did you find it?"

"On the front porch across the street. The old bitch over there poisons cats because she doesn't like them. She works mornings. I saw this poor thing just before noon and went over and got it. I also saw a tuna can under her carport. She laces tuna with rat poison or antifreeze, the cats eat, then they die. They hemorrhage to death. The bitch has a dog. How would she like somebody to poison that foo-foo piece of hers?"

"This isn't your cat?"

"I don't keep pets. What's next, are people going to poison coons and deer and coyotes just because they roam around?"

"Have you talked to the woman?"

"No. I might punch her lights out."

"Where's the tuna can?"

"Still under her carport. She must've been in a hurry this morning. She usually hides the evidence. You going to do something about this?"

Service nodded. "Put the cat in a trash bag, leave it by my truck, okay?"

"You going to bury it?"

"First I'm going to have a necropsy done, then we'll cremate it."

"This is real good of you."

Service walked across the street and knocked on the front door of a neat white house with black shutters and flower boxes with bright red geraniums. There was a gaudy plywood bend-over stuck in the lawn by the porch—a cutout of a fat woman bending over, from the rear. On the porch there were two cement geese dressed in identical red gingham dresses.

The woman was seventyish with thinning blue-white hair and alabaster skin. She looked like the archetypal grandmother with a gentle smile and soft mannerisms.

"Ma'am, I'm Officer Service."

"You're with the DNR, right?" She clasped her hands over her heart. "You people do such a wonderful job."

"Yes ma'am, thank you. There was a dead cat found on your porch this morning."

"Oh my," she said. "Who found the poor thing?"

"I have it," he said. He saw sweat pop out on her forehead. "It's pretty rare for a cat to die a natural death in a public place. When they get sick, they usually go off alone to die."

"I don't understand," the woman said, her facade cracking.

"Well, when they die in the open like this, we assume there's been an accident or foul play and we investigate." He was stretching the truth a bit, but he did this all the time in order to encourage people in one direction or another. There was no law that forbade telling lies to uphold the law.

"I didn't see a cat," she said.

"Do you have a cat?"

"Well, no. I have a dog. I just love dogs, don't you?"

"Not especially," he said. "I prefer cats. In fact the one on your porch looks like one of mine."

The woman said, "Oh my."

"Do you mind if I look around outside?"

"Look around for what?" she asked defensively.

"It's just our common practice to look around in cases like this."

"Well," she said. "Maybe I should call my husband."

"You do that and ask him if I can look inside too. Meanwhile, I'll look around out here."

He didn't wait for her to respond, heading immediately for the carport. Beside the side door he saw a tuna can that still had bits of tuna in it.

The white-haired woman appeared at the door as he put on a latex glove, picked up the can, and stuck it in a clear plastic evidence bag.

"What are you doing?" she asked through the screen. Her eyes had turned hard.

"I saw this can," the conservation officer said. "Cats love tuna. They can't resist it. It might have spoiled and made the cat sick."

"I ate some of that tuna myself and it didn't hurt me."

"So this is yours?"

"Yes, and I want it back."

"Why was it here?"

"It probably fell when I took out the trash this morning."

He walked to the trash can. It was galvanized steel and the interior was immaculate. She obviously didn't put trash in the can unless it was in a bag.

"Ma'am, there's no trash in here."

"Well, it must've been picked up."

"When did you eat the tuna?"

"I had some this morning. Yes, I remember eating tuna this morning."

She was lying. "Is today your regular trash pickup?"

Her face went blank and her color drained away.

"Ma'am, did you put this can here by your step?"

She plastered a new smile on. "Yes, now I remember. I was going to put it in the trash, but I was in a hurry and there was no trash bag, so I just set it down."

"So you put it here this morning?"

"Yes, but now I have trash bags and if you'll just hand it to me, I'll throw it away. It won't do to have trash lying around. I'm not a litterer."

"Ma'am, I'm going to keep this can."

"You can't do that."

"Yes ma'am, I can. Do you have rat poison or antifreeze in your house or storage shed?"

The smile was gone now. "No."

"May I look?"

"No. I'm going to call my husband."

"Please do. I'm going to take this can and we are going to put it under scientific analysis. If there's rat poison or antifreeze, I'll be back."

"I'm not talking to you anymore."

Service placed the bag with the tuna can in the back of the truck with the dead cat, drove around the first bend in the road, pulled down a two-track, got his binoculars, and walked through the woods to the field behind the woman's house. He left Newf in the truck with the windows partly down. The woman would either put the rat poison or antifreeze in a trash bag and throw it out, or bring it back in the field and try to bury it, which would then put other animals in jeopardy. It was amazing how many people could kill or torture animals without guilt. Technically animal control would be called in to handle a poisoning, but if she put the rat poison or antifreeze into the environment, he could make the pinch.

He perspired heavily in the midday sun, but after an hour the woman came out of the back door, carrying a trash bag and wearing pink rubber gloves that reached up to her elbows. She had a small shovel and walked into the field about a hundred yards, stopped, and looked around nervously.

Service advanced through high grass toward her as she dug. When she had a small hole, she took another look around and dumped out a bag with the poison and then sprinkled the poison into the hole.

"Ma'am," he announced. "You're violating the dumping ordinances and you are putting poison into the environment."

She squawked and stood shaking as she glared at him, her mask of innocence gone.

"Ma'am, I want you to use your shovel to dig up all that poison and put the dirt in the bag you brought."

"I'm not wasting a trash bag," she said angrily. "They cost money and my husband and I are on a fixed income."

"Do you want me to call for backup and have a bunch of people out here digging up this field? I suspect there are other cats buried back here."

She was shaking badly now and looked ready to cry.

"Dig," he said.

"I have arthritis," she whined. "This isn't my fault. My husband makes me do this. I'm a good Christian woman and I do what my husband tells me to do."

"Lady, if you put that tuna out and a dog or kid got it, they could die. You want to be responsible for killing a kid?"

She sobbed and dug, showing no evidence of arthritis. He couldn't stand to look at the woman. He had seen people like this so many times before. Appearances told you nothing about a person's substance.

When the bag was filled, he made her shovel other dirt over the hole, then escorted her back to the house where he wrote a ticket for obstruction of an investigation, illegal dumping, poisoning the environment, improper use of a dangerous substance, and poisoning a cat. He couldn't think of other charges or he would have dropped those on her too.

He told her she had to appear at court within a certain period and plead guilty or not guilty. "If you plead not guilty, I am going to get a warrant and we are going to come out here and go through your house and we are going to dig up the entire back area and then we are going to throw the book at you. Do you understand?"

She said, "Why are you being so mean to me?"

"Ma'am, you are getting off light."

People like this disgusted him nearly as much as Limpy. People like this spouted Christian doctrine, went to church, ran PTAs and school boards, and all the while killed innocent things because in their twisted minds the only things that mattered were those they wanted to matter.

He left the woman in tears and didn't care.

When he got home, Kira wasn't yet there. He put the bagged cat in the freezer and left the bag of poison dirt in the truck. He'd have to take care of that tomorrow. He locked the back of the truck to be sure nothing got in. Newf hopped onto the porch and Cat hissed at her. Service said, "Knock it off, you two."

He made corn bread with diced habanero peppers and Vidalia onions and a pot of Texas chili, which came out differently every time he made it.

Kira came in, shed her coat, kissed him, and changed into shorts and a halter. "It's hot," she said. She went to the fridge for ice water, but while she was there she opened the freezer. He saw her jump back.

"What the hell is *that*?"

He laughed. "Evidence. A woman poisoned a cat with rat poison. I was going to ask you to do the necropsy."

"In *our* freezer?"

"It was too far to the office or your clinic. I thought we'd just keep it overnight."

She turned and looked at him. "I suppose our freezer will be used for *evidence* other times?"

"Yep."

"God," she said.

"Hungry?"

"Yep."

Kira wolfed down two bowls of chili and they each had a beer.

"Do you know Cece Dirkmaat?" she asked after dinner. They were sitting on the porch, looking out at the creek.

"I don't think so."

"She teaches art at Northern and makes the most incredible jewelry. I gave her the pebbles to polish and see if she could make a bracelet or necklace for me."

He made a face. "Those ugly pebbles?"

"Leave it to a woman to find beauty in the mundane," she said. "I like it that you gave them to me, and Cece thinks they'll polish up nicely."

"You drove up to Marquette?" He didn't think she had time.

"Cece lives at Little Moose Lake with Glynnis Fayard, a librarian at Northern. Cece brought their cat in this morning. The poor thing has a sour tummy."

"She and this Glynnis are roommates?"

Kira looked over at them. "Yeah, and they also sleep together. Is that a problem for you?"

"Nope," he said. "Might be a problem for them, but not for me."

"Cece and Glynnis are university people."

"Little Moose Lake is not liberal territory."

Kira smiled. "True."

Cat jumped onto the porch with a headless chipmunk and purred loudly. Kira complimented the cat and scratched her chin.

Newf came up from wading the edge of the creek and curled up at Service's feet.

"How was your day?" Kira asked.

"You know about the cat. That kind of shit makes me sick."

"I'm a vet. I see it all the time."

"I'm still on that fire thing," he said. He hadn't told her about Jerry Allerdyce. Once again, he wasn't sure why he was holding back on her. "Radar painted a chopper over the Tract two days before the fire, but they don't know who it was or where it came from. ATC has radar tapes."

"Well, it's not an alien," she said. She took off her sandals, turned her chair, and put her feet in his lap. "Rub?"

He began rubbing her feet. "What's that mean, not an alien?"

"If the chopper exists, it has to be somewhere. *You're* the tracker. So track."

How did you track a chopper? In Vietnam they either came to extract you or they didn't and you humped out on foot. How many hours had he and Tree spent in the belly of a Huey? A heap of trips, but not that many hours. Why? Limited range. The more people, cargo, and weapons the bird carried, the shorter the distance it could fly. Range, he thought.

"Grady?"

"I'm just thinking."

"*Rub* the foot, honey. Don't squeeze it to a pulp."

He looked at her foot and saw that it was red. "Sorry."

What *was* the range of a Huey? Three hundred miles, give or take? At a speed of 120 to 130, slower if it was lower. If you flew somewhere and didn't refuel en route, it was an out-and-back and your range was limited by the fuel you carried. Some choppers, he knew, carried extra fuel in internal and external tanks, but how much? How much fuel was their reserve? The three-hundred-mile-range figure stuck in his mind. He had heard it during the war probably. Without refueling or extra tanks, your distance was halved. Not to mention wind and other variables that could affect range. Half to go out, half to come back. One hundred and fifty miles one way. Add in two hours of hovering and take away twenty percent for reserve fuel for emergencies and that reduced theoretical range to 120.

"Earth to Grady," Kira said.

"One hundred and twenty miles," he said.

"What?"

"This chopper probably didn't refuel en route. The pilot wouldn't want people to know, so he flew from its base to destination and back. That limits it to a distance of about 120. That means we can draw a circle around the place where it was seen and its base has to be inside that circle, more or less. This gives us a pretty good search area."

"Pi r squared," she said. "With a radius of 120, that makes for an area of about eleven thousand square miles."

"No," he said, his excitement growing. "Remember, we're on a peninsula. Lake Superior is north, Lake Michigan is south." Service closed his eyes to visualize the map. "Let's say that thirty percent of the area is water, maybe more. The 120 radius reaches to Canada, and we can be pretty sure the chopper didn't come from there. You can't just bop across the border in an aircraft, free-trade agreements or not. It also stretches down to about Traverse City but there's only a small arc of land, sweeping northeast to the straits, and the chopper isn't likely to have come across Lake Michigan because radar would have an easier time painting it over water, even if it was wave-hopping. To the west, the area stretches down as far as Green Bay, and out into the western U.P."

"Grady, it's still the *whole* U.P."

"No, the glass is half full. Listen to me. The bird surely didn't come from Canada because of the border, or from the Lower Peninsula because radar would have painted it over Lake Michigan. So it had to fly east or west. East of the Tract, the land is as flat as a stamp and easier to see on radar. To the west there are hills and ridges a chopper can use to hide itself from radar until it gets here. By coming from the west, the radar can't easily track its route in; from the east it can. We used to do this in Vietnam, use the hills to avoid detection. We know the pilot was low. He knows what he's doing. So he had to come from the west, which means we can draw the arc in that direction and now we have really reduced the search area."

"You're guessing," she said, wiggling her toes.

"You said I should track. What do you think tracking is? It always involves a lot of educated guesswork."

She took his hand and slid it under her halter. "Track this for a while."

He began to caress her, but suddenly jumped up and her feet banged the porch.

"I'm *so* stupid," he said.

He went into the house and picked up the telephone.

"Mister Voydanov, this is Grady Service. Fine, thanks. I need for you to concentrate. Exactly how long was that chopper in view?"

Lehto walked inside and ran her fingernails along Service's stomach.

"You told me an hour, are you sure?"

He hung up and looked at Kira. "He said the chopper hovered for forty-five minutes to an hour, not an hour or two, which is what he told me when I first talked to him. The radar paint was around forty-five minutes, so now we have two observations that corroborate. A stripped-down Huey can run about two and a half hours, a heavily loaded one a lot less. So we subtract one hour from the two and a half—to give ourselves a margin. That leaves ninety minutes, meaning he could fly forty-five minutes each direction. But this guy is not going to pop up where he can get max speed, so he's on the deck and probably doing 100, not 120 or 130. This means our chopper could cover about seventy miles on the outbound leg. There's no way he came from the east because of the flatness, so he came from an arc within seventy miles to the west. He *has* to be in the west, Kira. That's where the hills are!"

Service hugged her and swung her around and she laughed.

But as soon as he put her down, he was on the telephone again.

Joe Flap sounded half asleep.

"Pranger, this is Service."

"I ain't seen that beer yet. You're not a welsher, are ya? Your old man never welshed on anything."

"You want to shoot for a case?"

"Hell yes."

"How many choppers are based in the U.P., say, west of Escanaba within a hundred miles?"

"Hell, I don't know. Not many, I'd hafta guess."

"Who uses them?"

"Rich pricks. Seems like they always got the best toys. Loggers. Miners. Construction companies. The USFS. State police. Aerial survey people. Maybe some flight instructors. Hell, I don't know. I heard a guy from Hurley used one to haul hookers up from Milwaukee to service the red jackets in November."

Hurley was a town in Wisconsin once famous for prostitutes, drugs, and booze during the November deer hunting season in Michigan. In Wisconsin you could drink at eighteen, but not till twenty-one in Michigan, so they got thousands of crossovers.

"Can you find out?"

"Will sure give 'er a try. When do I get that case?"

"Tomorrow."

"Pranger is on it."

Service then called Nantz and gave her Flap's address. He asked her to take the man a case of beer in the morning.

"This will cost you," she said.

"I'll pay you back when I see you," he said.

"Is this guy hot?"

What the hell was she talking about? "He's sixty-seven."

"You didn't answer my question," she said before hanging up.

Service and Lehto went back to the porch with fresh beers and halfway through hers, Kira set her bottle on the deck floor and stood up.

"What?" Service asked.

"I'm going to unplug that Goddamn phone," she said, walking into the house, shedding her clothes.

Service left his beer unfinished.

It was early morning and still dark. Newf sat at Service's feet, patiently waiting to be let out while he talked on the telephone.

"Seton Knipe now lives near Crystal Falls," Gustus Turnage said. "He moved down there sometime in the early eighties. He owns a company called Wildcat, Inc. Land speculation is what I hear. Knipe is in his eighties and semiretired. His son Ike runs the show, day to day. The son would be about sixty, I think."

"What kind of land speculation?"

"Nothing big. Forty acres here, forty acres there. Bits and pieces. Parcels, mostly. I guess it pays, but I don't see how. Call Simon del Olmo in Crystal Falls. He's a real bird dog."

CO del Olmo had been with the DNR about four years. He had been born near Traverse City to Mexican parents, migrant workers who spent summers in Michigan and winters in Texas. Simon had a degree from the University of Michigan and had been in combat with the air cavalry during the Gulf War in Iraq.

"Thanks, Gus."

Knipe, mining, Crystal Falls. Scaffidi's contract with a mining company in Crystal Falls. He hoped del Olmo could tell him.

He let Newf out. She quickly took care of business, tried to cover the spot with weeds, and raced back to the porch. She followed him inside and curled up on the floor beside the bed. She was okay for a dog, he decided.

"You knew that dog wasn't going anywhere," he said to Kira. "Don't pretend you're asleep."

She giggled and pulled him toward her. Kira was still always in a hurry. Living together hadn't changed that.

After making love, Service made breakfast while Kira took a shower. He was buttering Dutch whole-wheat toast when he realized there was someone at the screen door in front. He went instinctively toward the door before it dawned on him that he was nude. Suddenly he felt himself blushing. He grabbed for something, anything, to cover himself, but all he could find was a sock. Then he heard the woman at the front door laughing, and he began to laugh and just dropped the sock. He walked back to the bed and grabbed his trousers, which were draped over a chair. He tugged them on as he went to the door.

"That sock just didn't cut it," the woman said with a smile. "I'm Cece Dirkmaat," she added. "I'm sorry to startle you. I thought you'd hear my car door close."

Service looked at Newf. "Great watchdog," he complained to the animal.

"Come in," he told the woman. "Coffee?"

"You bet. Black."

The woman sat at the small kitchen table. She had short silver hair and several silver earrings in each ear.

"Where's Kira?"

"Bathroom," Service said. At that instant Kira padded naked out of the bath area, wrapping a towel around her head.

Cece said, "You two aren't big on clothes."

Kira squealed and retreated.

Cece laughed. "Maybe I ought to strip. That way we can all say we *really* know each other."

Service said, "Let's leave it at this."

Kira came back in a bathrobe. She was blushing. "What are you doing here, Cece?"

"I know it's early and I'm sorry to intrude, but at least I waited until sunrise. I wanted to come over in the middle of the night, but Glynnis wouldn't let me."

Kira glanced at Service, who gave her a look of bewilderment.

Dirkmaat dumped pebbles on the table. Service saw that they had been polished. All but one of the stones were reddish purple. The one was sort of opaque with a yellowish tint and a greasy appearance. Cece picked up the odd stone.

"Do you know what this is?"

"Glass," Service said. "The moving water rounds it off."

Cece Dirkmaat smiled and held the stone out to Service.

"Not glass, but a glass cutter."

Kira grinned. "What?"

"It's a diamond," the art professor said. "An honest-to-God diamond."

Lehto and Service stared, their mouths agape.

"Where in the world did you find these?" their visitor asked.

"Newf found them," Service said.

"Come again?"

Service nodded at the dog. "Newf," he said. She dutifully wagged her tail.

· 14 ·

Service waited for Simon del Olmo at Alpo's, a run-down coffee shop in the village of Sagola, ten miles west of Crystal Falls. Sagola dated to the nineteenth century, when some Chicago investors formed a lumber company to capture the local white pine. All the yellow DEER CROSSING signs on the road into town were shredded by bullet holes from high-caliber slugs, a definite indication that you were in the UP.

The younger officer arrived in khaki shorts, sandals, and a green body shirt that said CASTRO SUCKS. Del Olmo was tall and thin with jet-black hair and a neatly trimmed black mustache. He grinned and nodded when he saw Service, who was also out of uniform.

"Thanks for coming," Service said.

"A chance to work with the great Grady Service."

Service cringed. They ordered coffee and cinnamon rolls. In the UP there was intense competition among towns to see who could make the best rolls, with size more than flavor the deciding factor. These rolls were not as large as the one-pounders in the central part of the peninsula.

"Do you know Seton and Ike Knipe?"

"I don't think anybody really knows them," del Olmo said. "They've been here since before my time, but they don't mix much with the people from town. Sort of do their own thing. Rich people are like that."

"What about their company?"

"I know they have one. Wildcat, Inc. They have an office downtown."

"Can you show me?"

"Sure. You want to tell me what this is about?"

"I would if I knew. It may be nothing, but you know how it goes. You have to move like a snail. Can you find out what land they own around here?"

"Shouldn't be a problem, *jeffe*. Them or their company?"

"Cut the *jeffe* crap. Both them and the company. If they have land near anything else, I want to know that too."

162 · JOSEPH HEYWOOD

"Like houses?"

"Not necessarily. Businesses, factories, other property investments, big lodges, summer camps, resorts, unusual stuff. Also, I want you to look at Wixon Inc. They have a contract with a mining company. Is it Wildcat?"

When they drove into Crystal Falls in del Olmo's vintage Volkswagen bus, Service saw that the offices of Wildcat, Inc., were directly behind an office front with a small sign in the window that said LABO-RATORY.

"What's that?" Service asked as they eased by slowly.

"You don't know?" Del Olmo seemed surprised. "There were supposed to be diamonds around here, I shit you not. Hell, maybe there are. Dow Chemical got involved back in the eighties, then sold majority rights to some sort of subsidiary of an Australian mining outfit, called Crystal Exploration, I think. This was in the early nineties. Crystal has a Colorado-based subsidiary and they have some people here now, but the word is out that they're closing shop. The lab, I think, was set up by another company to serve all the needs of the diamond searchers."

"Diamonds, huh?" Service's heart was racing. "Many people?"

"Actually there were several outfits in the diamond race and God knows how many wildcatters." Wildcatters. Interesting word choice, thought Grady. Did Wildcat, Inc., connect to this in some way?

Del Olmo continued, "From what I read and hear, Dow and Crystal found formations associated with diamonds, and more than half of them held microdiamonds. But it's my understanding that microdiamonds aren't where the big bucks are. The companies were after gem-quality stones. Still, finding micros in more than half the formations was apparently an unexpectedly high percentage, and this got the diamond folks excited. They drilled samples to decide if they had something with real economic potential. I've heard rumors that based on the early results, the local formation had the potential to be the biggest diamond field in the world, but that might have been beer talk. Can you believe that? Biggest in the *world*? The chamber of commerce had an official stiffy over the whole deal. I've also heard that there's a lot more formations around, but most of them tend to be down toward Iron Mountain from here. All moot now. These companies are all pulling out, so I guess the whole thing was wishful thinking. The thing is, they were really tight mouthed about what they were doing around here. The stakes must be huge in that business."

When they got back to Sagola, del Olmo said, "You think the Knipes are connected to this diamond business?"

Service looked at the younger man. He was smart. "What makes you ask that?"

"I believe in hunches, and my hunches are almost always good."

Service understood. "Maybe, but you have to be quiet about this. With our people, with anybody."

"No problem, but I gotta say it's not against the law to go for diamonds."

"That depends on how you go after them," Service said. "And where."

"How it is," del Olmo said with a sly grin. "Be cool, *compadre*. You call, Simon hauls."

Service drove north toward Houghton. He had an appointment in the morning with petrologist Dr. Kermit Lemich. When he called Michigan Tech and got the name, it seemed vaguely familiar to him, but he couldn't peg it. Definitely not a violator. He remembered the names of violets forever. He had invited Kira to come to Houghton with him, but she had too much work and begged off, telling him she would miss him "terribly." He was on his own. Gus Turnage was going to meet him tonight for dinner.

He was still chewing over the diamond discovery. When he'd told Cece Dirkmaat that the dog had found the stones — which was the truth — she had laughed this off as a nonanswer. She could think what she wanted for now. Kira too.

The diamond was high quality, Cece had insisted. *Very* high. She was almost passionate about it. She said a professional gemologist should do an official analysis with X rays, but she felt she was pretty much on target with her assessment. Under X rays diamonds showed a distinctive blue color. She said the garnets appeared to be first rate as well.

Diamonds and garnets in the tract? It was still pretty hard to believe. But his life had been filled with strange events. Service found his mind drifting backward to another time on the other side of the planet.

Major Teddy Gates had awakened them in their bunker one night near midnight, told them to gather their gear, walked them down to the helipad at Camp MagNo, put them in a chopper, and said, "Don't get your asses killed."

The chopper had taken them to Da Nang, where they were met by a full colonel who escorted them to an unmarked C-119, a model that the flyboys called a crowd killer because of its history of crashes. They flew to an air base in northeast Thailand called Naked Fanny. There they were fed in an air-conditioned club and given air-conditioned rooms to sleep in. "Fattening us up for the kill?" Treebone wondered out loud while they ate.

The next morning they were taken to a briefing room and surrounded by men in civilian clothes. The only other person in uniform was a two-star navy admiral.

"For a number of years," the admiral began, "we have been air-dropping ARVN commandos into North Vietnam. They were carefully selected men, well trained and well equipped. Of nearly one thousand men we have inserted, we have yet to get a single radio response after the drops. We are certain that someone in the South Vietnamese government is an agent for the north and tipping off Hanoi. We can't let this keep happening. We are sending you two in to observe and document the next drop."

Treebone said, "I don't think I like this, sir."

The admiral said, "You two have been handpicked. Your participation is voluntary. And if you say no, it will not be reflected in your records."

"If a thousand men have been lost, what makes you think we'll be able to make it?" Service asked.

"Because nobody in the South Vietnamese government knows about you or what you will be doing. Your job will be to shadow the ARVN commando drop and report back. I won't blow smoke up your asses, men. This is going to be dicey even if all goes the way we think it will."

After nearly a whole day of briefings and discussion, Service and Treebone agreed to go.

Three days later they were parachuted into eastern Laos, from where they infiltrated the North Vietnamese border, descending through a brutal range of mountains.

Along the way they saw a herd of a dozen animals that looked a bit like antelope, but were unlike anything they had ever seen before. They took photographs.

Days later they witnessed the ARVN airdrop and watched in horror as the parachutists were shot while they descended in their 'chutes. The North Vietnamese had rolled into position only an hour before the drop and were waiting. They used a small camera to record the entire disaster, then retreated to Laos for their pickup, which went uneventfully.

Based on their evidence the infiltration program was terminated and a hunt begun for the traitor in the government who was tipping the North Vietnamese, where no questions were asked.

They never heard another word about any of this and were returned to their unit.

But the strange animals had piqued their curiosity. They showed the photographs around, but nobody could identify them. They eventually gave the photos to a UPI reporter, who sent them to university contacts, who in turn declared that the animals were a previously unknown species. The lesson stuck in Service's mind. There were a lot of things in the world yet to be discovered.

When it came to natural phenomena, you just never knew. So far in this diamond deal, there were a lot of peculiar circumstances, but no conclusive evidence. Which was not unusual in a complex case, he reminded himself. Case? There was no case yet. The cops would handle the murder of Jerry Allerdyce. All he had was a bunch of stuff.

And alarms in his gut.

Service stopped at a small general store in Amasa, which sat west of the Hemlock River where iron ore had been found before the turn of the twentieth century. Amasa somehow remained one of the few villages in the UP not yet invaded by downstaters and outstaters. A developer had once tried to attract rich Japanese to the shore of Lake Superior between Marquette and Munising, but the locals had not been receptive and the whole thing had died. He had read about moneyed Californians invading Montana and Idaho, buying huge chunks of land, bulling their way into local and state politics, trying to reshape or abolish local customs and ways of life. In Michigan the relocation influx was primarily from suburban Detroit, but the disruption was not appreciably different than what Montana was experiencing.

Amasa had fended off such an invasion in part because the old town was surrounded by the Copper Country State Forest, a tough, dirt-poor, isolated region.

Sometimes Service wished he had the power to declare the entire UP a wilderness and limit human occupation to a few large towns, the way things were already done at Cape Hatteras. Outside the towns there would be no development, and all the villages and places there now would be let go to be reclaimed by nature. There was too damn little wilderness left in America and when it was all gone, America would no longer be America. Something had to be done. He felt it almost as a rising panic.

Governor Sam Bozian sure as hell wouldn't do the right thing. Bozian believed that previous incompetent state governments had prevented the sort of investment in Michigan that would put it in the top tier of the lower forty-eight economically. He repeatedly reminded the public of the Arab oil boycott of decades ago and how that had crippled the state, which had only one major industry: cars. If Clearcut had his way, the whole state would be reduced to concrete and factories.

There was a huge blaze orange billboard across the street from the store. LET THEM GO. LET THEM GROW. The DNR knew that habitat supported only so many animals and unless the herd was reduced, the animals would be stunted. The DNR wanted hunters to shoot does and small bucks in most UP areas, but some self-styled experts from know-it-all sportsmen's groups that vehemently disagreed had run their own campaign against DNR policy. Real men shot only big bucks, and you couldn't have big males if you shot all the small ones. It was all baloney, bereft of science, one of those situations where science seemed to be counterintuitive. The no-kill bucks crowd reasoned that the more small bucks you had, the more big ones you would eventually get. This wasn't true, but the sportsmen refused to believe the studies and considered the deer their own, not the charges of distant bureaucrats. Too many residents of the UP seemed to think they knew more than the professionals in the DNR, and Bozian's careless disregard of the environment just served to embolden others.

A middle-aged woman and a girl of eight or nine were sitting on the sagging wooden steps outside the store, eating ice cream cones.

"Nice day," the woman said when Service came out. She had thin, pale red hair and patches of freckles peeking through sun-reddened skin. There were gold rings on several fingers, and her wrists were weighted down with bracelets. Fifty, sixty? It was hard to tell her age.

"It's a beauty," he said.

"How come you don't wear a uniform?" the tiny girl asked.

"What makes you think I should?"

"Game warden, ain'tcha?"

"How do you know?"

"Your truck." She pointed with her dripping cone. "I can *read*, you know."

He laughed. Since joining the DNR he had never owned a car. He lived a simple life that revolved around work and he had saved a lot of money despite what most would think was not a handsome salary. He supposed the money he had saved would come in handy if he and Kira decided to make things permanent, but that was a big if. Was he ready for marriage? The first time hadn't worked out at all, and in the years since he hadn't met anybody he cared enough to try again with.

"We got a bear at my Grampa's camp and he poops all over," the girl said.

Service loved how candid children were and how easily they segued from topic to topic without the slightest transition. He wondered what kind of a father he would have been. At forty-seven, he probably ought to stop thinking about that.

"A bear, huh?"

The girl gave an exaggerated nod. "And know what?" she said excitedly. "He *bites* Grampa's tires! Tell him, Grandma."

"You know bears," the woman said. "Like ill-tempered dogs."

Service knew that most bears were timid and wary of people. "Where's your camp?" he asked.

"East, near Premo Lake."

Service sort of knew the area. It was pretty wild. "Have you called us about the bear?"

"My grampa will shoot that *damn* thing!" the girl said. She had ice cream smeared on her chin.

The woman said, "Mind your language, Mary Ruth. Be a proper little girl."

The little girl pouted. "Grampa says it."

Service looked at the grandmother. "Is your camp new?"

"We had it built last summer," she said.

Had it built. He was not surprised. "There's no point in killing the animal."

"He's punctured three of my husband's tires. You know how much new tires cost?"

Meaning the state paid for his. "Your camp is probably in the bear's territory. The males can be pretty aggressive and the new camp is a threat, but they seldom attack people. They just want you to go away." *The way I do.* "Call Officer Simon del Olmo in Crystal Falls. He'll drive over and trap the bear and move it far away."

"We've heard they always come back."

This was one of the myths that conservation officers repeatedly faced in dealing with the public. "Some do, but they're rare. If this one keeps coming back, then we might have to destroy it, but why kill it before we have to?"

"Three tires, for starters," the woman said. "It's only one bear. They're all over the place up here. Just pests."

"Where are you from, ma'am?" Service asked.

"Grand Rapids. My husband sold his dry-cleaning business and we retired up here. We love the summers. We bought a little house here in town and built the camp. Wouldn't do to live out there, but eventually we're going to build our dream house there and make the county improve the roads. It's just dirt and mud now."

Just like Montana. He had been wrong. Even Amasa was being invaded. He wrote del Olmo's telephone number on a notepad and gave the number to the woman. "It's against the law to kill a problem animal without a permit. Talk to Officer del Olmo and he'll help you."

The woman looked at the paper. "Seems like a lot of useless red tape."

"It's for the animal's benefit *and* yours."

It was not that he didn't like people, he tried to convince himself as he drove north. It was just a shame they had to come up here. The more people who came, the more problems there would be, and he and other officers were already strapped. Animals needed space and space was shrinking, a major threat to all the progress they had worked so hard to achieve.

When he reached Covington, Service called del Olmo on his cellular and told him about the woman in Amasa, suggesting he get over to the woman's place before her husband killed the animal.

"They make you some kind of roving three-striper now?" del Olmo asked, half joking.

"Me, a sergeant? No fucking way."

Service concentrated on the problem in the tract as he drove toward L'Anse. He needed to sort things out.

Superficially nothing added up, but he could feel something big was under way, and he needed to find a way to tie it all together. No doubt it all fit; the question was how. His gut was rarely wrong, but it had taken him most of his life to learn to trust it. A slow learner in some ways. Maybe in all ways, he thought.

What had the stranger been doing in the tract and why had he been so evasive? He'd had a camera and a hammer. Geologist? Prospector? Had he been looking for diamonds? Had he been upstream at the log slide before he encountered him?

First a fire at the Geezer Hole, then at the log slide.

Neither fire had been an accident.

Connected to the granite formations? At this point there was only conjecture. His. If this all finally came together in a case, he was going to have to go upward for assistance. But not until he knew what he was dealing with.

A mysterious helicopter had been seen by Voydanov north of the log slide, and Voydanov might be a little addled in some ways, but he seemed to know choppers pretty well. Granite up there too. Just one outcrop, a phallic shape. He was surprised Nantz hadn't pointed this out. It fit her mind. Surely she noticed, because Nantz didn't seem to miss much. Granite at the log slide, but not the Geezer Hole. How did these three locations fit together? Did they? The chopper had taken pains to not leave an imprint. In at daylight, flying low, no call sign, no flight plan. Shadowed by a goose? Voydanov was a nice old man and might know choppers, but the conversations with him reminded Service how useless eyewitnesses were on most counts.

The pebbles were a diamond and several garnets. Maybe the dog had found these downstream of the lone outcrop. In the water. The clay and gravel there were brownish red, same as he had seen near the log slide and Geezer Hole. Related geologically? Maybe, but he would have to learn more about this from the professor tomorrow.

Limpy had suggested that the tract was not all publicly owned, and he was technically wrong; the state did own all the land. But he was also right in that the state had leased a few parcels to citizens. This was a technicality, Hathoot had tried to assure him. Maybe. How did Limpy know this, and why had he put him on this scent? Seton Knipe held two of the leases, the only ones not on the perimeter, and Knipe had moved to the Crystal Falls area about the same time Dow Chemical had gotten into the hush-hush hunt for diamonds. Was this more than a coincidence?

Diamonds in the UP. He vaguely remembered something about this years ago but had never seen or heard anything more since then. He figured it had fizzled, and if del Olmo was correct it had. But what about Knipe and his office attached to the laboratory? There had been silver and gold in the UP's past, but a real diamond find would create an unwanted, uncontrolled rush. He wondered how Bozian would handle this. Had Dow Chemical briefed the governor? Probably. He was an outspoken supporter of big business and considered environmental impact something between a minor consideration and a pain in the ass. Had Dow's political action committee contributed to Bozian's campaigns? Service felt vaguely irritated.

Knipe's businesses were involved in industries that potentially might use a helicopter for one task or another. Did Knipe own one? Or Wildcat, Inc.? Could they lease one somewhere? If so, there had to be a record. There was always a paper trail of some kind. Knipe, speculating in small land parcels. Why? Was Knipe in the diamond hunt? If so, his parcels in the tract seemed too far from the granite formations to serve a purpose. If the granite had anything to do with diamonds, which remained a major if. What were the Knipes up to, and did Limpy know Knipe?

If the pebbles were really gems, what was he going to do about them? A stampede could start on no more than a rumor. These sorts of things traveled underground and took on their own lives and power. Yukon, Keweenaw, Black Hills, Sutter's Mill: these had all been stampedes for easy riches, all deeply rooted in the American psyche. In this country you could start with nothing and get everything through smarts and hard work. Or luck. Usually luck played the greater role. You could have a fortune, lose it, get it back, lose it again. No need to lose hope in America. If there were diamonds in the tract, what would Bozian do? Simon said there had been talk that the Crystal Falls diamond find could be the richest in history. Bigger than South Africa or Siberia? Jesus. Bad news on all fronts, except that the diamond hunters seemed to be gone. What if the real diamonds were not near Crystal Falls, but in the tract? Or in both locations?

Service cringed and gripped the steering wheel.

He had all sorts of puzzle pieces but no clue if they all fit the same puzzle. So many things could be linked intellectually and instinctively, but without evidence you had nothing but something to worry about. Jerry Allerdyce had worked for Ralph Scaffidi and Jerry had been murdered. Jerry had continued to see Scaffidi's niece even after banishment. Jerry had taken his chain saw to do some logging, and now they had Jerry in a bag. The saw was still missing. A chain saw had been used at the log-slide fire, where Jerry's body had been found. He felt certain he could assume Jerry had been working there for somebody, then killed. Why? His womanizing had created a lot of hard feelings over the years. But Jerry was also a skilled logger, a good choice to help somebody put a protective line around a small fire. Finding out who Jerry Allerdyce had worked with in the Mosquito was crucial. Did Limpy know something more? Maybe.

He would need to find answers before a situation developed that couldn't be controlled. Once you had a full-blown crisis, your only option was damage control, which meant damage was inevitable, no matter what you did. The trick was to stop events from becoming a crisis.

Driving toward L'Anse, Service turned west on M-28, bypassing the downtown area. He passed under the outstretched arms of the golden statue of Father Baraga, standing on a bluff above the highway. So many people up here on welfare, but the Catholics built golden statues. When he reached Pelkie Road, he headed north to the village of Pelkie, where he stopped at a gas station next to a restaurant called Finn's Fins. The sign out front said HOMECOOKED WHITEFISH. They were probably illegal, but he had other things to think about, and this wasn't his turf. As a CO, your first lesson was that you couldn't do everything. A professional learned to pick and choose. Sometimes you had no choice but handle what came up, but there were other times when you had to ignore some things and stay focused. It was a tough balancing act, one he still struggled with.

Gus told him that Knipe was an old name in Pelkie, a town founded by French Canadian fur trappers and loggers. The gas station had one ancient pump under a sagging wooden roof. There was a handmade sign in the window: SPRINKLE DONUTS: YAH. BAIT: YAH, PRETTY ALIVE LAST MAY. AMMO: SHOOT, YAH! Yooper humor with one-stop shopping. He filled the truck's tank with gas and went inside to pay. It was a hot day and getting hotter. If this weather stayed and there was no rain, the fire threat would escalate rapidly. Some summers it was terrible. Other summers the temperature might climb to seventy degrees only twice between Memorial Day and Labor Day. He could remember three times when there was snow on July Fourth. But this summer had the earmarks of a hot one.

Bozian's policies had cut hell out of the state's forest fire-fighting resources, chopping the state staff twenty to thirty percent. Now the governor bragged to reporters about how he'd downsized deadweight bureaucrats.

A man in greasy white coveralls was behind a glass counter that hadn't been cleaned in a long time. There were half a dozen yellowing pike heads on the wall and a five-year-old calendar with a painting of a bull moose.

"Any granite around here?" Service asked.

The man looked past him at the truck and its emblem.

"I don't know from rocks." The man had not shaved in several days and had black grime under his fingernails.

"Nice pike," Service said. "Spear?"

"Yah," the man said.

A woman in her late twenties came out of a back office. She wore faded denim coverall shorts and no shirt. She was in danger of spilling out of her bib.

"Are you a rock hound?" she asked. She had short black hair streaked with blond highlights and a tattoo of a purple rose on her left shoulder.

"He's a fish cop," the older man said.

A warning to her? It often was. Yoopers could smell a CO out of uniform. To a Yooper, a CO's job was regulating outsiders, not locals.

"Hey," the woman said, adding, "Far out!" She had a square face and thick, full lips. "Are you new? We haven't seen you around here before."

"I'm passing through," he said. "Somebody asked me about granite formations over this way and I said I'd look around."

She smiled. "There's granite hereabouts, for sure," she said. "Limestone Mountain and Sherman Hill. You take Papin Road west to the mountain and Pelkie Road north to Mantila Road and turn west to get to the hill. It'll be on your right."

"Thanks," he said. "Were these places ever mined for iron or copper?"

She asked sarcastically, "You one of those ice hunters?"

The question was so unexpected that Service stammered in his response.

"Ice hunters?"

"Diamonds," she said.

"Diamonds?" he asked, his heart racing.

"Exactly," she said. "There aren't any."

He was puzzled. "Why did you ask me about diamonds?"

She studied him for a minute, then laughed. "Sorry. It's sort of a local joke," she said.

"Mind your mouth," the man said as he went into the office and slammed the door.

The young woman cringed and frowned. "I hate the mindset up here," she said disgustedly. "I can't wait to get out. I started at Suomi and finished up at Minnesota Duluth. My degree's in forestry and horticulture. I want to open a nursery, but banks up here won't loan piss to a toilet and you can't get money unless you already have money. It's the same everywhere, I guess. Them that has gets more. I want to make some real money. Pop has had to struggle for everything. I want a cushion in my life, eh? The way people scrape along up here, there's no safety net. You make a mistake and you're screwed. I want more than that."

She was clearly talking about something specific, but he sensed this wasn't the time to ask. "You're working here now?"

"Summer off. I teach in Chassel, but that's just for now. I'm probably going to head for Colorado or New Mexico. There's nothing up here for me."

It was a familiar story. The U.P.'s youth left first chance they got. And rarely came back.

"Do you know the Knipe family?" Service asked.

"Assholes," she said, tightening her jaw.

"Do a lot of people share your opinion?"

"I speak for myself."

He wondered what her beef was and wanted to pursue it, but he had to see Gus Turnage in Houghton and he was still thirty miles away.

On the road north, he thought: Diamonds again. Out of left field this time. It was a non sequitur, but the woman clearly had no use for the Knipes. What had happened? He decided he would make it a point to visit the woman again and talk at more length.

Gus Turnage, the CO stationed in Houghton, was one of Service's closest friends. Gus was an elf of a man with the shoulders and arms of a blacksmith. Turnage had once been CO of the Year in Michigan and nationally in the same year, but shrugged off honors. He was the scoutmaster of a troop that won national awards nearly every year, but you would never hear this from him. Gus's wife, Pracie, had died in a head-on collision with a logging truck ten years ago and he had raised three sons alone. Good kids. Gus had become a CO the same year as Service and over the years their paths had crossed continuously. They'd had a lot of fun together.

Service pulled his truck into the YOOPER COURT MOTEL, two miles south of the center of Houghton. The manager was Yalmer Wetelainen, who worked only to pay for his hunting and fishing obsessions. Wetelainen was forty, bald, thin, short, and partial to beer, especially his homemade, which he drank in copious quantities, mostly because it was cheap. Service and Turnage had once used a Breathalyzer on Yalmer at an all-night nickel-dime poker game: The Finn drank a case of beer and shots of straight vodka in a fairly short time, but never registered legally drunk. Neither CO could figure it out. Yalmer drank like a fish and ate like a pig, yet he was an ectomorph with not even the hint of a paunch. Turnage and Service decided their friend didn't fit any known human physiological profiles and because of his unique metabolism, they nicknamed him Shark. It stuck.

Shark was waiting outside his office and waved as Service pulled in.

"Good, you're in civvies," Wetelainen announced in his booming voice. "We're gonna go meet up with Gus."

"Where's my room?" When he was in Houghton Service always stayed at the Yooper Court, and Shark always gave him a cut rate. In fact most COs got cut rates on virtually everything they bought; just recently the governor had tried to tube a senior DNR official over this. The official had disagreed publicly with Bozian on a wildlife resource issue and next thing he knew, the state attorney general's office charged him with buying for his personal use at a discount from a DNR-approved vendor and not paying tax on what he bought. The whole case got thrown out, but Bozian made it clear that anybody who got crossways with him was going to feel the full heat of state government. Service knew his name was on Bozian's hit list.

"Chuck your gear in my truck," Shark said. "We're gonna bunk out to my camp tonight."

His camp was a shack he called Valhalla, a small log cabin set near the Firesteel River, an area that could be tough to get into and out of, even if you had a good sense of direction, a compass that worked, and knew where you were going. The soil was mixed with clay and with even a modest rain, the roads were slipperier than black ice and nearly impossible to negotiate.

Gus's truck was already at the cabin when they arrived before sunset, but despite fast-moving evening shadows, the cabin was dark.

"C'mon, c'mon," Shark said excitedly. He got out of the truck and took off into the woods without bothering with bug dope, but Service doused himself as he followed along. His pals were up to something. Shark was a unique man who made ancient weapons the way prehistoric Indians had. He hunted with a flintlock rifle he had made from scratch and a bow made from Osage orange wood he had gotten in Montana.

They walked for twenty minutes until they got to an area of steep ridges covered with pungent firs and mixed hardwoods. It was growing dark fast.

Nighthawks roared down from the light sky into the shadows, hunting mosquitoes.

"Where's Gus?" Service asked.

"Quiet," Shark whispered almost inaudibly. "Geez-oh-Pete, for cryin' out loud, we're in the bloody bush, eh?"

Service shut up. The woods were Shark's church and his god was nature. You didn't talk in Shark's church.

At the edge of a ridge Wetelainen put out his arm and pointed for Service to sit down. They hung their legs over.

There was an open, grassy area below and a nearly full moon rising in a pink-orange sky. The two men sat in fading light and silence.

After an hour Shark tapped Grady's shoulder, leaned over, and mouthed, "Soon." Then, grinning, he grabbed Service's arm and pointed down.

A dark shadow loped into the open area below and was followed by four lighter colors that danced and pranced and rolled and circled in tight coils. The larger animal carried its tail out straight, not down. Not a coyote. Service's heart raced.

Shark poked his arm hard. "Geez!" he whispered huskily. "Iszatsompin?"

A female wolf and her four pups played below them. When she sat and howled, her pups yipped and tried to copy her. Service felt a chill. These were the first gray wolves he had ever seen in the wild and they left him speechless. It was a glorious and beautiful moment, witnessing something few human beings ever saw. Especially in this state.

After thirty-one years as a territory, Michigan had become a state in 1837. By the early 1950s there were few deer left and no elk, moose, or wolves. Now, because of DNR action, there were two million deer in the woods, a thousand elk, five hundred moose, and more than two hundred wolves. The transplant programs had been tenuous, but they had all taken hold and the animals were spreading and prospering. In some ways seeing these wolves reinforced his faith in the system: Despite all the conflicts between so many petty interests and all the nasty politics, the DNR was making headway in restoring the state in ways that only future generations would fully appreciate.

Someday, he hoped, he would hear the howls of wolves in the Mosquito.

The animals cavorted for fifteen minutes in the open and then disappeared as silently and quickly as they had arrived.

"I need a beer," Shark said, popping a tab and handing the warm can to Service. "You like my wolves?"

"Yours?"

"Fucking eh. I found the den and been watchin' over 'em. I'm their grandpappy."

"Where's Gus?"

"He'd better be catchin' our dinner."

The three friends ate a salad of fiddlehead ferns and fresh brook trout salted and peppered and pan-fried in butter with a pinch of brown sugar. They had canned corn mixed with red potatoes and sautéed with scallions and red peppers. They ate while kerosene lamps hissed and frogs chattered outside in the trees and somewhere in the distance coyotes yipped at each other.

"The wolves are the future," Gus said, sipping a beer.

A future not yet assured, Service thought. Not by a long shot. All of this, so magical to behold, could be erased in no time.

Kermit Lemich, Ph.D., had a cluttered office in the basement of an old building called Schoolcraft Hall. The building sat directly above the Portage Ship Canal, smelled of mildew, and looked like a cellar that had once housed custodians, but Lemich seemed to have taken it over. His desk, phone, and gray metal file cabinets were in the center of a sort of open hub, surrounded by mounds and stacks of boulders and rocks of all sizes and colors, piled up to eight feet high. Every stone, Service saw, was marked in a code with some sort of white paint.

Service had to wind through a narrow canyon in the rocks and round a final sharp bend to enter Lemich's inner sanctum. The man was stocky with a gray crew cut and a bushy white handlebar mustache. He had an unlit cigar in his mouth and wore shorts and a red Hawaiian shirt. Overhead hung several colorful silk pennants, the sort that ice hockey teams and players exchanged at national and international tournaments. There were also three pairs of dusty goalie skates and some dog-eared goalie leg pads suspended from wire hangers overhead, and on a small space on the wall, several faded black-and-white team photos.

"Doctor Lemich?"

The man looked up and motioned the CO forward, using a wet-tipped cigar as his pointer. "Pull up a chair and call me Rocky," the professor said.

Service sat gingerly in a rickety wooden chair at the side of a battered oak desk piled with papers and rocks. There was an antiquated Japanese laptop computer on the desk, and beside the desk a dented metal cart containing all sorts of computer components.

Lemich stared at him and after a few seconds said, "I'll be go to hell. *Banger* Service!"

Service stared at him.

"You don't remember me? Sudbury Wolves," Lemich said. "You were playing Junior B with the Marquette Ironmen. Your coach set up a scrimmage with us and we thought it was pretty funny, some American Junior B snotnoses coming to play a Tier I OHA team. I'll never forget it. You were six-four, 230. You don't look much different now, which is better than most of us can say. You were what, sixteen, seventeen? And all our guys were licking their lips ready to give you snotnoses an ass kicking."

Service did not recall the game. It had been nothing special, just one more among the hundreds he had played. His coach, Okie Brumm, was always taking his teams against superior competition. Usually older too.

"We won 4–3," Lemich said, "but you won the war and we called you Banger after that. You were a legend; we all expected to see you in the NHL. Not your team, *you*. None of our guys had ever been hit that hard before, and every time one of our guys ran you, you lined 'em up and blasted 'em. I played some games with Boston, enough to qualify for a pension, but left hockey and got myself into Harvard. Rocks and pucks, both inanimate things. God, you were a helluva player, Service."

"Just a journeyman."

Lemich laughed and swallowed cigar juice and coughed. "Yeah, you sent a whole bunch of guys on journeys to bloody lala land. You were All-American at Northern Michigan. The Red Wings drafted you. See, I remember all this shit. How come you didn't go?"

Service hadn't thought about hockey in a long time. "I looked at the organization and it looked pretty shaky and disorganized and I didn't want any part of it. I joined the Marines."

"Officer?"

"Grunt."

"You get sucked into that Vietnam shit?"

Service nodded.

Lemich grimaced. "Figures. Still wantin' to crash the corners. Now you're with the DNR?"

"Twenty years."

"Long time," the professor said. "You were a helluva player, Service. I mean that. I've worked as a volunteer coach here with goalies. Johnny McInnes and I were pals. Johnny told me about the time you flattened one of his stars in a fight. You made an impression, Service. I've been around hockey all my life. If you'da gone to the NHL, you'da lasted twenty years up there. There's never been a checker as tough or as ferocious as you." Lemich suddenly laughed. "I guess it's a good thing none of the Wolves tried to pick a fight with you that time!"

Service was embarrassed.

"You still skate?" Lemich asked.

"No." He had simply walked away from the game. He no longer owned skates and had no idea where his mementos and medals were.

"You ought to. Maybe coach some kids. It'll keep your ass young, and there's nothing like kids to remind you how wonderful our game is."

Service didn't want to talk hockey. That life was done, just like Vietnam, and he wasn't one to dog-paddle in the past. His old man had played for the Chicago Black Hawks in the 1940–41 season and had started the next year in Chicago, but the morning after Pearl Harbor he had gone down to the recruiting office on State Street and joined the Marine Corps, not returning until 1945. His old man never went back to Chicago; he had returned to the U.P., married, and three years later Service was born. But it was a hard delivery for his mother, and within a year she had died. The old man had become a CO when he got back from the war and, after his wife's death, had begun to drink too much and bury himself in his work. The old man had done his best for him, but Service knew that playing mother and father was too much for him. Often when the old man was out all night chasing bad guys or drinking, Service was dropped at various neighbors. Or with his Grandmother Vonnie, who thought he was crazy. Even before the shotgun deal.

He didn't like thinking about his past, except as it related to his job. What was it about work being a living and not a life? He tried to block out his ex-wife's words and refocus on his purpose in meeting with Lemich.

"Maybe we can take in a game sometime," Lemich said.

Service agreed, only to get the subject changed.

Lemich chewed his cigar. "Okay, if this isn't about hockey, what the hell do you want?"

Service opened a plastic bag and put the aerial photos on the professor's desk. He had never owned a briefcase. He used grocery bags to haul around what he needed.

"Tell me what you see."

Lemich drummed his fingers and leaned down close to the photos. "Granite. Was there a fire?"

Service nodded.

"Geologists are dirt-grubbers, not flyboys." He pushed the photos back to Service. "Circular formation, but it's hard to say if that's significant or serendipity. I need to analyze the rocks chemically. Rocks are real. Appearances can mislead you, but chemicals rarely lie. If you make a mistake, it's your fault, not the rocks'. They are what they are. At an eyeball, this stuff looks vaguely volcanic, but I just can't tell for sure. Have you got magnometer readings?"

"What're they?"

"They measure the strength of magnetism. You chart the lines, you can pick out highs, lows, shapes of magnetic structures. Good shit, can tell you heaps."

"How do you measure?"

"Well, first it has to be a planned, methodical survey. A chopper carries a package of instruments, and the pilot goes up and down the plot. Then the readings get translated and mapped by a computer."

"Always by chopper?"

"Usually. It's the fastest and most economical way."

"What's the instrument package look like?"

"I can show you," Lemich said. He went to a file drawer and pulled out a pamphlet. "This is a book about geology for kids, but there's a good photo."

Service blinked when he saw what the professor was pointing to.

"Weird, eh? A lot of people in the business call it a bird, but I sure as hell don't see a resemblance to any bird I know of."

"Canada goose," the conservation officer said.

Lemich looked. "A honker? I'll be damned. You're right."

The chopper over the tract had been measuring magnetism. Right where the gems had been found. Not a coincidence, Service thought.

"That's a Huey in the picture," Service said. "Do they always use Hueys?"

"Not always, but pretty much. They're old pieces of shit, but they're roomy, they still fly, and they're cheap and fairly reliable if you don't push 'em too far or too high."

"Does the university do magnetic surveys?"

"Shit no. Can't afford to keep a chopper on staff, or even the magnometer. We rent what we need and bring it in. Some of the faculty do some as part of their work, but we always have to go get most of what we need."

"Including the instrument package?"

"Yep. We have the computer programs to translate, but not the hardware."

"Are there places that rent this stuff in the U.P.?"

"Nope. I know outfits in Boulder and Butte. There might be half a dozen in the whole country. 'Course, if you get one of them in, you still need a technician to calibrate the instrument package and make sure you have an accurate interface with the computer program. That stuff can be touchy, especially in a chopper, shaking all over the sky. Otherwise, you get gobbledygook and pixel snaps."

"Do the companies have these kinds of technicians?"

"Most do, but when we do surveys, we use our own people."

"Tech has such people?"

"Three, I think. What're you after?"

You had to read people, Service thought. Take a chance.

"It's complicated," the conservation officer said. "Might be easier if I showed you. Got a couple of days for some fieldwork?"

Lemich grinned, dug a specimen hammer out of a desk drawer and held it up. "Can I crawl around in the dirt and whack some rocks?"

· 15 ·

Gus Turnage was waiting for Service at Shark Wetelainen's motel office. Shark had a fly-tying table crammed into his office; hackle capes, snowshoe hare fur, jungle cock feathers, and tail feathers from turkeys and pheasants, patches of moose, deer, and elk hair were scattered all over the place. It was a pure sportsman's chaos, no place for everything and nothing in its place, but it only looked a disaster to others. He was actually meticulously organized and always operating a season ahead in preparing his equipment and tying flies.

"Good meeting?" Turnage asked, offering a cup of fresh coffee.

"Ain't no good meetings!" Shark barked, not bothering to look up from a tiny vise where he was fashioning a gaudy steelhead fly with holographic flash above.

Service gave Turnage three names. "These people are technicians. They measure magnetism and they all work for Tech. I need for you to talk to them. I want to know if they've done a job recently on the Mosquito, either for Tech or freelance. All these university types freelance and consult."

Gus grunted. "Can do. Posthaste?"

"Please."

"Piece of cake," Turnage said.

"Cake?" Shark said, looking up suddenly. "Who's got cake?"

As soon as he left Shark's place, Service got on his phone and dialed Harry Digna. A woman answered the phone.

"DNR, Officer Service. Is Harry there?"

He heard the woman pass the phone. "DNR. What have you been up to this time."

"Nothin', just keep your nose out of my business, eh?"

The woman cursed and her voice receded.

"Yeah?" Digna answered.

"You've been quiet, Bird."

"I've been asking around," Digna said. "It's not easy, eh?"

He didn't expect Digna to come up with anything, but pushing helped keep him in line and there was always the possibility of luck. Bird-man ran with lowlives with loose lips. "Tougher than the alternative?"

"I told you I'd do it."

"That your wife who answered?"

"Don't push," Digna said nervously.

"This is a friendly chat," Service said. "When I push, you'll feel it."

"You get your rocks off fucking with people's minds?"

"Only if they have minds," Service said. "Be in touch, Bird."

Near Assinins, Keweenaw Bay nearly touches Old Des Rochers Road, now a segment of US 41. The morning was sunny with some clouds, the wind calm. Cloud shadows moved majestically over the calm water of the bay. As Service drove south he looked toward the water's edge and saw a man walking with a rifle. He parked immediately, got out, and walked down to the gravelly beach.

The rifle had a scope. The man carried the weapon in one hand; the sling drooped, dragging the stock along the gravel. The man was stark na-ked, moving slowly. Service used his handheld radio to call the state po-lice post in Baraga, identified himself, told the dispatcher the situation and location, and requested backup. "Tell them no bells and whistles." A naked man stumbling along a beach suggested mental illness, perhaps even a potential suicide. A siren might push him over the edge. Take no chances, he warned himself, stumbling along.

Backup on the way, Service paralleled the man's route and observed. The man's feet were bloody from the sharp edges of the rocks, and he walked stiff legged.

When the man halted, Service stopped and looked back to see if backup had arrived. It hadn't.

A seagull soaring overhead let out a grating squawk. The man fum-bled with the rifle and aimed it in the air. He tried to pull the trigger sev-eral times, but the weapon didn't discharge. Drunk, Service decided. The rifle's safety was on and the man couldn't figure it out. This was good.

A glance told him that backup was still not there.

"Sir?"

The man didn't react.

"Sir?"

The man looked over his shoulder at the conservation officer. "What the fuck do *you* want?"

"Sir, please put the rifle on the ground and step away from it."

"My rifle."

"Place the rifle on the ground, please."

Another seagull sound caused the man to swing the rifle skyward again.

"Sir, don't shoot. Just put the rifle down."

The man jerked at the trigger and, when nothing happened, took the rifle by the barrel and flung it spinning into the water.

At least he was unarmed now. "Sir, I want to help you."

"Got mead?" the man asked.

Mead? "No sir, just sit down. Your feet are bleeding."

The man lifted a foot and looked at the blood. "Who took my shoes?" he asked.

"Sir, sit down so you don't cut them anymore."

Service looked back and saw a state trooper jogging toward them. Service moved cautiously toward the man on the cobbled beach. "Sir?"

"Okay, okay." He bent his knees to sit and fell backward. His head hit the rocks with a loud thunk and the man's arms spread out.

The trooper caught up. Service pointed. "He had a rifle and threw it in the water." "I saw."

Service nodded and approached the prone man.

"Sir?"

"Yah, I can hear."

Service knelt nearby but did not get close. The trooper traipsed into the water, found the rifle, and picked it up. He stomped over to Service. "I hate getting wet. Now I'll have to change uniforms."

"Call EMS. He's cut bad on the feet." The trooper talked into the radio microphone attached near his collar while Service spoke calmly to the man.

"We're gonna get you a doctor, sir."

"Got no insurance," the man said.

"Don't worry about that now."

The trooper stood behind Service. "I don't need *this* today."

"You know him?"

"Unfortunately. Name's George Stix. He used to be a lawyer, but he lost his license. He's psychotic. Last we knew he was in a rubber room in Grand Rapids. Let's get cuffs on him. He can be unpredictable. Don't let his age fool you."

The naked man suddenly sat up. "You may not touch royalty."

Service looked at the trooper, who said, "He thinks he's a king."

"George the Forty-Third," the man said haughtily.

"Your Highness," the trooper said, "roll over on your stomach and put your hands behind you."

"I only obey God," George said.

"Which god?" the trooper said.

"What day is this?"

"Roll over, George."

The prone man exhaled deeply and started to roll, but he quickly changed positions and shot forward like a crab, catching the trooper just below the knee and knocking him down.

Service grabbed the man by the hair and dropped on top of him, but the man pulled away and head-butted the conservation officer in the face. The pain blinded Service, but he still had hold of the man and pushed him down. The trooper yelled, "Roll him over!"

When the man was over, the trooper cuffed him and stood up.

Service was still seeing stars when the trooper said, "Shit," and fell beside him.

"My fucking ankle," the trooper hissed. "I think the bastard broke it."

Service rubbed his face. His hand came away covered by bright red blood. He felt his nose and knew it was broken and off center. The pain in his face was not relenting. He pulled up the trooper's wet pant leg and felt along the bones. The man winced.

"We'll let EMS take care of it," Service said. "Don't move."

The trooper said, "Your faced is fucked up."

When the Bay Ambulance Service vehicle arrived, the techs gave Service a towel to hold against his face while they worked on George the Forty-Third and strapped him onto a stretcher. One of the emergency techs went for another stretcher for the trooper.

The EMS team wanted Service to ride in the ambulance, but he refused. The blood had stopped flowing. Now he felt numbness in his cheek and a headache taking root. He followed the ambulance to Baraga County Memorial Hospital on Main Street in L'Anse. When he got inside, the trooper and George were already in examining rooms. A nurse looked at Service and shook her head sympathetically. "Bad day?"

"It's just beginning," he said.

"A doctor will be right here." She showed him to a small room, sat him on the examining table, and attached a blood pressure sleeve. "We're going to need some X rays."

"I've had broken noses before."

"It's your cheek I'm worried about," she said. "Your blood pressure's up," she added, storing the sphygmomanometer after she had taken his pressure.

The red-haired doctor wore a pale green smock and sandals with no socks. The exam took about fifteen minutes. "I need to get moving," Service said.

"Let's just get some pictures, then we can talk, okay? Meanwhile, stay still and remain here."

"What about the trooper?"

"His ankle's broken. We're setting it now."

While Service was in X ray, a logger was brought in. He had severed his hand with a saw. The entire emergency team focused on that.

Service was taken back to the exam room, where he lay down. His headache got progressively worse. He lost track of time and felt sleepy.

The next thing he knew, he was on a gurney and being taken somewhere. He tried to ask questions, but words wouldn't come out.

When he awoke, the doctor was beside his bed. "You're back."

Service looked around. "When did I leave?" The doctor laughed. Service looked around the room, which was a sterile white. There was an IV stand beside the bed. A clear plastic line snaked down into his arm. "What happened?"

"Concussion," the doctor said. "Moderate. Your nose is broken, but that should heal if you don't bang it again. There's a hairline crack in your cheek. You're gonna need to stand down for a few days."

Service lifted the arm with the IV. "Get it out."

The doctor nodded to a nurse and she set about freeing him.

"When you get home, see your own physician," the doctor said. He placed two prescription sheets on the table by the bed. "Get those filled. They're for pain. If headaches persist, get to your physician. Concussions aren't minor injuries."

When Service got outside, the sky looked wrong. He checked his watch. It was the next morning. "Shit," was all he could say.

On his way east, he called Sergeant Parker and explained what had happened.

"You're okay to drive?"

"I *am* driving."

"You will see another doctor before you return to duty."

"Right," Service said, signing off.

Kira was going to be worried.

Newf raced out of the house when Kira opened the door and Kira came flying right behind the dog. She stopped when she looked at his face. "My God, Grady!"

"I had a problem," he said.

She showered him with gentle kisses. "You've been gone a month. No, a year!"

"It was just two nights."

"I was worried," she said in a tone he couldn't read. Was she criticizing him?

She insisted he go to bed and made an ice pack from plastic bags.

After his nap, she made a salad of romaine lettuce, arugula, and avocado, and a small pizza with yellow squash, mozzarella, and lemon thyme on a crust no thicker than paper. He took a couple of sips of a glass of beer, then pushed the glass away.

He told told her about the mother wolf and her pups and eating fresh trout. He was about to tell her about his encounters with the grandmother, teacher, Lemich, and all the rest, but the telephone interrupted him.

It was McKower. "Rollie Harris died this afternoon."

Service felt weak and grabbed the chair for support. Harris was the district's lieutenant, a forty-year-old who led his people intelligently and held his ground against the muck-a-mucks in Lansing with diplomacy, never selling out his COs.

"What happened?" Rollie had been a fanatic about conditioning and was always on everybody's ass to keep in shape.

"He was fishing with Lanny and had a heart attack. They were up on the Yellow Dog. Lanny used their cellular to call for help and gave him mouth-to-mouth, but he was dead when the emergency team got there. Poor girl," McKower added.

"Damn," was all Service could say. Lanny was Harris's fourteen-year-old daughter, his only child. "How's Jean?" Rollie's wife.

"Strong for the moment. You know how she is. The burial will be at Big Bay the day after tomorrow, no church service. Jean and Lanny want you and me to be pallbearers."

"They can count on me," Service said.

"We all count on you, Grady."

Why did she have to say that? As long as he had known McKower she had always put him on a pedestal and tried to make him out to be more than he was.

Kira asked, "What's wrong?" after he hung up.

"Rollie Harris died today. Heart attack."

She looked shocked. "He's *so* young."

"His number came up."

"Fatalism," she said sarcastically, "from the same fool who jumped in front of his grandmother's shotgun."

He said, "I'm going to let Newf out," He needed time alone.

Kira didn't object.

Rollie had been a grunt at Khe Sanh and had seen men killed for nothing. As an LT in the DNR, he would not allow history to repeat itself, even when his people were eager to take chances. Survey after survey showed that COs were eight to ten times more likely than any other kinds of cops in the country to be assaulted and injured in the line of duty, and the inherent risk was high enough without his people pushing the envelope. Service didn't doubt the surveys. He touched his face, which served as a reminder of the uncertainties the job held.

Rollie Harris would be hard to replace, as a boss and as a friend.

Service wondered when his number would come up. Newf watched him for a while, then loped into the woods with her nose down, sniffing everything until she halted in the darkness and began snarling and barking.

Service made his way to the dog, found her staring up, and and saw three black bear cubs on branches. They were staring down like live teddy bears.

"Shit," he said out loud. "*Newf.*" The dog looked over at him. "*Come!*" he said. The dog obeyed. His head ached and he looked around carefully before backing slowly away. He was certain the sow was nearby, and if she thought he was threatening her cubs she could get aggressive. Sows were unpredictable. Male bears, like male gorillas, put up an aggressive front but rarely attacked. Females with cubs attacked without warning—maternal instinct at its deadliest.

They got back to the house without incident and Service made sure that Newf was inside. The bear would take her cubs and move on. He needed time to think, but he was tired and dozed off in his chair, only to be awakened by a motorcycle roaring by the house and headed down the trail where he had seen the bear.

Christ almighty! He grabbed a 12-gauge shotgun and a spotlight and ran after the dirt bike. He found it in a heap not far from where he had seen the cubs. The motorcyle was on its side, the front fender bent, handlebars twisted, front tire popped.

"Help me," a voice called weakly.

Service pointed his light up and saw a young man in the tree, frantically trying to climb. A large bear was behind him. Oh fuck, Service thought. Was this day never going to end?

Service moved closer to the tree and shone the light up, but the bear ignored him. He checked the ground, found a rock, and threw it, hitting the bear in the rump. She looked down and clacked her jaws angrily, a warning for him to butt out.

Then the animal turned and came straight down the tree. Service backed away.

"Help!" the man shouted again from above.

"Be quiet!" Service ordered.

The female landed hard on the ground and shook as she looked at him. Her eyes were red in his light beam. He braced the light against the forestock of his shotgun and fired into the dirt under the bear, spraying her with dirt fragments. As dry as it was, the bits would sting like shrapnel. The bear took a couple of steps toward him, shaking her head from side to side, then pivoted suddenly, cut sharply right, and crashed through tag alders. He heard her land in the creek with a splash as loud as a depth charge. And as deadly.

"Climb down fast," he told the climber. "Now."

Before the man got most of the way down, he fell and collapsed on the ground. He was bleeding from the head and whimpering. Service couldn't tell if the bear had gotten to him or if the injuries came from the accident and the fall. This was no place or time to make an assessment; he had to get the guy to safety. Now.

"I hurt," the man said.

Service grabbed him by the collar, lifted him up, and dragged and helped him toward the cabin. When they got there, Kira took his flashlight, took one look, and went into action rendering first aid while Service called the county sheriff and an ambulance. The man was bleeding badly from slashes from the bear's claws, but worse from a compound fracture in his leg. An hour later the man had a ticket for riding without a helmet, trespassing, riding off a designated trail, and reckless driving; he was on

the way to the hospital. It would take the surgeons hours to put his leg together, but at least he was alive.

"My God," Kira said. "What happened out there?"

"Tomorrow," he mumbled wearily, waving her off. No time to even
mourn Rollie. He was exhausted, and he would worry about the bears and
the broken motorcycle when he had daylight and backup. Right now, he
needed sleep. *Just* sleep.

As soon as he felt himself sliding into deep sleep, an ORV roared up
his driveway and he was up again, dressing and out to his truck and following at breakneck speed, but he lost the trail within a mile. Goddamn assholes. North woods summer fever was setting in.

Back to bed again. The phone rang. This time it was central dispatch
at the county. A deputy had a B&E and a possible intruder at a house near
Skandia and needed backup. He was closest. Service got dressed again,
drove down to the house four miles away, and met up with the cop, a man
named Avery. Service took the back of the house and Avery went to the
front door. Minutes later, Avery was yelling for him. Service went back to
the front and found the deputy shaking his head and lighting up a smoke.

"No B&E," Avery said. "The woman's granddaughter came home late
from bowling and the old lady panicked. Sorry."

"No problem," Service said. It was always something in this job.

Less than a mile away from his cabin a van raced up behind him, fish-
tailing back and forth. Service pulled to the right and slowed, and when
the van finally passed it was swerving all over the road ahead of him.

Not my day, he thought angrily. He turned on his blue lights and
followed, careful not to press too close. No siren. That could spook anybody on a dark, country dirt road. The van didn't get far. Rounding a
tight curve, Service saw dust rising and headlights pointed up into some
oak trees and blue spruces. The damn thing had flipped on its side. A
wheel spun lazily. The van was baby shit brown and badly rusted. Dust
hung in the air.

Service scrambled up on the van and jerked a door open. He could
smell gas and fumes. Not good. The engine was still running.

"Shut the motor off," Service barked.

A male voice said, "I know, I know, I shunt drink an' drive. Jus' had
one, I swear."

One: a bottle, a keg, a tanker off the back of an eighteen-wheeler?

At least he got the engine off. Service helped the man out and down.
He stank of alcohol and had a nasty cut on his forehead. He was seeing a

year's worth of blood today, and summer was just starting up. The man tried to stand but fell.

"Are you alone?"

"Yup."

But Service heard more sounds from inside the van. He climbed back on top and used his light. There was a woman in back.

"Are you hurt?"

"Where's Roy? I need Roy."

"The driver?" Why had the man said he was alone?

"Roy!" she shouted. "You know Roy?" she asked Service.

The light showed a nasty knot on her forehead, and it was growing.

Drunks. He helped her out and looked for the man, but he was gone. Service took the woman to his truck.

"Stay right here."

The woman began to sob and shake. "Where's Roy?"

He wanted to tell her that the chickenshit was trying to leave her high and dry, but he kept quiet. Using his light he spotted the man on the road, stumbling along and falling every few feet. He ran to Roy, who suddenly turned and held up his hands and toppled backward on the loose sand road, raising a small cloud of dust.

When Service got him to his feet, the man stuck his hands in his pockets and weaved. Service led him back to the truck and put him inside with the woman.

The woman said, "Where's the van, Roy?"

"I don't know nothing about a van," he said. "I was taking a walk."

She began to slap him and he struck back in defense. Service wedged himself between them and immediately became their joint target. The woman punched him hard three or four times on the back of the head before he could subdue her. He held the man off with one hand on his bloody forehead; he was too drunk to resist.

Service radioed for Avery, who this time came to his assistance.

They administered Breathalyzers. The woman blew .22 and the man .31. They were way over the legal limit. The man's name was Boven, the woman Daviros, both from Mackinaw City.

Service read them their rights and Avery drove them away.

He was glad that Kira seemed to be asleep when he got back. It was nearly 4 A.M.

"Everything under control?" she asked in the dark as he crawled onto the bed beside her.

Everything except the world, he thought. Nights like this were a lot more common for a CO than most people could imagine, much less cope with.

"It's fine," he said, kicking off his boots.

She tried to caress his face. "Well, we're awake . . . ?"

He said, "I need sleep, Kira." She rolled over with a loud sigh.

He knew Kira was miffed and he lay there for a few minutes, then got up and called Candy McCants. They quickly made a plan for the morning.

McCants pulled up to his house before sunrise, as promised, towing a steel barrel trap, which they moved down into the woods and baited with a mesh bag loaded with smoked bacon.

"You think she'll come back?" she asked.

"I hope not," he said. It was depressing how much time was wasted trapping and moving nuisance bears in summer. August was the worst because the tourist traffic was heaviest, and they all had food along and didn't know how to take care of it. Bears and idiots: It was a bad combination.

"Your face looks like a waffle," McCants said.

"You ought to see the other guy," he said, trying to make a joke.

McCants stayed for breakfast, which Service cooked. While bacon fried, he awoke Kira, who came to the table in her robe and eyed them sleepily.

"Did I miss something?"

When breakfast was done, Kira whispered to McCants, "Tell him to take the day off."

McCants said, "You tell him."

Kira was cool when he and McCants went out to their trucks.

"She up to this life?" she asked.

"Is anybody?" he answered.

His formal workday began at the Marquette County Sheriff's Department, where he made out reports on the drunks and cycle rider. Avery, of course, was off duty and home sleeping, while he was back on duty. Normal. The drunks had told Avery they had left Mackinaw City, "just for a drive," and begun drinking road beers. They had come well over a hundred miles and were still alive. God watched over drunks. Sometimes.

The cycle rider was still in the hospital in serious but stable condition. After writing his reports and affixing it to Avery's Service called Sergeant Parker and told him about the bear and the trap and asked for a suggestion of where to put the sow and her cubs if she cooperated and got into the trap, which was far from a given. Parker told him he expected COs to handle such problems on their own initiative. Classic Parker, never taking responsibility, just credit.

He went to Rollie Harris's house in Marquette to see Jean and Lanny. Several COs and neighbors were already there, and the kitchen was piled with food. In an emergency people tended to pull together. Why couldn't they behave this way when there was no emergency?

Jean Harris hugged him tight but didn't cry. A CO's spouse was the same as a soldier's spouse. You kept it together.

"Rollie said you were the best," she whispered. "He said no matter what happened, no matter how crazy things got, he could always count on you."

That shit again. "We'll miss Rollie," Service mumbled. He thought there might be a creator, but doubted heaven or hell. Dead was dead.

He talked to Lanny for a while. She had puffy eyes but was trying to be brave. Service left Harris's and went to a pay phone, using a prepaid phone card. He was always picking them up in convenience stores: They were impossible to trace.

Simon del Olmo reported that he had visited the Iron County deeds office. The Knipes had a quite a number of small parcels and lots, all located haphazardly around Lake Ellen, the general area where diamond-bearing structures were rumored to be.

"They're in the hunt, *compadre*," del Olmo said.

"Find out if they're trying to peddle or lease their parcels, okay? And find out if they have mineral rights for the properties."

"*Bueno*, Bubba."

Service stared at the phone. *Bueno*, Bubba? He laughed out loud. Del Olmo was brash.

The next call went to Joe Flap.

"How we doin' on that chopper?"

"Hey," Flap said. "I got the beer. That Nantz broad is a real dilly."

Dilly? What the hell did that mean?

"No blue chopper yet, but I'm not a quitter," Flap said.

Service rubbed his eyes and called Gus Turnage but got his machine; he left a message asking him to call tonight. The way his luck was running, Gus would wake him up.

McCants met him for lunch at a pasty shop called Shovels. It wasn't far from Marquette Prison, where the worst prisoners in the state penal system were housed.

"You had a hell of a night," she said. "You see Jean?"

He nodded.

"I was over there earlier," she said. "Pretty damn sad. I can't believe the LT's gone. How come death always takes the good ones first?"

"Thanks," he said. He was nearly a decade older than Rollie.

"Not you," she said. "Don't be so sensitive. You think Lisette will get his job?"

He hadn't thought about it. "Only if no other LT wants it. She's low man on the totem pole."

"But she's perfect for the job, yes?"

He nodded. It was true.

They ordered gravy with pasties. Service drank three cups of black coffee and smoked several cigarettes. The pasties were too dry, but filling. Brought to the U.P. by Cornish miners in the previous century, they were the area's dish of choice. In essence potpies filled with pork, rutabagas, and onions, the pies folded over to form a half moon, a shape that let miners heat them in the mines on their shovel blades over fires and torches. Service ate only a few bites of the pasty and lit another cigarette.

"You need to cut down on the smokes," McCants said.

"Are you my mother?"

"You never had a mother," she said, putting out her hand. "You were born of wild animals in the woods. Can I have one?" she asked meekly.

Lemich would meet him tomorrow morning. How much should he tell the man? Without the hockey-crazy professor's knowledge, he wasn't likely to learn much. He thought momentarily about inviting Nantz but decided against it.

He stopped at Silver Creek on the way south and checked the licenses of three men using Mepps spinners for brown trout. They had two seventeen-inch dandies. Their fishing licenses were fine and they were respectful. They were up from Mount Pleasant for a few days and happy to be fishing instead of working.

Service was glad it was summer. In late spring and into June warmwater species spawned and made people crazy. In fall cold-water fish moved up the streams and hunters started in. More craziness. Summer had its share of nuts, but the weather was better.

His thoughts about weather told him he was getting punchy on too little sleep and too much caffeine.

Central dispatch in Lansing called him on the radio when he was on US 41 and told him a man in Ladoga wanted to see a CO right away.

"About what?"

The dispatcher wasn't sure, which was typical. Lansing wanted control, but didn't have a clue about what COs needed in the real world where they operated. He got the name and address and headed for Ladoga.

The village, such as it was, was east of US 41, south of Gwinn. The call came from a two-story house across from a fourplex that looked like a cheap motel that had been modified. When K. I. Sawyer Air Force Base had been active the locals had built apartments, hoping to harvest some easy military cash. Now the Air Force was gone, the base decommissioned, and most of the apartments vacant.

The man at the house was named Alping. He owned the fourplex.

"Something I want you to see," the man said. He was short and obese and badly needed a haircut. He wheezed and puffed as he walked.

There was a terrible stink coming from an end apartment. "Have you been inside yet?" Service asked.

"No way."

The smell was organic, rotting, but not human. In his experience, dead people had a unique scent.

"Open it."

"You gonna take out your gun?"

"No." When people looked at a uniform they tended to see only the badge and sidearm. TV made it seem as though cops shot people every day. Unlike cities, up here everybody was armed. There were fewer burglaries than in cities because northern property owners knew how to shoot and would. The downside was that there were more accidental shootings too.

The smell that rolled out the open door was nauseating. Definitely not human, but *definitely* something dead and decomposing.

The owner remained outside.

The smell was strongest from the cellar door. Service flipped on the cellar light and crept gingerly down the wooden steps. The floor was littered with the carcasses and viscera of skinned raccoons. Service counted up to twenty and stopped. Skinned and dumped. He trudged back up the stairs and looked at the carpet runner, looking for blood. None was in evidence, meaning they had been brought downstairs and skinned. Where were the pelts? None of this added up.

"Who's the tenant?" Service asked Alping.

"An asshole four-flusher named Bowin, behind in payments. I told him he had till the end of the week or he'd be evicted. Then he run off and didn't pay."

"How do I contact Mr. Bowin?"

"You tell him I'm keeping the damage deposit and I'm gonna sue his ass."

"Sir?"

"I don't got a number."

"How long has Bowin been your tenant?"

"They come last fall."

They? "Does he work around here?"

"Don't know. He and his whore were in and out at all hours. I'd see 'em one day, then not for several days. One time I never seen 'em for a month or more."

"Is the woman his wife?"

"I don't know and he never said. You want my opinion?"

"Did he have a vehicle?"

"Yah, a brown van with a lot of Bondo. Piece of shit was falling apart."

Service closed his eyes. Could it be?

"What is Bowin's first name?"

"Roy," the man said. "Or so he claims."

"Did Bowin have a lease?"

"Nah, he paid cash, three months in advance, but now he's been here for six more and he owes me."

"You never saw his driver's license?"

"Didn't need it. It was cash up front and at first he seemed decent enough. A few years back I'd never have taken him, but those assholes in Washington closed the base and a body has to recoup investment, right? What's the state gonna do for me? That's what I want to know. You can kill only so many raccoons, right?"

"There's no limit on coons."

"That don't sound right to me."

Service was not going to dig out his regs. "That's the law. Please don't move the carcasses until I get back to you."

"You just gonna let them stink up my place?"

Service said, "We'll take care of them later. Right now they're evidence."

Alping was still boiling when Service left and drove to the county jail. Alping had given him the name Roy Bowin and described a brown van. At the jail he had a Roy Boven and a brown van. These were not likely to be coincidences.

The couple from the previous night were still in jail. They were not going to be arraigned until this evening. Service arranged to talk to them separately.

The man looked sick, his skin pallid gray-green; he had the sweats. "You remember me, Mister Boven?"

The man half looked up, muttered, "I'm so sorry about this."

"You have no previous OUILs. Why this time?"

No answer.

"Is the van yours?"

"Yeah."

"Do you hunt or fish? Trap?"

"No, never."

"You live in Mackinaw City, right?"

Boven nodded unenthusiastically. A bandage stretched across his forehead where the cut had been repaired.

"Ms. Daviros too?"

Another nod. He was obviously hurting.

"Are you married, Mister Boven?"

Boven looked up with panic in his eyes. "Did you call my wife?"

"No. Ms. Daviros isn't your wife?"

The only answer was a hangdog look.

"Do you like raccoons?"

Deep sigh, no answer, no response.

Service met the woman next. She was charged with drinking in a vehicle and could have been released last night, but refused, saying she wanted to remain with Boven. Not an unusual request. The deputies had housed her in the jail. She was midthirties, a little plump, looking better than Boven, but she had a nasty blue-and-violet knot on her head.

"How long do we have to stay here?" she asked.

Time to push. "Not much longer. I had a call today from a man named Alping. You and Boven have been using different names. He claims you owe him rent for an apartment in Ladoga. He's filed a complaint and can come in and identify both of you, if that's what you want."

She looked past him, looking weary. "You don't have to do that. It was us."

"He says you left without paying back rent."

"That's a damn lie," she said, her head snapping up. "Roy paid him ahead in cash. We have receipts. He's a total jerk, that guy. When we weren't there, he turned off our heat and electricity. Once last winter the pipes froze and he tried to stick Roy with the bill. We told him we were moving out. Yesterday was our last day."

"What about the coons?"

The woman had a blank look. "What coons?"

"Never mind." She didn't know anything about them. Neither did Boven. "You two aren't married."

"We're married . . . just not to each other."

"You drove a long way."

"We wanted to be careful."

"But you told Alping you were moving out?"

She sucked in a deep breath and let it out slowly. "We've both told our spouses we want divorces. There's no sense driving all this way anymore."

"How'd Alping react when you told him you were moving out?"

"He flipped out. The man has a temper and he's a bully. He said we had a one-year lease and he was going to sue. But there was no lease, I swear. He's trying to hold us up. He said he was going to get us and make big trouble for us. We're in trouble," she added.

Service tried to reassure her. "This is Boven's first OUIL. He's going to get hit hard, but it's worse for repeat offenders."

"I'm not talking about that trouble," she said. "I'm pregnant."

Service blinked several times.

She said, "Not by Roy or my husband. By *another* guy," she said with a catch in her voice. "God, I can't believe this has happened."

Service had heard enough. "Roy used the name Bowin to rent the apartment?"

She nodded.

Service left her and made some telephone calls. He found out that Alping had a fur harvester's license from the previous autumn.

When Service got to Alping's yard, the man came out quickly. "I called your superior," he said. "Now we'll see who does what."

Sergeant Parker pulled in moments after Service. He looked smug. Parker wouldn't leave his office unless he thought he could get something on Service.

Alping ranted about his no-good tenants and the conservation officer.

Service kept quiet. Parker listened politely, then the sergeant asked for the key. When Alping said he would come along, Parker told him to stay where he was.

Service wondered what was up.

Parker looked at the rotting carcasses with an impassive face. "What's your read?" he asked his subordinate.

What game was he playing? He had expected Parker to gloat, cajole, or threaten.

"The renters are from Mackinaw City. By coincidence I got the man and the woman last night on an OUIL. They're married, but not to each other. This has been their little love nest. They told the landlord they were moving out. He claims they have a lease and owe him. They insist there's no lease and they're paid up. The landlord said he smelled this and called us. I responded. I just got back from talking to the renters. The driver will be arraigned tonight. I think the landlord is trying to extort money. He wants revenge because they're moving out."

"Is that conclusion based on a hunch or on evidence?"

"Hunch so far."

"Proceed," Parker said haughtily.

Service knocked on a door at the end of the building and a woman answered. She had a baby in her arms. "DNR: I'm Officer Service and this is Sergeant Parker. Did you know the neighbors at the other end of the building, a Mister Bowin?"

"They was just shacking up," she said. "They didn't mix much."

"Have you smelled anything from their apartment."

"About noon today I did."

"Not before this?"

"No sir."

"Do you have a lease with Mister Alping?"

She laughed cynically. "In these dumps? People come and go. We pay ahead, and Alping is a cheap bastard. I got three kids and no old man and he's always claiming my kids broke this or that and demanding I pay."

"Did he ever mention a lease?"

"All the time. He says it's a verbal lease, but that's crap. He says if I don't have the money, I can work it off in trade."

"Doing what?"

"You figure it out," she said.

Service was irritated, but kept it under control. He and the sergeant went back to the house.

Alping was in the yard, pacing.

"Did Bowin have a lease?" Service asked.

"No. Did that bastard tell you that?"

"Did you tell the woman at the other end of your building that she has a verbal lease?"

"No, she's a slut. Don't believe no cunt like that. She's got three brats by three different men."

Alping was red in the face.

"What do you trap?"

The landlord exploded. "This is bullshit," he yelled at Parker. "I'm the fucking victim here."

Service said, "You bought a fur harvesting license last fall."

Alping grew quiet. "Yeah? What of it?"

"It's in our computer."

"I follow the law."

"Did you trap those coons?"

No answer. Alping was weighing his positions.

"Look," Grady Service said, "your apartment dealings are none of our business. You called us because of the coons. I can see you had trouble with tenants. That's not my concern. Maybe you put the coons in there because you were mad, but you have a license to trap and shoot coons. There are no bag limits on how many you take and they're pests, right?"

"I shot 'em all legal," Alping said. "They did a lotta damage to my gardens and they keep trying to move into my garage. Law says I can shoot 'em and that's what I did."

"That's right," Service said. "That's the law. Where are the pelts?"

"Out in my shop."

"Can we see them?"

"Why?"

"Just closing things up."

Alping led them back to his shed. The building stank of tanning chemicals. There were coonskins tacked to all the walls. Service stood silently, taking it all in.

"Okay, thanks."

"What about my money?" Alping asked. He was starting to get confident again.

"That's for a civil suit. Get a lawyer."

Alping said, "I sure as hell will."

Walking back toward the house, Service said, "You need to be a good shot to knock down a coon at night."

"I do okay," the man said.

"Harder this time of year, with all the foliage."

"Sometimes."

"You like night shooting?"

"It's the best time to pop coons."

Service said, "Even in this heat?"

"Heat don't bother me," the man said.

Service stopped walking and pivoted to face the man.

"Mister Alping, do you know that it's against the law to shoot problem coons or coyotes at night up here until July 15?'

Alping stumbled. "Say what?"

"Sir, where did you shoot these animals?"

"On *my* property," he said.

"Show us, please. We want to see the damage to your garden too."

"Fuck you, you backstabbing bastards."

Service took out his ticket pad and wrote the man up. "I have to do this," he said. "If Sergeant Parker and I do any more looking, there might be more."

Alping shut up.

Parker walked to the truck with him.

"We really nailed him," the sergeant said.

We? "We're not done yet," Service said. "You want to stay?"

"Sure." Parker looked and sounded pleased.

They drove their trucks away from Ladoga, parked, and walked cross-country to the fields and woods behind the apartments. "He'll bag the carcasses and dump them somewhere. We'll get him again."

Parker smiled. "You don't miss any tricks."

They didn't have to wait long. Alping made several trips through the field into the woods behind the fourplex, dumping carcasses a third of a mile behind the apartment building. On state land.

On the blowhard's fourth trip, Service made his move.

"Mister Alping?"

The man was sweating and puffing, his eyes bulging, too tired to move.

"Sir, you're dumping illegally on state land. It's littering."

"Cocksucker!" Alping roared. He clumsily swung the bag but Service ducked, sidestepped, grabbed the man's arm, pushed his hip out, flipped the man, and immediately rolled him over on his face, jamming it into the bag with the dead animals.

"Night hunting out of season," Service said. "Illegal dumping. Obstructing a police officer and assault. That's a hat trick for sure."

Service read the man his rights and called the county. He grinned when Deputy Avery showed up. Avery looked at him funny and, when Parker wasn't close said, "Did they fucking clone you, or what? Man, you are like . . . *everywhere.*"

Parker stood beside Service while he called central dispatch in Lansing and reported the bust. He ended the call-in with "TOT, Marquette County Sheriff." Meaning he had transferred custody of Alping to another jurisdiction.

The sergeant said, "We make a pretty good team."

Service hoped that Parker had not taken or passed the LT's exam. What the hell was he buttering him up for? Then it came to him. Parker was thinking McKower was going to get Rollie's job, and he was trying to cover his ass and erase the past.

"Thanks for your help, Sarge."

"Maybe I've been wrong about you," Parker said. "I have a feeling things between us are going to be different. You're going to see your doctor, right?"

Service stifled a laugh. Things sure as hell would be different if McKower got the job. She loathed Parker.

He stopped at a grocery store and bought some staples for the next day.

He showered when he got home. Kira was late. By the time she got there, he was in deep sleep.

· 16 ·

As soon as Service's eyes opened in the morning he saw Kira, propped on an elbow, hovering over him. He thought she would reach for him, but she only stared. Neither of them spoke.

Professor Lemich's headlights flashed in the yard.

"My God!" she said in exasperation.

"It's a professor from Tech. We're going into the Tract today. I don't know when we'll be back."

She sat up, dropped her feet to the floor, and grabbed her robe, snapping the cloth as she put it on.

"You're either not here or if you're here you leave and then you're not here again! The state can't expect people to live like this. I *don't like this.*"

"They don't expect me to live like this."

"Then why do you?"

He didn't have an answer she'd understand. "We can talk later."

"*When?*" she asked. "Now? Can't. Tonight? You'll be gone again. Tomorrow? It'll be something else. I need order, Grady. A modicum of predictability."

"Not now, Kira."

She stalked behind the bathroom screen.

It was their first fight and he had neither the desire nor the time to indulge her.

Lemich sat in his Eagle, but Service went out and invited him in for coffee.

When Kira was dressed she came out and was polite, but not especially friendly. She was not the Kira he knew.

She did not hug Service when he left and didn't stand in the doorway and wave.

When Service saw Maridly Nantz's truck parked at the trailhead, he did a double take. What the hell was *she* doing here?

She grinned and waved as he rolled to a stop.

"Why're you here?" he asked when he got out.

"Your face is hamburger!" she said. When she reached out, he recoiled. "I needed to talk to you," she said.

"How did you *find* me?"

"Intuition."

Was she serious?

"Who's this?" she asked, eyeing Lemich.

"Rocky," the professor said, sticking out his big hand.

"Maridly Nantz," she said. "I didn't catch your last name."

Service growled, "*Nantz.*"

She said, "I called your house, Grady." She added, "But you were gone."

He looked at her.

"Who's the woman?" Nantz asked.

"None of your business."

"Wife?"

"No."

"Fiancée?"

"No."

"Cohabiting?"

"Give it a rest, Nantz."

"Doesn't matter," she said dismissively. "I brought my gear."

"You're not invited."

"Why're you being so secretive?"

"I'm not."

"I want to know what's up, Service. I know my way around the tract as well as you."

"I doubt that," he said. She could be a pain in the ass. He'd been watching over the Mosquito for nearly twenty years and she had spent a little more than a summer here. She was as arrogant as she was relentless and maybe too damn smart for her own good.

"Don't be so . . . *male*," she said. "Face facts, Service. Six eyes beat four."

Lemich watched the exchange with a puzzled but amused look. "Give it up, Banger. You've met your match."

"I'll get my stuff," Nantz said enthusiastically, opening the door of her truck. As they hiked toward the river, she moved close to Service and lowered her voice so Lemich couldn't hear.

"Banger?"

"Leave it be," he said, trudging forward.

They started work at the Geezer Hole.

Lemich scooped up some of the unusually colored gravel with a trowel and put it in a fiber specimen bag. Mostly he stood and surveyed the area, making faces.

"Is the granite near here?" The gregarious professor seemed distracted.

Nantz showed him the formations. "There's more upriver."

Lemich took some samples and the trio hiked at a fast clip up to the log slide, breaking into a heavy sweat as they clambered over the second burn.

As before, Lemich stood motionless studying his surroundings. After a while he began to collect samples from the granite outcroppings, the gray ground stone between them, and more from the gravel in the river. He worked steadily and silently.

Nantz prowled around, burning nervous energy.

Service sat, thinking a nap would be nice. Why didn't Nantz park herself? She had ants in her pants. She had spoken to Kira? Would've liked to have heard *that* exchange. No, you wouldn't, he corrected himself.

It was late afternoon when they hiked farther up the Mosquito River to the site with the single column of granite. Once again Lemich collected samples and studied the area with intense concentration.

While Lemich worked, Service and Nantz made a camp on the west bank of the river. Nantz built a fire. Service took two slices of venison tenderloin out of the cold pack in his ruck and braced a small grate over two logs with the fire in between. He hadn't counted on three for dinner. Nantz disappeared for more than an hour and returned with wild strawberries stuffed into a two pint-sized Baggies.

They worked, side by side, saying nothing, each seeming to know what the other was going to do before they did it.

As it neared dark Nantz said, "You want me to fetch Rocky?"

"He'll be along when he's ready."

Nantz sat down and poked the fire with the toe of her boot. "Level with me, Grady. What're we doing here?"

"Remember the glass Newf found?"

Her eyes said she remembered.

"They were several garnets — and a diamond."

"Right," she said as she grinned and poked the fire again.

"I'm serious," he said. Her eyes narrowed.

Lemich came into camp with his sample bags bulging. His face was

flushed and he looked dusty and tired. He dropped the bags unceremoni-
ously, sat down, and slumped back on the ground.

The fire crackled. Service watched tendrils of campfire smoke rise
and drift.

Lemich sat up and looked at the CO. His voice was stern yet assertive.
"Why did you bring me here?"

Service exhaled. "Because a man was murdered on the river over
where the fire was. Things are going on here that we don't understand and
I think the rocks are somehow connected."

"I think there's kimberlite here," Lemich said, sucking in a deep
breath. "It shouldn't be here, but it is kimberlite. I'll need to do chemical
assays and such, but it's kimberlite. One pipe for sure, maybe a pair. And if
we can see two, you can bet there are more around here. These things
always occur in clusters."

"Like genital warts," Nantz said.

Lemich chuckled. "That's a good one."

"Kimberlite?" Service said.

"Don't play the goofball with me," the professor said.

"A chopper was seen here, possibly carrying a magnetometer, flying a
pattern just across the river. A while before that, I ran into a stranger with a
hammer like yours and as soon as I met him, he got nervous and bugged
out. Two fires have been set around here since then. Two parcels of land
in the Tract are leased by a man named Knipe. He's originally from
Pelkie."

"Pelkie?" Lemich had a sly grin.   ·

"What?" Service asked.

"Back in the eighties the US Geological Survey published a paper by
a couple of geologists who believed there might be cryptovolcanic structures in the Pelkie area. This was based on their finding Paleozoic rocks
that are often found covering kimberlites."

"Were these pipe things found near Pelkie?"

"Not that I know of, but that paper no doubt got the corporate and
wildcat diamond hunters' attention. They started looking at geologic formations and ended up moving their focus southwest toward the Wisconsin border."

"Dow Chemical?" Service said.

"They were just one among several companies," Lemich said, nodding. "Exactly how they were involved is not at all clear."

Service said, "Dow Chemical moved into Crystal Falls to look for diamonds in the eighties. Knipe moved down there about the same time, and
now he owns a lot of land in the area where pipes have been found."

"The word is out that the mining companies haven't found gemstones and are cutting their losses," Lemich said, "though it's always hard to figure out exactly what these outfits are up to."

"Knipe hasn't left," Service said. "Diamonds scare me, Rocky. All it takes is a rumor to start a run of prospectors. If that happens here in the tract, it will be a disaster for this place. I'm not going to let that happen."

Lemich grunted and lowered his voice. "Who said anything about diamonds here? We're talking about kimberlites, and this is pure speculation on my part. We have a pipe here, maybe two. Or none. Over by Crystal Falls they have a heap of pipes and reportedly found microdiamonds in more than half of them. Let me tell you, that defies the hell out of geologic odds. Usually one in ten kimberlite pipes has micros, but maybe one in a hundred has real gems. Of three thousand diamond mines in the world, maybe twenty are paying off. Diamond hunting is a humongous gamble. The odds just plain suck. Even if you find gems in a rich pipe, you have to dig and move fifty thousand tons of rock to get five thousand carats. On the other hand, if you actually find gem-quality stones, you can forget the odds."

"What makes you think there's kimberlite here, and what exactly are these pipes you keep talking about?"

"The technical term for pipe is diatreme. It's a volcanic eruption. Lava shoots up a hundred miles or so from the earth's core and explodes on the surface. Understand, this happened during the Paleozoic period. We're not talking hot news and we're talking about small structures, not major volcanoes. And this usually happened in hours, which is the geologic equivalent of the speed of light, eh? I'm talking *fast*. After the Paleozoic, glaciers came down from Canada, then retreated, leaving the bedrock and pipes under hundreds of feet of debris. Kimberlite is dark green, but exposure to weather and erosion turns it reddish brown. When the lava rises it brings all sorts of smaller rocks, which mix into the kimberlite. By the time it gets spit out on the surface, it's like a funny-looking purple clay. I've seen some evidence of this stuff at all three sites today. The amazing thing is that these formations are nowhere near Crystal Falls or Pelkie. Not even close. Probably it's all connected underground, but this is the first time I've seen evidence that maybe we can correlate aboveground connections of this kind up here."

Scientists loved theories, big-picture crap.

"How long will tests take?"

"A few days."

"Then what?"

"Not all pipes have diamonds. Most don't. To find out you have to drill down two or three hundred feet with a five-inch-diameter bore. You take a couple of tons of rock from each boring, break it up, examine the contents, and analyze."

Nantz listened attentively, but didn't interrupt. Not even with her usual one-liners.

Service said, "Chances are there's nothing here?"

Rocky Lemich nodded. "If you believe the odds, that's right, but I've been in this game a long time and you just never know. People in the diamond hunt take it real slow. And they tend to be very cautious and extremely thorough. It doesn't cost much to send out mineral cruisers to scope formations, but it costs heaps to do even rudimentary exploratory drilling."

"But if somebody got a wild hair and started to drill here, it could start a rush."

Lemich agreed. "True enough. Diamonds send dreamers off the deep end. But," he added, "this is wilderness and the law doesn't allow drilling."

"Laws can be changed," Nantz said.

Service looked at her and turned back to the old goalie. "What does a diamond mine look like?"

"Well, it's somewhat like standard hard-rock mining, like copper and iron used to be up here. A kimberlite pipe tends to be ragged and ziggy-zaggy. The pipe is twisted like a strand of broken DNA and narrows the deeper you go. Think of an askew funnel, all bent to hell during the violent uplift. You never know exactly where diamonds will be in the pipe. Usually they're dispersed and found in pockets in different parts of the pipe. Magnetic readings can help identify target sites. You bore sample holes. Poke around, look in water for evidence of gems being spit out and eroded by hydraulic pressure. Most diamonds are first found by some schmuck, and then engineers follow the diamond trail back to the original source. If you decide you want to dig for real, you offset and dig vertically. Once you have the shaft in, you dig sideways to intersect the pipe. Some mines in Africa go down three or four thousand feet. Here in the U.P. we have old iron and copper mines that go down as deep as nine thousand feet. But you don't sink a shaft until you know you have a bloody good chance for the gems."

"How far away from the pipe would the shaft be?"

"That can vary. Three hundred yards, four hundred. The farther away it is, the more expensive the cost of engineering and extraction. In mining, depth and distance are money."

"Is there a limit?"

Lemich pursed his lips and squinted into the smoke. "If you have stable bedrock below you, the only limit is how much dough you want to spend to get at it."

Meaning the leased properties Knipe had were close enough to where Newf had found the diamond. If Knipe had his eye on diamonds here, he had access. A chopper could bring in construction equipment and people and haul out rock. They would never have to touch public land, so they couldn't be gotten for trespassing. And there was nothing to stop them from digging if the DEQ approved a development plan and granted them a permit, which under the Bozian regime was a paper requirement. This was shaky ground. Knipe had a loophole and Bozian had weakened the state's environmental agency to the point where it was rubber-stamping everything. Service felt his stomach roll.

"What about garnets?"

"Nature's way. If you find diamonds, you usually find garnets. Yin and yang." Lemich looked at Service. "Do you want my opinion? I couldn't care less if there are diamonds here or anywhere in the Yoop. I like it the way it is and I know history and what a bloody mess copper and iron brought. You want me to forget all this, it's forgotten. But it's gonna cost you."

Nantz and Service glanced at each other. "What's the price?" he asked.

"You gotta get back into hockey, eh? Coach some kiddies."

Nantz frowned. "What hockey, you guys?"

Kids? Service thought. "Deal," he said reluctantly.

The two men shook hands.

"What hockey? C'mon you guys," Nantz said with a mock whine.

Service grilled the tenderloin steaks for them, cutting his in half to share with Nantz. Lemich ate heartily while Nantz chattered away in the flickering light of the fire. The wild strawberries were so sweet that the three of them closed their eyes and let themselves get lost in their thoughts.

After dinner Service walked into the woods and used his handheld radio to get a phone patch to Kira. There was no answer at his place. He wondered if she was still ticked off.

When he got back to camp, Nantz was helping Lemich put up his tent. Hers was already up. Service put his on the other side of Lemich.

When they were in their tents Service doused the fire, leaving a pall of smoke lingering over the camp. Frogs peeped. Way off in the distance a coyote yipped. Sometime in the night he heard a rustling sound and woke up, but before he could react a hand closed over his mouth.

"Not a word," Nantz whispered as she wriggled into position beside him. "Are you serious about diamonds?"

"One diamond," he said.

"Don't niggle," she scolded. "Where there's one, there may be more."

"Get out of my tent," he whispered.

"Okay, call me crazy, then live with it. I listened patiently all day and kept my mouth shut, now I want answers." She was behind him, her breath on his neck. "How many of the stones were garnets?"

"Seven of them," he said.

"Jesus," she whispered.

"You heard what Lemich said. There are pipes here."

She said, "This could be a disaster."

"If the governor gets wind of this, all he'll see are dollar signs; he'll make all the usual political noises about environmental safety, then order the DEQ to make sure mining companies get what they want as long as the state gets a fat cut."

"Fighting the governor could be risky. He likes to get his way, and usually he does," Nantz said.

She was right about that. "We have to fight silently and smart until we're forced to go public. When that happens, we want to be set up so there's nothing anybody can do to get at these pipes."

"Don't underestimate Bozian," she said. "He looks and talks like a clown, but he's a heavyweight. There's talk in his party that he could eventually reach the White House."

How did she know such things? "I'm not underestimating him." He remembered Bozian's warning that he had a long memory.

"Can we trust the professor?" she asked.

"We have to," he said. His gut said yes.

She murmured and nestled closer, and he tried to pull away.

"What's wrong?" she asked.

"You can't stay."

"Don't be a worrywart. I'll be out before daylight."

"We have a neighbor."

"He'll never know," she whispered.

"Good night, you two," Lemich called pleasantly from his tent.

"Oh well," Nantz said, laughing softly.

She was warm and soft, but he slept restlessly, thinking about Kira. When he awoke in the morning Nantz was gone, just as she had promised.

The three of them had coffee while Service scrambled Egg Beaters with bacon bits, garlic powder, and onion flakes.

When they packed up, Nantz got Service aside. "Drop him off and come back, okay?"

"Why?"

"We need to look for more pebbles. If we find any we need to cache them until we figure out a more permanent solution."

She was right. "Quick as I can get back," he said pulling out his folding knife and handing it to her. "Notch a boot."

Nantz stared at him. "Why?"

He showed her the sole of one of his boots. It was marked with a tiny triangle. "When I see your tracks, I'll know it's you."

She grinned. "You'll know mine!"

Lemich promised to get back to him with test results in a week to ten days. He expected Kira to be at the clinic, but her truck was parked at the end of the cabin. Service took the professor to his vehicle and went inside. Newf and Cat were both glad to see him. Kira was sitting at a table looking troubled, her eyes puffy.

"Hi," he said.

She answered, "Grady, I'm sorry. I think I know now how your ex felt. I'm really sorry," she added breathlessly, "but I'm just not cut out for this. I can't live with you. I just can't. It's not your fault, Grady. I think for now we shouldn't see each other. You can keep Newf. She was yours from the beginning."

They'd only lived together for a week and she was already bailing out.

"I can't take Newf today," he said. The dog nuzzled his leg.

"I'll take her for now, but I want you to keep the bed. Sleeping on footlockers isn't healthy. I am really sorry to do this so abruptly. You made a wonderful gesture for us, and I appreciate that, but I'm just not as strong as you."

He hated beginnings because they inexorably led to endings.

Her speech done, she took her purse, called Newf, went out to her truck, and drove away. Service watched until the truck was out of sight. He considered going after her, but what would that accomplish? Her mind was made up. He wished he could just sit and let Kira's words settle in, but there was no time. He had to get back to the tract. Nantz was waiting and duty called.

He telephoned del Olmo. "What have you got?"

"I can't figure it out," the younger CO said. "Knipe has a lot of parcels, maybe twenty-five of them, but none of them is closer than a quarter mile to any of the suspected pipe areas."

Service knew why. A slanted mine could intercept a pipe. "But all the parcels are in relatively close proximity?"

"So far."

"Any that are miles away?"

"Nope. If you listen to rumors over here, they're all adjacent to kimberlites, but nobody can say for sure because the exact location of the sites is being held close."

It figured. Knipe was going to try to cash in, one way or another. The question was, How?

"Here's a good one," del Olmo said. "He's got one site fenced in and electrified. There are motion sensors all around, and security people are on duty around the clock. Dogs, too."

"Where?"

"Not far from Lake Ellen and one of the Dow properties."

Did Knipe have a pipe on his property or was he trying to burrow into somebody else's? Why the fence and heavy security arrangements?

"Simon, how well do you know your DEQ counterparts?"

"Well enough."

"We need to know if Knipe has a permit to drill."

"He'd need an approved plan first."

"Exactly."

"Si, *jeffe*."

"Be circumspect, Simon."

"Hey," del Olmo said. "That's my religious preference."

The next call went to Gus Turnage. There were no messages on his answering machine. Cleaned out by Kira?

When he reached Gus, he sounded tired. "I was out all night."

Service said, "Did you call?"

"I'm just getting in," Turnage said. "I've been dogging those names.

One of the three no longer works at the university. His name is Fox and he left maybe six months ago. People over there seemed pretty nervous and evasive about him. Could be he was canned. I'm trying to nail that down. The other two haven't done a job in a year and never up here in the Yoop."

"Where's Fox now?"

"He left to quote 'pursue other interests' end quote. That sound like personnel-puke talk to you?"

It did.

"I don't have the foggiest where he went, but I'll stay after it, okay?"

"Thanks."

The final call went to Joe Flap.

"No blue chopper, but I found us a black one."

"Unmarked?"

"Pretty much. Got a small red WC near the tail rotor. Hard to see from any distance."

Could WC stand for Wildcat? Service wondered. "Where were you?"

"Way the hell up by Skanee. Buncha grumpy old Swedes up that way."

"Who owns the chopper?"

"Some guy. He's an outfitter, I think. Fishing and hunting guide, wildlife photographer, jack of all trades. He seems to jump around like a damn grasshopper. You know the type."

"You got a book on him?"

"I'm working on that. He hasn't been in this spot all that long. A few months, from what I gather. And he's not here often."

"What about a name?"

"Will Chamont."

WC. Will Chamont, not Wildcat. So much for wishful thinking. When would he ever learn? In college his coach had made all the players take personality tests to type their styles. He had been classified an "intuitive," a style that applied to fewer than one in twenty people. His mind tended to jump from rock to rock, rather than following the paved road.

"You want me drop in on this bozo? I could tell him I'm looking for work."

"Can you fly a chopper?"

"Hell, I can fly a fart if it has an engine."

Service laughed out loud. Pranger had never lacked confidence.

Maybe that was what had kept him alive through all his crashes and close calls.

"Did you see that Nantz broad?" Flap asked.

"Why?"

"Just tell that little gal she can come see old Joe Flap anytime."

Service felt his neck hairs bristle. "I'll tell her if I see her."

A small lie.

"I'll head back up to Skanee tomorrow, scout around, see what I can find."

"Thanks and take care, Joe."

"This'll cost you another case of beer."

"No problem."

Service got out his topo maps. Skanee was on the northwest side of the Huron Mountains, and south of the village were the two highest elevations in the state, Mounts Arvon and Curwood. There were hills stretching almost all the way down to the Tract from the helicopter's location. The situation looked right, and it was within the helicopter range he had calculated. There were still too many loose ends, but it felt like some of them were starting to tighten up.

He left food and water for Cat. When he got into his truck he noticed the sky was overcast and darkening. The humidity was oppressive and air too still. He could smell rain coming. He went back into the cabin and hurriedly grabbed a rain slicker.

He stopped at Voydanov's on his way back to the Tract. The old gent was on the porch in a handmade rocking chair. It was sprinkling and there was no wind. Service grabbed his slicker from the backseat and realized he had grabbed the wrong one. He wanted green but had taken his bright blue one. Put it on, dummy, he told himself.

Voydanov waved and called out, "Howya doin' son? Nice rain comin' in, eh? We can sure use her."

There was no sign of the old man's dog. The rain felt like a sprinkle, not a soaker, but predicting weather in the Upper Peninsula was a form of roulette at best. It could pour without warning. They would need plenty of rain to knock back the summer fire threat.

"Sir, are you sure about the color of that chopper you saw?"

"Sure am. You still fretting about that?"

"Just following up."

"I read in the papers about that DNR lieutenant who died. That why you're in black?"

Service was confused. Black? He looked down at his slicker, and said, "This is blue."

"Looks black to me," Voydanov said.

Service returned to the truck and grabbed a black backpack, which he held up for the old the man to see. "Was the chopper more like this color blue?"

"She's pretty darn close," Voydanov said with a solemn nod.

Voydanov's color vision was screwy. Service immediately called Joe Flap on the cellular and told him the chopper they wanted was probably black, not blue. It was sprinkling a little harder when he reached the trailhead and parked and locked the truck.

There was no sign of Nantz when he got to the river, but her tent was still up. She had added a rain fly and dug a neat runoff trench around the tent. He stashed his gear in the tent and wandered around for a while. He wished she had stayed put but guessed her nervous energy made that impossible. He could relate.

There was still no sign of her by late afternoon, and no letup in the drizzle. He admitted to himself that he was getting worried and decided it was time to look. To hell with what she might read into it.

He took his pack and moved quickly along the river, almost at a jog, feeling like a hound with no scent and eager to get on it. He went all the way down to the log slide and up one of the fire lines before he paused. East of the burn he found a small, blurred bootprint with a tiny and unreadable mark on the heel. Farther east, under a maple tree where the ground was protected, he found a patch of damp clay with a pristine track. The mark was shaped like a Coke bottle with exaggerated breasts. He smiled. *Nantz.* She said he would know her mark. He was certain the print in the clay had been carefully placed for him, but why had she come all the way down here?

He soon had a possible answer, a second set of tracks offset twenty yards from hers. Was she shadowing someone? The rain made it difficult to tell what was happening. The second prints were much larger, those of a man. Service found a place where moss had been disturbed on a fallen tree. Only humans stepped on logs that fell across trails. In his mind, he could see Nantz and the other person. All trackers could see like this. It helped make the trail real. Visualization, a big-shot psych once termed it, one word as good as another.

He tried to check his compass but it was still spinning under some sort of iron ore deposit in the area. Obviously Lemich had used a miner's compass, one designed to ignore magnetic disruptions. Nantz's course looked like she was following a consistent heading, more or less east-northeast. A lightbulb came on. It was about the right course to the general area. Was she headed for one of Knipe's leases? Damn.

Instinct and experience told him to make himself invisible; he removed his blue slicker and hurriedly stuffed it in his pack. He felt a pressing need to hurry but restrained himself. A tracker had to control his emotions, keep them as far out of the work as possible. He moved track to track, not jumping ahead, this a cardinal rule. He compromised only by not taking time to mark the tracks with tape; instead, he broke small branches, or set twigs in crooks of trees, Indian pointers. The Shadow Wolves could read sign as easily as most people read books.

Now and then he made a side jaunt to the second set of tracks. There was a steady course there too.

Suddenly Nantz's tracks veered sharply to the left. Why?

The other tracks mirrored hers. Had one of them spotted the other? Maybe. If you were alone in the woods enough, you learned to feel when you weren't alone. You didn't need sound. The knowledge came from something else, something inside and finely tuned. This took many years to develop; most people never caught on. Which made it pretty easy for most COs to walk up on violators.

Nantz's tracks pivoted ninety degrees back to the right for fifty yards, then ninety degrees left and right again on the original course. It was like a Crazy Ivan, a submarine maneuver he had seen in a movie. Smart Nantz. Good going, Nantz. He thought the sign showed that she was the follower, but her maneuver suggested a different scenario.

Cat and mouse was a dangerous game, especially in the woods. Smart could be dumb if you got too confident, but Nantz wasn't the type to back down. You learned to retreat when it was the best option. He had learned this when Grandma Vonnie or the old man was mad at him, and the lesson had been magnified and reinforced in Vietnam and as a CO.

When Nantz's prints got to firmer ground they grew faint. He slowed his pace. Continuing on, he found torn spiderwebs, the breaks too high for an animal unless it was one from a circus, trained to walk on two legs. He had her again.

A dark line of massive northern white cedars loomed ahead, their fresh scent heightened by the rain. It was a huge cluster of towering conifers, their tops so intertwined that light could barely penetrate. He found where Nantz had hunkered down, waited. Had she seen something?

He moved to find the other track and found evidence of some stones being knocked loose, as if the man had turned suddenly. Service stopped to look, reminding himself to let his eyes do the work. You learned to look for what doesn't fit. There. He saw young ferns wilted and drying up. The rest were verdant and upright. He approached them cautiously, careful not to disturb anything.

What the hell? There was a metal pipe in the ground covered over with uprooted ferns, a clumsy attempt to conceal. The pipe was ten or twelve inches in diameter. Was it an old water well or new one? It was hard to judge unless a pipe was quite old or brand new, and this one was neither. He looked around the immediate area, where the terrain was pancake flat and appeared to be a clearing in the process of being reclaimed by nature. There could've been a cabin at one time, but no ruins were in evidence. In time the forest always took back its own. The larger prints came nowhere near the pipe but angled eastward, drawing away from Nantz and the grove where he had last seen her prints. Maybe the two sets of tracks were coincidental. His mind kept switching between her being the follower and then the followed.

Still, he dogged the larger tracks for about a hundred yards, where the trail began looping back to the south, then eventually turned northwest, the equivalent of a 270-degree turn. The tracks were doubling back on Nantz.

An alarm sounded in his head: He told himself to get back to the cedars and find Nantz *now!*

Her prints led into the grove and disappeared. Where had she gone? He looked up into the trees, remembering the way he had guessed that their firebug climbed into the trees to rest, leaving no trace. He stretched to the lowest branch on the nearest trunk. She could jump to this easily enough. Examining it carefully, he found freshly scuffed bark.

He climbed up. The branches were grown together overhead, forming some semblance of a platform. On this she could have moved laterally above the ground like a little monkey. He founded broken branches here and there, little stuff dried out, and the occasional green branch, broken purposefully, all of them pointing west. Now and then he saw where she had scuffed her boots on the bark. He followed the faint sign all the way to the northwest edge of the grove. Now what?

There were some smaller straight-trunked birches below, not too far to reach and not too many branches, which would make for a tricky descent. They were shinnying trees, as smooth and beckoning as white poles. He used the nearest birch to lower himself quietly to the ground and look around.

She had known he would follow her. She had marked her trail this far and wouldn't fail him now, but if something or someone had spooked her into the trees, the next sign would not be easy to find. Nantz was as cool as she was smart. No panic and no quit, qualities rarely found in men *or* women. He guessed that she had been a star for FEMA.

He made a half circle, moving only a pace or two at a time, studying everything around him, trying to think the way she would think. There was a cluster of nasty-looking slash to the west where ice or wind had battered the forest. Trees died the same as people, and sometimes just as violently. Old age, too. Usually it was a combination of the two.

Think, he told himself. If you chased an animal, it would invariably head for cover. Slash was cover.

He approached the slash, bending low to minimize his profile, poking here and there, looking for anything to tell him where she had gone. There was no blood and he chastised himself for looking for it, but old habits were ingrained.

Where would she leave the next sign for him? Where would he leave it for her?

Deeper, not near the edge, he told himself. He entered the dense slash and looked backward. Most people kept looking ahead, rarely looked back. In war this got you killed. In hunting you missed meat.

He saw it under a log, clear as a *Free Press* headline. Good thinking, Nantz. The track couldn't be seen from the outer edge. You had to crawl into the jumble and look back. Clever move. Big Track had tried to double back on her, but she had caught on. Big Track might still be out there, but Service was getting desperate to find Nantz.

He could resume the follow now. It moved deeper and deeper into the slash. Was she looking for a hidey-hole or just seeking to cover her movements? It was an old Vietnam trick: Stay off the trails, head for the worst shit, every time. Where had she learned this?

She'd left sign but not much. Why? Was she feeling pressured? He was reduced to guesswork.

Then nothing. Nantz was damn good.

"Maridly?" He said in a loud whisper.

"Stay *low*, Grady."

He heard her voice drifting out of cover, but he couldn't see her. It was like a séance. "*Get . . . your . . . big . . . ass . . . down,*" she hissed anxiously.

He squatted and heard his knees creak. Great shape at forty-seven wasn't the same as thirty. To hell with John Glenn and his stunts. All he had to do was sit on his pampered seventy-year-old ass atop a rocket.

He looked around for a long time and saw a slight movement and a pair of eyes peering out from under a deadfall.

She came out tentatively crawling on all fours until she was close. She threw her arms around him and clung to him tightly.

"What big ass?" he asked.

"Bigger than mine," she whispered.

"It's getting dark," he said. "We need to get to the river." If they headed due west they would be above their camp, could move downriver from there, a basic navigational technique for hitting landfall by dead reckoning.

When he stood to look around he felt a sharp pain in his left shoulder. The pain merged with the sound of a rifle report and sent him sprawling.

Nantz crawled on top of him, trying to protect him. He had to push her off.

As the pain intensified he fought to remain calm.

He pushed her away and whispered, "Move it."

"Where?"

"Back where you were."

It was a tight squeeze and the pain in his shoulder was like fire, but he managed to get under cover with her.

"Check for blood," he whispered.

She gently unbuttoned his shirt, moved her hand up his chest, onto his shoulders, and down his sides. She pulled the hand out and showed it to him. Either she had the touch of a spider or he was numb.

"No blood," she said with relief in her voice. "Where *is* he?"

Another mistake. "I don't *know!*" he snapped. He was so focused on finding her that he had committed the cardinal sin of not guarding his six o'clock position. Dumb, he chided himself. He was making too many mistakes in too short a time.

"Do we move?" she asked.

"No, we sit tight," he said.

She nodded. "How long?"

"At least until dark."

"I'm sorry," she said. "I thought I lost him."

"You did. He followed me."

She touched his cheek tenderly.

Night took its time in settling in. Clouds hung overhead; a heavy rain continued to fall. There were no stars and the temperature was dropping. They were wet but had good cover, which afforded crude shelter.

"It's time," he said in the darkness.

"Can you move?"

He grunted. There was more stiffness than pain now. He wondered how much more of a beating he could sustain. Not as much as when he was younger. Then he could will the pain away until it was convenient to deal with it.

"Can you see?" he asked

She tugged on the bill of her hat. "Like a bat."

Nantz didn't lie. She had night eyes the equal of his.

At the river camp they got into her tent. He rationalized that it was too wet to put his up now.

"What were you doing out there?" he asked.

"I saw a guy with a rifle headed down the east bank and I followed him. He checked out the log-slide burn, right where we found the body, then he headed out. I thought, Weird, and wondered if it was the same guy you talked about seeing. I followed him. When he got to that rocky area he didn't do much, but he disappeared. He was there and then he wasn't. I thought, Uh oh. The mouse had become the cat. I tried to lose him when I got lucky and saw him cutting back on me. I knew it was time for me to get upstairs. I *knew* you'd figure it out. Take off your shirt," she added.

She helped, using a small flashlight with a red lens to examine him. "Not a bullet."

"I think it was a tree branch," he said. "The bullet must've knocked it down."

"Jesus, Grady. It's a nasty bruise. Does it feel like something's broken?"

"Right now it's just stiff."

"*Stiff* can be good," she said, teasingly.

"Nantz."

"Okay, okay, I'm just trying to lighten us up. I'm scared shitless and we need to get you to a hospital."

She dug a small leather pouch out of her pocket, dumping the contents on her sleeping bag. There were more than a dozen small stones. He picked them up. Three were yellowish, clear, and greasy.

"Goddammit," he said.

"I was sick when I found them. Then I caught a glimpse of the guy while I was in the water. Grady, there are pebbles like this all over in that one spot. That guy tried to *kill* you!"

She was reacting to overlapping realities. He shared the feeling.

"Maybe," he said. The light had been bad and getting worse. It was also possible he meant to miss, though a reason for this eluded him. "Did you see a rifle?"

"Yes."

"Scoped?"

"It looked that way. It was one of those black rifles."

Not enough to identify it, and he cautioned himself against assumptions. "How well did you see the guy?" he asked.

"Real."

"Describe him."

"I don't need to."

"Nantz."

She reached into her pack, took out her camera, a compact 35 millimeter with a 75- to 150-millimeter lens.

"He's in here," she said, tapping the body.

"You got pictures?"

"If the rain doesn't get to them." She poked him playfully and he winced. "Oh God. I'm sorry."

She tried to hug him, which made him hurt more and recoil. "Shit," he said.

"That does it, Service. I am taking your stubborn ass to a hospital."

He pointed up. The rain was pummeling the rain fly above the tent. "We're staying put until first light," he said.

"Last night you couldn't wait to get rid of me," she said.

He smiled. "You handled yourself damn well today."

"Don't shine me, Service."

He laughed, even though it made him hurt. "The chopper we're looking for? It's probably black, not blue. And Joe Flap may have found it. Voydanov has some sort of color blindness."

"That would mean he couldn't see any color or would have red-green abnormalities."

"Christ, are you always a nitpicker?"

"I'm a perfectionist," she said. "Is *that* a crime? If I do something, I do it right. And I expect the same from others."

He rested but did not sleep and kept his sidearm by his hand. The pain came and went. They lay side by side in her unzipped sleeping bag and awoke to a clear sky and bright blades of sun knifing through the tree-tops. Raindrops lay on leaves, gleaming like diamonds.

Ironic, he thought.

"Now can we get you to the hospital?"

The shoulder was stiff and painful to move.

"Okay, but we say nothing about the shooting."

"Why?" She was skeptical, which was a good way to be.

"If we report it, it's out of our hands. If the cops move in, they'll start poking. But if we keep it quiet for now, nothing happens, and the other side will be wondering what we're up to."

"The other side won't be alone," she said.

They drove to the emergency room at the hospital in Escanaba. The doctor's verdict: a slight shoulder separation. The doctor taped Service tight and told him to rest. His arm was put in a sling to lessen the pull on the shoulder. As soon as they were outside, he took off the sling and dropped it in a hospital trash bin.

"Macho," she said. "That's Spanish for stupid."

He grinned. "Let's get that film developed."

They went to Big K and the one-hour photo counter.

When the pictures came back, Service fanned them out on the counter and looked at them. "Damn," he said.

"What?"

"This isn't the guy I saw on the river." How long did they have to wait for a break? Just one. Driven by habit, he asked for six prints of the man.

When the prints were done, Nantz drove him to his cabin and dropped him off.

"I'll come back tomorrow. We'll fetch your truck then."

He didn't invite her in and she didn't make an overture. He ignored his answering machine, took six Motrin tablets. He didn't bother to take off his clothes, just eased himself onto his footlocker sleeping pad. He needed real sleep. More than that, he needed luck. But the footlockers felt like shit and he got up and went over to Kira's bed and immediately dropped into deep sleep.

17

H e was unshowered, unshaven, and aching. Nantz stood in the doorway, looking at him.

"You have a funeral today," she announced.

"How do you know?"

"Word travels in the family," she said.

He had been so absorbed with the previous day's events that he had forgotten. No wonder Kira had made a run for it. He could hardly move his arm.

Nantz was not in uniform. She wore a plain black dress with a short hemline and black pumps with low heels.

"What?" she asked, walking in.

"Nothing."

"Liar," she said. She helped him out of bed and led him back to the sink in the shower area.

"Shirt off," she said, an order, not a request.

When he didn't react she said, "Off."

He did as he was told, accepting her help. He stood in front of the little mirror eyeing the gray in his whiskers.

She soaped and lathered his face, shaved him. She had sure hands, moving the razor confidently and quickly. "You've done this before?"

"None of your business. Point your chin up."

When she was done she gently urged him to the shower, pushed the curtain aside, and turned on the hot water. She undid his belt and zipper and used her thumbs to drop his trousers and underwear. She held the curtain back for him. He stepped in gingerly and used his good hand to shampoo his hair. The hot water felt good.

The shower curtain snapped open. Nantz held out a cup of coffee, examining him with her eyes, looking skeptical. "Hurry it up. We'll get your truck after the funeral. At your speed this morning we'll be late as it is."

"Nag."

She snapped the shower curtain shut.

When he stepped out, she was holding a towel and a suit on a hanger. His only suit, basic black and at least a decade old.

"Get my uniform," he said. "I'm a pallbearer."

"With that shoulder?"

"I have two," he said. "Uniform. Please."

She toweled him dry and helped him dress. She was gentle and all business.

Nantz was exasperated when he insisted she stop at the Marquette County Jail. Limpy Allerdyce looked under the weather and, for once, he could sympathize. He showed Limpy the photograph Nantz had taken.

"Who's that?" Allerdyce asked.

"Don't bullshit me, Limpy."

The prisoner looked away. "I want out of here."

"You know the rules. Why did you point me to the tract?"

"You're the fish cop. Figure it out."

"This asshole took a shot at me." Service slapped the photo against the edge of the table.

Allerdyce still didn't look at him. "Guys who shoot at people don't usually miss."

There was no amplification of the statement. Meaning? A warning shot? He had already considered that possibility and dismissed it. What was Limpy's point?

"I don't back off," Service said.

"Big fucking secret. I got me a lawyer. He says you can't hold me like this."

"There's a backlog, Limpy. The wheels of justice turn slowly."

Actually, he was surprised that all Doolin had done was arraign Limpy.

"Trey Kerr," Limpy said. "But you didn't hear that name from me."

"Where do I look?"

"I gotta do everything for you?"

Service fought back tears at the cemetery and felt a terrible sadness enveloping him. He took a handle of the casket and gutted it out. His right shoulder still hurt like hell. McKower watched him like a hawk.

A flag was folded, presented to the widow by Captain Ware Grant, the U.P. field boss. Volleys of shots were fired by an honor guard. "Taps" moaned. The whole thing left him sapped and feeling exhausted.

Kira was there, smiling halfheartedly in his direction. She mouthed, "I really am sorry," but made no attempt to approach him. Was she feeling guilty or relieved?

He saw Doolin and got him aside. "What's with Limpy?" Service asked.

"We're hanging on to him, which is what you wanted." Doolin lit a cigarette.

"He says he has a lawyer."

"So what? He's a parolee and he broke the rules. We have enough on Allerdyce to hold him. His lawyer can make legal music, but it won't come to anything. Limpy's charged. That gives us a year to work with."

"Can you check a name for me?"

"No problem."

"Trey Kerr." Service spelled it a couple of ways.

Doolin made a note. "Is this from Limpy?"

"A little bird."

Doolin grinned. "Fuckin' stoolie bird, I'll betcha."

Service hugged Jean and Lanny Harris, nodded to Rollie's father, chatted idly with some of his brothers and sisters, others. Family, Nantz had said, and she was right. It was a sad family, trying like hell to be brave.

Sergeant Charlie Parker looked haggard but sidled up to Service as if they were now asshole buddies. McKower caught this and cocked an eyebrow. Service shrugged. He looked for Gus Turnage but didn't see him. It was unusual that Gus would miss the funeral.

Flap was there, Hathoot, Sergeant Ralph Smoke. At least thirty field COs, their spouses, friends, relatives, other cops. It was a good turnout; no less than Rollie deserved.

There had been no eulogy. Rollie wanted it that way, Jean told him, and he understood. What did Rollie care now? He wanted to say it was before Rollie's time to go, but your time was your time. There was no logic to it. If there had been a logic he and Tree would have never gotten out of Vietnam. When his own time did come he wanted his friends to get drunk and forget all the mumbo jumbo. He had five grand earmarked in his will just for this. It would be a hell of a party, one he'd hate to miss.

Joe Flap stood next to him. "When your old man kicked off, we were all drunk for three days. I'm headed for Skanee now for a little recce."

Kira made her way through the mourners to him, eyeing him critically. "Newf is in my truck," she said.

He followed her. Newf bounded out and jumped up, knocking him off balance. When he winced Kira said, "What's wrong?"

Newf leaned against him, licking his hand.

Kira opened her purse and gave him a large plastic vial. "Your stones," she said, quietly adding, "Under the circumstances, I don't feel like I can keep them. I've talked to Cece and she promises to keep quiet."

"Thanks for watching the dog." He wondered if he could trust Cece. Secrets like this had a way of getting out.

"Anytime," she said. "I mean that."

When the mourners began to depart for the wake Nantz tried to help him into the truck, but he pulled away and got in on his own, not wanting anybody to see he was hurt. The funeral had sent him into an emotional spin. Newf jumped in back and went from side to side, looking out.

"I hate funerals," Nantz said. "Everybody is going back to Jean's for the wake," she added.

"Just drive," Service said. Rollie was dead. Jean and Lanny had insurance, but not Rollie. It was a shitty trade. He had been to too many funerals of good people and what did it all amount to? You worked twenty-five or thirty years, retired, faded away, and died, this last part a mere formality. The truth was that you first died when you turned in your badge. Your physical passing was anticlimactic. Was it worth dedicating yourself to something most people didn't give a shit about? He was lost in his own thoughts, feeling morose. Had the bullet in the tract been a warning or a try? The jury was still out, but warning or not, he had once again been inches from his own funeral.

"We're here," Nantz said.

Service saw his truck and couldn't recall anything of the long drive from Big Bay.

"Lost in your thoughts?" Nantz asked.

He nodded.

"It happens," she said.

It hadn't happened in Vietnam. Only here, and only in recent years. There, life had meant nothing. But perhaps life was an illusion here too.

He began talking without thinking about what it was he was trying to say. "I quit hockey because I nearly killed a guy from Michigan Tech. He was their tough guy. We fought in those days, just like pros. Vicious fights, like animals. He never played again. I finished that season, got my degree, and told myself, That's that. I pitched my skates in the garbage."

"We all feel vulnerable at funerals," she said. "We think about paths already taken and paths that lay ahead, and wonder if any of it means any-thing."

"I don't feel vulnerable," he said.

She shook her head, backed up her truck, and headed back down the dirt road.

"What about my truck, Nantz?"

"Yada yada," she said. "I'm driving."

They drove thirty minutes to Gladstone and down a hundred-yard-long driveway through white pines to a large house on the cliff called the Bluff. It would be a pain to plow in winter. The bluff faced Little Bay de Noc. There were no neighbors, and the house was set back in from the road a couple of hundred yards. When she stopped in the driveway, he stared at the house. It was old fashioned in style, with two stories, painted pale blue with white accents. It had gables and a cedar-shingled roof. There was a wraparound porch and a detached garage painted the same as the house. He saw lumber and sawhorses on the lawn. A face-lift was in progress.

"Mine," she said, sensing his curiosity.

"Yours?" How did she afford this on a government salary?

"From my dad."

He took Newf by the collar and followed her into the house, which was filled with antiques, the walls covered with paintings. The wall-to-wall carpeting was light colored and deep.

"Comfortable," he said.

She got a bottle of Jack Daniels and two shot glasses. She sat on a long yellow couch and patted a cushion. He sat down with her as she filled the glasses. The dog stretched out on the floor and put her head down.

"Rollie Harris," she said, holding up her glass. She drank it in one swallow.

"Rollie Harris," Service said, doing the same.

She poured a second shot and then a third.

"To life," she said after the fourth one. "Not death."

After pouring the fifth shot she said, "Here we are."

"Everybody's got to be somewhere," he said. They clicked glasses.

"Profound," she said, refilling the glasses. "To the Mosquito."

And so it went, her face growing red, his mind fogging over.

She unfolded her feet from beneath her and flipped a shoe, which tumbled end over end across the room. Then she stood, lifted her dress, and peeled off her pantyhose, tossing them in his lap.

"This is not an invitation to boom boom," she said, slumping down beside him.

He laughed.

"It's not technically true," she said wistfully.

"What's not?"

"Cornell."

"Where you're from."

"Pffff," she said, blowing air through her lips. "Grosse Pointe, Lake Shore Drive — an address in the hundreds. Glanceys, Fords, Old Lady Dodge, piles of car money. Old money, old ways, shopping on the Hill, proms at the War Memorial, parties at the Yacht Club, Hunt Club, the Little Club — so exclusive the membership list was top secret. My dad had an advertising agency. GM was his main client. My mom loved the trappings, but Dad was always a country boy. He bought a farm near Cornell. We spent summers there, Mom and me. Us there, Dad in Detroit. Free-range hormones. She went one way, he went another."

She added, "Actually, they both went all the way, just not with each other. When the Japanese began to cut into the US car biz, Dad sold his agency. He took half and Mom took half. They split the money and the marriage. "He divorced my mom and moved up here. Then he met a woman and he was like a kid again. They married and headed for Colorado."

"Did the divorce bother you?"

She thought before answering. "Not really. I never could see my mom and dad together. It was better this way for both of them."

She poured two more shots. "Then he died. Last winter. I was there. The last thing he said? 'I'm not sure I'm ready for *this* audit. I laughed out loud. My dad could always make me laugh."

"Sorry," Service said.

"He left me this house and I was fed up with FEMA's gig."

"And here you are."

She lifted her glass in salute. "I'm loaded," she whispered.

"We both are."

"No," she said. "We are both drunk, but I am *loaded*." She rubbed her forefinger and thumb together. "Like that. Geidas, long green, shekels, buckaroos."

"Poor little rich girl."

Her face turned serious. "Kira seems nice. What's with you two?"

"Nothing," he said, the truth in one word.

He sort of remembered stumbling up stairs together and falling onto a king-sized bed.

There were no memories after that. He awoke naked with an equally naked Nantz beside him, her leg draped over his, her dark hair mussed, her eyes swollen. His shoulder ached.

"We buried your LT," she said. "And we could have been killed. Your lady moved out. We got drunk, end of story. We had to sleep somewhere."

She blinked and rubbed her eyes. "You know what your lady said? 'Good luck.' How do you like being a baton that gets passed?"

He said nothing. Nantz said, "She's nice enough, but too soft for you."

She rolled over on her side. "Now I need more sleep. Don't wake me unless there's food."

And she was out.

He had never met anyone like her.

Which could be good or bad.

He slept too.

Doolin answered his phone later that morning. "Doolin here."

"Trey Kerr," Service said.

"Where are you? I've been leaving messages. This Kerr is a *piece of work*. You name it, he's done it. Rap sheet as long as a muskie. He was in Jackson but the conviction was overturned on a technicality and they had to let him walk. Right out of sight. There's another warrant out on him now. He had a fight in a bar, and the other guy croaked from a heart attack. Nobody's seen Kerr in months and guess what: That little bird you talked to was his cellmate for a while."

Limpy *did* know something, maybe a lot more than he was letting on. "Jerry's autopsy?"

"Done, ruled a homicide. You don't sound well."

Service said, "Can we release the body?"

"If that's what you want."

"I do, and I also want you to withdraw charges on Limpy and let him go."

"Are you nuts?"

It was a distinct possibility. "I need him out. Tomorrow. I'll pick him up."

"It's gonna be hell getting a judge to buy this."

"Talk to Onty Peltinen. He'll play ball."

"What the hell is going on, Grady?"

"I'm trying to maintain momentum."

Pause at the other end. "You're a crazy fucker, just like your old man."

Service smiled at the association, hung up the phone, and opened Nantz's refrigerator.

Nantz drove him back to his truck after a lunch of pancakes and sausages.

"Thanks," he said. "For everything."

"Anytime, anyplace," she said. "What should I do with the pebbles?"

He gave her the packet Kira had given him. "Hang on to all of them."

What *should* they do about them? Not just those they had, but all those just lying in the stream, awaiting discovery?

"Are you okay?" she asked.

"Yep," he said. It was not quite true. What was happening between them? He wasn't sure he wanted to know.

"You know, you don't have to carry the whole load," she said.

"What's that mean?"

"You have good people you can depend on. People who maybe know how to do things you don't."

She flipped him a half salute, started to walked away, stopped and came back.

"I don't want to leave this hanging and I can see in your eyes that you don't get it. The answer is no, we did not do the deed. When we do, and please note I said 'when,' not 'if,' we will do it when we are both completely sober and in full possession of all our faculties. Any further questions?"

He shook his head dumbly and watched her get into her truck and drive away.

Was Maridly Nantz real?

Service let Newf run around outside while he called Gus Turnage, who picked up his phone on the first ring. "We missed you at the funeral," Service said.

Turnage sounded harried. "No time. Rollie would understand. This Fox guy? He's a rotten apple for sure. He got grants on false pretenses, embezzling money from the feds and the university. Tech kicked him out in the standard academic way. No blame, just git. And they don't want publicity. They hope it will just go away. And here's a kicker: Fox has done work for Knipe's company."

It figured. Disparate atoms orbiting the same flawed nucleus.

"Great job, my friend."

"That's it?"

"For now."

"You want a photograph of Fox?"

"You bet."

"Bearclaw is headed over to HQ today. I can give it to her to bring to you."

Bearclaw was Betty Very, the CO in Ontonagon. She was a very tough lady who had handled more trouble bears than anybody in the history of the DNR and had a terrible set of scars on her face as proof.

"Ask Betty to leave an envelope with my name on it. I've got a photo for you too. The name is Kerr. He's tied into all this, I just don't know how yet."

"Consider it done. How're Jean and Lanny?"

"Coping," Service said.

"That's about all they can do," Turnage said.

Limpy nodded when he saw Service.

"This your doing?"

"Yeah, and I'm your taxi. I win all the prizes today."

"You shoulda sent Honeypat," Limpy shot back.

"I'm a cabbie, not a pimp."

Limpy grinned.

They headed south in the truck. Service had picked up a six-pack of beer and gave it to Limpy.

"You were Kerr's cellmate."

"Yah, he's a crazy fuck, eh."

"What's his connection to Jerry?"

"Kerr called me, said he needed help for a couple of jobs. Nothing serious. He needed a pulpjack. I figured they were going to snatch a little lumber, you know?" Service knew. Timber theft was a continuous problem. "Said he'd pay good. I gave him Jerry's name."

"You think he killed Jerry?"

Limpy looked straight ahead, said nothing.

"You're out, Limpy, but I can park your ass right back inside."

"My kin is *my* business."

"You had an arrangement with my old man. Now we're going to have one, you and me. You give me information and I'll guarantee the cops get Jerry's killer. You're out, but if you get out of line, you're going back in."

"You mean not even the occasional chop of high-speed beef?"

"I didn't hear that."

"I don't like depending on others," Limpy said.

"That makes two of us. You're out for the moment, but it's up to you to keep it that way."

Limpy popped the tab of a beer and took a long pull. "I don't wanna go back inside, eh? But I won't wait forever. Family means something. I don't got much else."

"You find something out, you tell me."

"I'll do 'er, but mark my words, not forever."

Limpy wanted to be dropped on a two-track so he could hike cross-country into his compound to arrive unannounced. The old man took the empty beer cans with him.

"Dime's a dime, eh?" Michigan had a deposit law for bottles and cans.

Allerdyce was a hard case, but he had some values. If his old man had worked with Limpy, he could too. A CO didn't have to like someone to work with them. You learned this early or perished, and it didn't hurt to remind yourself from time to time. In the years ahead Limpy could be a useful source. Maybe. Right now he needed to find Jerry's killer and make sure Limpy didn't skulk off with revenge in mind. There was too damn much going down.

A green double-cab truck was pulled into his yard. Betty Very was sitting on his porch with a thermos of coffee.

"You look like crap," she said.

The scars on her face were magenta. Said she wouldn't have plastic surgery until she retired. Why get it done only to have to get it done again? At six feet and 180, she was physically imposing, a big woman with square lines, no fat, and the legs of a pulling guard.

"You didn't have to drop the envelope here."

"Stop bitching."

He laughed. "How's Bearclaw?"

"Sick as hell of blackies. I'm thinking about giving the critters contraceptives."

He smiled and accepted the envelope.

"Take care," he said as she got up to leave.

"The less time I have to spend at HQ, the better I like it," Very said. "You hear anything about McKower getting Rollie's job?"

"It's mostly speculation. She passed the LT exam."

"Well, I hope she gets it," Very said. "As a rule, I don't like dinky women in these jobs, but McKower works bigger than she looks." He gave her a print from Nantz's roll and asked her to drop the photo with Turnage on her way home.

When she was gone, he opened the envelope and removed the photograph.

"Fuck!" Fox was the shooter, not Kerr. Had he been snookered by Limpy?

Limpy was surprised to see him again so soon. He shuffled barefoot onto the porch in soiled, striped boxers. "Now what?"

Service showed him the photograph. "That's *not* Kerr."

Allerdyce glanced at the picture. "So?"

"This guy took a shot at me."

"I never saw this asshole before."

"You bullshitted me."

"Don't be blowin' no gasket."

"You're going back in."

Limpy looked shaky, yelled into the screen door, "Honeypat, bring us beer, woman."

"I don't drink on duty," Service said.

"Your old man did."

"And it cost him his life, too."

Honeypat came out with beer cans in hand. "Hey," she said, "Limpy told me you got him cut loose. That was real nice of you."

"He's going back."

The beers fell to the floor, shooting foam onto Limpy's feet.

"Hold on just a damn minute!" Limpy snapped. "I give you my word, and Limpy don't break his word."

"You lied to me."

"I said I knew Kerr. The picture ain't Kerr." He turned to Honeypat and said, "Scoot your ass inside."

Service wanted to smack him but refrained.

"Where's Kerr?" Service asked.

"Figure it out: Jerry's dead and Kerr done disappeared."

"He ran."

" 'Course he ran. He's a con and they was on his tail. But guys like Kerr, they don't run for for long. He ain't been seen, so maybe he ain't findable. You following me?"

"Talk plain."

"Maybe Kerr got himself whacked too."

Service rubbed his face, sat down. "I guess I will take that beer."

"Honeypat," Limpy barked. "Get your sweet ass back out here."

"I give you my word, sonny," he said to the CO. "Limpy ain't worth beans, but his word is."

Another game? Service's instinct said no. This seemed to be from the heart, an earnest little black heart. He suspected Allerdyce would now do anything to stay out of prison.

"Shoulda got yourself a mug shot," Allerdyce said. "You brung me a picture and I give you a name and you added one and one and got thirteen or something. I never said it was Kerr in that picture of yours. You screw up, don't come rattling my chain."

He hated to admit it, but Limpy was right. He should have gotten a mug shot to compare with Nantz's photo.

"I'm sorry," Service said.

Allerdyce flashed a crooked grin. "You're a lot like that old man o' yours, sonny."

Honeypat brought two more cans of beer. She patted Limpy's head, said, "I'll be waiting," and went back inside.

Limpy's sleeping with his daughter-in-law was sick. Service took a beer and drank. It was tepid. More and more he was like his old man. He wasn't sure if he should be pleased or depressed. Would his old man have missed checking a mug shot? He doubted it. The old man was hell on mistakes, his or anybody else's.

Jerry Allerdyce had been murdered in the tract. Limpy had tried to setup Kerr and Jerry. Had they connected? Fox had been in the tract, and taken a shot at Nantz and him. Too damn many coincidences to ignore. So where was Fox now? All this had to be connected.

He thanked Limpy for the beer and called Nantz on the way out of Limpy's.

"How's the shoulder?" she asked.

"It hurts. Are you up for company tomorrow?"

She laughed happily. "*Dumb* question, Service. What's wrong with tonight?"

"I'll pick you up tomorrow morning, bright and early," he said. She was a pip.

He drove south to Escanaba and the Delta County Sheriff's Department and asked one of the deputies in the dispatching office to pull a mug shot of Kerr off the state computer. Service stuck the photo in his pocket, went home and fed Newf and Cat, and spent a restless evening thinking about Kerr and Jerry Allerdyce.

18

Nantz was surprised when Service pulled up to her house and told her to get her gear. Newf sat in the space behind the seats and hung her head over, seeking Nantz's attention. As they drove northeast, he told her everything about Limpy, Kerr, the whole thing, start to finish. She listened attentively and asked no questions.

They were in the Mosquito Tract again. As it usually did, yesterday's rain had cleaned the landscape, washing away prints and signs.

They secured the truck, took their packs, and hiked back into the area where he had found the odd pipe protruding from the ground. Newf ranged ahead of them, crisscrossing their path.

"Definitely a well," she said, with no more than a cursory glance at the pipe.

"How can you be so certain?"

"It's not rocket science, Service. Look at the weld, type of pipe. That dates it."

How did she know so much? "Dates it to when?"

"It's Scorzi pipe, which was used in the fifties."

"You weren't born then."

"Dad's agency handled more than GM. I used to go to trade shows with him. It's Scorzi pipe, commonly used for wells. What are we looking for?" Nantz asked.

"I'm not sure," which was technically true, but not entirely accurate. Jerry Allerdyce had been dumped in the fire. There had been a definite attempt to cover up, but it wasn't the work of a pro. This killer was an amateur. With a pro, you rarely found bodies.

They searched methodically.

Service saw a coyote trot by, tail down, glance over its shoulder at them, and keep going. Newf also saw the animal, but looked at Service. He told her to ignore it and she did.

East of the pipe area there were dozens of ravens in pin oaks. The birds were black and shiny, as if they had been recently polished. Ravens roosted in groups at night, but usually split up by day.

Guard birds squawked warnings, tree to tree. A din of discordant sounds echoed through the woods. There was nothing pretty about a raven's voice, he thought. Maybe they were telling jokes. No way to know. Only Indians claimed to speak raven.

Nantz was advancing along the edge of a semi-open area, ferns up to her thighs, when he signaled for her to stop.

There were lots of messengers in the woods if you knew how to look and listen. Parents taught their kids to cross streets this way: Stop, look, listen. It was the same proposition out here. What were the ravens saying today?

A few of the black birds fluttered down toward the ground ahead, then lifted up, spewing feathers. Back and forth, up and down. They seemed to be expending energy for nothing. Birds and animals seldom wasted efforts. He waited and watched as they flitted about. Nervous birds? Curious was more like it.

About what?

He pointed and Nantz nodded and started walking again. They merged in the woods, walked through some cedars and paper birches toward a blackwater swamp.

"What's wrong?" she wanted to know.

"Ravens don't flock by day."

"I do," she said. Then, "Oh, you said 'flock.' "

He laughed.

She looked ahead and squinted. "Ravens. They like dead stuff, easy pickings on the roadsides. Fast food." Her pale green shirt was damp with sweat.

He nodded. What were the birds thinking about? Hoping for something? No, animals didn't have hope. Animals dealt solely with facts. Except Newf. It was too early to tell about her.

The swamp turned out to be a pond made by beavers. In other parts of the U.P. the DNR spent a lot of time dynamiting beaver dams, but not here in the tract. The birds were clustered in trees ringing the edge of the water.

Nantz looked down at the still black water and made a face. "Loon-shit bottom," she said.

Service slid off his pack, and took out nylon rope, moving deliberately. He fixed the rope in two loops, using carabiners. Bought by him, not the DNR.

"You're going in that?" she asked.

"Think I have to," he said.

"Why?"

"I'm not sure. All I know is something is telling me to do this."

"Let me do it," she said. "I'm lighter."

"I'm taller," he said, countering.

"I'm more buoyant." She cupped her breasts with her hands and lifted for emphasis.

He grinned. "The water will be cold."

"Women have extra fat to insulate them."

"You don't."

"A compliment, Service? God almighty. How about this, I have *two* good shoulders."

"There'll be leeches," he said, as he took a rope from his pack and began tying a large loop and two smaller ones off the main one.

She blinked and held up her hands. "You win."

They both laughed. He stripped to his skivvies, placed one leg in each of the small loops and fastened the larger one around his waist, securing it with a half hitch to a metal carabiner. He anchored the rope to a tree and stretched it out toward the water. "If I get stuck," he said, "I'll pull myself out."

"If you get stuck, I'll empty the whole damn swamp to get you out," Nantz said.

He got himself a long stick, held the rope in one hand, and waded in one tentative step at a time. He had never been crazy about water, even when it was clear and clean. When his feet dug into the muddy bottom, a terrible smell rose to the surface. From the waist down he was freezing in muck. His stick hit weeds, debris, the usual stuff in beaver ponds.

He moved deliberately, sweeping ahead with the stick like a blind man, probing for obstructions, finding plenty, mostly rotting logs, under water a long time, nature recycling itself.

It was hard work. Freezing below, sweating on top.

Nantz watched in silence, not taking her eyes off him.

He was on the verge of getting out to warm up when his probe hit something solid.

Nantz yelled, "You're going to freeze."

He took a deep breath and dropped quietly below the surface, following the stick down, using his hands to feel around, then surfaced, blowing water.

Nantz moved toward the edge of the bank.

"There's another rope in my pack. Throw it to me," he said when he popped to the surface. Rope in hand, he slid under the water again, and when he came up sputtering and pulling himself hand over hand along the rope anchored to the tree on shore, his legs splayed behind him, a frog with no kick. His injured shoulder burned. Nantz helped him onto shore and felt his legs. Newf bumped against him. Service stretched his aching shoulder and winced, then stood and began hauling the second rope. A yellow saw eventually came to shore dripping black muck. He pulled the chain saw onto the bank and stepped back into the water. He went to the end of his rope and began diving, staying down for short periods before surfacing for air. "I can't see down there," he said. "I have to feel my way."

Twenty minutes later he came ashore.

"You're blue," she said, rubbing his legs vigorously. "What's down there?"

"A body," he said. Kerr, perhaps, but he kept this to himself.

"Jesus," she said. "Now do we call the county?"

"I guess there's no choice this time. The muskrats and fish will eat the evidence. If there is any."

Two bodies to account for now. He had a strong feeling that this body was Kerr. It had to be Kerr. Both men had presumably been working together. If so, where was Fox? If this was Kerr, why wasn't he killed at the fire with Jerry? Allerdyce, the ridgerunner, was not too bright, but Kerr was a hard con. Kerr would smell out a threat or double cross and make a break. This could explain the distance from the log slide, and Jerry's body. But if this was Kerr, Fox had been able to run him down and finish him. Fox knew the woods, how to track, a pro at finding and an amateur at killing, a dangerous combination.

"No leeches," Nantz said.

"What?"

"No leeches."

"I guess I was lucky," he said.

"Liar," she shot back.

They hiked back to the truck and waited for the county, whose people responded quickly, bringing recovery gear. As he knew they would, they looked to Service to recover the body. COs invariably drew this duty: accidents, suicides, murders, kids, adults, it didn't matter who or what. If you were a woods cop, you were supposed to be able to find and fetch bodies from the woods. They led the people from the sheriff's department to the pond. Service put on a dry suit and harness and began the grisly work. The body was stiff and blue and bloated. Cold water helped preserve remains, but the fish and other aquatic animals had started in on it. The dead man was shot in the back, same as Jerry. Fingerprints and teeth would confirm the identity, but he already knew it was Kerr.

They told the cops the find was accidental, which was technically true, but not the whole story. A fib would have to suffice until he could figure things out, see where to take this thing next.

They looked at the body in silence.

"No leeches on him either," Nantz observed sarcastically.

"They prefer live flesh," he said.

"I didn't need to hear that," she said, making a sour face.

Service pulled into Nantz's driveway. She invited him in for a shower and hot coffee, but a call came in from Joe Flap, his cellular patched through to Service's radio. Nantz went inside.

Flap's radio technique had been honed over decades. He understood the lack of security over the cellular and reported, "Nobody home, but the blackbird is in good shape."

"Any problems?"

"Nope, just got myself lost like a flatlander and walked up to the place to get directions, which could happen to any dumb bastard from down below, right?"

"Right," Service said. Flap knew all the tricks.

"You want me to stay put?"

"I'll meet you." Flap explained where they should meet and they broke off the call.

Nantz came out of the house.

"I've got to go," he said.

"You need rest. Your eyes are sunk in your head and you have a weird stare." She gave him a kiss. It started as chaste, on the cheek, but she moved her mouth to his and they locked on, the effect that of a red-hot poker shoved sharply into his brain, blurring his vision. He was left with near-total disorientation, a first: carnal vertigo.

"I'm not leaving forever," he told her.

"I just guaranteed that," she said.

"You're pretty sure of yourself."

"A lot of people say the same thing about you," she said.

He had no idea what would come from his meeting with Flap, but suspected a stakeout was in the offing. "Could you take Newf?"

She smiled. "That's a pretty big step for a man, trusting the girlfriend with your dog."

" 'Girlfriend'?"

She opened the truck door and said the dog's name. Newf jumped out, her tail wagging. "Girlfriend. Got a better word?"

"I guess not."

"That's not exactly a ringing endorsement, Service."

He wasn't sure what to say, so he said nothing.

Nantz rubbed his shoulder tenderly. "Be careful, okay?"

Joe Flap looked surprised when Service crept up to his surveillance site in a dense stand of popples along the edge of a swale that faced the cabin and helicopter.

"You got here quick."

"I flew on four wheels."

Pranger frowned. "I never speed on four wheels. Too many damn fools out there."

"Anybody show?"

"Not yet," Flap said with a devilish grin. "The Huey's well maintained, but it looks to me like nobody's been in the shack for a while."

Service used his binoculars to survey the scene two hundred yards away. The chopper was at the edge of a field, covered with a camo tarp made of rubber ribbons, the stuff they made ghillie suits from and now favored by bow hunters. The shack was unpainted, set back in the woods, which made it pretty much like most backwoods camps in the U.P. Somebody had flown in and left the chopper here. Why? If the flights to the Tract had originated here and were done, wouldn't they move the chopper to a secure site? There were no parts here, no gas, no maintenance, no options. Could there be more flights ahead?

Service warned himself to be careful about what he said next.

"How reliable's a Huey?" Service asked the old pilot.

Flap looked at him, his leathery face creasing. "If it's on the ground, the worst thing can happen is a broken fuel line. No gas, no go."

Good old Pranger. He was cagey and understood the reason for the question.

"Did you find any fuel at the camp?"

"No aviation fuel, but these old heaps will fly on most anything, plain old gas, diesel fuel, anything made from petroleum, you name it."

"Why don't you take a break?" Service said.

He needed to disable the chopper and Joe needed to be able to testify he knew nothing, saw nothing, and was not part of what happened. Flap knew the score in such matters. Some of the newer COs were book people and neither worldly, nor wise. Some would learn and some wouldn't. The horseblankets learned from doing, not books.

Service scouted the area cautiously. All he found that looked to be relatively new was a two-hundred-gallon fuel oil tank behind the shack. A new tank at an old shack, a nonfit. Everything Flap mentioned was petroleum based. Could the Huey fly on fuel oil? Maybe. Better be safe. He checked the gauge on the tank. It was full. "Damn," he said out loud. "This valve seems open. Better close it, be a Good Samaritan. Honest mistake, Your Honor." Sometimes you bent little laws to keep the big ones from getting broken. He heard the oil go *glug-glug*. Nice sound. He checked the gauge again and saw that the volume was falling slowly. Good.

He went to the chopper, crawled under the camo cover, and looked around, opening panels. There was a confusing maze of lines and pipes inside the machine. By process of elimination he located the main fuel line and a pressure lock. It was tight. He used the butt of his .40-cal to knock it loose, then twisted it. He hand-tightened it again, but not all the way, creating a small leak. In a few hours the chopper's fuel tank would be bone dry. The pilot would come back, find no fuel in the tank behind the cabin and none in the Huey. The pilot might siphon gas from his vehicle, but what good would that do? Forty-gallon tank, max, 6 pounds per gallon, 240 in fuel, barely enough to make the Huey fart.

A reasonably intelligent person would conclude sabotage and he would be right. Would he call for help? There was no phone line to the shack. A cellular? Not likely. Too easily eavesdropped. No, he'd size up the situation and bug out. The big question was how long they would have to wait. Hours, days? He had to prepare for the worst. It was time to babysit the chopper.

He tried McKower at the office, but she had gone off duty. He used his cellular instead and caught her at home. He heard her daughters squealing in the background.

"I'm on the chiller," he told McKower. Chiller was their term for the cellular because it chilled and retarded official conversations. "I need assistance. Those two probies, Sarah and Dan, can I borrow them?"

"Call me back on a secure line."

She was perturbed. He had always been able to read her moods.

"No time for that. I'm sort of in a bind here."

"Where are you?"

"They should meet me at Mossy Camp." Mossy Camp was an area on the west slope of the Huron Mountains he had named years ago when she was his probie, a long time ago. It was a great place for brookies, and a name only she knew. The place had been good for more than brookies back then.

"I'll do what I can," she said.

There was no emotion in her voice now. He checked his watch.

"They should meet me at nine tonight. If the fishing's good, we may have to stay a while."

"The fishing *better* be good," she said firmly.

Ouch. A threat, and not an idle one either. There was no way he could explain all this. She was about to become an LT and would have to walk the straight and narrow even more than she had as a sergeant. A CO working the field had more room to maneuver.

"Thanks, Lis."

She hung up. She was pissed at him, not for the first time.

He called Nantz. "It looks like I'm gonna be out of pocket."

"Why tell me?"

Her unexpected tone made him stop. Now what? "I thought you'd want to know."

"I've got no claim on you, Service."

What the hell?

"I just wanted — "

She cut him off. "But I do have your dog. You'll be back."

Left, right. She was like a jabber.

"Try not to leave any pieces out there," she added.

"What?"

"You heard me," she said with a chuckle. "Be careful. You want to talk to Newf?"

"She's a *dog*."

He heard the dog panting into the phone and said, "Hi girl," and began laughing.

Talking to Nantz was like trying to catch smoke with your hands. She had him spinning.

Mossy Camp lay beside a gravel road, six miles south of the helicopter. The West Branch of the Huron River flowed around the site, which was on a flat area with small cedars and pines. The river spilled over a series of natural slate steps. Boulders and rocks along the bank were covered with soft moss, giving the whole area a soft and fuzzy appearance. Upriver Service had seen moose, and twice while he was fishing black bears had ambled by. South of camp the roads turned bad and eventually impassable. Vehicles could not get through, but in winter the road was a thoroughfare for snowmobiles. It was unlikely that Will Chamont would venture down this way, but if he did he would see a camp and assume they were fishermen.

Probationary Conservation Officers Sarah Pryzbycki and Dan Beaudoin arrived in an old Ford and a newer Camry. Beaudoin drove the Ford. Service had hurriedly shopped in L'Anse and had just driven into Mossy Camp with several cartons of food and supplies. The young officers looked weary. They had driven a long way fast on little notice with no idea what lay ahead of them.

"We couldn't believe you asked for us by name," Pryzbycki said.

"No?"

"Word is, you crush probies," Beaudoin said.

Service frowned. The genesis of this was the situation with Trip Bozian. "Knock off the tag-team drill," he said.

The probies laughed. They'd do well, he thought.

Service helped the probies build lean-tos with poles he had cut years ago and kept nearby. Roofs were made from camo green tarps. The probies worked efficiently and cheerfully.

"Did you bring sleeping bags?"

The rookies nodded.

He took time to explain the procedure he wanted, but not the reason for it. Having four watchers reduced the likelihood of detection. One vehicle seen regularly might arouse suspicion, but four vehicles alternated would not. They would work twelve-hour shifts, 6 A.M. to 6 P.M. If someone came to the chopper, the on-duty watcher was to call for backup. If that someone drove off, they were to follow and call for backup. He tested their knowledge about following vehicles and gave them a couple of pointers to add to what they already knew, the main thing being not to get too close and crowd the target vehicle.

Tonight he would relieve Flap. Base camp was here, close enough to the target yet far enough away. He hoped this surveillance didn't take too many days. Sooner or later, he had to have some luck with this crap. The chopper was well maintained. It wouldn't stay like that without attention. Somebody would come.

He hoped it would be soon.

It was stupid to wish for luck. The Indians said never to let out your fears in summer, when all the spirits were alive and anxious to interfere in men's affairs. Better to talk in winter when everything was frozen, especially spirits. Most of them, anyway.

Unable to reach Turnage or del Olmo, Service called Nantz.

"Everything okay?" he asked.

"Newf and I are bonding. You may not be able to get her back without me. We're that close."

Nantz. Cast and reel, set the hook. He was willingly on the end of her line and grinning.

On the third day of the stakeout, Joe Flap had the watch. Pryzbycki and Beaudoin were parked next to the river, trying to sleep in their vehicles with the windows up. The mosquitoes were thick, and there were remnants of early-summer blackflies lingering. Chiggers and no-see-ums were in the on-deck circle. He hoped his probies had patience and crossed his fingers that Lisette didn't recall them for other duty, but if she did, they would have to go. After this stint, the pair would begin to know if they were patient enough for this kind of work. This was real CO work, sitting and waiting. Most nights you sat in the dark, getting cold or bug bitten, and went home empty handed. Lansing didn't like to talk about sheer hours spent unproductively. Perception was the prevailing reality in Lansing. He got a rash if he got closer than a hundred miles.

A radio call from Turnage interrupted his reverie.

"I've acquired that target you've been looking for," Gus said.

Fox. "Where?"

"Pure luck. I sent a copy of your photo to Simon and he spotted Fox outside Crystal Falls and followed. He handed him off to me about thirty minutes ago. How do you want me to play this?"

"Where are you now?"

"Uh, south of L'Anse."

Was Fox headed for the chopper?

"What's he driving?"

"Dark blue Ford Bronco with Michigan plates. I ran them through the computer. The vehicle belongs to Wildcat, Inc. Simon said to tell you that Wixon and Wildcat are not connected."

Dark blue Bronco and Wildcat! But no link to Wixon. Scaffidi was not part of this. Fox was and he was probably in the Tract the night of the first fire too. Things were beginning to come together. But who had the stranger with the rock hammer been? Service felt his heart revving.

"Can you see him?"

"I'm hanging well back, but I have him."

"What direction's he headed?"

"North. He just got on Skanee Road. Where are you?"

"You're both headed for me now."

"I didn't know."

"I haven't been able to get through to you. You can break off and we'll take it from here."

"No problem. I'm pulling off now."

Good, finally. "Thanks, Gus. Call Simon and let him know what's going on."

"Roger, pal. The Bronc's all yours now. Don't let him buck you off." Service drove north and parked down a two-track off Skanee Road so he could see the Bronco when it passed. Pranger would see what went down at the helicopter site.

When the Bronco came by him, it was traveling the speed limit. Service called Joe Flap. "You're about to get company," Service said.

The answer was two clicks on the radio. Flap was ready.

Service smoked, ate an apple, and gnawed a tough piece of venison jerky. The radio was silent for nearly thirty minutes. Then a patch came through.

It was Pranger, his voice calm. "Blue Bronco, headed south. Checked his birdie and cut out. I'm in his six, not pushing."

"Good job," Service said. "Did he get out and look or just swing through?"

"Just a drive-by."

Why hadn't Fox stopped? Had he seen something and spooked? "Stay with him. I'll be in your six if you need me." If Flap felt he was being made by Fox, he would pull off and Service would move up to be the primary follower.

Click-click.

When Fox came by he was still keeping the speed limit and didn't seem spooked. Flap passed three minutes after Fox, grinning as he drove by. Service headed for Mossy Camp to release the PCOs. Flap could handle the tail for the moment.

Service radioed Turnage and del Olmo, told them what was going on. They would both join in when Fox reached a destination.

Fox led them to a one-story house two miles east on the outskirts of Crystal Falls. Service, who hurried to the area after meeting the probies, kept everybody back. He couldn't take Fox yet. It was too soon. He met with del Olmo and Turnage about a mile from the house, asking del Olmo to get rid of his official vehicle, get his VW, and be ready to tail, but not make an arrest. "We need to know where Fox goes, what he does, who he meets with. If he breaks the law, grab him, otherwise just stick to him."

Service made a mental note to look up the probies later, fill them in on what this was all about, share some beers. Maybe he'd ask Nantz to come along.

It was tough to get this close to Fox without moving on him, but he didn't have the evidence he needed and when he dropped this one on Fox's head, he meant it to stick. He was sure Fox was the killer, and this made him uneasy. Letting a killer run loose was a risky proposition, but it was in Simon's hands now and he trusted Simon.

With the surveillance organized, and del Olmo in place in his VW, Service called Flap and Turnage and told them they could leave.

He called Nantz as he departed Crystal Falls.

"I'm on the way," he said.

"I'll believe it when I see it," she said.

On CR 422 just before Ralph he saw four pickup trucks and a car parked along the road. A fistfight was under way. He stopped and parked, got out, and waded in among the combatants. All but one of them stopped when they saw his badge. He had to knock down the recalcitrant one. "What's going on here?"

The question prompted a barrage of garbled words, accusations, anger, blue-streak swearing, red faces.

"Everybody put a cork in it!" he shouted. With control established, he tried to get the story, one liar at a time.

The woman had hit a deer and went to call her husband to come get it.

While she was at the pay phone, a passerby stopped to claim the deer.

When she saw the latecomer dragging the carcass toward his truck, she ran over to him and pushed him. Then her husband arrived.

An argument ensued.

Mine.

Not yours.

Meanwhile another man stopped, assessed the situation, and tried to grab the carcass while the others fought.

The first bunch then turned on the last guy, angrily pounding him.

Everybody had a bloody nose and torn clothes. Even the woman.

Service was too tired to deal with it. Nearly seventy thousand deer were killed by cars in the state every year and more often than people might think, this was the sort of fiasco that resulted. It was worse during hunting season when armed people sometimes argued over who shot what.

He sent the lot of them on their way, flagged down a logging rig, and gave the surprised driver the venison.

Farther down the road he saw a dead mother coon with five dead babies, all flattened, probably last night, a poignant example of where blind obedience could take you. Nature had taught him much, and so far all the lessons had been brutal.

About ten miles from Gladstone, he got a call from the county, the kind of call cops hated most: he was needed as backup in a domestic dispute, in Trombly.

He got to the scene first and cursed his luck. Dammitall.

It was a nice house, lawn cut, flowers in beds, real homeowners, none of this a clue to what went on inside.

There was a woman sitting on the steps of the front porch. Her face was swollen, nicked and bruised, one eye puffed closed, her sundress torn, and she didn't seem to care to try hiding any of what hung out. He listened for sirens of responding units and heard none. He would have to handle it.

"I'm Officer Service," he told the woman.

"Harold's inside," she mumbled with blood in her mouth.

"Are you okay?" he asked.

She waved him on. No venom in her body language, which might be a good sign. Maybe the worst was over. Where the hell *were* the county people? COs plugging holes. Did that little Dutch boy die with his thumb in the dike? He couldn't remember.

He peered into a small foyer and went inside, easing open the door but not closing it. He didn't want it swinging shut and alarming anyone. He looked into the living room and saw an immense man, shirtless, sitting on the couch with a pistol in his lap. It was a a big-bore revolver, a serious hogleg.

"Sir . . . Harold?"

"I've had enough," the man said wearily.

"Are you okay?" The man had no visible damage.

"I can't take this shit anymore."

"Yessir," Service said. Humor him. Come on, county.

"I do everything around here," Harold said, "while she sits on her ass all day, then goes visiting neighbors at night. She didn't drag her ass home till four this morning and now she thinks she's going out again. Did you see how she was dressed?" Harold looked up to make eye contact and Service didn't like what he saw in the man's face.

Don't take sides, Service told himself. "Well, she came home safe. That's good."

Harold looked up. Rheumy eyes. "You buying her bullshit?"

Damn. "Sir, you look pretty tired." Change the subject. Neutralize the pistol first.

"I know what I'm doing," Harold said. "*She* knows too."

"Harold, can you help me get an ice water?"

"Let her do it. She likes men." Harold pursed his lips and made a sucking sound.

A voice behind Service said, "Hi Harold, how ya doin'?"

It was Deputy Alice Hadanak. She stepped beside Service but kept her eyes on the man on the couch. "I saw Mabel outside, Harold. She doesn't look so good."

"I just marked her up," Harold said. "I figure the neighbor won't want her, all those marks."

"You know me, Harold. I want to hear your side, Harold, hear everything you have to say, but you know I don't like guns. They make me antsy."

Hadanak was very cool, very professional. Her holster was also unsnapped.

She moved away from Service and he knew what that meant. If Harold started shooting, he'd have a difficult time getting both of them.

"I won't shoot the slut," Harold said. "I'm a decent Christian, and it's against my religion."

Hadanak said, "Put the pistol on the couch beside you, Harold, and get up slowly and let's go get us something cool to drink. Officer Service is thirsty, right, Grady?"

"Parched," Service said.

Harold leered and grinned. "I know this drill."

Service sensed Hadanak tensing.

What occurred next happened fast, but seemed like slo-mo while it was going on. Harold lifted the pistol from his lap, turned it at his head, and fired. Pieces of wall plasterboard and dust showered the room. The smell of cordite spread.

Hadanak dived onto Harold and knocked his gun away. Harold was much larger than her and retaliated by smacking her hard with a forearm.

Service swept the revolver down a wooden hallway with his foot and jumped in, getting Harold by the hair, pulled him off the couch and slammed him to the floor, twisting an arm behind him, and felt breathtaking pain in his shoulder. The man struggled with surprising strength, but Service pressed his knee to the man's spine and stilled him.

Hadanak looked dazed, but managed to crawl over and put her cuffs on the man. Her nose was gushing blood.

Another deputy came rushing in, stopped and stared dumbfounded at what he saw. It was Avery.

"Jesus Christ, Service! You *are* everywhere."

Service didn't stay. As first on the scene, new state regs said he had to fill out the report, but Hadanak told him not to sweat it, that she would take care of it.

He helped get Hadanak's bloody nose stanched then drove directly to Nantz's house and stood on the front porch, his shoulder screaming.

He saw the door open and felt Nantz's arm around his waist. Newf's tail banged against him.

"We need to get you to a doctor," Nantz said.

"No doctor, no hospital," he said.

"Where are you hurt?" she asked.

"I'm not qualified to give medical opinions."

He tried to move but couldn't. He had gone numb. Nothing seemed to work and he felt frozen in place. The old man wouldn't have liked this.

When was it? Seven, eight, playing up against twelve-year-olds, the old man's idea. Push push push. Hit by a puck behind the knee. No padding there. Just scrawny leg, sinew, bone. Left leg numb. Carried off the ice, fussed over. The old man had been there, in his face, pushing others away, hovering. Whiskey breath. "What's your problem?"

"My leg." Probably whined. The old man hated whiners and complainers.

"You got two, eh? Get your butt back out there and play through it."

Which he did.

That night he punched his pillow and cried until all his energy was gone, the anger ebbed away like a slow tide. The pillow as his father's head, adolescent Yooper voodoo. Why the hell didn't his father care?

But he had cared, believing in lessons, not words. Pain, injury, and sorrow were all part of life. You lived or gave in to it. He would have liked to tell the old man that he understood. Too late. Story of his life. Always too damn late for the important shit.

"What was that about your father?" Nantz asked. "You were mumbling."

"I'm fine," he said gruffly as he stepped inside.

She studied him the way a bug doctor looked at a Japanese beetle. "Yep, you look real peachy."

"Stay out of my hair," he said.

"First I'd have to get in it."

He couldn't even look at her. "Nantz . . ."

He shook his head, grimacing to swallow a laugh. It would hurt too much to laugh.

"Take a hot shower, Service."

He showered in pain, put on his dirty clothes, and made his way downstairs to the kitchen. Nantz pulled out a chair and said, "Sit."

She brought him an omelet unlike any he'd ever seen.

"Nice omelet."

"I do it all," she said.

He didn't doubt it. "What's in this?" he asked, reaching for ketchup.

She grabbed his hand, sending pain up into his shoulder. "Eat it the way I cooked it, barbarian."

He tasted it. Delicious. He ate with his left hand, dropping a lot.

"Tomatoes," she said. "Garlic, onion, green pepper, red pepper, teaspoon of minced jalapeño, a little cayenne, black olives, parsley, sour cream."

The list made him dizzy. "It's great."

"Unlike your right arm," she said. "You winced when I grabbed your wrist and you're eating with your left hand."

"I'm ambidextrous."

"Than can be proven only in bed," she said. "Raise your right arm. Go on."

He put down his fork, looked at her, and exhaled. "I can't."

"The old housemate give you a romp?"

He told her about Harold and Deputy Alice Hadanak, the backup call, the half-assed suicide attempt, the scuffle, his dive, the earlier fracas over the deer. "I should've waited for the county," he said.

"Right, and old Harold might have blown his brains out."

"His wife might've preferred that."

She said, "You walk the walk, but you can't handle the talk."

He looked up at her.

She was smug. "It means, my dear Officer Service, that you are one dedicated and heroic sonuvabitch and you can't deal with it."

"I suppose you have a degree in psychology."

"Nope, but I went to a shrink for years."

"For what?"

"To humor my mother."

"Did it work?"

"Nope, all the man wanted to do was bounce me on his wee-wee."

Service rolled his eyes. "Do you *ever* tell the truth?"

She batted her eyes, lifted a hand, crooked her little finger. "He was bent like this, one of those banana types, dinky and curved."

"You're sick," he said.

"I thought you men liked stories."

"Not today."

She said, "It's your day off and we're not wasting it."

"Day off," he said, "*means* waste."

"That's truly pathetic, Service," she said.

"What?"

He called Simon del Olmo. So far, Fox was staying put. Service said he would check in later. He told Nantz about Fox and the stakeout.

"You think Fox killed Kerr and Jerry Allerdyce?"

"I don't know he didn't."

"If he did, you're taking a big chance leaving him alone. You know what your problem is?"

"No," he said.

"*That's* your problem," she said disgustedly.

She took him upstairs to the spare bedroom and he must have registered surprise.

"You need rest," she said. "I don't fuck crips, gimps, or grumps."

Newf looked from him to the door and followed Nantz.

Service said, "Traitor."

"Don't pick on the dog," Nantz yelled back at him.

19

He awoke at six the next morning thinking about Fox, Nantz, and his father. The old man had gone his own way, oblivious to opinions. Hell, he had been oblivious to *life*. His job had been everything and nothing, all at once. It didn't make it right, but he was beginning to understand him.

The shoulder was cement again, pain replaced by near-total numbness. It had been a slight separation to start, but he knew it was worse now. He had never been good about following the directions of doctors. Damn Harold what's-his-face.

He labored out of bed and went tentatively downstairs. Newf came out of Nantz's bedroom and followed him. He made two pieces of toast and took them outside. Newf joined him, her tail wagging. She ran around while he got into his truck and switched on the radio. "Marquette, DNR 421 is on."

"Roger, have a nice day!"

Nice day? Not in *this* body.

It took a while to get through to del Olmo. "Do you still have Fox?"

"He's sitting as tight as *el gato* with narcolepsy. The cops say we ought to tap the phone."

"Negative." He didn't want a judge brought in yet. The case was still circumstantial. "Just stick to him."

"The cops are asking why such a long watch. You know how cops are."

He knew. "Fox is a prime suspect in a case that we're making. That's all they need to know. Did you talk to your DEQ counterparts yet?"

"I'm assured that no development plan or drilling permit for Knipe came through the Crystal Falls office. But they say he could go around or over and bypass them."

"Thanks." Bypass the locals? If so, how high would Knipe have to go? Damn Bozian. His splitting DEQ out of the DNR had politicized all the environmental stuff. Service hated Lansing but decided he would have to go down there and do some squeezing.

He called McKower and asked for a meeting at the roadside park on US 41. Nantz padded out to the truck in running shorts and flipflops, carrying two cups of coffee. She thrust one toward him and stood outside the driver's window, sipping and blinking with sleep.

"How's the shoulder?"

He moved it and tried to hide the pain.

"I thought so," she said. "You're at work already?"

"In a case like this, you can't let up. The breaks come from small details that suddenly take on a new importance. If you let up, you can lose it all."

"Don't I know it," she said wistfully. "Do you want Newf to stay with me today?"

"Do you mind?"

"I face a day of scut work. She'll be fine at the office."

"I don't know when I'll be back," he said.

"My door's always open," she said. She ducked her head in the window and kissed him passionately. When she pulled away she stroked his cheek and said, "Kick some ass out there today, Officer Service."

"Yes ma'am."

He looked in the rearview mirror and saw her wave from the driveway. Then he shifted his mind to business and headed for the meeting with Lis.

With her name added to the lieutenant's list, McKower wore gleaming new silver bars on her collar. It was strange not to see stripes on her sleeves.

"Do I salute or bow?"

She snorted, "Bow and you'll get a feel for my boot size. What was the deal with Pryzbycki and Beaudoin?"

LT McKower was like Sergeant McKower, right down to brass tacks.

He pointed to the picnic bench. "Let's sit." Service took a deep breath and let it out. "Here it is, Lis, the whole thing. Jerry Allerdyce and probably a man named Kerr were murdered in the Tract by a man named Fox. Fox engineered two fires in the tract. Allerdyce and Kerr were helping him. He killed them to cover what they were doing. I believe Fox works in some capacity for Wildcat, Inc., a mining engineering company owned by a man named Seton Knipe. I know he's done work for Knipe in the past. What Fox has done, he's probably done for Knipe, not solo. I don't have all the evidence yet, but I'd bet on it. Simon del Olmo has Fox under surveillance in Crystal Falls. That's what Mossy Camp was about. We got lucky and intercepted him near there and we've been on him ever since. The cops in Crystal Falls are assisting Simon del Olmo. He has ninety-nine-year leases to two land parcels in the tract and I *know* he's planning something there. I just don't know how or what or when. Not yet."

"Leased land in the Tract?" she asked as if she were trying to classify the information. Then she added, "Murders are not our jurisdiction, Grady."

"Fox took a shot at me in the tract and any felony there is my business."

"Let the blue suits handle this," she said in her stony supervisor's voice.

"No."

"Grady, you are a loose cannon and if you keep going, you're going to leave me no choice. We have rules and procedures. We're law enforcement officers, not freelancers. We are a team and we are disciplined. *You* do not own the tract."

He wanted to rip up her damn book, but he also understood the threat: suspension without pay, or worse. There were various DNR officials in Lansing who weren't exactly his fans, which meant he could expect the worst. And if Bozian jumped in, he could be out on his ear, with no pension.

He told himself he didn't care.

"Are you getting Rollie's job?" he asked. There was enough speculation circulating.

She made eye contact and nodded. "You want to know why? Because there is not one lieutenant in the state who wants to put up with your shit, Service."

Ouch. "You accepted?"

"Yes."

Service sensed a moment of truth for them. If she wouldn't help, he might as well walk away. "There are diamonds in the tract, Lis."

She started to grin, but this quickly faded when she realized he wasn't joking.

"Where?"

He fetched his maps and charts, showed her the locations, walked her through the whole situation, one step at a time, omitting nothing except for his suspicions about what the governor might do.

She thought for quite a while. "Fox shot at you?"

He nodded and showed her the photograph Nantz had taken.

"This is pretty wild, Grady. You got Limpy out of jail. Why?"

"He's got more value to us outside than in."

"How?"

"He pointed us to Kerr and to Knipe's leases in the tract."

"That's thin. You know where Fox is but you haven't sworn charges. What if he kills again? You're being impetuous and endangering public safety."

"Fox isn't a serial killer, Lis. He murdered Jerry and Kerr to cover his tracks. The shot at me was meant as a warning." Probably, he thought. "Kerr was Limpy's cellmate in Jackson. Limpy set Jerry up with Kerr and I believe Kerr had the connection to Knipe."

"Is Limpy part of this?"

"I don't think so. He simply provided the lead."

She shook her head. "I don't like this."

"Goddammit, Lis. You know how a case gets made. We have a puzzle, we put the pieces together, get the picture straight, find and assemble the evidence, make the arrests."

"Don't lecture me."

Her temper was surfacing.

"Then stop being a fucking lieutenant and think like a CO and listen to me!"

Her face flushed. McKower stared at him in disbelief. "What . . . do . . . you . . . propose . . . to . . . do . . . next?" she asked with great deliberation.

"You've heard about diamond exploration around Crystal Falls?"

"Vaguely."

"I believe Knipe's company is part of that. I'm going down to Lansing. I need to know if Knipe is getting permitted over the heads of the DEQ in Crystal Falls."

"And if he is?"

"That depends on where he's permitted. If it's for his Crystal Falls property, that's one thing. If it's for the tract, we have a different problem. If they issue permits in Lansing, he can drill and we can't do a damn thing about it except encourage a lawsuit going from outside groups."

She nibbled the inside of her cheek. "You're stepping on all kinds of jurisdictions, Grady. Permits are the DEQ's business, not ours. And you shouldn't have told me any of this," she added.

"You asked."

"I'm new at this crap."

"I can't take it back."

McKower stood up. "Stay away from Lansing, Grady. If you show up down there, they'll try to chop off your head. I'll get a fix on Knipe's permit status. This meeting never happened, understood?"

He nodded, overwhelmed by a surge of affection for her.

"If Knipe has the legal right to drill, Grady, you *will* uphold the law."

"I know what the law says. Mining is illegal in the tract, but given the way things are under Bozian, I wouldn't put it past Lansing to give Wildcat a green light there."

"If they get permits, they can go forward."

"They are not going to drill in the tract."

"If Lansing permits the Mosquito, the operation can go forward."

"Bullshit. Lansing can't give permits to drill where the law doesn't allow it."

"Such arguments are in the purview of lawyers, not cops."

"If DEQ is pressured to grant permits, their lawyers won't fight. Somebody else will have to file for an injunction and get the thing into court."

"How do you always end up in tangled cases?" she asked.

"Must be luck," he said. "All bad. But when I make a case, it always sticks."

"One of these times it won't. I'll handle Lansing and check the permits for you, Grady. After that everything you tell me will be on the record and by the book."

"Yes Lieutenant Ma'am."

"Do you seriously believe there are diamonds in the tract?"

"I do." He didn't tell her that he had the best evidence there was.

She put an arm up to his neck, pulled him down, and kissed him gently on the lips. "If this Fox was warning you off with a shot, that's one thing. If he had something else in mind and screwed the pooch, that's another. I think you should push to pick up Fox now, but I am not going to interfere. Yet. As long as Fox is loose, you watch your step, hear?"

McKower walked toward her green jeep and stopped. "If there really are diamonds in the tract, you still have a problem even if you stop Knipe."

He nodded.

When she got into the driver's seat, she put her window down. "If you stop Knipe and there's no diamonds to be found, no problem."

McKower gazed meaningfully at him a long time before driving away.

No diamonds, no problem. He understood what he needed to do, not how.

He lit a cigarette and tried Nantz on his cellular and radio, but she had her ears off or was ignoring calls. With her, either was possible.

Service got on the road. He had a lot to do.

His first stop was at OSF St. Francis Hospital to see Vince Vilardo the Delta county medical examiner. In the old days coroners had been elected at the county level. Now a state medical examiner law allowed for the appointment of an ME in each county. Service had known Vilardo and his wife for many years. The internist owned a parcel of land with a small stream that filled with steelhead every fall and spring and was overrun by poachers. COs were there so often during those two seasons that the Vilardos gave them open access to their home. Vilardo could have made much more money practicing medicine just about anywhere outside the U.P., but chose to remain.

Service found the ME at his clinic in the hospital.

The doctor's receptionist fetched him as soon as Service arrived. They walked outside, where both of them lit up cigarettes. "Do we have an ID on the body from the Mosquito?" the CO asked.

"I don't have the file here, but the man's name is Kerr. We identified him with dental records and fingerprints and several small tattoos. I heard you found him, eh? And not too far from where you found Allerdyce."

"Yep." Vilardo understood the possible link.

"I don't know which is worse, scooping up a corpse or opening it up," the ME said.

"Probably depends on when your next meal is," Service said.

The doctor smiled. "So true, so true."

"Did you recover a bullet?"

"We harvested one good one and some fragments."

"Enough for comparative ballistics?"

"You'd have to get the definitive answer from the state lab people in Negaunee, but I'd say it should be adequate. We took a good one out of Allerdyce."

"Caliber?"

"Looked like 5.56-millimeter to us, but the official ruling will come from ballistics. A caliber of this type is likely to go all the way to the lab in

Lansing for confirmation. I can't say when we'll get it back. You know how that music plays."

He did. Law enforcement and prosecutors were extremely finicky about the chain of custody of bullets. They had to be moved to the lab in such a way that there would not be even a theoretical chance of tampering. Too many cases had failed because the chain of custody had not been adhered to. In Detroit such movement was no big deal, but in the U.P. you had to contend with long distances, which slowed down the process. And if Negaunee decided to seek additional help from the state police forensics lab in Lansing, the time multiplied.

"Is the bullet the same as what you got out of Jerry Allerdyce?"

"The ballistics lab will make that call officially, but I'd say yes," Vilardo said.

The caliber, 5.56-millimeter, fit the M-16 A1 Armalite rifle, a weapon that was entirely black and matched what Nantz had seen.

"Thanks, Vince."

"Anytime."

More facts established. The dead man was Kerr, and he and Jerry Allerdyce had probably been killed by the same-caliber bullet; Service guessed ballistics would show it was the same weapon. If they could get Fox's weapon when they got him, they might get a ballistics match.

McKower radioed him late that afternoon while he was checking the license of a man fishing Silver Creek.

"There are permits for Crystal Falls only," McKower said. "They were issued at the behest of a member of the NRC and the superintendent of the Mosquito."

"What?"

"You heard me: Doke Hathoot lent his support. Now we go by the book, right?"

"I hear you," he said. She had done a lot more than verify permits. That she had managed to get such inside information so fast told him she had real connections downstate. He was both impressed and surprised. McKower had always been more than she seemed.

Hathoot and somebody from the Natural Resources Commision running interference for Knipe? Bastards. The NRC was supposed to provide oversight for the DNR and DEQ, not act as a damn lobbyist.

When he confronted Hathoot at the tract headquarters building, Doke wore a stupid grin but wasn't the least evasive or apologetic. "Sure I went to bat for Knipe. Why not? I got a call from Ron Novotny from the commission. He said the governor wants to make certain Michigan gets its fair share of the diamond business. Dow sold fifty-one percent of its interests to the subsidiary of some Australian company. The governor believes we ought to be taking care of Michigan companies first. What's wrong with that?"

"You don't even know Knipe, and all the other companies have abandoned the diamond search."

"I never said I knew Knipe. Big fucking deal, Service. I did a favor for Novotny, a quid pro quo. You think my wife wants to live here forever? You think I do? I'm just scratching a back. That's politics. Look, Service, I know the difference between politics and principles, and if somebody tries to fuck with the tract, I'll be on them before you. But this has nothing to do with the Mosquito, so why are you so bent out of shape?"

Hathoot was slick but not that slick, and he had met plenty of liars you couldn't detect without a lot of effort. He didn't like what Hathoot had done, but the man's explanation sounded plausible, which didn't guarantee that it was.

"What do you expect from Novotny?"

"He said he'd push for the NRC to have its planning retreat here. If we do a bang-up job and impress them, he whispers in the governor's ear and he whispers to the DNR brass and maybe the wife and I can transfer south."

"Novotny's close to the governor?"

"He's a major contributor. When Bozian's family vacations at the mansion on Mackinac Island, Novotny and his wife are usually with them. He's a key adviser in Bozian's kitchen cabinet, a real behind-the-scenes power broker."

Another thread: Knipe to Novotny to Bozian. Service was glad he came to see Hathoot. Knipe was pressing forward near Crystal Falls, but he wouldn't have had two people killed in the tract if he didn't have his eye in that direction too.

The telephone connection was lousy. "Knipe has approved permits for his Crystal Falls operation," Service told del Olmo. "Can you get one of your DEQ pals to take you out there for an inspection?"

"What inspection?"

"Hell, I don't care. Tell Wildcat it's routine and that permits require photos of facilities for the records."

"You're bent," del Olmo said.

There was admiration in the younger CO's voice. "Yeah, you too."

"What about Fox?"

"Not yet."

When he got back to Nantz's that evening she was gone. There was a note: "I have Newf and we will be 'out of pocket' for a while." He headed for his place to check on Cat, who was happy to have her food replenished but otherwise ignored Service's presence. He wondered where Nantz was, but expected she would call when she could.

He spent the next day on routine activities. Time dragged by. Service tried repeatedly to contact Nantz through her office, but she wasn't there and the office would say only that she was "unavailable," the standard bureaucratic kiss-off. Where she was was none of his business.

Del Olmo called him and asked him to drive over to Iron Mountain tonight.

What the hell was Nantz doing? And why did she have to be so damn independent? With all that money, the older she got, the more independent she'd be, he guessed.

He met del Olmo at Ruggers in Iron Mountain. The two men ordered fries with malt vinegar, grilled whitefish, and coffee. There were photographs of Steve Mariucci and Tommy Izzo on the wall, local boys who now coached the San Francisco Forty-Niners and Michigan State's national champion, basketball team. Del Olmo had brought photographs, glossy eight-by-tens in black and white.

There was a photograph of Fox and another man he had seen once before — the stranger from the tract!

"Our Fox finally left his den," Service said.

Del Olmo smiled. "God's hand. That's what my mom always said about coincidences. He moved the same time I went with the DEQ people, and when we got out to Knipe's property, there he was. It was sweet."

"Where did you get this?"

"At the Wildcat compound."

Service tapped a finger on a photograph. "Who's Fox with?"

"Ike Knipe. Fox met him at the compound."

Finally! It was Ike he had met in the Mesquito that night. Ike Knipe and Fox. Seton Knipe's son and his hired gun. "Did they have a problem with you being there?"

"They weren't real happy to see any of us, but the DEQ guys were cool and said it was just routine and not to get their bowels in an uproar. They let us poke around and that was that."

"Anything they didn't let you see?"

"Nope, they gave us free run of the grounds."

Meaning there was nothing there to hide? If so, why the fence and extraordinary security? Something didn't jibe. Sometimes the truth lay buried between people's actions and words.

"Any evidence of drilling?"

"Didn't see any. Just lots of equipment."

"Any excavation, digging?"

"*Nada*."

A woman in a very short red skirt and gold sandals approached their table. She had one wrist loaded down with gold bracelets and gaudy rings on all her fingers, even her thumbs.

"How come they let fish cops wear guns?" she asked, challenging. Her voice was a raspy and guttural.

She was middle aged, well preserved, proud of her legs, and more than a little tipsy. A spiderweb of blue booze veins showed through the skin of her cheeks.

"You never heard of shooting fish in a barrel?" del Olmo said.

The woman looked confused.

"Sometimes the fish have water guns, lady."

She stared daggers at del Olmo. "You a greaser?"

"No ma'am, spick-American." He gave her one of his white-toothed smiles.

Her lips curled down nastily. "You're not *real* cops," she said disgustedly, coasting away on her twisty course.

Service looked over at del Olmo, who was still smiling.

"Gee, and somebody told me once that COs never have fans," del Olmo said.

"Doesn't anything get you down?"

"No, jeffe. This is America, not Cuba. You think that lady would run us off if she had a problem and we were first on the scene?"

Service laughed.

"Is it time for the poor hens to take down the Fox?"

"Soon," Service said. He needed to see Rocky Lemich in Houghton before he moved against Fox and Knipe.

*   *   *

Lemich wasn't in his office. The secretary who answered the phone said he was "out—eating biscuits."

"Ma'am?"

"It's *his* juvenile language. He's at the rink playing hockey."

"In summer?"

"Year-round," she said disparagingly.

Service watched Lemich finish up. Age took reflexes, but added smarts based on experience. Lemich played the angles, and didn't have to do much work, easily smothering three shots from the point. When the teams were banging into each other in the neutral zone and other end he busied himself sweeping snow out of his goal crease with his big paddle.

Lemich came off the ice smiling and flushed. The scoreboard read 4–0.

"Who had the four?"

"Not us," the professor said. "Screened on one, and three rebounds."

Goalie talk for not his fault. Service grinned. "Tests done?"

Lemich waddled over to a skaters' bench in his unwieldy equipment and plopped down heavily, his back against the yellow cinder-block wall. "It's kimberlite," he said. "Heavy olivine, clasts showing chrome pyrope, pridot, ilmenite."

Clasts and olive oil? "Is there an English translation?"

"Looks diamondiferous, eh? It could hold diamonds."

"Does the formation have to be the source of the stones we found?"

"No, it could be that your stones rode down from Canada with glaciers. Diamonds have even been found in Indiana, and no doubt how those got there, eh? Theoretically, your stones coulda hitched a ride down this way, but I'd hafta say this is unlikely. Sorry."

Service got out the photographs of Knipe's compound.

"Anything in these stand out?"

Lemich shuffled through the photos like they were playing cards. "What's the question?"

"Are they drilling?"

"Based on these?"

Service nodded.

"Looks to me like they're stockpiling equipment, but haven't gotten down to the dirty work yet. Who is this?"

"That's not important. Thanks for your help."

"No problem, bucko. Remember what you promised me in return for amnesia."

Kids, Service remembered. "I keep my word."

"Knew you would," Lemich said. "Banger."

Service drove past the cemetery across the street from the rink. He saw pure white statues of the Holy Family with their backs to the rink. Maybe they didn't like hockey.

On his way out of Houghton Service got a call from Gus Turnage. "Where are you?" his friend asked.

"Headed out of Houghton on US 41, aiming south."

"Great timing. Grab a coffee?"

"Sure."

"Drake's Café." The restaurant was nondescript, with standard deep-fried Yooper fare.

"I'm almost there."

After getting coffee Turnage said, "I don't know if this fits, but I thought you should know Fox bought and sold a lot of property down in the Pelkie area. The university's lawyers finally decided to tell the feds about Fox's grant fraud and now they're digging into his assets, trying to freeze them."

Service let his friend continue.

"What's interesting is that he bought the land way below assessed value from Wildcat, Inc., and sold it all off over a five-month period. Even with capital gains, he made a very nice profit."

"When?"

"Last year. He took the money he made and parked it in Cayman Island banks. The feds say it will be tough to get at. Does any of this compute?"

"Not yet."

They ate a quick lunch. Service went out to his truck and called Wink Rector at his office in Marquette.

"FBI, Special Agent Rector speaking."

"It's Grady. Are you involved in an investigation of a man named Fox at Tech?"

"Why?" the agent asked suspiciously.

"Other agencies may have their own interests in him."

"For what?"

"A number of things. I'll fill you in later. Right now I'm curious about his land dealings in Pelkie. He bought land on the cheap and sold at a considerable profit."

"Who the hell have you been talking to?"

"Is it true?"

"Yah."

"How much land was involved?"

"A thousand acres, give or take."

"Sold in pieces, not as a chunk."

"Right."

"How did he do it?"

The FBI man said, "Scam. People in Pelkie got the cockamamy idea that the land might contain diamonds. Can you believe that?"

"Where did the people get the idea?"

"From Fox, using an alias. Will or Willie Chamont."

WC. Things were starting to close.

"You're sure it was Fox?"

"We had a complaint and we were following up. Since he was making noises about diamonds, we wondered if there was some sort of connection to Tech."

"And when you got there, you found more problems?"

"Who is your source, Grady?"

"The guy scammed money off grants at the university and off the land deals in Pelkie. How come this didn't hit the news?"

"We've only recently gotten into this. People down there talked to some lawyers about suing Fox, but the land deals were legally binding and there was nothing on paper about diamonds. The people were had and didn't want others to know."

"But somebody came to you guys."

"Yes, an infuriated young woman. Her father lost a bundle, and she wanted to help him. Her call started the ball rolling."

Service inhaled and shook his head, remembering the young woman he had met in Pelkie.

"Fox has a long record of scams. He's been inside twice, once in California, once in Missouri. How he got hired at Tech is beyond me. Damn universities don't check backgrounds for shit." Neither did federal grantors, Service thought.

"Does Fox have a degree?"

"Two engineering degrees from the Colorado School of Mines. Now it's your turn to answer some questions."

"Later, Wink."

"Asshole, you milked me."

"I'll get back to you," Service said, signing off.

Would Knipe sell land he knew to contain diamonds? Not likely. The question was, Were the Knipes part of the scam or had Fox acted alone in Pelkie?

Passing through Chassell, he decided to visit Pelkie again.

The old man was in the gas station and looked like he hadn't washed his coveralls or hands since the last time Service had seen him.

"Is your daughter around?"

"What's it to you?" Fatherly concern or misanthropy? A little of both, Service guessed.

"Just thought I'd say hello." She was a good-looking woman and probably he wasn't the first man to come in asking after her.

"She's out back," the man said disgustedly. "Catchin' rays, whatever the bloody hell that means."

Service found her on her stomach on a bent, rusty chaise lounge near a lime-green Rambler on blocks with weeds poking up through the chassis. The young woman wore a two-piece bathing suit, faded by the sun. She was covered in tanning oil, her top undone in back.

"Hi," he said. "Sorry, I never caught your name. I'm Grady Service."

She looked over at him calmly, pushed up tiny sunglasses, and grinned. "Tish. You looking for rocks again?"

"Not rocks, but I'm hoping you can help me with something."

"Sure." She started to sit up, realized her top was undone. "Whoops," she said, grabbing hold of it.

"Will Chamont," he said.

She said in an accusatory tone, "The FBI guaranteed my name wouldn't be made public."

"It hasn't been made public, but I am looking at Chamont for something else. Would you tell me what happened?"

"The FBI has my statement."

"You want Chamont caught, right? Work with me, okay?"

She nodded reluctantly. "Chamont showed up last summer. He hung out at Skidreams, that's a bar not far from here? He passed himself off as an amateur rock hound. He was good looking and smooth as all get out."

"He told people about the diamonds?"

"No way, eh. There's a woman who waits tables at the bar, Vicki Baily. They started going out. That's a euphemism," she added. "Chamont showed Vicki some sort of government report saying they found the kind of rock near here that could contain diamonds. Vicki told her brother and pretty soon everybody around here was whispering about it, you know, a secret that takes on its own life?"

"Then what?"

"Chamont said that the land the government report talked about was owned by the Knipes, but that he had bought most of it and had put himself in hock. He was looking to unload some of the land to get some of his investment back. He offered some to Vicki and her brother and pretty soon he was selling to all sorts of people."

"Your father included?"

She frowned, then sighed. "My dad, too."

"Did it strike anybody as odd that he was selling land that might have diamonds on it?"

"It sure struck me that way and I told my father so, but he wouldn't listen. You know parents. They don't want to hear kids' opinions."

His old man had been the same way. "Why did people buy?"

"You're asking a logical question. But you get people's minds filled with treasure and they don't use logic. Chamont sparked greed. You know people up in these parts. They like being able to get something for nothing."

"After they found out the land was worthless you'd think somebody would have gone after him."

"Some people talked to their lawyers, but the contracts were legal and there was no mention of diamonds on paper. A rumor got started and people started buying. It was a scam, I think, but not a scam, if you know what I mean. I talked to a lawyer and he just threw up his hands."

"So you called the FBI."

"Somebody had to step up."

"Is Chamont still around?"

The woman laughed and tossed her hair. "He's long gone and it wouldn't be healthy if he showed up again, eh?"

Service went back to his truck and got the photographs. He gave them to Tish, who set them on the chaise lounge and went through them slowly.

"Hey," she said, holding up a photograph. "This is Chamont."

Chamont was Fox. Fox was connected to the Knipes. Knipe to Novotny. Novotny to Bozian. It was shaping up as a neat chain. Now all he needed was evidence to make the case.

"What about the other individual in the picture?"

"I haven't seen him in years," she said. "but he looks like Ike Knipe. Been a while since we saw him and his father. They moved down to Crystal Falls some years back."

She paused to reflect and continued talking. "I've thought about this a lot. The Knipes weren't real popular here, but they had money. Chamont told people they shouldn't talk to the Knipes about this, that he was just going to put one over on them. He said rich folks deserved to get outhustled sometimes."

"Did he say specifically that the the Knipes didn't know about the diamonds?"

She looked up at Service. "I guess they wouldn't have sold if they knew." She rubbed her mouth. "This is too sick," she said. "This guy spins a buncha bull and everybody jumps in and maybe the Knipes didn't have a damn thing to do with it. Maybe Chamont was legit. Maybe he was just a dreamer and everybody got sucked into his dream?" She began to laugh. "Yoopers," she said. "We're dillies, eh?"

"Thanks, Tish."

"I don't want my dad's name in the papers," she said, but he did not respond. He wouldn't use her name, but he could make no promises for the FBI.

Service sat in his truck thinking. It had nearly been a perfect scam, entirely worthless land sold on nothing more than rumor with no trace of the rumormonger to the landowners. If rumor alone could do this, what could it do to the tract? Destroy it.

Crossing the southern end of Keweenaw Bay, Service swung the truck north from L'Anse, taking the road up to Skanee. It seemed like ages since the stakeout of the black helicopter.

This time Service had no concerns about entering private property. He now had evidence of crimes, and Fox had been seen on the property. The black chopper was still under its camo net. He checked under the net and smelled fuel. From what? Not fumes from when he had been here. Those would have evaporated. This was something new. He checked the connector and found that it had been tightened. Somebody had found his tampering and the chopper had been refueled. He wished he'd had the manpower to have maintained the stakeout, but they had gotten onto Fox and there was no compelling reason to spend more resources. He looked around for fresh tire tracks, but the summer was already dangerously hot and the ground brick hard. If this kept on, it was going to be a terrible fire season. He'd *never* see Nantz. Indians danced rain dances, which were mostly baloney and wishful thinking. Still, he might try one. Just in case. He wondered if Nantz would appreciate his effort.

If the chopper was refueled, that meant it was ready to go.

More flights ahead?

Yes, and he had a disturbing idea where. When, was the question that lingered.

He called Nantz's house and got no answer. Frustration was replaced by concern. It was late afternoon when he drove to his cabin to take care of chores he had been neglecting.

Donning shorts, he went down to Slippery Creek with his fly rod, threw half a dozen casts over the head of the pool below the house, hooked a foot-long brown, played it in fast, whacked it on the head, cleaned it, went back to the house, and cooked it.

He sat at his table, picking at the fish and looking at the photographs from Simon. There was more there than he was seeing, but whatever it was, it was refusing to declare itself and his mind wasn't cooperating.

He gave the remains of the trout to Cat, who bumped against this leg the whole time he ate, and went outside to water his tomato plants. While he watered, he decided he needed a couple of bags of fertilizer. Manure, not chemicals. Gardens up here were a gamble. He always waited until after Memorial Day to plant. Downstate it rarely froze after that, but U.P. weather was different. He kept the plants covered at night until after Independence Day. Most people who had tried to farm in the Yoop had gone under. The growing season here was too brief to grow almost anything of value.

He drove to a store called U-Name-It-We-Got-It. It was not false advertising. There was a crowd of people in the sprawling store even though it was out in the middle of the boonies.

Owner Rune Forsberg drove by in a forklift with a pallet of potted blue spruces. He waved and kept going.

Service got two bags of manure. Forsberg's daughter, Sissel, was working one of the cash registers. She was six-five, a sophomore at Wisconsin on a basketball scholarship, a big change since he was young. Newspapers in the U.P. said Sissel might be on the next US Olympic team, but up here they touted anyone with the slightest possible Yooper connection to glory. National pride in an area that was neither a nation nor a state, but very much its own place, four hundred thousand independent-minded people in an area the size of Vermont and New Hampshire combined.

On his way out, he saw Rune headed back to the nursery for more trees, the pallet dancing on the metal forks. Service stopped the truck and watched until the man was out of sight. Why this fascination? His own mind was sometimes as much a mystery to him as to others.

He was sweating when he finished spreading the manure.

Cat lay on the porch watching him. A chipmunk ran across the porch. The feline scrambled, got a paw on the tiny creature, picked it up in her teeth, and trotted across the yard like a mother carrying a wayward pup. The cat dropped the rodent near the trees and began batting it with razor-sharp claws. He thought about rescuing the chipmunk, but this was nature's design and he let it take its course.

"May have to change your name to Bad Mama," he told the cat, who was busy eviscerating the animal.

Unlike Newf, Cat was content with proximity. The dog needed contact and affection. Where the hell *was* Nantz and where was *his* dog?

Pallets, chipmunks, pallets, chipmunks, images moving and undulating in the subconscious swamp, popping out suddenly as something else.

What had he missed in the photographs?

He looked again, spreading them out on the porch.

Pallets with equipment on them. Big deal.

Pallets with huge U-bolts.

"I'll be damned," he said out loud. Choppers in Vietnam hauled cargo on pallets suspended from the aircraft, using cables affixed to the pallets with U-bolts. Just like these.

A quick check of the photos showed that every pallet had the bolts. The pallets were awaiting chopper transport. And the black chopper was refueled and ready.

It didn't matter that Knipe had permits for the Crystal Falls area; the equipment had to be headed for the Tract. There were no diamonds in Crystal Falls, but he knew there were diamonds in the Mosquito, and somehow Knipe knew too. He had encountered Ike carrying a rock hammer, and now he knew why. Ike had been scouting. The chopper had been used to take magnetic readings. Equipment would be flown into the tract by chopper, equipment to be used without a permit and in an area where all mining was against the law!

He called McKower at home.

"Service."

"Do I want this call?"

"This is another of those things that never happened."

"I thought I told you that was done."

"Lis, Knipe has a compound near Crystal Falls. He's gathered mining equipment on pallets equipped for chopper transport. I think he's going to drill in the tract. I have photos of the pallets. It took me awhile to figure this out. The site at Crystal Falls is a red herring."

"He can't drill without a permit."

"He can't drill *legally*," Service said, correcting her.

"Evidence, Officer Service?"

"Everything points to this, Lis. And if he does, I'll be there to stop him. What worries me now is if some of his pals in the NRC or Lansing suddenly push through a permit for him in the Mosquito. We need to know what's going on down there . . . and stop it."

"You're out on the edge, Grady."

He knew that. He'd been there one way or another his whole life. "Are we going to let this jerk do whatever the hell he wants? Bozian has crapped on the state and on us and if he knows about this and lets it go through, he's a partner in rape. Somebody has to step up and say, 'No more.' If it costs my job, so be it."

"You'll go that far?" she asked in a quiet voice.

"I will."

He knew she was thinking it through.

"All right," she said. "What's the point of being an LT if you don't fight for what's right? Get them, Grady. I'll deal with Lansing."

He wanted to cheer. "I love you, Lis."

She laughed. "Yeah, and the next time I get in your way you'll hate my ass too. Anybody this dumb should never be promoted," she added before hanging up.

Okay, Knipe.

The gloves are off. Now we rock 'n' roll to *my* music.

20

Del Olmo called early the next morning. "Bad news. We've lost Fox."

"When?"

"Sometime yesterday. His Bronco is still at the house, but he's not. We usually see him come out to the mailbox for the morning papers, but he didn't come out yesterday and we figured he was just sitting tight. I sent a mail carrier up to the house this morning and nobody was there. I have no idea how he slipped past us. What do you want us to do?"

"Give everybody a heads up, leave somebody at the house, and keep a tight watch on Knipe's compound."

"Sorry, Grady."

"Don't be," Service said.

He immediately telephoned Joe Flap.

"Can you get up to the chopper ASAP and watch for activity?"

"What kind?"

"I checked yesterday. It's been refueled and it's ready to fly." Was Fox headed for the chopper? "If it lifts off, radio Simon del Olmo and call me on my cellular."

"That's it?"

"It's important, Pranger."

"Where are you going?"

"Hunting the hunter."

"Good luck, son."

As he drove south, Service sensed he would soon have a rendevous with Fox. He parked his truck outside the tract, got his pack and sleeping bag, and headed into the forest. He didn't want to leave his truck where he usually parked, so he picked another location about ten miles from Knipe's parcel. Figuring three miles an hour hiking cross country through the bush, he would be there in three hours, give or take. He moved as quickly as he could, leaving little sign that he had passed. In the woods Grady Service was just another animal, silent and invisible. He was in his natural habitat.

The hike took longer than he expected. The air was humid, the temperature unseasonably hot.

He was certain that if Fox came, it would be by chopper, which meant he could lay back a distance and move in when the bird appeared. This was the most likely scenario, but over twenty years he had also learned the hard way that he needed to cover all options because criminals and violators didn't use normal logic. Fox might have given surveillance the slip, but Service knew that sooner or later he would come to the tract. Everything pointed to it. While the chopper was his most likely means of arrival, he also could come in on foot. Either way, Fox was going to find a surprise.

An hour before he reached Knipe's parcel, Service called McKower on his cellular.

"I'm on the chiller. Call me when you get word from down below. Blue sky today."

Blue, their code for can't talk.

"Be smart," his lieutenant said.

Meaning, Stick to the book.

He would. Or he wouldn't. As it always did, the situation would dictate its own rules.

Service's eyes searched the area, methodically recording details. Somebody had taken trees down with a chain saw, trimming and stacking them. The open space would make an efficient landing zone. He had seen too many LZs not to recognize it for what it was.

At 8 P.M. Joe Flap called on his cellular. "The bird has flown."

"Thanks, Gus."

Service smiled as he took out a Snickers bar and bit off a piece.

Ninety minutes later del Olmo radioed him. "Our boy is back," he said. "He landed in a helicopter at the compound about nine. The engines are shut down. They're attaching a pallet now."

"Did Fox fly it in?" Service asked.

"Ike Knipe had the stick. What now?"

Another link. Knipe was a chopper pilot. It was unlikely they would risk a night flight. "Call me when they lift off. It will probably be around first light."

"Later, *jeffe.*"

Service's exposed skin had become a patchwork of welts from mosquitoes. He used no bug dope, no smoke, no scents to keep the bugs off or give him away. Fox was an amateur killer, but woodswise. Blend in, wait. Around midnight Service moved to the river and splashed himself to reduce body odor.

Time inched along. Service kept checking his wristwatch, cautioning himself to be patient and not overfocus on the terrain. Most hunters made the mistake of tensing up and concentrating too hard, but if you were hidden and if you were still, there was no need. He'd see what he came to see when it was time. Probably he would feel it even before he saw it.

Settling in, he set his watch alarm and allowed himself to slide into sleep.

The voice startled him. *"Hey, kid. When you hit the edge, follow a straight line."*

"I know my job." Was the voice real or inside his head?

"Don't fuck up," his old man said. *"The way I did."*

"I don't talk to ghosts," Service said out loud.

"What ghosts?"

The old man had been superstitious. "Go away. I don't have time for this bull."

"This is how you treat your dearly departed old man?"

"Beat it."

"Wherever you go, they got rules, son. You gotta learn how to bend 'em, but not break 'em."

"You broke plenty."

"No way, kid. Not one, not once, leastways none of the important ones. You know me better than that."

This was crazy. "What the hell do you want?"

"To see my son kick some ass. Is that a crime?"

"Okay, you've seen me. Now leave me be."

"My son, the hardass. You know what you have to do here?"

"Whatever it takes."

"Good boy. I'm proud as hell of you, Grady. I shoulda said that a long time ago. Finish your check, kid. Stick this s.o.b. good."

Dream, hallucination? Either way, it was a first. It sure sounded like the old man, though. Service grinned. Cracking up. Nut case, son of the alky.

What time was it? Wait till morning. Don't move. Finish the check.

McKower called on the cellular just before midnight. "You were right, Grady. A permit was issued for the tract."

Service's anger rose. "It's against the law."

"The governor is going to issue an executive order and let special interests fight it out in court. He says the diamond business is too important to ignore. The permit allows for exploration only." Lemich had made it clear that exploration would in itself be a major operation.

"Have the permits been signed?"

"Tomorrow."

"You have to stop it. We can eliminate Knipe and Wildcat, but if the permits get signed, the precedent will let others in. This cannot be allowed to happen, Lis."

"You're asking for the moon, Grady."

"There's a lot at risk, Lieutenant McKower."

"I'll do what I can, Grady. Where are you?

"In the henhouse," he said.

He could not sleep all night. Every time he moved to change position his shoulder ached.

The eastern sky began to lighten to a pale lavender at 5 A.M.

The radio crackled at 6:20 A.M.

"This is Simon. They've just lifted off."

"They?"

"Knipe, Fox, and two others."

"Thanks, Simon."

"Be careful," was all the younger CO said.

The air was fresh and still, no hint of rain. Mosquitoes walked on his ears and neck and he swatted them quietly. Fox had to be headed here and when he came, he would nail him, but what about the diamonds in the river? He needed to shut it all down, everything. Lis had said, No diamonds, no problems. Where the hell was Nantz?

Rays of twilight glowed faintly in the eastern sky. Three deer walked past him and spooked when they caught his scent.

The sun rose into a clear sky. Estimating an hour's flight time, Service moved east to get the rising sun at his back. Every little edge mattered.

Service heard ravens awaken. Wild turkeys talked on their roosts along the river to his west. A small bear lumbered by in the direction of the beaver pond where they had found Kerr. Several deer grazed past him, unalarmed by his scent.

At 7:30 he heard *thrump-thrump*, a distant sound, disturbed air, beaten air, turmoil boiling above. You could feel a chopper before you

heard it, feel it in your bones. Air movement preceding sound, past inter-
cepting future, forming the present.

Chopper.

LZ-bound? Listen and feel.

Wait. There. He felt his adrenaline rising.

Watch.

The chopper grew louder and appeared suddenly, its rotor wash whip-
ping the trees, spraying leaves and detritus. He watched it hover while Fox
and the other men quickly deployed the pallet and winched the cables
into spools in the helicopter's belly. He hoped McKower could stop the
permits from being signed, but he was not going to be able to wait.

When the bird landed, Fox and Knipe shook hands, and Knipe and
the other men got back into the Huey.

Twenty-three minutes after touchdown the chopper lifted away.

Only Fox remained, sitting on a canvas bundle, an M-16 slung tightly
over his back, drinking a can of beer.

Fox was sixty feet away, with his back to the sun. Service left his pack
and crawled slowly forward, his eyes alternating from the ground just
ahead of his knees in the dewy ferns to Fox.

Twenty feet.

Ten.

Fox swiveled and shielded his eyes from the sun with his hand. He
looked tense and suspicious as he stared into the glare. Finally he
shrugged and took another slug of beer.

Amateur, Service thought.

Five feet.

Finish the check.

Fox sat still, unaware.

Service rose to his feet and took two steps forward, his hands poised.

Grabbing the stock of the slung rifle, he pulled hard and twisted,
hauling the killer off his perch.

Fox's beer can made a burping sound when it hit the ground, spewing
foam.

Service jammed the man's face into the ground and got a knee on the
back of his neck. Twisting one arm behind him, he attached one of the
cuffs, then pulled the other wrist behind Fox and with a sharp *click*,
the bracelet was on. Service gave the handcuffs a tug to make sure they
were secure.

With Fox face down and neutralized, Service popped the clip out of the M-16 and stuffed it in his pocket. He used his belt knife to sever the leather sling and tossed the rifle away.

"What the fuck?" Fox asked in a muffled gasp as he fought for air.

"Save your breath." Service felt fire in his shoulder again and cursed silently. As he rolled Fox over, he stood up and stared into the killer's eyes. "DNR. You're under arrest."

"Where did you come from?" Fox muttered.

"I grew here."

He sat across from his prisoner, too tired to move, hurting beyond description. He turned on his tape recorder, took out his cheat sheet, read Fox his rights, and wrote the time in his notebook, D805.

He activated his handheld radio. "Delta County Sheriff, this is DNR 421. I have a murder suspect in custody. Request transfer." He added his coordinates.

"Can you get out to a road?" the dispatcher asked.

"No way." It was time for the county do some work. He suggested the fastest route to the site and left his radio in receive mode. Fox stared and said, "You fucking people are crazy!"

Service was weary. "You think *we're* crazy? Wait till Limpy Allerdyce gets here."

"He's in Jackson," Fox said smugly.

Service smiled. "I got him out."

Fox blinked, looked shaky, and began to talk. "I didn't do this alone."

"Save it for your lawyer. My tape recorder is on, so you'd better be careful what you say."

"I don't give a shit," Fox said. "I did just what old man Knipe wanted. Don't let Allerdyce near me."

"Which Knipe?"

"Ikey doesn't shit, his father don't tell him to."

"The Knipes were part of your Pelkie deal too?"

"Seton's idea, start to finish."

"And now you're here."

"Ike says there are stones here, not in Crystal Falls."

Service grunted. He'd had enough. "Gonna be murder one for you, pal."

"I'm not taking the fall alone."

Service made a quick decision. If Ike Knipe returned in the helicopter and found Fox gone, he could spook. Service radioed del Olmo. "I've got Fox. Don't let that chopper take off again."

"Roger, do we arrest Ike?"

"Yes, and no phone calls for him until I get there, understood? I don't want him talking to his old man."

"Thy will be done," del Olmo said. "You okay?"

"Yeah."

Fox would make a deal, even if Knipe got him a lawyer. Check finished. Almost.

"These cuffs are too tight," Fox complained.

"Shut up," Service said. "I need sleep."

"I'm wide awake," Fox said.

Service drove the heel of his hand hard into the side of Fox's head, knocking him groggy. "That's for shooting at Nantz and me," he said.

Striking a prisoner. The old man never broke a law. He did. So it went. Different time, different scumbags. He was a cop, not a Boy Scout.

Service stared at the murderer. "Don't let the bedbugs bite, asshole."

McKower called while he waited for support from Delta County.

"The permits are not going to be signed," she said.

Service exhaled in relief.

"What's your status?" she asked.

"I have Fox. I'm waiting to transfer him."

"Great job. What about the Knipes?"

"Del Olmo will take Ike Knipe and I will personally see to his father."

Congratulations Brett!
Niles High School
Class Of 2006

You are invited to join
in our celebration at
an Open House
Saturday June 24th
2:00—8:00pm
1638 Sioux Trail
Niles, MI 49120

· 21 ·

The Crystal Falls police chief's name was Pallaviano. He was a tall man with long hair and a scraggly salt-and-pepper beard that made him look more like a logger than a cop. He wore a T-shirt; his badge dangled around his neck from a purple shoestring.

Pallaviano and del Olmo met Service late in the afternoon at the Jewel of Iron County—the Romanesque county courthouse that sat atop Superior Street, overlooking the Paint River Valley. They met with a judge named Hjalmquist. Pallaviano made a brief introduction and Service quickly outlined the evidence, finishing with the tape of Fox's confession.

Fox was housed temporarily in the Delta County Jail; Ike Knipe was in Iron County's facility. It was time to move against Seton Knipe before the arrests hit the news.

"Seton Knipe is well connected," the judge cautioned.

"Not for long," Service said.

The judge signed the warrant and a writ allowing them to search Knipe's house, Fox's place in Crystal Falls, and the Wildcat compound outside town.

Service, del Olmo, Pallaviano, and one of his deputies drove to Knipe's house, which was perched on a steep hill above Mastodon Creek near Buck Lake, south of the old mining village called Alpha. It was dark when they got to the house, which sat above them.

"No fence," Service said. And no shrubs or trees around the place, which meant no cover.

"This ain't fence country," Pallaviano reminded him.

Service didn't like the looks of the place. Anybody in the house would see the headlights of approaching vehicles.

"It's your bust," Pallaviano said magnanimously. "You've earned it."

Service shook his head. "Take Simon and serve the warrant."

Pallaviano looked surprised. "And you?"

"Leave your man with the vehicles and I'll go around back and come up from behind."

"You're one of those overly suspicious types?"

Service laughed. The Knipes had bailed out of Pelkie and didn't seem the kind of people to willingly face the music, unless they were the conductors. The CO circled the house through jagged rocks that made for slow and tricky footing. His shoulder ached and every time he used his right arm for balance, pain shot through him.

There were no lights in the citadel above.

In back he could hear Mastodon Creek tumbling lazily along. Pallaviano had to be at the door by now, but the house remained dark. Not a good sign.

The CO climbed down through the rocks to the creek's edge. Caddisflies were thick in the night air, and a couple of small trout were splashing the surface as they grabbed at emergers. Service edged north and saw the shadow of something in the water. It was more than a plank and less than a bridge. He used it to cross the creek. A narrow trail led from the water's edge on the other side up to a flat area and a low cinder-block building with two garage doors and no windows.

He stood in darkness against the side of the building. After ten minutes he saw lights come on in the house and from the direction of the creek heard shoe leather scuffing gravel. The shuffling was slow and halting.

"Evening," Service said when the man drew close.

"Who in blazes are you?" a startled voice asked.

"Mister Seton Knipe?"

"Who the hell else would I be?"

"Did you talk to Sheriff Pallaviano?"

"I don't chew the fat with wops."

Service turned on his flashlight and the old man raised an arm to block the beam.

"Turn that thing off."

"Mister Seton Knipe, you are under arrest."

"Is that a fact?" The old man was not easily intimidated. Service activated his tape recorder.

"Yessir."

"I expect it's my son you want. He runs things."

"Is that so?"

"He did it all."

"All what?"

"That diamond business."

"You knew about it, but did nothing to stop him? That's conspiracy at a minimum."

Knipe coughed. "I want my lawyer."

"You're gonna need him," Service said.

While the elder Knipe was being processed into the Iron County Jail, Service went to see Ike Knipe in his cell.

"You," Ike said, his face betraying surprise.

Ike obviously remembered the night they had met in the tract.

"Your father says the whole deal was yours and that he had nothing to do with it. He called a lawyer for himself, but not one for you." Service turned on the tape of his conversation with Seton Knipe.

Ike glowered. "That bastard."

"Fox says it was all your old man's doing and that you both just followed orders."

So much for familial bliss. Seton would sing. Ike would sing. Fox would keep singing. A jury would hear the tune and name it in three notes. It would be a hit—for the Mosquito Wilderness. He hoped his father was watching.

· 22 ·

McKower sat behind her metal desk, her hands primly folded on the blue paper blotter. She looked distinctly unhappy. At least Captain Ware Grant wasn't with her. Grant, the U.P.'s law boss, was a straitlaced, by-the-book iron jaw who had once been in army intelligence.

Service made a show of checking his watch as he stepped into her cubicle. "Hey, I'm even on time."

"Sit down, Grady."

Not a request; a calm order, in her somber in-charge demeanor.

"That bad, huh?"

"If they were doing psychological profiles back when you joined, they wouldn't have hired you."

Uh-oh. "They wouldn't hire the people who made up the tests either. What's that tell you?"

McKower's head moved slowly, side to side. "You have made a shambles of law enforcement jurisdictions."

"This isn't the old days. Jurisdictions are approximate now. We all share. We ebb and flow, cooperate."

"Don't play semantic games."

"I don't play games," he said, defending his honor.

"Not the ones you should play," she said.

Okay, the blow was coming. "Spit it out, Loot." Was she enjoying this?

"If the lawyers in Lansing could figure a way you wouldn't sue the state, you would be out and unemployed."

Service said, "I'd never sue."

"*They* don't know that," McKower said. "To them you are a loose cannon capable of anything. Lansing hates unpredictability."

Lansing, not their DNR bosses. "Hell, Lis. It was you who squeezed Bozian's balls."

She looked across the desk at him for a long time. "It wasn't me, Grady. Somebody else got to him—and just in time."

Service winked. "Right, LT."

"It's the truth, Grady. Somebody got Bozian to withdraw his support, but it wasn't me."

If not McKower, who?

"Lansing would terminate you, but you solved two murders and a host of other crimes and they can't ignore that or sweep it away. But they want you punished and I quote, 'put in his place,' end quote."

"And you get to be the messenger."

"I'm your lieutenant."

"Okay," he said. "Give it to me. I can take whatever you dish out."

"Whatever I decide, you will accept it."

"Right."

"I mean it, Officer Service. I want your solemn promise."

"You've got it," he said, wincing.

"Effective immediately, you are on a sixty-day suspension without pay."

Shit. He had money in the bank, so that part was no big deal. But sixty days? Usually suspensions lasted a few days at most. This wasn't a slap; it was a two-by-four between the eyes.

"When the suspension is over," she said, "you will report back here to me."

"That's it?"

"Most of it," she said.

"Money doesn't mean much to me," he told her.

"I know that."

"Anything else?"

She stared at him.

He got up. "You want my badge and sidearm?"

She nodded. "Under the circumstances." He placed them on her desk and started for the door, but stopped. There was something peculiar in her voice and manner.

"Most of it?" he asked, turning back.

"Thank you for your cooperation . . . *Special Investigator* Service."

He stared at her with an open mouth. "What did you say?"

"You heard me."

He charged her desk. "No fucking way, Lis."

"You gave me your solemn promise, Detective." She was grinning.

"You snookered me."

A smile stretched across her face. "I did, didn't I."

"I am a CO, pure and simple."

"Grady Service, you are anything but simple and I will not even attempt to address the purity issue."

"No way," he said.

"Chief O'Driscoll has decided it's time to extend the special investigations mission to the Upper Peninsula. You'll report directly to me, with a dotted line to Captain Grant."

"Jesus H. Christ! What are you trying to do to me?"

"We're trying to save your ass," she said. "And harness your power." She formed a steeple with her fingers and sat back. "Captain Grant and I figure that since your cases always turn complex, why not just immerse you in complexity from the get-go? You'll be doing what you always do and now nobody can bitch."

"What about the tract?" he asked.

"Day to day, it will no longer be your concern."

"Whose?"

"McCants."

He grunted. She would do a good job and he could always check on her. "You think you're pretty smart."

"No, Grady. I *know* I'm smart."

He shook his head in resignation and flipped McKower a casual salute. "Maybe when I get back in the saddle, the first thing I'll do is take a long, close look at the governor."

His long-ago protégé held her head in her hands and began to laugh uncontrollably.

· 23 ·

S ervice had checked Nantz's house on his return from Crystal Falls
   but there had been no sign of her or his dog. When he got to his
   cabin he called her but she didn't answer. Nobody at the district
office in Escanaba knew where she was because she had called in to
take four vacation days. Just before fire season? Service thought. She
was up to something.

Out of desperation he drove to the Tract, but found no sign of her
truck. He hiked the contour trail to the log slide and headed north along
the river. She was not there either and he chided himself for hoping
she would be. He poked in the water where Newf had found the diamond. He had to find the source and do something about it. What this
would be he had no idea, but he had to look, and get his mind off
Nantz.

The bottom here was shallow and the river a series of rocky ledges,
like steps. He had gone a mile or so when he sensed something and
froze, looking up a slight rise on the eastern bank.

There sat a grinning Maridly Nantz with Newf beside her. Nantz
wore running shorts, a gray tank top, and her work boots. Her hair was
in a green doo rag and she was glistening with perspiration. The dog
wagged her tail.

"What the hell are you doing out here?" he asked. "I've been calling
for days!"

"I've been waiting for you," she said quietly.

"You didn't tell anyone where you were."

"I knew you'd find me."

"And if I didn't?"

"You did."

Unassailable logic. Newf bolted down the embankment and jumped
into the water, barking and splashing him. They climbed up the incline
together and he saw Nantz's tent pitched about twenty yards back. She
had dug a firepit and neatly lined it with stones. He saw a white plastic
cooler and two foldable camp chairs.

"You look pretty smug," he said.

"Do I?" She said, rubbing Newf's ears.

"I know you, Nantz."

"Not biblically," she said. "Yet."

"Don't tease."

"Believe me, I'm not. Teasing time is over, buster." She got up took his hand led him north. As they walked, he told her what had happened.

She stopped them at a small, rocky outcrop above the water's edge.

He looked at the color and frowned. "*Another* pipe?" Service felt his belly roll.

"No, my dear. This is *the* pipe."

The eroding outcrop barely protruded from the bank, about five or six feet over the water. She knelt beside it. Service joined her.

"The stones come from here," she said. "And tumble downstream."

"It's a tiny," Service said.

"Some good things come in small packages."

"We have it all now," he said. "I just wish I knew who put the muscle on Bozian."

She grinned mischievously.

Suddenly he understood. "*You.*"

"I've known that jerk forever. Dad had known him since he was in the legislature. Sam said he was happy to see me when I went over to the island, but he wasn't so happy when I left. I told him the Knipes were involved in two murders and it wouldn't look too good if he was seen as trying to cut red tape for murderers and thieves. Not with his political stance against crime and criminals."

Grady Service suddenly had no words.

"The deal is this," she said. "The rock erodes a little each winter. Water gets into the cracks, freezes, expands, and causes pieces to break off. Some of the pieces have gems in them."

She stood, held out her hand, and led him into the forest to a little clearing where there was a green tarp. Under it were bags of cement, two shovels, trowels, and buckets.

"It took me two days to lug all this stuff in here. The gravel for the cement we take from the Mosquito," she said.

"You brought all this in here? Alone?"

"If we cap the rock, we can stop the erosion. We just need to check on it from time to time and do some patching."

"The weather will get to it."

"Not if we keep capping."

"You've got this all figured out."

"No diamonds, no rumors. No rumors, no stampede. I called Rocky, who told me what to do."

Service peeled off his shirt and hoisted two bags. The pain was agonizing. One more time, he told his shoulder. Don't give out now.

They worked all afternoon. First they covered the outcrop with thick plastic. Then they installed wire mesh over the plastic. Finally they poured the cement, and Nantz finished it by placing other rocks and logs in the wet cement to make it look more natural.

"I don't know," Service said when the work was done.

"Don't worry," she said. "Nature always takes over."

"Always?"

"Yeah and right now she's saying forget work."

They hauled shovels and empty bags and other gear back to the campsite.

"I'm suspended for sixty days," he said as they walked.

"Did you deserve it?"

"Probably," he said.

Nantz smiled. "You mean you have two months of summer with nothing to do?"

"Looks like."

"I hope it rains cats and dogs," the fire marshal said. "I think you are going to have one hell of a lot to do inside."

They both laughed and kissed tenderly.

Dark was falling. They cooked freeze-dried pasta and Italian vegetables over a two-burner Coleman stove. Nantz opened a bottle of Brunello di Montalcino and cracked two loaves of hard bread into pieces.

After dinner they went down to the river and bathed in the icy water. It felt good.

"Tree huggers would kick our asses for using shampoo in the water," Service said.

"Let 'em kick," Nantz said as he rubbed shampoo into her hair.

They carried their clothes back to camp. Nantz added wood to the fire.

Nantz produced a bottle of champagne and poured it into tin cups. "To an end or to a beginning?" she asked, raising her cup.

"To us," he said.

She touched his arm. "Okay, *Banger*, it's time we determine the validity of that handle."

The sky was filled with stars and Service lay beside the fire on an air mattress, Nantz on top of him. He had no idea how long they had been making love. Time was suspended and even his shoulder no longer ached.

In the distance a bottle rocket flashed up from treetops and burst into a shower of gaudy sparks.

"Somebody's shooting fireworks," Service said.

"We're making our own," Nantz whispered.

"They could start a fire."

"Let 'em. It won't be anything compared to the one we've lit."

· EPILOGUE ·

I t was nearly daylight. The rain fell softly and steadily as it had for nearly a week. Cat meowed to be let out and Newf sniffed at her as they waited impatiently.

Maridly Nantz let the two animals out, stretched and yawned.

Service began to dance slowly around the porch, looking out on the creek.

Nantz poured two cups of coffee and sat on the glider she had bought the day before at Forsberg's store.

She watched Service for a while and said, "Is that a dance or a palsy?"

"Rain dance," he said, continuing.

"We have rain," she said.

"I want more," he said.

She smiled and raised her cup in salute. "Dance, baby, dance." After a pause she added, "I have to fly down to Lansing at the end of the week."

Grady Service stopped dancing and sat beside her.

"For what?"

She looked smug. "I took the CO test," she said.

He stared at her.

"I've already talked to Lis and Captain Grant and now they want me in Lansing."

"You never said anything about this."

"There was nothing to say before now. How do you feel about it?"

He had no doubt that she would be good at the job.

"I was thinking about this before we met. I want work that counts all year."

Service said, "As a probie they'll move you all over the state for a year."

"Whatever it takes," she said. "Does that bother you?"

It did and he said so.

She reached over and rubbed his neck. "Good answer."

They had been taking it a day at a time and not talked seriously about a future together. Since their time in the Tract they had split time between their places.

Nantz kissed his cheek, patted his hand, and whispered, "Don't worry. We're going to be just fine."

"We are?"

"Damn right," she said, giving him a long passionate kiss he wished would never end.

"Hungry?" she said, breaking away.

"The cupboard is empty."

She went into the house and got his fly rod but didn't hand it to him. "Nature always provides." She picked out a size-eighteen Adams and tied it on quickly. He followed her down to the creek and sat down on a log.

"Tough casting down here."

She ignored him, stripped out some line, and cast across the creek and slightly upstream, mending automatically. On her fourth or fifth cast a large fish sucked the fly under. The rod immediately bent under the fish's weight. It took a few minutes to get the fish to the bank, and by then Service had fetched a net, which he slid under the struggling trout. It was a good eighteen inches.

"Perfect for two of us," he said.

"Let it go," she said. "Others need its genes." Newf came down, sniffed the fish, and galloped back up the bank.

Service gently released the trout into dark water and felt her arms slide around his neck. "I won't kill a fish like that, and I won't do anything to kill us either."

She felt good in his arms.

"What do we have?" he asked.

"A very interesting future, Service."

When she went back to fishing, he returned to his log and watched her silhouette as she worked the water gracefully and efficiently.

After a while he said, "Is there anything you can't do, Nantz?"

"I think we are in the process of finding that out," she said as she deftly threw another cast.